MOONLIGHT AND MURDER

Sarah Lightly huddled against the parapet at the far end of the building. She was sobbing quietly, but as soon as she saw them coming she started to laugh. She laughed and laughed, her mouth horribly stretched over her teeth, tears streaming down her face so that it shone in the pale moonlight.

'What's happened to her? Paul, what have you done?' cried Kate, terrified and repelled. 'Sarah, be quiet! Sarah!'

'I haven't touched her!' yelled Paul. 'God, you don't know what's happened! You've got to help me, Kate. Get her out, downstairs. Come on, come on!' And he began tugging and pulling the girl's heavy body, trying to make her move.

'Paul!' Kate shouted, his panic shocking her almost as much as Sarah's hysteria did. 'Leave her alone! I'll get Tilly. I'll get—'

Sarah jerked her head violently. 'Get Tilly!' she shrieked. 'Get her? Oh, God! Look over . . . down. Down. Look!'

Kate looked over the parapet, into the narrow laneway that ran beside the building, and her stomach lurched. Around a garbage bin, far below, something white and shapeless was crawling. She almost cried out, and then she saw it for what it was—Tilly's Chinese shawl, flapping in the wind. She almost laughed in relief, and then her eyes moved on and the laugh choked in her throat. There was something else in the alley, twisted and broken, pale limbs sprawling, and still as death. . . .

MURDER
by the
BOOK

Jennifer Rowe

CRIME LINE ™

BANTAM BOOKS

New York   Toronto   London   Sydney   Auckland

All characters in this book are entirely fictitious, and no reference is intended to any living person.

MURDER BY THE BOOK
A Bantam Crime Line Book / January 1992

Printing History
First published in 1989 by Allen & Unwin Australia

CRIME LINE and the portrayal of a boxed "cl" are trademarks of Bantam Books, a division of Bantam Doubleday Dell Publishing Group, Inc.

ISBN 0-553-29373-7

Published simultaneously in the United States and Canada

Bantam Books are published by Bantam Books, a division of Bantam Doubleday Dell Publishing Group, Inc. Its trademark, consisting of the words "Bantam Books" and the portrayal of a rooster, is Registered in U.S. Patent and Trademark Office and in other countries. Marca Registrada. Bantam Books, 666 Fifth Avenue, New York, New York 10103.

PRINTED IN THE UNITED STATES OF AMERICA

RAD   0 9 8 7 6 5 4 3 2 1

FOR NORM

CONTENTS

CAST OF CHARACTERS

Berry and Michaels Staff

QUENTIN HALE, MANAGING DIRECTOR
EVIE NEWELL, PUBLICITY MANAGER
MALCOLM POOL, EVIE'S ASSISTANT
AMY PHIBES, QUENTIN'S SECRETARY
SYLVIA DE GROOT, ROYALTIES MANAGER
KATE DELANEY, MANAGING EDITOR
SID, MAN OF ALL WORK
DAVID, ART DIRECTOR
LULU, DESIGNER
MARY, EDITORIAL SECRETARY

Authors and Illustrators

SIR SAUL MURDOCH, NOVELIST
TILLY LIGHTLY, CHILDREN'S WRITER
JACK SPROTT, GARDENING WRITER
BARBARA BENDIX, BIOGRAPHER
PAUL MORRISEY, STRUGGLING FIRST-TIME NOVELIST
PATRICIA PENN, ILLUSTRATOR

VISITORS

SARAH LIGHTLY, TILLY'S DAUGHTER
VERITY BIRDWOOD, ABC RESEARCHER, FRIEND OF KATE

Police

DETECTIVE-SERGEANT DAN TOBY
DETECTIVE-CONSTABLE COLIN MILSON

MURDER
by the
BOOK

1

End of an Era

'Evie, they can't do this!' raged Kate. 'They can't just tell a man to get out of his own company like that! In one afternoon!'

'They've done it, haven't they?' said Evie Newell slowly. 'They own the thing now. They can do what they like.' She stood up and walked to her office window, leaning heavily on the wide sill. The windows buzzed slightly, picking up the vibrations of the peak hour traffic, rising on gusts of hot, humid air from the shimmering roadway below. But Evie was staring across the road, at the green park slipping away to the Harbour behind black iron railings.

'So,' she said softly, 'that's that.'

'We should all just leave. Just walk out,' insisted Kate, determined to get a response. 'How can you be so calm, Evie? You of all people?'

Evie turned to face her, stocky, tired and pale with anger. 'For God's sake, Kate, what's the good of going on like this? Brian knew when he fought the takeover what he was risking. He knew, I knew, you knew— everyone knew! Now the Gold Group's got Berry and Michaels, and they wouldn't want Brian Berry as mail boy, let alone managing director. That's it. The fight's over. Brian lost, and he's out.' She turned back to the window.

There was a knock on the door. Little Sylvia de Groot, the royalties manager, crept into the room. Her eyes were red and puffy under her heavy black fringe, and her nose was shiny pink under a thin film of powder.

'Brian's gone,' she whispered. 'Did you see him?'

Evie made no movement, but Kate nodded. Sylvia sniffed, and her eyes filled with tears.

'We waved him off,' she said. 'The girls from the order room, and accounts, and the computer room. He kissed everyone and just went. I couldn't believe it was happening.' She cast her eyes in Evie's direction and raised her eyebrows. 'How is she?' she mouthed. Kate shrugged, and shook her head.

'I've had authors on the phone all day,' Sylvia said aloud. 'They saw the piece in the paper. They say they'll leave Berry and Michaels if Brian goes.'

'They say that now,' said Evie, without turning around.

'Oh, they mean it, Evie, really!' said Sylvia earnestly. She brushed back her fringe. 'Some of them have been with us since his dad's time—and *his* dad's in the estates' cases. We keep saying what a crime Gerald Berry ever made Berry and Michaels into a public company. If he hadn't this could never have happened.'

'It probably seemed a good idea then,' replied Evie. She hunched her shoulders, turned away from the window and walked back to her desk. 'How was he to know a mob of greedy shareholders, and half his family, would sell his baby to the highest bidder one day—and that his son'd be tipped out on his ear.'

'An English company, too,' breathed Sylvia. 'Berry and Michaels being owned overseas. I mean, it's terrible! He'd turn in his grave. And this Englishman they're sending out to replace Brian—this Quentin Hale . . .'

'What about him?' said Evie through tight lips.

'Well, he won't know anything about us, or our authors or anything, will he? And someone said he was really awful.'

'He's a hatchet man,' snapped Evie. 'He's some marketing heavy who's been angling for the job. Brian met him in London. He says he'd sell his grandmother for sixpence if that was all that was offering.'

'How old is he?' asked Kate curiously.

'Early fifties. Aging *wunderkind*, Brian said. He's spent most of his time in stationery, apparently. Great, eh?'

'Stationery!' Kate exploded.

Evie almost smiled. 'Thought the managing editor'd like that,' she said. 'Brian thought he'd get the job. The Gold Group's awfully old school tie these days, you know, and Hale's not quite quite, apparently. Not pukka enough, or something. Didn't go to the right school, doesn't talk proper. And there was some nasty domestic scandal he was involved in, about a year ago. Someone died, and it got into the papers. The Gold Group people look down their noses at that sort of thing. Puts them off their polo.'

She looked under her eyebrows at Sylvia's shocked face. 'Well, it wouldn't be the first time the poms have sent their embarrassments to the colonies to stop them lowering the tone at home, would it?' she said. 'You'd think the immigration laws'd stop them doing it.' She laughed bitterly. 'Great, isn't it? They make all these eager beavers wait years for residency, and they let Quentin Hale and his missus in just like that!'

Sylvia blinked, looked at Kate, sidled to the door and slipped out.

'What do you think's going to happen now?' asked Kate.

Evie shrugged, her eyes hard. She indicated a sheet of paper on her desk. 'I know exactly what will happen. They faxed me—or rather, they faxed "Miss Edie Newen, Publicity Manager", and we assume that's me.

Anyway, Miss Edie Newen has her orders. The illustrious Mr Hale will be arriving on Monday, and will be in the office by lunchtime. He will be welcomed at a management lunch, which I am to organise. He will stay in a hotel, which I am to organise, until Brian's things have been removed from the apartment upstairs, which I am to organise, and then his wife, the illustrious *Mrs* Hale, will arrive, and they'll take up residence.

'Then I would say the illustrious Mr Hale will begin to lay about him, sack a few people, appoint a few new ones, throw his weight around a bit and then settle down to charm everyone into submission—especially the press and the authors. His big job'll be to make everyone happy with the takeover, defuse the criticism, all that.'

'He'll want you to help,' said Kate quietly.

'I suppose he will. I always said public relations was the second oldest profession.'

'You're really not leaving? You always said that if Brian went you'd . . .'

Evie put her head in her hands. 'I don't know,' she said. 'Now that it comes to the crunch . . .' Then she looked up. 'The fact is,' she said fiercely, 'I've been thinking that I'll be damned if I'll just let them take this place over and have it all their own way. Push the authors around, muck everything up, break it all up because they don't know anything about our market, or the people, or any bloody thing! I care too much about it to just walk off. Twenty years, Kate. Twenty years I've given to this company. Even if I could find another job just like that, and I suppose I could get something . . .'

'Oh, Evie, don't be ridiculous! Anyone would want you!'

'Be that as it may, and I'm not as confident about that as you are, I just can't do it. The company's been good to me. I'll stick around. I'll wait and see what Hale's like. Then I'll decide what to do. He might be OK. He might, mightn't he?' For the first time her voice faltered. Her eyes strayed to the memo on her desk.

'He might,' said Kate doubtfully. 'Maybe he will, Evie. I'll wait too. We'll wait and see. We'll all wait and see.'

2

Big Plans

The meeting was not going well for Evie. She felt it, and so did everyone else, but typically, thought Kate, not a glimmer of uncertainty crossed her face. She just hunched her shoulders, stared at the smooth, polished surface of the conference table, and doggedly went on.

Kate stole a look at Quentin Hale at the head of the table. He was leaning back in his chair, his plump fingers carefully pressed together, his broad, pink face politely interested. He's hearing her out, she thought. He's the new boss being courteous to a long-serving staff member, showing that he's not just a savage new broom. But he's making her feel dusty just the same—dusty and old hat. The last thing a publicity manager should feel.

She looked back at Evie's familiar figure. She didn't have to listen to the proposals for the public relations campaign to 'celebrate' the company's takeover and 'promote its vigorous new image', as Quentin had put it on arrival. Evie had discussed them with her weeks ago—the party for Berry and Michaels authors and staff and the rest of the publishing community as the centrepiece, the children's competition, the advertising campaign with the new company slogan, the university prize in the founder's name—a steady, sensible campaign which would involve not too much expense.

Nothing there to set the world on fire, but after all what would? It would all work, anyway, and it would succeed however ordinary it sounded. Evie's campaigns always did succeed. She hadn't been with Berry and Michaels for twenty years for nothing. She knew the place inside out and knew how to promote its mixed image of sober literary merit and sound commercial judgement. Everyone knew that.

But Quentin doesn't, thought Kate suddenly. He only arrived a month ago, and he'd never heard of Evie Newell till then. With new eyes she looked at the Evie that Quentin Hale was seeing—not a familiar, eccentric figure, part of the office furniture, veteran of many an all-night work binge, many a marathon office party, closest advisor for years of the flamboyant Brian Berry whose shoes Quentin was now filling.

He was seeing a short, dumpy, middle-aged woman, with a toneless voice and slightly truculent manner. Not very impressive, no doubt, to someone like him. In fact, it was hard to imagine someone like Evie ever inhabiting Quentin's office world before. Amy Phibes, the intensely groomed, even glamorous, blonde secretary at his elbow was more his sort of thing—the sort of office furniture he would see as befitting a go-ahead publishing house. He'd hired her a week after his arrival. No doubt her cool English efficiency made him feel at home. It made everyone else extremely uncomfortable.

Evie glanced at her notes, folded them and began winding up. Beside her, angelic and attentive, a slight flush on his downy cheek, her new assistant Malcolm Pool moved slightly, with a suggestion of restlessness, and ran a hand over his close-cropped hair. Kate watched him catch Quentin's eye for the briefest of moments, watched his eyebrows rise ever so slightly, heard him take a deep breath that was almost a sigh.

Disloyal little go-getter, she thought. He's making the most of this. Evie'll regret she ever agreed to take him on, if she doesn't already. We were all taken in by those sweet little-boy looks, and the big blue eyes. Oh, what idiots! You can smell the ambition on him. For sure he's read one of those poisonous books on office strategy and Getting On. He's got Hale well and truly bluffed.

'Thank you, Evie.' The man at the head of the table sat forward and smiled briefly. 'Well done. We're not quite there yet, I don't think, but I'm sure everyone at this table would agree that you've given us plenty of food for thought.'

Evie blinked at him. 'I considered . . .' she began.

'Now,' Quentin interrupted smoothly, holding up his hand to silence her with the smile never leaving his face, 'perhaps we can hear some ideas from some of the other people here.' He looked around. 'Could you take some notes, Amy?' The woman beside him nodded and crossed her elegant legs. Her pen hovered over the shorthand notebook, her pale green eyes flickered up to regard the room with a cool stare. They waited together.

A small ripple of panic washed around the table. This had always been Evie's project. Anyone who'd had anything to say had said it to Evie weeks ago and those ideas, if they were good ones, were already incorporated in the carefully and fully worked-out plan that had just been dismissed as 'food for thought'.

Kate looked at the blank and fearful faces around her, realised her own must be just as revealing, and tried to pull herself together. Out of the corner of her eyes she noticed Sylvia de Groot leaning forward, small and eager, eyes intense under the black fringe. For sure she was going to put forward yet again that loopy plan of hers about the doves and her local church choir dressed up as book jackets. The man would think they were parochial idiots.

'I think, Quentin, that Evie has really summed up most of our thoughts,' she said quickly, to forestall the impending catastrophe.

'Ah, yes, I see. Well. Very good.' He looked neither

disappointed nor pleased. Amy made a couple of squiggles on her pad, and studied a fingernail.

'As it happens, though, you're not quite right, Kate,' Quentin went on casually. 'I believe the newest member of the team has a few points to make. He tells me he's been thinking about the project in his own time.' He nodded and smiled briefly at Malcolm Pool.

'Well, for goodness . . .' Evie spun round to glare at her assistant.

The cynosure of all eyes, Malcolm blinked with a false modesty that deceived no-one. He opened the bright yellow folder in front of him, and cleared his throat. His perfectly clean fingernails rested lightly on the table top.

'I haven't been with you all long, I know that,' he said. 'A month is no time at all. And I wouldn't dream of saying that I could offer to this discussion anything like the knowledge or experience of an Evie, or a Kate, or anyone who's been with Berry and Michaels since I was a kid in short pants.' He smiled around beguilingly. 'But, just as an exercise, because I know I've got so much to learn, I thought I'd put together a few ideas. As a newcomer I'm seeing things fresh, you see.'

Quentin nodded. 'Exactly. The fresh view. One of the reasons I hired you, Malcolm. New blood's never a bad thing. As, I hope, you'll all decide in my case.' He looked around and smiled, showing all his teeth.

'Fair enough,' muttered Evie. 'Let's hear it, then.' She gave Malcolm a sharp, appraising stare and settled back to listen, arms folded.

Malcolm raised his clear blue eyes. He spoke directly to Quentin Hale. 'As a newcomer, it seemed to me that quite a few things here are taken for granted.

'This marvellous old building, for instance. It's one of the oldest in the city, isn't it? What a place for a publishing house to operate from. It's a landmark. I thought the whole promotion should be centred here.'

'It's much too small, Malcolm,' said Evie impatiently. 'The reception rooms don't hold more than a couple of hundred. The place I've booked has space for . . .'

'I'm not talking about the party you suggested, Evie,' said Malcolm softly, turning to her. 'If I can just go on?' Evie shrugged.

'The party Evie has suggested,' Malcolm went on, to Quentin, 'is basically a party to which our authors and staff and people like literary agents are to be invited. And I'm sure a good time would be had by all. The thing is, what benefit do we gain from it?' He looked around enquiringly, wide-eyed.

'Surely the benefits are obvious!' snapped Kate, very irritated by his self-possession. 'It's a PR exercise—a good-will event.'

'Will the press be invited?'

'Of course they will—the book reviewers and so on. Evie told us all that. Features and social page people too, of course, but nothing much will come from that.'

Malcolm leaned forward. 'Why not?'

'Because,' Evie said in a bored voice, 'it'll be a bun-rush, and not necessarily all that glamorous. They might come, but they won't write much about it.'

'Well, what a wasted opportunity,' said Malcolm coolly. He brushed a speck of dirt from his cuff.

'I disagree!' barked Evie, very red in the face. 'The purpose . . .'

'Evie, I'd like to hear what Malcolm has to suggest,' said Quentin Hale calmly. He glanced at his watch. 'And I have an appointment at three.' He nodded to Malcolm, whose mouth tightened slightly to conceal his pleasure as he turned a page before continuing.

'All our authors are very wonderful people, but of course as far as the press is concerned, most of them are of marginal interest,' he said. 'There are exceptions, however, and of these, four are notable exceptions. And I think here again I've stumbled on something that's been taken for granted. The Big Four.'

He held up a photograph neatly mounted on cardboard, and laid it on the table. A fragile-looking woman, holding a single daisy between her fingers, smiled enigmatically up at them from the polished mahogany.

'Tilly Lightly,' he said with a proprietorial air, as though introducing this household name to them for the first time. 'The author and illustrator of our all-time best-selling children's book, *The Adventures of Paddy Kangaroo*. A modern classic, constantly reprinted in multiple editions for nearly twenty years, and the first in a string of Paddy stories, every one a great success—for her and for us.'

He placed a second photograph, mounted as the first, on the table. A romantic studio portrait of a sensitive-looking man with a gaunt face, silvery hair and what used to be called 'soulful' eyes. If you looked at the photograph too closely, you could almost see the lips tremble.

'Saul Murdoch, our most famous and distinguished novelist. Again, there would be few who hadn't heard of him, studied him at school, or whatever. Winner of every award you can think of, published internationally. A great name.'

'His royalty cheques aren't so great anymore,' muttered Sylvia de Groot, still a little miffed because her publicity plan hadn't been aired.

Ignoring the interruption, Malcolm laid his third picture down. Jolly Jack Sprott, the gardener's friend, twinkled gnomishly through the branches of a camellia in glorious flower.

'Half a million copies of Jack Sprott's *Gardener's Almanac* sold, ten other gardening books in print. Newspaper and magazine columns, a named range of gardening tools, fertilisers, sprays. By far our most outstanding practical author,' said Malcolm briskly, already reaching for his fourth and final offering. Keeping the pace going, thought Kate. She glanced at Quentin. He was still leaning back in his chair, hands behind his head, but his expression was approving. He liked Malcolm's style, obviously, and of course, to him, this information about the company's leading authors was relatively fresh and therefore, possibly, interesting.

'Of course you all know who's next and last,' Malcolm was saying. And of course all of them did, but all looked nevertheless with unwilling fascination at the photograph of the redoubtable Barbara Bendix, all eyes, cleavage and exotic jewellery.

'Our lady of the knife jobs,' smiled Malcolm Pool, resuscitating the old office joke and offering it to them as newborn.

Quentin laughed heartily.

'A relatively recent arrival to our stable, Ms Bendix, but a very valuable one,' Malcolm continued, tapping Barbara Bendix's image with a pink finger. 'In barely eight years she's become one of the most frequently quoted women in the country, all on the strength of three books—biographies, warts and all, unofficial biographies, of prominent people. Every one's been a sensation—major newspaper serialisation, huge bookclub sale, and massive hardback distribution. According to records I saw, her last book reprinted in hardback *four* times, and the paperback, I know, is still on the bestseller lists. Her wit is famous . . .'

'Her malice, you mean,' said Kate drily. 'She always writes about people after they're dead, and those books are really the most scandal-mongering, scurrilous . . .'

'Sell for us though, don't they?' Malcolm cut in brightly. Barbara Bendix might have been his personal invention.

'We're quite aware of her value, thanks, Malcolm,' snapped Evie. 'We ought to be. There's a huge advance out on her next book. Which she's spent, I might add, and not a chapter of the new thing have we seen! We don't even know what it's about!'

'I think she's got interested in someone who's alive and kicking,' said Kate. 'And she's been spending all her time on that, and now she's stuck because of libel, and can't deliver. She's . . .'

'Sure. Yes, of course.' Malcolm glanced at Kate placatingly. You could see that busy, disciplined mind under the short-clipped hair giving itself a little slap—you must remember to be more tactful, Malcolm!

'Let's get on, shall we?' said Quentin, rather crossly.

'Yes, ah . . .' Malcolm flushed slightly, spread the photographs on the table into a neat fan, and began again.

'The Big Four, as I've called them, have good news value because they're famous, and their books are very widely read. Evie told me the presence of three of them at our celebration is in fact not expected, because they live in different parts of the country—Tilly Lightly in Western Australia, Saul Murdoch down south in Victoria, Barbara Bendix up north in Queensland. Only Jack Sprott lives here in Sydney. Evie didn't seem too worried.

'But think of what we have here—a children's author, a novelist, a practical writer, a best-selling writer of popular non-fiction. They represent the four great strengths of the Berry and Michaels list. Furthermore, they represent the country's North, South, East and West. And—two men, two women. See? In these four people, *all* our authors are represented!

'What if,' he drummed his fingers on the photographs before him and leaned forward, his eyes very bright, 'what if we abandon the idea of a huge "bunfight", as Evie called it, and instead spend the money on bringing our Big Four together here. Flying them in for three or four days of group interviews, seminars, book signings. They can stay here, on the premises in the apartments upstairs. Now we've tipped out *News & Views* magazine, they'll be alone on that floor. The four together would be some package to offer, especially if we do the thing in style—first class travel, hire cars to drive them round. Really give them the star treatment for once.

'We'll get press features and profiles, radio and TV, everything! And all focused on this building. The ABC have already been onto us, wanting to do a story on the takeover. They want to send a researcher here to the office for a few days. We'll say, sure, we've got nothing to hide, be our guests! And we'll time the researcher's visit to coincide with the Big Four promotion, and let them do some filming at the party. Not a huge affair everyone and his dog gets invited to, but a really elegant affair downstairs, with the Big Four as guests of honour.' He pressed his fingers together and leaned forward.

'In my opinion, the idea can't fail. Except for Barbara Bendix, none of the Big Four, would you believe it, has made any personal public appearances for at least five years!' He spread his hands, palms up, and made a little moue of noncomprehension. 'Maybe they've been taken for granted. I frankly find it hard to understand why they haven't been pushed and pushed again. But this fortunately works to our advantage now—people will be so curious they'll fight for tickets to that party, and for interviews. And the whole project, most important of all, will make it clear to everyone that there's new management now at Berry and Michaels. An energetic, go-ahead management that's determined to do things in style and promote, promote, promote!' He closed his folder and waited.

'Malcolm . . .' Evie began slowly.

'That's more like it!' Quentin leaned forward, ignoring her completely. 'That's the thinking that's going to drag this company into the twenty-first century, Malcolm. Bold, and simple, and eyecatching. That's good promotion. Good work!'

Malcolm flushed with pleasure.

'It can't be done, Quentin,' Evie was shaking her head. 'It just isn't . . .'

'Evie dear, for God's sake, we're all on the same team here I hope,' Quentin interrupted firmly. 'You had your say, and Malcolm simply had a better idea. That's all there is to it.'

'It all sounds terrific in theory, Quentin,' said Kate, glancing at Evie who was determinedly drawing lines on the pad in front of her. 'But unfortunately . . .'

'Kate, please don't be negative about this,' said Quentin seriously. 'Any details can be taken care of. I'm sure, in fact, that Malcolm's already thought them through. He's put a great deal of work and clever thinking into this plan of his, that's obvious, and I think he deserves all our support. He certainly has mine. We mustn't ever fall into the trap of rejecting fresh ideas just because they're new and different, Kate.'

'Quentin!' Evie's voice was ominously quiet.

He shook his head at her decisively and put his hand on Amy's arm.

'Get this written up as a minute, Amy, please. Malcolm will give you any details you missed. Copies to everyone present. I'm putting Malcolm in personal charge of the implementation of his plan. Evie will give him what assistance he needs. Some aspects of her original plan can be retained—the children's competition, for example, and the scholarship, as long as they're tied in with the central idea. You give that some thought, Malcolm. I'll leave it to you. You'll have to get a move on. Ideally I'd like you to plan for no more than a month from today. Fast work, but you'll manage.'

He smiled briefly, placed his fingers on the table and rose. 'I'm sorry to break this up but, as I said, I have an appointment. Thank you all.' It was a very firm dismissal.

As she left the beautiful old room, the scene of so many boisterous, jokey meetings in the past, Kate looked back once. Malcolm, head bowed, was listening as Quentin made some final remarks to him in an undertone. Ah, how times had changed.

Evie hadn't waited for the lift, but had bolted straight down the stairs to her office, an untidy cubby hole on the first floor of the building. She had complained for years about its size, but somehow always

found a reason not to move when a change of office
was suggested.

Kate found her looking out her window, leaning
against the deep sill. Perhaps that green view of the
park was the magnet that had held her in this small
room for all these years.

Berry and Michaels was—had been—the centre of
Evie's life. For years she'd handled its publicity with
confident aplomb. Mondays to Fridays she bristled
with energy and activity, teasing, cajoling and bullying
her contacts and her authors; endlessly on the phone,
endlessly running from one appointment to the next.
On Saturdays she shopped, did housework, read. And
on Sundays she slipped quietly back to town, let herself into the silent old building, and peacefully dealt
with her paperwork, while the shadows lengthened under the trees she could see through her windows.

It had been a life she relished. She had seen no reason why it should not continue forever—or at least
until she chose otherwise. But in a few short weeks,
everything had changed. Kate, hesitating at the door,
saw how much it had changed. Evie's bowed shoulders
had a defenceless look.

'Evie.'

'What?'

'You know what. Evie, you've got to tell them.'

'Why should I?'

'Evie, if you won't, I will. Quentin's got to know.'

'I tried to tell him. He shut me up. You tried to tell
him. He shut *you* up. That's it, as far as I'm concerned. He and that little swine Pool can stew in their
own juice.'

'We'll stew too, Evie. The whole company'll stew.'

'The company'll be OK. It's lived through plenty of
disasters in its time. One more won't kill it. But what
will kill it is the sort of thing we saw just then—a total
lack of respect for experience, snap decisions, shallow
thinking, sneaky one-upping, all that.'

'Evie, it all sounded very convincing. You can understand Quentin . . .'

'You can understand Quentin Hale listening and being impressed. It sounded good. Of course it did. But
can you understand him refusing to let us comment,
and putting a little twirp who's twenty-two, if that,
and who's been here *two weeks* in charge of such an
important event, and asking *me* to assist *him*?'

'I know, Evie, it's awful, but . . .' Kate touched her
friend on the shoulder.

Evie whirled round to face her. Her eyes were puffy
and red, her face blotched with uneven pink patches.

'Kate, you know and I know. With Brian gone and
just about all the other old hands moved on or given
up the heave-ho, we're the only ones here now who
do. So you keep quiet. This is my responsibility, not
yours.'

'Maybe they won't come,' said Kate hopefully.

Evie snorted. 'Of course they'll come! Not one of
them could resist the star treatment. They'll welcome
the opportunity anyway. They've always wanted more
personal promotion than I gave them. They'll love it!'
She laughed a little hysterically.

'Let them try their wings for once outside the gilded
cage I've kept them in. They might find I wasn't so
silly and boring after all. And won't our pretty boy
scout Pool have his hands full. Tilly Lightly, anorexic
whimsy queen, vain as a cat and bored to tears with
her blasted kangaroo, meets face to face, after twenty
years of mutual hatred, her ex-lover Saul Murdoch,
now, by all reports, heading for his third nervous
breakdown. Lovely stuff. Jolly Jack Sprott, Jolly Jack
Drink-like-a-fish, ghost-written for years because by
lunchtime he can't hold his trowel straight, will add to
the fun. He should come up well in group seminars. I
hope Malcolm organises a literary lunch.'

'Evie!'

'And of course not forgetting Barbara Bendix. She'll
have a field day! Material for half a dozen nasty little
short pieces about the other three to tide her over while
she finishes the book. Oh, and she's so charming, too.
So sweet and endearing. So compassionate. So refined.

And all of them tucked up in the flats upstairs to-gether. Malcolm couldn't have chosen better. Kate, I'm looking forward to this. I really am!'

'Evie, it'll be appalling. It'll be murder!'

'I wouldn't be a bit surprised!'

3

Countdown

FROM *The Sydney Morning Star:*

Amid continued controversy concerning the takeover of Berry and Michaels, one of Australia's oldest publishing houses, by the giant UK-based Gold Group, Quentin Hale, recently-appointed managing director, has enlisted the help of the company's best-known authors in an attempt to defuse the issue.

Mr Hale, 51, replaced long-serving managing director Brian Berry, grandson of the firm's founder, eight weeks ago. He was previously marketing director for the Gold Group publishing subsidiary Allprint, based in London.

This evening, the Manchester-born Mr Hale and his wife Dorothy will be hosting a small cocktail party to welcome to 'Carlisle', the Berry and Michaels headquarters, Sir Saul Murdoch, children's author Tilly Lightly, controversial biographer Barbara Bendix and *Sydney Morning Star* gardening writer Jack Sprott, whose name is synonymous with green fingers throughout the nation.

The Big Four, as the Berry and Michaels publicity handouts have dubbed them, will be worked hard over the next few days in a tight schedule

of seminars, literary lunches and interviews. They
will be the guests of honour at a gala event to be
held in the historic 'Carlisle' reception rooms tomorrow night.

'Carlisle', built by the company's founder,
Walter Berry, in 1899, has retained its original
character despite some internal alterations such
as the addition of the lift in the 1920s, the in-
stallation of four guest apartments on the third
floor, and the conversion of the whole top floor
into an executive apartment now occupied by Mr
and Mrs Hale.

A Who's-Who of Australian glitterati will be
present at tomorrow evening's festivities, but the
last Australian resident of the Berry family, Brian
Berry, will not be attending. Said to be shocked
and angered by the desertion of shareholders who
declined to stand behind his efforts to thwart the
Gold Group swoop, and his subsequent removal
from the MD's chair held by his father and
grandfather, Mr Berry is believed to be having
an extended holiday in Europe.

Tilly Lightly put aside the paper and smiled rather
grimly to herself. Now Brian Berry knew what it was
like to be on the outer. Well, good for the Gold Group.
He'd always been so cold and superior, not at all supportive. Not like his father, old Gerald, who'd been a
real sweetie.

Tilly had always been uncomfortable with Brian,
ever since his very early days in the company when
he'd rejected her third Bindi Mouse book. Said it was
'ordinary' and the pictures were 'a little unsophisti-
cated for today's competitive market'. It was ridiculous. Gerald had always been very happy with her
manuscripts. The fact is, Brian just hadn't understood
children's books and, presumably, putting her down
gave him a sense of power, since she'd been a pet of
his father.

It would have served him right if she'd gone elsewhere. The rejection was such a shock, after two successes. Alistair had been dead for barely a year, and she had Sarah to support on a pension. She'd been counting on that book for a little bit of help. She really should have gone elsewhere. But then dear old Gerald had written that sweet, sympathetic note and said, leave Bindi aside for now, Tilly, and try something new. You can do it. So Paddy Kangaroo was born, and the rest was history.

Dear old Gerald. He'd had a soft spot for her, always. She still remembered the thrill of receiving his letter accepting her first book, *Meet Bindi Mouse*. 'Charming . . . delightful . . .' he'd written, and he'd loved the illustrations and published it just exactly as she'd sent it, with not a word or a line altered. So exciting for a nineteen-year-old—still a student, too. To have her first book published at that age, no-one could take that away from her. None of those snobs at university could ever have hoped for that.

Not that they were impressed. Oh no. They were on far too high a plane to be impressed by a children's book. They probably thought that children's books were beneath contempt. Like Brian Berry, they probably thought any fool could write one. And that included Saul, who'd always acted embarrassed about *Bindi*, and never wanted to talk about it, especially in front of them, his so-called friends. Tilly lifted her chin proudly. And what had any of them done since? Nothing! They'd all disappeared into oblivion, every one. Except Saul. So it seemed that she and Saul had had something in common after all, something they couldn't begin to understand. A creative urge their bitter, barren, academic little minds couldn't muster up if they tried for a year.

Tilly became aware that she was clutching angrily at her seat belt, and breathing hard. She glanced quickly at Sarah, sitting tall and patient beside her. But her daughter was staring out the window, her face masked by a tangle of black hair, daydreaming as usual. She seemed, these days, to be slipping away into her own world more and more often. Tilly touched her arm and Sarah turned slowly and blinked at her, smiling slightly, like a child just waking.

'You OK?' asked Tilly brightly, casually.

'Sure, Mama. You?' Sarah's smile broadened to reassure, and she touched her two long front teeth with her tongue—a childish trick that belied her twenty years.

Tilly nodded and laughed, a little nervously. There had been a time when Sarah was as clear as crystal to her. All through her childhood and adolescence they'd been so close, but lately she'd had more and more the feeling that Sarah was thinking . . . her own thoughts. Thoughts that shut her mother out. It was uncomfortable. She'd been writing, too. She locked herself in her room and typed now, instead of coming in after dinner to read in the studio while Tilly worked. It was disconcerting. Maybe now the book was finished things would get back to normal. This trip to Sydney was sure to help.

'You did put your manuscript in, Sarah, didn't you?' she murmured.

Sarah's shoulders moved a little. 'Yes, I told you, Mama,' she said peevishly.

'Oh, yes.' Tilly controlled a sigh. Sarah was so touchy these days. 'It's just such a good chance, sweetie,' she said, 'because we can give it directly to Quentin Hale, and cut out all the waiting and so on.'

'Mama, they won't want the book,' muttered Sarah, hunching her broad shoulders. 'You've as good as said they won't.' The fine Liberty-lawn blouse she was wearing strained at the seams.

'I didn't say that, Sarah, I just said they might want you to do a bit of extra work on it. You can't expect to get it exactly right first time.' Tilly turned away. 'And of course they'll take the book, sweetie. I mean, they're not going to reject my daughter's book, are they?'

Sarah turned to her, dark eyes furious and horrified.

'I don't want them to take it because of you, Mama! That would be the end! I'd rather burn it!'

Tilly looked baffled. 'Well, I don't see why,' she said reasonably. 'Everyone's got to start somewhere.'

Sarah bit her lip and looked out the window again. Tilly sat poised to continue the conversation for a moment, then slowly subsided into her seat. She was surprised to find her hands trembling, and she clasped them together nervously. The palms were damp. Now she felt she'd been crass. Saul Murdoch had always been able to make her feel like that, too. She shivered. Well, Saul wouldn't be able to get at her like that now. She was older now. She was older, she was really, really successful, and she was still, she knew, quite attractive. There was no reason now for Saul to be able to feel superior to her.

She remembered the last time she saw him, his face mean with contempt, the bitter, callous words, the absolute, pig-headed failure to see her point of view, or understand her needs. So obsessed by his own version of things, his own precious view. So convinced of his own superiority and so aware of the amazing sacrifices he'd made to have a relationship with her against the combined disapproval of his rigid, snobbish friends. Well, now he'd see what a mistake he'd made.

Saul Murdoch lay back in his seat with his eyes closed, and tried to let the aircraft drone fill his mind, blot out all those confused, jangling thoughts, loud as shouting voices, that wouldn't let him rest. Had he been right to make this trip? The doctor seemed to think he should. Keeping busy, that was the key, the doctor said. No point in sitting alone with one's thoughts, was there? Funny . . . Saul Murdoch's still beautifully shaped lips tilted in a smile. Once, being alone with his thoughts had been his idea of paradise. And in those days, thoughts merged and linked and turned into books. But that was a long time ago. Now thoughts remained disjointed, wry little pieces of insight, wincing recollections, unformed fears that chased round and round in his soupy mind like clothes in a laundromat machine, getting nowhere, resolving nothing, exhausting, terrifying.

This summons from Berry and Michaels, though . . . For a few days after he received that, everything had calmed down. He'd seen clearly, for the first time in years, what he could do, what he could still do, with his life. He was a considerable presence even now. A symbol, the Berry and Michaels letter had said. He was an influence. He could be an influence for good. For disciplined, rigorous thought. For integrity, high standards, everything that was being neglected and even sneered at in the pursuit of easy money, power and prestige on the one hand and easily-satisfied quests for self-fulfilment on the other.

Everywhere, sentimental trash was being lauded, sloppy thinking treated seriously. He could be a voice speaking stern sense in that wilderness. He'd seen that, and it had given him, frankly, a reason to go on living at a time when life had seemed to hold no purpose for him. So, he'd accepted the invitation, made his usual precise arrangements for the care of his house and his dog during his absence.

But a few days before departure, like unwelcome guests at a feast, the doubts had started sidling in to the clean, silent and uncluttered room he had created in his mind. They'd reminded him of the other guests at this fiesta. The other authors, who, presumably, had also been told they were symbols of national importance.

Jack Sprott, some gardening fellow, apparently, who lent his name to pesticides and fertilisers, was one; then there was Barbara Bendix. He had never read one of her books, and never wanted to, but he had seen her interviewed on television. That excruciating experience had been enough to convince him that she was a woman to be avoided at all costs. The dirt she'd dug up on poor Frederick Manners! A fine writer, Fred, occasionally sentimental, even mawkish, but generally someone fairly special, in a country this size. One of the few who richly deserved his popular hero status.

Saul Murdoch winced. All that was gone now. Poor old Fred was the butt of every loudmouth's pub joke since that woman's book, prepared before Fred died and whisked into the typesetter's, he'd heard, within weeks of the old man's funeral.

Funny that the libel laws here, so easily pressed into service on the most trivial of grounds while a person was living, made no objection to the wrecking of a reputation after death. Fred had been robbed of his privacy, his dignity and his pedestal by Barbara Bendix. Of course, everyone who knew him knew about his lovely young men. Maybe not everything—men were fools when it came to sexual matters, embarrassing fools, thought Saul, with an ascetic's complaisance. Certainly some of the things Bendix had said about Fred's habits made one raise an eyebrow. But the work was what counted, not what a man did, discreetly and hurting no-one, in his private life.

So what was Barbara Bendix a symbol of? The national hobby of tall-poppy cutting, of course. And for Berry and Michaels, the power of big sales, big money, in the mass market.

Saul sighed. He wondered if it had cost Brian Berry any heart-searching, publishing such savage tripe. If Fred Manners had been a Berry and Michaels author, would the company still have gone ahead with the book? Maybe it would. One should have no illusions about publishers—and for all his charm, Brian was a ruthless man when the chips were down. Not like his father, a gentleman in every sense.

Well, Brian was on the outer now. None of his charm, or his ruthlessness, had saved him. The shareholders had gone for the money.

Saul Murdoch mused pleasurably for a moment on human folly. And then, unbidden, another face swam into his thoughts. A soft, pointed face, enigmatic smile, chin resting on two small hands. Tilly Lightly. Tilly Lightly, as he'd known her twenty years ago. He frowned. Tilly Lightly, pretty as a picture, hard as nails. How could he have been so fooled?

His friends had tried to tell him, God knows. But he'd swallowed it whole; the flitting elusiveness of that slender body, the clinging pressure of those predatory little hands, the fey, wayward manner that had so entranced him and that had been the screen behind which a remorselessly ordinary mind schemed. Tilly was the one who always, somehow, found a flower to carry, to twist in those soft, white fingers, to play with or stick in her hair. Tilly was the one who always threw herself down on the floor on entering a room, eschewing chairs like a charming child. Tilly was the free spirit who never walked on the beach, but ran, with arms outstretched.

He'd swallowed it whole! He'd been besotted. It was Tilly and Saul against the world, playing on the swings in the park, writing in the sand on the beach at sunset, eating Chinese takeaway, luminous with love, on the faded floral carpet of his bedroom floor.

She painted, in those days. She wrote poetry, too. He winced, remembering. She endlessly sketched and made notes, curled up, waif-like, in corners at parties and in coffee shops. She talked a lot, secretly and low, when they were alone. About creativity, and integrity, and being true to oneself, and how lost and lonely she sometimes felt, with no family, no emotional support, but him.

And he'd talked, too. He'd told her things he'd never thought he could tell—about his cold, withdrawn father, and the mother who had overdosed when he was eight and left him, terrified of the dark. And the nightmares that still tortured him. And the fear that he was no good, second-rate, and a fraud after all. He had cried on her thin, white breast like a child. Fool!

Saul Murdoch tossed his head against his headrest, and gritted his teeth. Even now, twenty years on, the thought of her made his flesh creep. Her and her ludicrous buck-toothed kangaroo, who was everywhere he looked in books, cards, posters—even fluffy toys.

And she'd be there. She'd be there. An honoured guest, like him. A symbol, like him. Symbol of manipulative vanity and playacting and shallowness, that was Tilly Lightly then. That would be Tilly Lightly now. People like her never changed.

He frowned. The beginnings of a headache began to flicker behind his eyes. His lips moved soundlessly as the formless sound he had learned to fear rose in his head.

The woman across the aisle nudged her husband. 'Look at that,' she whispered. The man leaned to look. They exchanged glances and settled back in their seats.

'I told you,' said the woman. 'It is Sir Saul Murdoch. I knew it was, he's exactly like the photo in Viv's book. He must be thinking up a book right now.'

'He looks like he's in pain,' said the man.

'Well, that shows what you know about creative people,' said his wife. 'It costs them dear.'

'I thought he was dead, Saul Murdoch. Years ago.'

'Sshh.'

Barbara Bendix brushed at the flies darting round her face and decided against another dip in the pool. The turquoise water was warm and soupy, and made her eyes sting. Anyway, she should really get herself organised for this little affair tonight. She was supposed to be there in an hour and a half. She looked across at the young man sweating gently on the deck chair beside her. Simon was developing a bit of a paunch. And if she wasn't mistaken, his blond curls were a little thinner on top than the last time she'd seen him. Yes, there was no doubt about it—the damp gold strands were clinging together, and little flashes of pink scalp were showing through. She raised her eyebrows and sighed in genuine regret. He'd been so pretty, too. So eager, and so pretty. Well, he was still eager, but it was amazing how that particular characteristic became disproportionately, rapidly, unattractive as personal charms waned.

Perhaps it had been a bad idea to come to Sydney a day early to have this little holiday with him. One couldn't go back, after all. One should never try. It had been a delicious little fling they'd had two years ago. And how furious that girl Carol had been about it. That had made it even sweeter. But it was lucky she had to move on to the Berry and Michaels apartment now. The situation here could quite easily become boring.

Simon shifted in his chair and his flesh wobbled slightly under the golden tan. He murmured and felt for her hand. She evaded him gently and stood up.

'What's up, Barbs?' he said, struggling into a sitting position.

She smiled at him vaguely and blew a negligent kiss. 'Have to go, darling. It's work time. You stay there.'

She wandered into the house, trailing her towel behind her. She would have a shower. Then she'd read right through her notes on Saul Murdoch and Tilly Lightly before she got dressed. She didn't want to miss a single opportunity, over the next few days, to add to the Murdoch file. This was a gift from heaven, this Berry and Michaels extravaganza.

'Barb?' Simon stood at the terrace door, blinking into the dimness of the house.

But Barbara was busily making plans, and had already forgotten he existed.

4

The Final Ingredients

Dorothy Hale looked miserably at her reflection in the dressing-table mirror, and plucked at the waistline of her dress. The powder blue had looked so pretty in the shop, with its little tucks and softly gathered waist. And the salesgirl had said it suited her down to the ground. But now, suddenly, it looked all wrong. She looked sort of bunchy, like a bedroom cushion on legs. It was the gathered waist. It made her look fat, and the colour was too young for her anyway. How could she have made such a mistake? She sank down onto the elegant little stool that stood before the dressing table, and homesickness swept over her like a wave. At home she always went shopping with a friend—with Jean or Judy or one of the others. They'd never have let her buy a thing like this. Who did she have here, even to talk to, let alone to shop with?

The mirror reflected her plump, unhappy face with its straying, wispy grey hair in sharp contrast, so it seemed to her, to the view through the window of the Berry and Michaels penthouse flat—the sky, hot, cloudless, growing paler in preparation for the abrupt Australian sunset, the glittering Harbour, the white tops of the Opera House sails. Alien, all of it. Bright, shining, young, alien. Like the long-legged, harsh-voiced girls in the boutiques, the brash, characterless shops, the TV, the white light, the terrible heat . . .

'Dot, they'll be here in a minute. What're you doing?' Her husband stood in the doorway frowning at her, his hand at the knot of his impeccable tie.

She turned and blinked at him stupidly. 'I can't wear this. I've got nothing to wear,' she said, and shrugged helplessly.

In three strides he was beside her, bending close. 'Dorothy,' he said urgently, his mouth by her ear. 'Come on. We've got no time for this, girl. You look fine. It doesn't matter how you look. And anyway you look fine.'

'Quentin,' she clutched at his dark sleeve. 'Quentin, I hate it here. I'm lonely . . . it's so hot. I want to go home.'

'For God's sake!' He pulled away from her, scowling, whispering furiously. 'Dot, there's no time for this! We're supposed to be hosting a party. They'll be here any minute. The waiter's here. Amy's in there doing everything. Pull yourself together, Dorothy, or . . .'

'Quentin!' A low voice called from the next room, 'The lift's on its way up!'

'Coming!' Quentin spun towards the door and held out his hand. Dorothy, obedient, finally, to the habit of years, took it, and let herself be heaved from the stool and led into the living room.

Amy was standing by a crystal vase of lilies near the lift doors. Her cream-gold arms glimmered against the cool simplicity of her sleeveless white dress. Her straw-coloured hair was pulled cleanly back from her forehead, and her pale green eyes turned, expressionless, to her employer as he entered the room.

'Sorry, Amy,' he said. 'Everything ready?'

'Everything's organised,' said Amy. 'No problems.'

Dorothy felt her husband's hand slip away from her own.

'You're a treasure, Amy,' said Quentin Hale, in that special voice he kept just for her.

Dorothy plucked at the waistline of her dress, and watched the little gold arrow above the lift doors move slowly from 3 to 4. She knew the clanking brass cage below was bringing strangers. She knew it was bringing tension and embarrassment for her and strain for Quentin to whom this Big Four affair had become a symbol: his open declaration of taking charge. She knew all that, and braced herself, dumpily heroic, as she stood lost in the white, blue and gold of the executive suite that would never be her home. But she didn't know that it was bringing hatred and horror into her life as well. And she never thought of murder.

Kate sat in her cluttered office on the second floor, trying not to let her restlessness show. 6.15. She should be upstairs at the welcome party by now, handing things around, smiling, showing the flag, trying to keep the peace, if it came to that.

But Paul Morrisey seemed oblivious to the lateness of the hour. He talked on, jabbing long fingers at the air to make his points, going over his grievances again and again. Kate had given him all the answers—how glib they sounded even to her—but nonetheless they were true, and all she had to offer. No, the novel wasn't selling all that well, but slim, literary hardback novels by first-time authors were notoriously difficult, and *Unexpected People* was doing no worse than most. Yes, the publicity department had sent review copies to all the literary editors on his list, and more. Yes, it was true that one of the bookshops he'd mentioned had ordered his book and not been supplied, but that was because the proprietors hadn't paid their bills for some months now, and had been 'put on stop' by Accounts. The other bookshops on his list, sadly, had refused to re-order after their first copies sold, whatever they had told him, and his mother, and his friend in Canberra, about Berry and Michaels' unaccountable refusal to supply their urgent requests for further stock.

And, yes, Saul Murdoch's scathing dismissal of the novel in that long article about the year's literary offerings in *Book Review Quarterly* hadn't helped. Not at all. However unfair it had been, however bigoted and wrong-headed and filled with errors and misconceptions, however . . .

Kate's phone rang. She answered it with a sense of relief, raising her eyebrows in apology at poor Paul, who was leaning forward in his chair, a long, lank strand of dark hair falling into his eyes.

'Kate, where are you? You're supposed to be up here!' It was Malcolm Pool. He sounded rather ruffled. Kate almost smiled. Problems so soon? And Evie, presumably, unhelpful.

'I have an author with me, Malcolm,' she said smoothly, glancing at her watch, and at Paul Morrisey. 'I'll get there as soon as I can.'

Paul relaxed in his chair, and brushed back his hair unconcernedly. He was obviously not going to cooperate. He knew about Quentin's cocktail party. In fact, despite the obvious sincerity of his conversation during the last hour, Kate was sure that he had called at this time deliberately, as a protest against his exclusion from the select group upstairs. He'd been invited for the party tomorrow night, but he clearly resented the fuss being made of the 'Big Four'. Quite a few of the authors did, and Kate couldn't blame them.

'Kate, you'll really have to come. Um . . . just a sec.' There was a clatter as Malcolm dropped the phone. Subdued noises rose and fell. Over all one voice could be heard, rough, almost roaring, with the occasional bellow of laughter. Kate knew who that was—'Jolly' Jack Sprott, the gardener's friend, and in his usual form, by the sound of things. No wonder Malcolm was worried. This time she did smile, smiled while the tension and concern that had been mounting over the past weeks churned away in her stomach. It was so ludicrous, after all. Such an absurd situation.

The phone clattered again, and Malcolm was whispering hoarsely in her ear, 'Quentin says if you can't get rid of him—her—whoever it is, bring them up.'

'I have Paul Morrisey with me, Malcolm,' Kate said,

in that special, even, warning voice they all used when indiscretion or disaster was imminent.

'Who? Oh, *Unexplained Persons*. Yes, well, that's OK. New Breed. That's OK. Bring him up. Come now.'

'Malcolm . . .'

'Kate, look, I have to go. Come up now! Quentin says.'

The phone clicked, and Malcolm was gone.

Kate looked at Paul Morrisey, slumped back, staring sightlessly out at the park that now swam in thick, golden light, deep shadows forming under the trees and in the shrubbery.

'The royal summons,' she said, and stood, picking up her handbag. 'I have to go upstairs, Paul. Sorry.'

He sat still, and for a moment she thought he was going to refuse to move. Then he smiled bitterly and heaved himself out of the low chair. 'Of course, Kate. I'm sorry to have kept you from "Higher Things", as it were. I'll get off, then. See you with the rabble tomorrow night.'

'It's hardly a matter of the rabble, Paul! It's 150 people instead of the 500 it should have been. Invitations are like gold!' Kate realised she sounded sharp and shrugged in frustration.

'It's just that so many people are upset by not getting an invitation,' she said. 'They've been ringing up for weeks. I'm exhausted by the whole thing.'

'Oh, yes?' Paul remained unmollified.

Kate led the way awkwardly through the dim, deserted office to the lift.

'You go down this way, Paul. I'll go up the stairs,' she said, rummaging in her handbag for a mirror and comb. No time now to primp in the ladies' room, but she'd better make sure her hair wasn't actually standing on end, and that she had no white-out on her face.

At least she'd come to work dressed for the occasion. She'd known she wouldn't have time to change. Amy Phibes had found time though, she reflected sourly. She'd seen her gliding up the corridor, a cool vision in

white, as Paul came in. The well-organised Amy
Phibes. The well-organised Malcolm Pool. Scylla and
Charybdis, Evie called them. They were a pretty pair,
all right. Both of them had irritated Kate within a
week, and neither had improved on acquaintance.
Where was that mirror! Her handbag was a disaster
area.

'The lift's upstairs,' Paul was saying sulkily. He
stood with hunched shoulders, watching the gold arrow above their heads. As he spoke, there was a clatter,
and the lift started its downward journey.

'There we are,' said Kate brightly, thankfully closing her fingers around the elusive items in her bag. She
hauled the mirror out and began pushing at her hair.
Paul watched tactlessly, his head on one side. 'No point
in looking in on Evie, I suppose,' he said.

'She's upstairs too by now, Paul,' said Kate placatingly.

'Oh, of course.' His sensitive mouth twitched, and
again he brushed his hair out of his eyes with a bony
hand.

The lift shuddered to a stop before them. The outer
door slid open. The brass cage had been pulled back,
and the stolid figure of Sid, doorman, mailroom atten-
dant, and man-of-all-work at Berry and Michaels for
forty years, was revealed. He blinked at them.

'Sid, could you take Paul on downstairs, please?' said
Kate. 'I'll go up the stairs.'

'The young bloke said to bring you both up,' said
Sid flatly. 'In the lift. You *and* your friend.'

'Oh . . .' Kate stopped, flummoxed.

'Well, well . . .' Paul stepped lightly into the lift and
looked at Kate enquiringly, triumphantly. He ran his
hand through his hair. 'Coming, Kate?'

Hopelessly outmanoeuvred, Kate shrugged and
smiled. She stepped into the lift beside Sid. He turned
slowly to look at her, with his lowering red face and
dead grey eyes. 'He said bring you both up,' he said
loudly. 'You and—'

'Sure, Sid, terrific. That's fine. Thanks.' Kate felt

her cheeks burning. She wondered if Paul realised she'd been trying to avoid this. In the embarrassment and mild hysteria of the moment she found herself smiling broadly. Evie's face, when she saw the new arrival, would be a study. The recipe for disaster over which she'd so bitterly chuckled for six weeks was on the boil upstairs. Now Kate, who'd so disapproved of the mischief, was bringing with her the final, explosive, surprise ingredient. Evie would appreciate the joke.

5

Reunion

In the elegant apartment upstairs, the small, select cocktail party that Malcolm had imagined so pleasurably over the past month was in full swing. Barbara Bendix, décolleté in black, with jangling bracelets to the elbows and huge hoop earrings dangling almost to her shoulders, sipped champagne and smiled as Tilly Lightly, fair and fragile in a Chinese shawl, whispered, head on one side, to Quentin Hale and Sir Saul Murdoch. Soft music played, a waiter glided unobtrusively around as though he ran on little silver tracks, delicious morsels of food were being exclaimed over and accepted, champagne flowed. It was just as he'd planned it. Just as he'd imagined. But it wasn't quite right.

He gritted his teeth. Nothing was ever quite right. There were always problems. No matter what you did, how well you did your job, other people always mucked things up.

He looked with longing at Quentin's glittering group by the flower-filled fireplace. That's where he should be. This was his show. He deserved to be at Quentin's right hand, with the people who mattered. But here he was hanging round like a junior, having to deal with the misfits while that bloody cool piece Amy Phibes stood there, relaxed as you please, acting the hostess.

Tilly Lightly's daughter, Sarah, or whatever her

name was, was standing all by herself looking very down in the mouth. It was getting a bit obvious. Why on earth didn't she make an effort, he thought irritably. Great lump of a thing she was, and done up like Little Miss Muffet. Awful. Tilly had whispered to him, at the airport, that Sarah was a bit shy. Well, who wasn't? But you had to make an effort, didn't you? Not just stand around waiting for someone else to do it for you. That didn't get you anywhere. Oh damn, he'd better go over and look after her again.

But what about Jack Sprott? Malcolm glanced nervously behind him. Dorothy Hale was still there, backed against the wall. She looked irritatingly appalling as usual in some flouncy-looking blue dress. She was as bad as Sarah Lightly. Her hair was all wisps and frizz and her eyes were glazed. What a liability to Quentin that woman was! Still, at least she had the grace to keep a low profile. He supposed she and Quentin had a deal. Anyway, unlike Sarah Lightly, she was at least making herself useful.

Dorothy was coping, for the moment, with Jolly Jack Sprott, a short, red-faced gnome with an enormous belly, inexpressibly seedy in a green suit and stained tie. He swayed slightly before her as he went on with a convoluted anecdote about the Vietnam war. Each time he gestured, or demonstrated a tactical position, a little champagne would tip from his glass onto the carpet or onto his tie or foot. A few grains of caviar and a biscuit crumb clung to the corner of his mouth like a bizarre beauty spot. He, at least, was obviously enjoying himself hugely.

Malcolm watched him for a moment. Yes, there was no doubt about it. He was very drunk. How could it have happened so quickly? Good thing they'd decided not to have photographers here tonight, to keep everything friendly and intimate. And that ABC researcher, too. It was bloody lucky Quentin had decided against inviting her. The old guy must be overexcited, or something. Malcolm clutched his glass of tepid soda water and felt helpless.

There was a peal of high-pitched laughter from Barbara Bendix. Jack Sprott turned around to look at her, stumbled and tipped his glass down the front of his shirt. Malcolm hastened forward to help, aware of Saul Murdoch's fastidiously disgusted face, Quentin's stern pink one and Barbara's broad, malicious grin. He was suddenly, furiously angry. Why wasn't Evie Newell helping? Standing over there with her know-all look on, talking to the waiter, for God's sake! It was typical!

She was jealous, of course. Just because her pathetic, clapped-out ideas had been rejected in favour of his. And where was Kate Delaney? Wasting her time with some literary no-hoper downstairs when she could be making herself useful up here! No loyalty or sense of priorities, these people. He was horrified to find his eyes prickling with tears.

'Don't worry about it, mate, don't worry about it!' Jack Sprott brushed champagne from his loathsome tie and leered at Malcolm with red-rimmed blue eyes. 'Won't hurt. It'll cool me off, won't it, love?'

Dorothy Hale, thus appealed to, smiled and tittered nervously, her eye on the other people in the room. She felt somehow responsible for this man, who had attached himself to her so genially on arrival and clung like a barnacle ever since.

Truth to tell, she felt quite comfortable with him in one way. He reminded her of her Uncle Walter, back in the old days. Uncle Walter had always liked a drink. And he'd talked about the War quite a bit, too—the Great War, in his case. But he'd been a jolly, kind man who'd sweep you up in his arms in a bear hug at Christmas and other family get-togethers, crushing your cheek against his rough, tobacco-smelling coat and laughing with beery breath.

Dorothy half smiled. The old days. Dad and Mum's little corner shop, and the flat above. Not much money. Just enough to get by, she realised now. But still . . . happy days. She'd certainly been happy then. Young, and happy, and not bad looking, though her sister Daphne had been the pretty one in the family. Really pretty,

poor Daphne had been as a girl—fair as an angel. She'd
had boyfriends first, though she was two years younger.

But it was Dot, dark, sweet and twenty, who was
serving in the shop the day Quentin Hale walked in
the door, a sharp-faced, skinny, eager young man in a
shiny suit, selling chocolate biscuits. Funny to think
of now, looking at him, so prosperous, and pink and
polished. But chocolate biscuits it was, on commission,
too, and he didn't have two pennies to rub together in
those days. Dad bought some of the biscuits to try.
They sold, though they weren't very nice, really, Dot
had thought, and Quentin came again, and again. On
the third visit he asked her out, to tea and the pictures.
And that's how it started.

When he asked her to get engaged, Dad had been
pleased. 'He'll be a good provider, Em,' he'd said to
Mum, tearful by the cooker that night. 'He's as determined as they come, ambitious, and a good salesman.
He'll get on. Dot won't do better.'

But Dot hadn't cared about any of that. All she knew
was that her heart had turned over that first day Quentin Hale walked into her life and faced her across the
shop counter in the badly-fitting suit, and that from
that moment all he had had to do was hold out his
hand, and she'd have gone with him to the ends of the
earth.

Now, it seemed, she had.

Her gaze travelled around the blue and gold room,
taking in the waiters, the dressed-up strangers, the
flowers, the sunset view through the plate-glass windows. Thirty-five years on, and here they were, she
and Quentin. She hadn't changed. No reason to. She'd
spent those years on the house, their sons, her friends,
and Quentin's every domestic need.

But Quentin had changed. Switched from biscuits
to stationery, from stationery to books. Moved on,
moved up, into the Gold Group—sales, marketing,
management. He'd grown heavier and sleeker and
harder, and his eyes had grown more watchful. He

mixed with people you read about in the newspapers. He'd got on, just like Dad said he would. Despite his state education, his working-class accent . . . all those things he worried about so much.

Not that he hadn't had a battle. And, true, he'd never made it right to the top. Of course, here things like the accent didn't matter. Practically everyone spoke like old Jack Sprott, even the newsreaders, and the Prime Minister. Maybe that was one reason he'd been keen to come, take the offer to run this Berry and Michaels place.

Dorothy eased her plump feet in the tight little powder blue shoes she'd bought to match the dress. She'd thought if Quentin was happy, she'd be happy. She'd thought, too, that a change of scene would help. Well, it hadn't worked out that way, had it? Her faded blue eyes rested for a moment on her husband. He was standing, hand in jacket pocket, talking to the tall, worried-looking man who was the important writer Sir Saul Murdoch, that brazen, black-haired Barbara Bendix woman with all the jewellery, and the dainty little children's writer, Tilly Lightly, who seemed to have a lot to say for herself. Quentin looked very nervy, she thought.

She sighed. Nothing was simple anymore. Nothing was easy. Behind Quentin a cool, white figure hovered. Amy. She was leaning forward, saying something quietly, the soft lights gleaming on her straw-coloured hair. Quentin was leaning towards her, listening, smiling attentively now, while Tilly Lightly chatted on, oblivious, and Barbara Bendix watched, like a cat who senses movement in a mousehole. Dorothy's lips tightened unconsciously. Life could be very cruel. Especially for a woman.

'Here I am, going on . . .' Jack Sprott leered at her gnomishly, breaking into her mood. She realised with a start that they'd been joined by two more people—Kate Delaney, that nice girl from downstairs, and a tall, rather sulky-looking young man.

'Oh, no, not at all,' she flustered. 'Hello, Kate. I didn't see you before, dear. And is this your . . .'

'No, Dorothy, I was late. No, this isn't Jeremy.' Kate smiled. 'This is Paul Morrisey, one of our authors. Paul, this is Dorothy Hale.'

The young man nodded curtly, and flicked his lanky hair back with nervous fingers. He looked restlessly around the room.

'Been telling Dot some Vietnam stories. Boring her, I have, Kate. Can't help meself,' Jack Sprott nodded and grinned genially. 'You know me. See that waiter-fellah anywhere, Kate? I need a top-up of bubbly. Had a bit of an upset before.' He gestured at his champagne-stained shirt front.

'Oh, what a shame. Oh well, he'll be round in a minute, Jack,' said Kate hastily, glancing apprehensively at Dorothy. 'Have something to eat while you're waiting. What've you been doing?'

'Oh, you know, this and that,' said Jack Sprott vaguely. His watery blue eyes stared into space. 'Been waiting on you, really, Kate.'

'On me? What . . . oh.' Kate looked momentarily appalled, but recovered quickly. 'The memoir. Oh yes, of course, Jack. Won't be long now. I've been so busy, um, sorry we've kept you . . .'

'Ah, I know you women aren't too interested in war stories. I know.' Jack Sprott nodded and licked his lips, finally and mercifully removing the grains of caviar from the corner of his mouth. He winked at Paul conspiratorially. Paul nodded uneasily. You could see that the idea of enjoying male solidarity with the likes of Jack Sprott wasn't something he'd previously considered.

'Battles and raids and that, and men up against it . . . not your sort of thing. Give it to one of the blokes to look at, Kate.' He leaned over and spoke to her seriously, face suddenly solemn. 'All jokes aside, it's a valuable document, love. One man's Vietnam. Full of marvellous stuff, it is. God, it took me back, when I dug it out. All the blokes . . . You wouldn't believe

what we went through and the times we had. Look,'
he laid a stubby paw on her arm, 'females just don't
know, love, what life's all about, what men go through
in war, fighting for all you back home. Now, I know—
it was my choice. Regular soldier. Knew what I was
doing. But the others—kids, most of them. Bugger-all
training, shipped out there, lonely for home, fighting
for their lives in a strange country.' He shook his head.
'You sheilas don't have a clue what that's like. No reflection, love. You've never had to do it. You've never
been asked to do it.'

Dorothy Hale, dumpy in the regrettable powder
blue, raised tired eyes. 'Not like that, no we haven't,'
she said quietly. 'But there are other ways.' She stared
over his shoulder for a moment, then dropped her eyes
again. 'Women fight at home, where they have to,' she
murmured. 'They always have. When they want to
protect something they care about, they can.'

Jack Sprott smiled benignly. 'Oh, yeah, of course,
you're right there, Dot. Mothers protecting their young
and that. Oh yeah, any bitch with puppies'll teach you
that,' he said loudly.

Dorothy turned away.

Jack put his hand up to his mouth and leaned towards Kate. 'Nice old sport,' he whispered piercingly
in her shrinking ear. 'Had a few too many, I reckon.
Wouldn't you say?'

Kate covered her eyes with her hand. Paul Morrisey
sidled uneasily away.

'You read me book, Kate, and get back to me, eh? I
want to see it done. It needs to be done. I'll get it
bloody printed meself, if I have to. Ah, there's the
bloke I want. Bubbly for an old fella, son? Thanks.'
Jack helped himself to a brimming glass, and beamed.
'Now, Kate, let me just tell you one of the stories
I . . .'

The raucous voice droned on. Kate stood helplessly,
nodding mechanically, trapped by her guilt. She saw
Dorothy Hale, free at last, walk uncertainly across the
room, hover on the outskirts of her husband's group,

and then move to the solitary figure standing stolidly by the couch. That must be Tilly Lightly's daughter, though it was hard to believe. The older woman nodded and smiled brightly, inviting a chat.

One outsider to another, thought Kate suddenly. Still, Dorothy didn't have to make the effort. She was a genuinely nice woman. She really cared about other people, you could see that. In fact, her obvious love for Quentin Hale was the one thing that made Kate think there might be a pleasant side to his nature.

Kate had been very surprised, the first time she'd met Dorothy. Everyone had. She was so totally, so unexpectedly, matronly, motherly, kind and ordinary looking. The opposite of the sort of wife Quentin Hale might be expected to have. She looked ten years older than he did, for a start, and had a soft, pretty, English country voice and an unobtrusive manner. She talked mostly about her sons, and their wives and the grandchildren, and about their daily lives at home. She talked about Quentin himself as though he was a funny, vulnerable human being like everyone else, instead of the glossy-surfaced, chilly character who had cruised into the eccentric, friendly atmosphere of Berry and Michaels like a great grey shark into a small, busy, multicoloured aquarium, and had a similar effect on spontaneity and comfort.

Kate sighed inwardly. She wondered whether her time in this company was finally coming to an end. It wasn't too much fun anymore. Brian was gone. Evie was certain to go now. And there'd been other offers. Maybe she should . . .

'Oi!' Jack's elbow dug into her ribs. 'I say . . .' he swayed closer to her and she had to force herself not to avert her face. He was very drunk. He must have been well away before he got to the party. 'I say, I said, Kate, I'm just going to toddle over . . . Mohammed to the mountain . . . have a word with the great white chief. You come too. Give us some moral support.' He fixed her with watery pink and blue eyes. 'Want to get in good with him, don't I?' He grabbed

Kate by the hand and began stumbling towards the group standing around Quentin Hale.

'Jack! Hold on, I don't think . . .'

'Don't let the heavies scare you, Kate,' hissed Jack, in a stage whisper guaranteed to reach the furthest corners of the room. 'You should meet the ladies with him, anyhow, and the bloke. You publish books they've done. Kids' yarns, I think he said. Not the bloke, of course. He does real books. Never read them myself, but they say they aren't too bad. Young Malcolm's getting me one of them, to look at. The girls' books, too. You read any of them at all?'

'Oh yes, yes I have,' gabbled Kate, stumbling along in his sodden wake as he reached his goal and bobbed up, stocky and glistening, between Quentin and Tilly.

Quentin smiled, showing all his teeth. 'Jack!' he boomed heartily. 'Enjoying yourself?'

'How'ya going?' leered Jolly Jack Sprott, nodding and beaming at the circle of faces. 'Time of me life, yeah. Thought it was time to do a bit of a mingle, eh?'

'That's the way!' said Quentin, moving back a step, out of spitting range. 'Get to know everyone. We've got an exciting few days ahead of us. You've met everyone here, of course?'

'Too right!' Jack winked hugely at Tilly and put a stubby paw on her arm. 'Polly and Saul and Barbie and me met earlier, in the lift, didn't we, love?'

Tilly Lightly smiled and murmured, looking limpidly at Kate.

'No, no Jack,' corrected Kate, on cue. 'Tilly, not Polly.' She glanced nervously at Quentin, whose professional smile seemed to have frozen into position.

'Tilly put the kettle on! Doesn't go so well, does it?' hooted Jack, and snorted with laughter, very taken with his own wit. 'Me memory's going now. Tilly, right. And Saul. Right?' Saul Murdoch nodded uncomfortably. Barbara Bendix laughed, and reached for the last biscuit from the platter on the mantelpiece.

'Go on, Jack, test yourself,' she said, her mouth full. 'What about the others?'

Nodding happily, Jack spun round. 'You're on,' he said, and squinted across the room. 'Righteo, then. Now. There's young what's-his-name, the organising bloke, Malcolm, and your girl, Quentin, Amy, with him . . . ah, there's old Evie there. Who's that she's with Katie?'

'Paul Morrisey,' muttered Kate and glanced quickly at Saul Murdoch's stern face, seeing it settle into even harder lines.

'Ah, yes, and . . . and there's your good lady wife, Quentin. And she's talking to . . . now who's that? Big girl, isn't she, eh? She come up in the lift with us too. Who's that Quentin? Another one of your girls?'

Quentin cleared his throat.

'That's Sarah, my daughter, Jack,' Tilly Lightly said softly. She lifted her chin, with a warning smile.

'Fine looking girl,' said Jack Sprott heartily, and hastily. 'Never would have picked it, though, I must say. Would you, Saul?'

'She seems a very nice girl,' said Saul Murdoch coldly. 'No, I'd never have guessed it.'

Tilly's smile grew wary. Barbara's grew wider.

There was a brief silence. Jack looked around vaguely and then turned back to look at Sarah Lightly.

'Funny, you know,' he said, biting a thumbnail, 'I think I've met your girl before, or she puts me in mind of someone. Who, now? Who, who, who . . .' his voice trailed off. His eyes began to flutter closed and the hand holding the champagne glass to lower.

'Jack!' Kate put an urgent hand on his arm. 'Why don't we go and have a word with Evie? You haven't—'

The eyes snapped open. 'Just thinking, Kate. Think I was going off, did you? Think I'm a bit tiddly? Don't worry about me. I'm an old hand, eh? Now . . .' He focused carefully on the tall figure talking to Dorothy. 'Sarah Lightfoot. Sarah Lightfoot . . .'

'Lightly,' murmured Kate, in an agony of embarrassment, irritation and the need to laugh aloud.

'Lightly. Sarah Lightly . . . now . . . ah, no! Surely

not!' Jack spun round to face them, his face glowing. 'You wouldn't believe that!'

'What is it, Jack?' Barbara leaned forward, smiling encouragingly.

'By God, if she's Sarah Lightly, this must be Mrs Rabbit!' crowed Jack Sprott, and caught Tilly in his odoriferous arms.

6

RUCTIONS

Being hugged by Jack Sprott wasn't an experience most women would relish, and Tilly, shocked into forgetting her chosen persona for once, acted in the way that came naturally to her—screeching, wriggling and jabbing furiously at his chest with her elbows. Her audience, stunned at the sight of a short, red man who had apparently gone mad before their eyes embracing a tiny, writhing harridan who he seemed to think was a rabbit, and an old friend of his into the bargain, stood foolishly rooted to the spot, mouths gaping. Even Barbara Bendix was momentarily nonplussed.

Scarlet in the face, Tilly managed to free herself. She tossed back her hair, and scuttled to safety beside Quentin Hale, wrapping the Chinese shawl tightly around her shoulders and chest.

Jack, oblivious, was hailing Sarah who was, quite understandably, staring and refusing to obey his summons. 'Oi, oi!' he shouted raucously, wildly beckoning. 'Sarah Lightly! C'm'ere and meet your Uncle Jack!'

'Uncle Jack?' Barbara Bendix was agog, her eyes sparkling with mischief, her mobile face fascinated and intent. She leaned over to Tilly, earrings dangling, exposing a breathtaking cleavage.

'A long-lost relation, Tilly,' she beamed, patting the smaller woman's arm. 'How exciting!' Tilly drew back

further into the protection of Quentin's rigid shadow.
She murmured something to him.

'Jack,' Kate plucked at his sleeve desperately, but he
was intent on his quarry.

'Sarah, c'mon! I want a good look at you. I knew
your dad. Knew him! God, I'll say I knew him! Come
and say g'day!'

Sarah Lightly's pale, closed face was suddenly suffused with delicate colour. Her dull eyes widened, her
lips parted. Totally unguarded for a moment, her face
lost its heavy, sulky look. She moved quickly towards
the gesticulating Jack. He barely came to her shoulder
and in his present excited state looked even more
gnome-like than usual.

'Smile!' ordered Jolly Jack Sprott. 'Go on, don't be
shy, love.' She gave a surprised half smile, showing
her long front teeth and he pointed, grinned and turned
to the others.

'There you are! The image!' he chortled. 'Her dad,
just the same. I knew I knew that grin. See? Rabbit
Lightly, we called him, in the Unit—on account of the
teeth, see? Well, well, who'd have thought it? After all
these years. Twenty years. Sarah, the Baby Bunny
herself. Not so little now, eh?'

The girl was crimson. The brief moment of unself-
consciousness had passed. She shook her head unhappily and waited, very aware of being the centre of
attention and disliking it intensely.

'Your dad was a big, strapping bloke, too,' said Jack.
'A big bloke, wasn't he, Tilly? A lovely bloke. A great
mate.' He stopped for a moment, and in his eyes the
ready tears began to glisten.

'You knew Alistair in Vietnam,' said Tilly Lightly
softly. Her eyes were huge in her small-boned face.
She shivered slightly under her thin shawl.

'Ate with him, slept with him, fought with him,
nearly bloody died with him, love,' Jack Sprott rubbed
his eyes with his coat sleeve unselfconsciously. 'Rabbit
Lightly, eh? Always called him Rabbit, see, because of
these,' he tapped his own front teeth. 'Oh, I knew him

all right. Knew him as well as I knew meself for a while. Funny! He was funny as a circus, Rabbit was. Laugh! He'd have us in stitches, yarning away and playing the fool, sending us all up gutless, making up names, real humorous names. We got on like a house on fire.'

'How fascinating, Jack!' Barbara Bendix's dark, malicious face was alight with interest. 'He sounds awfully good fun. You must have been like two peas in a pod. Tilly's always been so quiet about him, too. I'd never realised, Tilly, that your husband was a life-of-the-party sort, like Jack. What fun for you.' Tilly flushed. Kate looked anxiously at Sarah Lightly, but she either hadn't picked up Barbara's tone or had decided to ignore her. She was staring at Jack with absorbed interest.

'It's nice to meet someone who knew Dad,' she said, not looking at her mother. 'We . . . I don't get much of a chance to talk about him. No one . . .' Her voice trailed off, and then she shook her head nervously and continued, 'He didn't get home from Vietnam till I was a toddler, and he was killed when I was only six, so I've only got the haziest memories. And a few pictures.'

'Shame we never kept in touch.' Jack shook his head. 'Funny how it happens, isn't it? Still, you know how it is—thousands of miles apart, girlie, once we got back. We all went our separate ways. All had our own lives and problems and that, back here.' He paused for a moment, then turned to Tilly and put out a reproachful red paw. 'But you should've got in touch, love, when he passed away, anyhow. Terrible. Young bloke like that. First I knew about it was at our ten-year reunion.'

Tilly bit her lip. 'I'm sorry,' she said, with an obvious effort. 'But I honestly didn't know you existed, Jack. I don't think Alistair ever talked about Vietnam once, after he got home.' She closed her eyes and shivered slightly. 'He was very sensitive underneath. I think it hurt him to even . . . even think about it. And he knew how it would affect me. Sarah knows. I've never been able to stand all that sort of thing. I just couldn't bear it. It's just not me. He knew that, and he knew what I'd been through, waiting and waiting. Lonely, so little money, so much time to think. If I hadn't had Sarah, and my work, I don't know what I would have done.' She shook her head and stared down at her little, flat shoes. Sarah looked distressed, and everyone else looked respectful. Everyone, Kate noticed, except Saul Murdoch, who was watching with a fastidiously curled lip, and Barbara Bendix, whose eyes were calculating.

'You survived, though, didn't you, Tilly?' Saul said coldly, breaking the spell. 'You found diversions to pass all that time?'

She jumped a little, and then her expression softened to one of helpless appeal. 'I had to do something,' she murmured. 'It's hard, alone with a baby to look after. I owed it to Sarah, and to Alistair, to keep going.'

'Course you did, love,' said Jack and patted her arm moistly.

But Saul's stony face didn't flicker.

Barbara Bendix leaned forward. 'You were married awfully young, weren't you, Tilly?' she asked, with more warmth and interest than Kate had seen her show previously.

Tilly smiled reminiscently. 'Oh yes,' she said. 'Only twenty. Still at university. Alistair was working—travelling round—selling, well, kitchen appliances, as a matter of fact. He was twenty, too. We'd loved each other from school. And he was called up and really I just said to him, let's do it, let's get married and I'll wait for you. It just seemed *right*. And we wanted a baby straight away, just straight away. I could never be sensible and practical about things like that.'

'No,' Barbara smiled admiringly, and warning bells began ringing in Kate's ears. She exchanged glances with Evie, who, attracted by the excitement, had drifted across the room to stand with Paul Morrisey on the outskirts of the group.

'Of course, Sarah doesn't remember what they were like, those early years,' Tilly went on, in her light, sighing voice. 'And she saw so little of Alistair after he came home. He had to travel a lot, for his work, and he was so broken, so terribly affected by what he'd done and seen.'

'I saw a lot of him, Mama,' Sarah broke in, flushing. 'Most weekends. And he wasn't sad like that all the time. I remember. I remember him when he'd come home from trips—playing with me, and going for walks, and telling me funny stories, and buying me things, and . . .'

'Oh yes, all that,' Tilly dismissed her daughter's memories with a flutter of a hand. 'It's only natural that he would have kept his real feelings hidden from you. Oh, but I mean the *real* Alistair. Only I knew him, the man I married. The man who came back to me, the man you knew, was just a shell.'

'Mama . . .' Sarah began, but Tilly shook her head. 'I know, darling, I know. It's easy enough to hero-worship someone you hardly know. Much easier than to understand and appreciate someone who looks after your baby needs day in, day out. The one who's got to keep things going. That's so, isn't it? That's always been so.' She looked soberly at the assembly, a half smile trembling on her lips.

Sarah turned away.

'It must have been very hard for you, Tilly, while he was in Vietnam,' said Barbara, shaking her head. 'I was wondering how you managed with the baby, with Sarah, while you were at university. You went back more or less as soon as he left, didn't you? In Perth?'

Tilly paused. 'Ah, yes,' she said finally. 'Yes, I did. I thought it would be best to keep busy, finish my studies and everything. My mother—'

'Oh, your *mother* looked after the baby,' Barbara nodded smilingly. 'How marvellous for you. But it must have been terribly awkward toiling backwards and forwards every day. I think your family lives, or lived, right out of Perth, and I don't suppose you had a car?'

Tilly stared at her uneasily and then pulled herself together. 'Oh, you know, we managed,' she said vaguely, and made a little movement as though to close the subject.

'Mama lived in town, actually,' Sarah blurted out. 'Sometimes she came home at the weekend to see us. Grandma said so, anyway. I don't really remember.'

'Sarah, you make it sound dreadful!' Tilly laughed a little shrilly. Her eyes were startled. 'That sounds as though I just abandoned you!'

'Oh, well, sorry,' Sarah mumbled. She looked up under her eyebrows with the half frightened, half defiant air of the weak creature deciding which way to dart next.

'I suppose, Tilly,' Barbara's throaty voice cut calmly through the embarrassed silence. 'I suppose it was at that time that you met Saul.' She smiled, cat-like, up at the tall man's grim face. 'I heard you two were the closest friends in those days. Intimate friends, really. What a shame you lost touch. Like Jack says, it's funny how it happens like that.'

'Not particularly funny in this case,' said Saul Murdoch, looking straight ahead. 'I finished my course and moved across the country to Victoria.'

'Still, I gather you two were inseparable for a while.' Barbara's claws were out now. She'd followed a pretty spotty trail over the past few months. She'd only had a few hearsay leads and a couple of dusty old record books to go by. But now her instinct was being proved right, and she pursued her quarry relentlessly.

Sarah gazed at her mother in simple surprise, and Tilly moved restlessly. 'I don't know what you're hinting at, Barbara, really,' she said defensively. 'I'm afraid all this is getting beyond me. I'm not much good at subtleties.' She shivered and drew her shawl around her. 'Saul *is* an old friend. It's no great secret. We had a lot in common in those days, didn't we, Saul?' She looked up at him and smiled conspiratorially. 'We were both loners, I suppose. Both shy, sensitive people. Both working for peace. Kindred spirits, in a bad, bad time.'

'And how did Saul feel about Alistair away fighting in Vietnam, and the baby, home at Grandma's?' The offensive politeness of Barbara Bendix was indescribable.

Tilly tossed her shining hair back, and her pale face grew pink. 'Barbara, I don't know what you think you're proving, or saying with all this. If you're trying to say there was some disloyalty involved, then you just don't understand the kind of relationship—'

'Oh, stop acting!' Saul Murdoch was white, the lines between his eyebrows and running down from nose to mouth charcoal grey. He pressed his hands to his temples. 'Stop acting!' he shouted and looked at her with loathing. 'Do you know what you sound like? You know it was the worst kind of betrayal!'

'I don't know what you mean, Saul.' Tilly looked honestly bewildered. Her big eyes were brimming with tears.

'Stop acting!' he groaned, in an agony of irritation and dislike. 'You know exactly what I mean. You know exactly!'

'You just be quiet!' flared Tilly, suddenly losing control. 'You just shut up! What do you mean by carrying on like this? You must be mad! I heard you were pretty near it.' Her eyes darted around, saw Malcolm Pool's wide-eyed, horrified face, Barbara's watchful smile, Jack Sprott mumbling in bemused fashion to a stony-faced Sarah. She caught her breath and put a trembling hand on Quentin Hale's sleeve. He looked as though he wished she hadn't.

Barbara took a sip of champagne and twinkled familiarly at Saul. 'Saul, really, we're all grown-ups. Good God, what's a spot of adultery these days? My second spouse, rot his bones, made a career of it! And twenty years ago? Ancient history! To tell you the truth it's a relief to find you were such a very human youth,

Saul. You're so grand and upright these days. Shame about the poor sod in the jungle, sure, but—'

'Barbara!' Evie was moving quickly. She spoke brightly, casually. 'Behave! Stop stirring the pot, you mischief maker! You're incorrigible!' She stood before Barbara Bendix like a stocky brown hen facing a butcher bird, and shook her head with a rueful smile. 'Come with me and look at the view, and stop behaving in character, will you?' She drew the laughing, flattered Barbara away with the ease of long practice, and Kate saw with relief the unlikely pair head to the other end of the room.

Saul Murdoch stood rigidly, looking at no-one. He looked dreadful. Someone should speak to him but Quentin had been commandeered by Tilly. Kate briefly considered doing something herself but in truth she'd barely met the man. Brian Berry had always dealt with him personally. Now hardly seemed the time to freshen the acquaintance. He looked exhausted, ill and bedevilled. As she watched, he drank the wine in his glass at a gulp, and took a fresh glass from the waiter.

The group began to split up as people drifted uneasily away to talk in couples. Black-haired, pale-faced Sarah Lightly and an emotional Jack Sprott had their heads together. Like Snow White and one of the seven dwarves, thought Kate wildly. Not Grumpy, or Sneezy or Dopey. Tipsy, of course.

Tilly Lightly was talking in a tense monotone to Quentin, Amy and Malcolm Pool. Her eyes were huge and shadowed in her pixie face, and the beautiful embroidered shawl, its fringe falling almost to her feet, was wrapped tightly around her shoulders. Now and again she'd glance worriedly in her daughter's direction and, taking advantage of her inattention, the other three would meet each other's eyes uneasily. Amy was as cool as ever, but Malcolm looked severely shaken, and Quentin's face was several shades darker than usual. Kate felt she should rejoice in their discomfort, but somehow she couldn't. It was all too awful. Poor

Sarah Lightly looked like a ghost. She'd clearly adored her father.

Obviously Evie had felt everything had got out of hand, too. She hadn't been able to keep out of it, when the chips were down. She was by the window now, chatting easily with Barbara, keeping her well away from the others. Now and again Barbara would throw her head back and laugh, gleaming white teeth flashing in the lamplight. A lean, loveless childhood, a long career in journalism, three husbands and innumerable clashes with authority had rendered Barbara impervious to social opprobrium. She was a forty-year-old woman with the sensitivity and greed of a determined five-year-old.

Dorothy Hale, frumpy in her unsuitable powder blue, stood looking from one group to the other, biting her lip. Her fingers fidgeted uneasily at the waistband of her dress. Then her tired eyes came to rest on her husband's rigid face, and she stared as if she was seeing him for the first time.

The light in the room was very yellow, now that it was almost dark outside. Saul Murdoch's face looked like a death's head, with deep shadows in the eye sockets and under the cheekbones. Kate took a step towards him, but she was too late. Mouth sulky, eyes determined, Paul Morrisey had beaten her to it. Kate saw him introduce himself and watched Saul reply coldly, without smiling. Paul ran his fingers through his hair, and began to talk. No possibility of joining them now. It would look too obvious.

Kate glanced at her watch. The waiter came around again. Soon they would all adjourn as planned to the restaurant a few doors away. They would sit and eat together, the good food dry and tasteless in their mouths, the waiters ingratiating, the traffic grinding on outside through the sticky night air. Then she would be free to go home at last, and Jeremy would be waiting up, ready to jeer at her for being out on the town stuffing herself with caviar and champagne while he babysat. The thought made her smile. She raised her eyes, still smiling, just in time to see Saul Murdoch, white with fury, dash the contents of his champagne glass hard into Paul Morrisey's face and stride, trembling, to the lift.

'Paul, what did you . . .' Kate caught nervously at Paul Morrisey's coat, watching in fascinated horror as Quentin and Malcolm abruptly abandoned Tilly and ran towards the tall figure by the lift, worried smiles and expostulations at the ready.

Paul smiled bitterly, and wiped his face with a shirt sleeve. 'He was bloody offensive, right?' he snapped. 'So I told him where to get off. Bloody arrogant ponce. Wouldn't even talk to me about that bloody insulting, one-eyed review that more or less wrecked any chance *Unexpected People* might've had. Just pontificated. More or less called me a degenerate. Said my thinking was sloppy, self-indulgent, everything. What would you expect me to do? Stand there with head bowed and worship at his bloody shrine?'

'But what did you . . . actually—'

Paul shook his head angrily, spraying Kate's face with drops of champagne which still clung to his hair. 'If you want to know, I said he was a tired old fascist has-been.'

'Paul!'

'And that anyway, as far as I could see, he was a fine one to talk about high moral tones. Someone who'd used the peace movement as an excuse to cuckold some poor bloke off fighting in a stinking war. That was when he threw the champagne and stormed off.'

'I'm not surprised.' Kate looked helplessly at the gesticulating group by the lift. The lift's outer doors opened and Sid stood, hulking and expressionless. Saul Murdoch entered, spoke to Sid and stood very upright beside him, his face closed, looking straight ahead. Sid ignored him and looked wordlessly at Quentin Hale.

There was an odd hiatus. One had the feeling that at a word from the boss Sid would just as soon manhandle Saul out into the apartment again, or knock him on the head, as take him where he wanted to go.

And he'd do it with no change of expression, too. But Quentin gave a slight nod, and with a clatter the cage doors shut. They saw Saul's death's head silhouetted for a moment through the window, before the lift began to descend. They watched the gold arrow move slowly around to stop at 3, the next floor down.

'What happens now?' Paul was looking stimulated and aggressive.

Kate shook her head. It was all too hard. She looked round for Evie, who held up a hand in greeting and raised her eyebrows in amused dismay. 'I suppose we go to dinner,' she said.

'Great!' Paul rubbed his hands together. 'I'm bloody starving.'

Saul Murdoch lay on the hard bed in his neat little room on the third floor and tried to hold back the tide that threatened to engulf him with a dam of new, hard, cold anger. That pipsqueak Morrisey. That crass phil istine Hale. That disgusting drunkard, Jack what's-his-name. That loathsome, insinuating woman Barbara Bendix. A whore in every sense of the word. And Tilly. Tilly Lightly. She hadn't changed. Self-ignorant, vain, stupid, manipulative Tilly Lightly. How dared they. How dared they! He gritted his teeth. His head tossed on the pillow. But he'd put them in their places. He'd do what he'd told them, the idiots, as they mimsied round him at the lift. By God, he'd let them all have it tomorrow. They couldn't cancel all those interviews now. He'd let the world know how he despised this charade, this vulgar, two-bit publicity stunt. They'd rue the day they decided to exploit his name to trumpet the demise of yet another Australian company, gobbled up by a multinational, putting him, *him*, on a level with those other three excuses for human beings, exposing him to . . . to . . .

The truth. The phrase was there, lying puddled at the foundations of righteous indignation. There was a leak in the wall. The warm, sickly-warm, self-doubt

began to trickle through. The truth. He gritted his
teeth and tossed his head again, but the trickle was a
flood now, and he couldn't escape it. His words, other
people's words, pictures from the past, overwhelmed
him. Paul Morrisey's insolent, sneering face. Tired old
fascist has-been . . . boring. Dead boring. Your trouble
is you're dead, and you hate anyone who isn't, and you
put your dead hand on their stuff and try to kill them
too. Hypocrite. Cuckolding some poor bloke fighting . . .
Sarah Lightly's white face, mouth pathetically hanging
open, the reflection of the man he'd wronged. He
hadn't known, hadn't known . . . He should have said,
told them he hadn't *known* about the husband, the
baby. It was so long ago. How could it still have the
power to humiliate him like this?

He groaned aloud, remembering the day he'd found
out, the thin little woman in the purple cardigan, Tilly's mother, sitting on the edge of the only chair in his
carefully bohemian room. The flat, nasal voice asking
him in a monotone to leave Tilly alone, to have some
respect for her family, her husband, her child. The
sickening realisation that he'd had it all wrong. That
the grand passion was based on the most squalid, the
most ordinary bourgeois sordidness. That the fey child
of nature, the lonely waif to whom he'd laid himself
open, had been lying. Lying! He remembered the
handkerchief, balled in the woman's left hand, dab-
bing nervously at thin lips. The eerie resemblance to
Tilly herself, aged and flattened and made ordinary by
time, circumstance, suburbia, unimaginative Catholi-
cism. The sudden physical revulsion. The shame, rising like a hot tide in his body. The shame. He felt it
now, as burning as ever.

He opened his eyes and stared at the ceiling. He
stared at the thing that he'd averted his eyes from for
twenty years. Humiliation, *not* because of the man in
the jungle, *not* because of the child, for after all he
hadn't known about them, but because he'd been taken
in, abominably, and everyone, *everyone* else had seen
it. He'd been ridiculous, doting on a counterfeit, like

a dolt treasuring up a worthless frippery and believing it gold.

They must have been feeling so superior to him all the time, as he resisted, thinking himself noble and a free spirit, their efforts to persuade him to drop the girl they knew was a poseur, an embarrassment and a bore. Their priggishness, their intolerance, their snobbery. How loathsome they had been, those so-called friends. And how right.

And *that* was what he couldn't stand. *That* was the source of the shame. He was as vain and worthless as she was, as consumed by pride, as self-absorbed. They'd been a perfect pair after all.

And now, by agreeing to come here, he'd done it again. Flattered, short-sighted, ignoring misgivings, he'd fallen for something cheap and humiliating. Well, he'd show them. He'd show them all.

He lay still now, his body relaxed. The room darkened.

7

Beddie Byes

'Thank you, Quentin. I enjoyed my dinner.' Barbara Bendix smiled. Dorothy Hale, crushed at the back of the tiny, airless lift, wished she wouldn't. She'd had enough of those malicious smiles over dinner. She eyed her husband's rigid back nervously. She hoped she wasn't getting a migraine. She hoped Tilly Lightly wouldn't start another interminable anecdote. She hoped Sarah Lightly wouldn't cry again. She hoped Paul Morrisey would get a taxi home as she'd advised. She hoped Saul Murdoch was asleep. She hoped Jack Sprott wouldn't fall over or be sick in the lift. They slowly climbed through the darkened building, past the first and second floors, the working office floors, to the third floor where the four guest apartments waited, beds made up with snowy sheets, kitchenettes stocked with biscuits, tea, milk, chilled white wine and soda water, and posies of scentless flowers in crystal vases.

Some famous men and women had stayed in those apartments in their time—foreign literary agents and publishers, Berry family and friends, visiting dignitaries summoned for book launchings, but most of all, authors. Authors visiting, passing through; overseas authors on tour to promote their latest offerings in this remote colonial outpost that so disconcertingly provided an outlandishly large percentage of British Commonwealth sales; poverty-stricken authors rescued

from disgruntled landlords, violent husbands, furious
wives, broken affairs, and, in a few notable cases, shel-
ters for homeless men. It was said that old Walter
Berry, Brian Berry's grandfather, had actually impris-
oned the balladist Tip O'Flannagan in apartment 3 for
six weeks, while he dried out and wrote enough poems
to work off his most recent advance. The resulting
book was still in print, as were all O'Flannagan's books,
in several editions, too, from paperback to illustrated
deluxe editions with tipped-on cover illustration and
ribbon bookmark. Kate, now on her way home, rejoic-
ing, could have told them about that. Probably Barbara Bendix could, too. But no-one else in the lift knew
the history of the place nor, at present, would they care
to know it. They were all much too concerned with
their own recent past to care about anyone else's, and
the evening had been interminable.

The lift jolted to a stop at the guest apartment floor,
where the dangling light fittings in the narrow hallway
cast weird shadows on the yellow walls. Malcolm Pool
pulled the doors open, stepped out, and stood waiting
like an angelic undertaker's mute. Tilly Lightly glided
out and stood, wan and waif-like, beside him. Her
daughter stepped heavily past her and walked towards
their room, fumbling for the key in her shoulder bag,
not looking back.

Tilly watched her for a moment, sighed and turned
back to face them.

'What a strange night,' she said softly, her eyes huge
and tearful, her handkerchief crushed into a ball, at
the corner of her mouth. 'I feel absolutely drained, I
really do.'

'We'll all feel better after a good night's sleep, won't
we?' said Quentin, his hearty voice at odds with his
strained smile.

'Jack won't!' said Barbara from behind him. 'And
Jack is presently standing on my foot. Could someone
give him a hand, for God's sake?'

''S all right,' mumbled Jolly Jack Sprott, swaying
forward. 'Give a man a break. I'll be fit as a fiddle

after a bit of kip. Ah, they're all the same, these women, son.' He grasped Malcolm by the shoulder for emphasis and support. 'Nag, nag, nag. Pretty ones, ugly ones—all the same.'

'Come on, Jack,' said Quentin, his finger on the 'doors open' button, his patience wearing thin. 'You're in flat 3, down the end there. Remember? Off you go.'

Jack fixed him with a bleary eye. He slowly raised one finger. 'In the jungle,' he said carefully, 'you get to know who you can trust pretty damn quick. You can tell a good officer by the way he gets things done. No balls-ups. No fighting in the ranks. No all-show-no-do. Get my meaning?'

Quentin's heavy face darkened.

Barbara closed on Jack and smiled her cat's smile. 'Come on, Jack,' she purred. 'Beddie byes. I'll take you, and Malcolm can help.'

He leered delightedly. 'Don't need any help, Barb. Plenty of life in the old fella yet!' he croaked.

'You're a terror, Jack!' Barbara hitched her arm firmly under his armpit and Malcolm Pool followed her example on the other side. She winked at him, and he looked confused.

'Ah, you should've seen me twenty years ago, Barb. Strong as a horse I was,' burbled Jack happily. 'All the blokes'd tell you, if they were here they'd tell you, Barb. Ah, those were the days. Tad and Rabbit and Wallaby and Slippy Joe—good blokes. Did I ever tell you about the time I . . .'

'Not now, Jack. Bed.' Barbara propelled the bulky little man forward. Malcolm, staggering slightly under his share of the weight, twisted his neck awkwardly and called back to his employer.

'I'll lock up, Quentin. You go on up. I'll fix every-thing down here.'

'Thank you, Malcolm.' Quentin Hale was steely. 'You do that. And I'd like to see you at eight tomorrow morning, in my office, if you don't mind. To discuss a few things.'

The boy showed the whites of his eyes and turned back to his task without a word.

'Tilly, goodnight,' Quentin said, looking edgily at the hovering, lonely figure. 'I . . . I'm sorry things haven't . . . have been difficult for you.'

Tilly hesitated, then stepped closer and put her hand on his arm. 'I probably shouldn't have come,' she whispered. 'Saul's obviously—well, he's obviously really stressed out, isn't he? I didn't dream he'd . . .' She gnawed at her bottom lip.

There was a short silence. Dorothy murmured something indistinguishable.

'Sarah will come round,' said Tilly, willing them to agree with her.

'Oh, yes!' said Quentin obediently, glancing at her briefly. The ghost of his confident smile flashed for a moment. Tilly smiled back quickly, looking up at him.

'And look, Quentin, really, just remember—whatever Saul says tomorrow, about the company, I'll do my best to counterbalance it. So please don't be too worried, and get a good night's sleep. You too, Dorothy. You both look so tired,' she murmured, patting his arm with exquisite condescension.

'Thank you, Tilly. Goodnight.' Quentin Hale had had enough. The lift door closed against the waif-like figure, smiling sweetly and sadly to the last.

Alone, the husband and wife looked at one another.

'Did Amy go home in a taxi, Quentin?' Dorothy's voice was flat and grey.

He nodded his head, with an impatient little jerk. 'Of course she did, Dot!'

'Did you pay for it? Did anyone see you?'

'I gave her a cab docket. Anyone would expect that. She was working late.' He looked at her. 'Why talk about that anyway?' he said with irritation. 'You're obsessed with the girl, Dot. For God's sake, focus on the trouble I'm in, *we're* in, will you? What a shambles. Malcolm's made a right muck of things. Young fool. And that old bitch, Evie Newell. She set me up, you know, Dot. She bloody set me up. She knew this would be a disaster. She knew it.'

'She may not have.'

'She did, I'm telling you.' The lift stopped. He pulled the doors open and they stepped into their blue and gold living room, restored during their absence to meticulous order.

He pulled at his tie and flicked open the top button of his shirt to release his strong, pink neck from its stranglehold. He looked around the spacious, softly lit retreat and Dorothy saw his tension slowly drain away. He chewed his bottom lip, moved to the drinks cabinet and poured himself a whisky.

'I'll talk to Murdoch,' he said, more to himself than to her. 'I'll talk him round. I'll crawl if I have to. I'll devote the day to him tomorrow. Malcolm can keep Jack away from the grog. Amy can keep the Lightly woman happy. And Evie can handle Bendix. She can bloody make herself useful. I'll deal with her later. We'll keep them separated. That'll do the trick. That'll do it. Keep them separated, and we'll be OK.' He drank his Scotch in a gulp, and then remembered his wife. 'Want a sherry?'

'No, thanks,' she said, watching him and marvelling at his resilience. Five minutes ago he'd been at the end of his tether. Now he had a plan of action, and his confidence was utterly intact again. He was amazing. She had no doubt that he was right. That it would work just as he said. She'd seen him prevail before, many times. The force of his will was irresistible. It would all work just as he said, if nothing else happened to deflect his intention.

The night was dark, and full of noises. Sarah Lightly, listening to the mid-city hum, the muffled sounds of shouts and sirens that penetrated the double-glazed windows of the flat, lay unsleeping. The air-conditioned room was cool, the sheet and blanket soft and light on her body, the firmly sprung mattress to her liking. But she felt that she was watching herself lying there amid the strange luxury. Her mind seemed quite separate from her body. Her mother, curled up in the bed on the other side of the room, was breathing softly and evenly. She had refused to take her pills. Could she have gone to sleep so quickly? Or was she just pretending?

Sarah thought that over. Funny how easily she could believe Tilly was pretending. She realised that she took a certain deviousness in her mother completely for granted. She'd lived with it since early childhood. There had always been, in her relationship with her mother, the element of pretence, of indulgence in private and keeping secrets in public. She realised that she had taken this as normal, always, as far as her mother was concerned. But of course it wasn't normal, was it?

Daddy. She thought about her father. She only had baby memories of him, really. But somehow she remembered looks, pauses, late-night, half-heard voices that gave her the impression that he had at least hadn't let Tilly's view of herself go unchallenged. Had he known all along about . . . about Saul Murdoch and everything?

She glanced at the shape that was Tilly, asleep or pretending. Outside in the corridor a board groaned under thin carpet. Someone was up. She wondered who it could be. Not old Jack Sprott, surely. He'd seemed to her almost out to it when he'd been put to bed so firmly by that terrible woman Barbara and Malcolm Pool.

Maybe it was Barbara herself, out prowling on some unnerving errand of her own. No need to go out into the corridor to use the bathroom. The bathroom was next door and both their rooms connected with it, so it couldn't be that. Maybe she was looking for something to eat. She was a greedy woman, eating ravenously, and happily cleaning up leftover salad and bread rolls from the centre of the table as though she couldn't bear to leave anything in sight undevoured. No more noise. Whoever it was had gone. Or was standing still. Suddenly she was glad the door was securely locked, and the door to the bathroom too.

Still no more noise. Maybe it had just been the old building relaxing its muscles after the long day, not a person walking at all.

But maybe it was Saul Murdoch, his haggard, handsome face pale in the electric light. He hadn't reappeared at all after the argument. Maybe he was up now, walking. But why would he be? He'd said what he was going to do. Make a mess of everything. In the morning. Saul Murdoch. Her mother's seducer, when she was a tiny baby, and her father was away fighting. What kind of man must he be, to do that? And now he was famous, and probably rich. And Daddy was dead.

She put her hands over her eyes, to shut out the room, and blinker her thoughts. How could she go on coping with Tilly after this? How could she face Murdoch? Old Jack had summed it up, slurring over dinner, his bloodshot eyes fixed on the tablecloth. 'A louse. Makes me want to spew, that sort of thing.' And Paul, Paul Morrisey, on her other side, intense and dark-eyed, had told her how Murdoch had slated his book, in arrogance and jealousy and spite, and ruined its chances. Murdoch must be utterly, utterly selfish. Like . . . like her mother. Like her mother was.

Sarah almost sat up, so great was the shock of the revelation. It was like a flash of light, illuminating all the stage sets in her mind, revealing them for the painted screens they were. She confronted them one by one, pushed them aside, till there was a clear space, and Tilly, her mother, sat there unscreened, unpropped, unlit by guilt and habit and sentimentality. She looked at Tilly unmasked, and lay very still. She could hear her own heart beating.

There was a stealthy creak from the bed on the other side of the room. She half opened her eyes, keeping her breathing even, and watched under her lashes, without surprise, as Tilly's white legs slipped from under the covers. She felt Tilly's eyes peering at her short-sightedly through the dimness, and eased her own eyes shut, lying perfectly still. Whatever her mother was up to, she obviously didn't want an audience, and Sarah had her own reasons for not drawing attention to the fact that she was awake and aware.

A few tiny creaks tracked Tilly's progress across the room. There was a click. Sarah risked another peep. Tilly was sitting at the desk hunched under the reading light with her back to the room. She seemed to be writing something. Sarah lay straining her eyes, struggling with a nervous impatience that threatened to make her limbs twitch. She realised she was holding her breath, and her heart jumped. But Tilly was quite absorbed in what she was doing and didn't turn her head.

The minutes crawled by. What time was it? Sarah didn't dare look at her watch, and suddenly it was agony just to lie there without knowing.

Then the reading light clicked off. Tilly glided, mothlike, to the door, a white glimmer in the dark. She unlocked it, glancing cautiously behind her as it clicked, and then quickly stepped out into the corridor, pulling the door almost shut behind her, leaving a thin bar of yellow light.

Sarah eased her cramped limbs, and quickly looked at her watch. Only five past eleven! Not too late after all. She felt a sense of her own power—the unseen watcher. She would have given anything to follow Tilly. What was she doing? Was it possible that she was, after all that had happened, going to try to talk to Saul Murdoch? She couldn't . . .

But even as the thought flashed through her mind, the crack in the door widened, and Tilly slipped back into the room. She was breathing deeply, and stood for a moment, quite still, clasping her hands in front of her. Then she tossed her hair back, straightened her shoulders, and moved softly to her bedside table.

Sarah watched her take a bottle from her bag, shake the tiny pills into her hand, and tip them into her mouth, swallowing them dry, one by one, like sweets.

Tilly had long passed the stage of needing to wash her little helpers down.

Another siren sounded from outside. Far away a car alarm began its rhythmic shrieking. Tilly shivered, slipped back into bed and pulled the covers up high, over her chin and ears. She hunched there, knees curled up, motionless. Sarah, with a surge of triumph, relaxed, watched and waited.

8

The Plot Thickens

The shadowed early morning streets were pleasantly bare and the parking station echoed, still three-quarters empty. Malcolm Pool raised his finger in greeting to the white-overalled man at the entrance, and swung his little red car into its cramped parking space, enjoying his own practised ease in the manoeuvre, and the little squeak of the tyres on the smooth floor.

He clicked off the ignition and sat back, with his hands resting lightly on the wheel. The car still had its delicious, clean, new-car smell. It had air-conditioning and a tape deck. It was as glossy and neat as Malcolm himself, from his fair, groomed head to his softly shining shoes.

Malcolm liked his company car. He liked the parking station. He liked the feeling of being a habitue of the city, at home and purposeful there, in contrast to the gawking tourists with their maps, cameras and timorous expressions, the women in from the suburbs for a day's shopping, with depressed-looking children in tow.

Malcolm remembered being one of those kids, trailing behind his mother, once every school holidays, even then embarrassed by her shy, awkward public manner, her dowdy clothes, the way shop assistants ignored her at first and then automatically offered her the cheapest, shoddiest goods in the range, assuming she could pay for nothing better, and had no taste. She always paid in cash, Mum. That had always grated on his nerves, too. It seemed so low-class. She would pick the notes and coins from her vinyl wallet with the big metal clasp and hand the money over with an ingratiating little smile, saving her complaints at the shop-girls' rudeness till they were out of earshot.

Once, on one of these outings, they had had lunch in the park, just opposite the Berry and Michaels building. Orange cordial and cheese sandwiches from the kiosk, and they sat on a park bench under a tree nearby to eat it, not even at a table, as though Mum had felt they shouldn't presume.

When he looked back on it, it was these expeditions that had made him see that whatever it took, when he grew up he wasn't going to live like that. He was going to be someone. He was going to have money, and power, and respect. People were going to jump when he said jump.

Soon he would walk through the streets to the Berry and Michaels building, as he did every day, his shoes tapping on the pavement, his briefcase swinging gently against his leg. This early in the morning he could smell his own after-shave cologne, his clean, ironed shirt. He walked, he could feel it, in an aura of well-being, health and confidence. Self-sufficient, ready for anything, he was insulated from the untidiness, dreariness and disorganisation around him: the workers queuing at snack-bar counters, the vagrants rootling in the rubbish bins, the heavily made-up girls clicking to work on high heels, clutching carry bags and cappuccinos in plastic cups.

For a moment Malcolm sat motionless, thinking of nothing, tapping the wheel lightly with his fingers. Then he climbed almost reluctantly from the car, slipped on his suit coat, grasped his briefcase and slammed the door. He tried to summon up the quick rush of excitement he'd felt at this time every morning since he'd presented his Big Four plan and swept all before him, surging ahead of Evie Newell on a wave of youth and energy. The sweetness of that carefully planned-for moment had lived on and strengthened in his memory, and many times in the last month he'd savoured it. But this morning it failed to rise within him, carrying him along the footpaths and across the roads to the office. Instead, as it mingled and churned with his feverish, muddled memories of the cocktail party and its aftermath, he felt his stomach twist and his heart flutter. A strange mixture of emotions chased around his mind, usually so clear, so focused: embarrassment, dismay, hope, elation, rage, fear . . .

It was a beautiful day. He saw that, as he reached 'Carlisle'. He didn't usually notice the weather, he realised. He did today, though, feeling almost helpless, watching the tops of the palms in the park gently stirring against the blue sky. Already the cool of the morning was seeping away. Already his collar and shoes felt a little tight, and his jacket a little warm. It was going to be very hot.

He tore his eyes away from the palm tree tops. Somehow this day was going to have to be got through, and the party tonight. He had to pull himself together, no matter how little sleep he had had, no matter what had happened. He had enemies and ill-wishers all around him. He had to protect himself, and all he'd worked for, from their jealous, spiteful manoeuvres against him.

He walked up the steps to 'Carlisle''s door thoughtfully. First, the meeting with Quentin Hale. Then, breakfast with the authors at the cafe as planned, and off to the first radio station. Nothing must interfere with that.

The meeting with Hale—the first hurdle. He set his lips, thinking of that. But surely Hale would see that it was all Evie's fault. He'd have to, because he himself had endorsed the Big Four plan, very publicly. Subtly, he could be reminded of that. It was his plan as much as it was Malcolm's, and it was Evie Newell who had spoiled it for them both, with her unprofessional behaviour. Malcolm paused, his key in the lock. Unprofessional. That was a good word. Hale would respond to that. And once they had an understanding, Hale could deal with the question of Saul Murdoch. He could cope with that alone, as long as they had agreed the plan could go ahead with three authors just as well as with four. To hesitate now would be disaster. Hale must be made to see that. The heavy old door swung open and Malcolm stepped, rehearsing calmly now, into the wide, dim hall.

'Malcolm . . .' Quentin Hale was sitting at his big, bare desk. He looked hazy in his grey suit, the morning light streaming through the windows almost dissolving his image as Malcolm blinked at him from the door. He looked colourless and rigid, like a dummy, sitting there. Malcolm moved cautiously closer.

'We have a problem,' said Quentin, through lips that seemed reluctant to move.

Malcolm's stomach lurched. 'Have you . . . ?' He couldn't go on. He waited, paralysed.

'Dorothy has gone on with Barbara Bendix and the others for breakfast, Malcolm,' said Quentin slowly. 'With Jack Sprott and Tilly, I mean, and Tilly's daughter. I couldn't wait for you. I needed them out. Right out. Dorothy's taken them.'

'Murdoch?' Malcolm forced the word out.

'You'll carry on without Murdoch, Malcolm,' said Quentin curtly. 'You'll say he's been taken ill. Understand? You'll just say he's been taken ill, and carry on as planned. Is that clear?'

Malcolm nodded. 'You've seen him, have you?' he said. He licked his dry lips. 'What did he say? Is he going to do what he said? Talk to the press? Is that the problem?'

Quentin Hale looked at him and a hint of a smile twisted his tense mouth. 'He won't be talking, no. We've got a new problem now.' He gazed at his shining desk top, and shook his head. Then he looked straight up into Malcolm's scared eyes. 'The new problem, Malcolm, is that he's dead! Stone, cold dead! The police are on their way.'

Detective-sergeant Dan Toby tugged at his collar. Eight o'clock in the bloody morning and already he was starting to sweat. He punched the button marked 'night bell' again, and glanced peevishly at his companion. Bloody Milson never felt the heat. He probably had cold water in his veins, instead of blood. He certainly acted like it.

Milson met his gaze disapprovingly. 'I presume he was told to listen out for us, sir?' he asked.

'I presume so, Milson,' snapped Toby. 'Sorry to keep you waiting!'

Milson smiled thinly and turned back to the door. They heard footsteps approaching. The heavy door clicked and swung open.

Mr Hale?' Toby waited for the man's nod. 'Detective-sergeant Toby, Detective-constable Milson.'

'Come in.' The voice was hollow in the grand, empty hallway.

Toby stepped gratefully into the cool gloom. Milson followed, his watchful eyes darting around, taking note of the antique splendour, the reception rooms on the right, the brass cage of the lift at the end of the hallway, and beside it the cedar staircase that curved gently up from the black and white marble floor. Toby saw these things, too, in his own time, as he followed Quentin Hale and stood impassively as the lift doors were opened to receive them. He noticed, too, the muscles of Hale's neck and face, massively tense and controlled over the tight, white shirt collar and the red tie, and was curious.

The lift doors closed and they began to rise through the old building. Up, past the first floor, the second floor, to the third, where the object and purpose of their visit lay in a darkened room, a single fly circling its head. Toby had seen many deaths. They no longer frightened or repulsed him, or made him sick, however gruesome. He'd been in the business too long for that. He felt other things, though. Murder made him angry, and put him on his mettle. Accidental death made him depressed, and prone to overeating junk food and drinking alone in his flat, finally ringing his grown up son, getting him out of bed, as likely as not, to check that the one person he had left to love in the world was safe, for one night at least. And suicides, like this one seemed to be? They worried him least of all, as long as they weren't kids.

Quentin pulled the lift doors aside and they stepped out into the third floor corridor. Two doors on one side, two on the other. The guest apartments. Three empty, one still, in a manner of speaking, occupied.

'He's in here,' said Quentin, stopping at the first door on the left. He pulled a key from his pocket and fitted it into the lock. Toby put his hand out to delay him.

'You've been in already, I gather?' he asked. 'Touch anything?'

'No.'

'Anyone else been in?'

'Not that I know of.'

'OK, let's go then,' said Toby briskly. 'Mind keeping right outside, sir, for the moment?'

Quentin nodded, unlocked the door and stood back. The two detectives entered the room.

It was dim and cool. Saul Murdoch lay on top of the bed, dressed in a royal blue, silky-looking dressing gown, which he seemed to have put on over his shirt and trousers. He was wearing his shoes. His eyes were slightly open, so that he seemed to be peering at them from under the half-closed lids. But the face and hands were cool and stiff to the touch. He was dead all right, thought Toby, and had been since the early hours of the morning, at least. A glass stood by the bed, and an empty bottle of pills, and an open book, with a paragraph underlined in fine black pen. He read the marked words, and looked unemotionally at the dead face.

Milson prowled the room. 'Where does this lead, sir?' he asked Quentin, indicating the door to the bathroom.

Quentin told him. Milson, handkerchief in hand, tried the handle. 'Locked,' he said to Toby.

Toby, nodded briefly, without looking up. He knew he was being unfair, snubbing Milson all the time. It was a weakness in him, but he couldn't help it. The man was a competent policeman, no doubt about that. But he was so officious! And so pleased with himself, in his own thin-blooded way. And Toby was uncomfortably aware that Milson didn't think much of him either. Not that he was ever downright disrespectful. Just disapproving, and sometimes amused, and sure, Toby was convinced, that his own future held far more promises, far more glittering prizes, than promotion to detective-sergeant, a rank that Toby seemed to be content to stick at till they shuffled him off with a gold watch to the Eventide Home.

Toby let his gaze wander around the room. The doctor, the fingerprint people would get here soon. Was there anything, anything here that indicated this was not exactly what it seemed to be? All the evidence pointed to suicide. And his own experience pointed the same way. That face, those hands. The haggard, sensitive face, the deeply lined forehead, the shadowed eyes, the sad, bitter mouth . . . all of them spoke of a haunted life, and death embraced with relief. Still . . .

He almost missed seeing the slip of paper. It was a folded single sheet, brushed aside as Quentin opened the door, and now caught between the bottom of the door and the carpet. Toby moved towards it hastily. Just as well he'd been the one to find this. It was the sort of thing Milson loved. He would have been sure to see it sooner or later. He saw Quentin look in curiously as he bent to pick it up. Hale had missed it too. He unfolded the paper and as his eyes flicked over the hastily scrawled words he stroked his chin thoughtfully. So . . . not so simple after all. Maybe.

'Saul, I hope you know what you've done tonight. Sarah had no idea about you and me. She was very attached to Alistair and she's incredibly hurt and angry. I know you always thought I wasn't good enough for you. You even said so, the last time I saw you. Well, as far as I'm concerned, you weren't good enough for me, and tonight you proved it. You're a twisted, bitter man. You never did understand my feelings, or motives. I was willing to forgive and forget, and be civilised about it, whatever you'd done to me. I wouldn't have come here otherwise. I had no idea you'd act like you did, in front of Barbara Bendix, as much as anything.

I'm just warning you, Saul. You'd better take back what you said. You speak to Sarah tomorrow and you tell her that she got what you said wrong. She'll believe you. She's easily convinced, when she wants to be. But she won't listen to anything I say. It has to be you.

You owe me that much, surely. I could kill you for what you've done to Sarah and me. You fix it, or I'll find some way to pay you back, if it's the last thing I do. I'm not joking.

Tilly'

Toby looked up, at Quentin looming by the door, at Milson, watchful and still, nose twitching with curiosity. He smiled slowly.

'The plot thickens,' he said.

9

The Slippery Slope

'Morning, Sid!' Kate grinned and nodded at the silent man at the mail desk. 'Tonight's the night!'

'Huh!' Sid raised his heavy head and glowered. 'If it all comes off without me having a heart attack I'll be surprised. Up and down, up and down those bloody stairs I've been since eight this morning. Lift tied up all the bloody time. You come up the stairs, I notice. It's a terrible muck-up downstairs, too. Did you see? No decorations up yet. Late as usual. Never be ready by tonight.' He shook his head.

As if to emphasise his point two young girls from the art department staggered past with a giant photograph of Tip O'Flannagan. Above their heads his image twinkled and swayed roguishly. Red and white ribbons trailed behind them and under their feet and every now and then one of them tripped and swore.

Kate and Sid watched as they stumbled and staggered down the corridor to the fire stairs.

'They're not going to try taking that down the stairs!' exclaimed Kate. 'Hey!' she called down the corridor. 'Hey, Lulu, take the lift!'

'Not working!' bawled the diminutive Lulu, skinny as a pencil with a voice like a wharfie. 'Bung or something. Typical!' She lunged down the stairs with her burden, bellowing at her companion to keep her end up.

Sid looked at Kate impassively. 'Two dozen to go, yet,' he said. 'And the lift's bung. You wouldn't believe it, would you?'

'Maybe you could help them, Sid. They look like they need a hand,' Kate hinted. It never did to try and push Sid around. He took his orders from the top.

'Not me.' He stared at her for a moment, then leaned forward across the desk. His red, stolid face was close to hers, his grey eyes narrow.

'They impugned me. They said I was rough with their stuff. Complained to Malcolm Pool, apparently. I said to him, I said, well if I'm not wanted I'm happy to stand aside. No skin off my nose. I got plenty to do, I said. Little twits. He was in a flap, looked like death warmed up, anyhow. Can't handle the responsibility, if you ask me. Couldn't stop and hear my side of it. Going off with these bigwigs upstairs to a radio station, or something. Could've spent five minutes. I never damaged the thing.'

'What thing?'

He shrugged his massive shoulders. 'One of the big pictures got scratched or something. Nothing to do with me. Now they're in a flap getting it done again. Lot of rot. Why leave it till the last minute anyway? Twits!'

Kate tutted, smiled and sidled away. She was late as it was, and party or no party there was work waiting to be done. With a pang she remembered Jack Sprott's manuscript. She must really make time for it today. He'd be bound to mention it again tonight. And there was Tilly Lightly's new thing too. Quentin had asked about that yesterday. And Jack Sprott's calendar. And all those letters, and . . . Her pace quickened, as though an extra two minutes was going to make a difference. She turned into the editorial corridor.

'Hello, Mary. Anything happened? I got held up.'

The editorial secretary looked at her drily over her half glasses and consulted a notebook.

'A Mr Ninish is here to see you. Says it's about a

manuscript. He's waiting in reception. Malcolm Pool called. Evie called. Your mother called. Mr Hale called. He was a bit put out. You're wanted upstairs. He's had Evie up there too. You're also wanted downstairs. The whole art department's down there, fixing up for tonight. They don't want to use the banner publicity organised, it clashes with the curtains David says. He wants you to see him about it. And your daughter called. She said to remind you about the green leotard for tomorrow morning. That's all.'

'All!' Kate sat down in the one visitor's chair by Mary's desk. 'It's only ten past nine!'

'Ah, well.' Mary placidly began opening the mail. 'Good to feel needed.'

'Needed! I feel besieged.' Kate got up. 'I'd better do Quentin first. Where upstairs?'

'His office, I think. He said go straight up. By the stairs.'

'Why? Oh, that's right. OK.' Kate turned to go.

'Why don't you leave your handbag with me, Kate?' said Mary kindly. 'You don't have to pay to get in.'

'Oh. No. Yes.'

'What about Mr Ninish?'

'Who? Oh. Ah, I don't know anything about him. He must be trying it on. Have we got his manuscript, or is he bringing one in?'

'He wouldn't tell me anything. And he's very deaf.'

'You'll have to get one of the assistants to do him, Mary.' Kate was already on her way. 'Melissa, say. She's got a good loud voice.'

She jogged to the fire stairs. It was going to be one of those days.

As she got to the top of the stairs Kate suddenly realised with a sickening little twinge what this early call from Quentin was all about. He was, of course, going to ask her if she'd known about Jack being a drunk, and Saul and Tilly being enemies and neurotics to boot. If she'd known all along that Malcolm's plan was going to be a disaster. And she'd have to say she had. She couldn't lie about it to his face, could she?

She slowly paced the carpeted corridor, through the little accounts department maze, past the shadowy conference room with its richly-coloured table and empty chairs, and the big cabinets where rare old books and memorabilia grew silently older and rarer behind glass. She stopped and looked in. The place was full of ghosts. Old Walter Berry, rambunctious, furious of eye, held court there. Benevolent Gerald, his son, beamed at his staff of plainly dressed women with round wire spectacles and slightly bohemian men with pipes. Brian Berry, the last of the line, wisecracked with a young and saucy Evie, a troop of earnest, admiring editors and one of a succession of splendidly eccentric marketing managers. And there she was herself, ten years younger, with long permed hair, so impressed by it all and scared to say a word.

And there she was again, a few weeks ago, managing editor, trusted employee, with Evie, and Malcolm and Quentin and the rest, hearing Malcolm's plan. How could she have gone along with Evie and kept quiet for all those weeks while the letters were sent and the money spent? She'd acted outrageously. How could she possibly explain her behaviour? It was practically inexplicable, even to her, now.

Her face was already hot as she turned the corner and walked towards Amy Phibes' desk, and the scent of flowers, perfume, brewed coffee and hot computer plastic that always surrounded it. Amy stared at her enquiringly. She supposed her cheeks were red, and cursed inwardly. She hated being thought badly of, that was her trouble. That was her great weakness. Other people, well, male people, anyway, seemed to be able to cope with making mistakes or doing the wrong thing. She never had been able to. It was so immature.

'Quentin has some people with him, Kate,' said Amy rather brusquely. 'Could I ask him to call you?'

Kate looked at her. 'Quentin called me. He said to come up.'

Amy raised her eyebrows slightly. 'Oh,' she said. 'That's strange. He didn't tell me.'

Smoothly groomed and polished as usual, her face had a brittle look today, Kate thought. What was up? She noted with what she knew to be malicious interest that as Amy moved to pick up the intercom phone, her hand trembled. A crack in the armour. Fascinating! Quarrel with Mr Hale, perhaps? Honeymoon over?

Amy jumped violently as the office door beside her clicked and Quentin's face appeared. He looked strained and tired. 'Kate! Come in!' he said, and his mouth moved in a rather ghostly imitation smile. 'Ah, Amy, could we have coffee, please? Two blacks, one white—Kate?'

'Black, please.'

'And another black. Thanks.' He held the door open and ushered Kate into the inner sanctum. As she went in, Kate glanced back. Amy Phibes was standing rigidly by her computer. Her perfect make-up couldn't disguise the paleness of her face, or the fear in her eyes.

Quentin's office was spacious and imposing. He had, as one of his first acts, moved out as much of the old furniture and personality as was possible, and introduced a leisured, modern, uncluttered and, to Kate's nostalgic eyes, rather bland atmosphere to the grand Victorian room where Brian Berry and his forebears had presided. The view over the park and the deep window sills were all that remained of the old days. Blinking in the grey and white silence, where the very pot plants looked disciplined and squeaky clean, Kate was surprised to see two strangers sitting, very out of place, on the squashy pale grey leather couch at one end of the room.

They rather spoilt the ambience. They looked rumpled and earthy, somehow, despite their suits and ties and serious expressions. One of them, an older, solid-looking man with a wrinkled forehead and balding head, looked vaguely familiar, but she couldn't think where she might have met him before. She smiled at them tentatively as they stood up to greet her.

'Kate, this is Detective-sergeant Toby,' Quentin said tightly, indicating the older man, who nodded seriously to her. 'And, ah . . .'

'Detective-constable Milson,' rumbled Toby. The dark, thin man beside him blinked acknowledgement.

Kate stared at them, her mind washed blank by shock and an overpowering sense of déjà vu. She tried to collect her thoughts. She'd met a policeman called Toby before, but this wasn't him. He looked like him, though. An imposter? she thought wildly. And then she remembered.

'I've met your brother, in the Mountains,' she blurted out, in her confusion. She felt herself blush. Hardly an appropriate thing to say under these circumstances. But what circumstances? Why were they here? What had happened? The important point, as ever, burst upon her last, and took her breath away.

Dan Toby's weathered face relaxed into an almost-smile. His assistant, Milson, glanced at him without changing expression. Silence.

'There was a . . . a . . . someone died,' Kate blundered on, feeling unreal. 'Where I was. Someone was . . . got poisoned, you see, and Mr Toby came and—'

Quentin made a small sound behind her, and she glanced involuntarily back at him, almost ricking her neck in the process. He looked grey. Her eyes widened. She spun back to face Toby, mouth open.

'What . . . ?'

The detective cleared his throat. He raised his eyebrows at her and sat down on the couch, leaning forward, his hands planted on his ample knees.

'Sit down, Miss Delaney, will you? May as well be comfortable, eh? We'd like to ask you a few questions. Just routine, as they say in the classics.'

Milson tightened his lips and flipped open a notebook. Kate looked again at Quentin. He made an obvious effort to pull himself together and put his hand on her shoulder, indicating a chair for her to sit on. He smiled at her briefly and she tried to smile back. She was suddenly grateful for his presence. He was an authoritative, reassuring ally in this situation.

The door opened and Amy came in with a tray. Silently she bent over the coffee table. She was pale and tense and looked at no-one. Dan Toby stared at her frankly and appreciatively. Quentin glanced at her once, and then fixed his eyes on the table and didn't look up again even when the slim hands, jerking slightly, spilt coffee into the saucer of the last cup, his own. Amy murmured apologies, produced a paper napkin to mop up, and withdrew, closing the door behind her.

Kate sat forward in her chair. 'What's happened?' she said, with dry lips.

Quentin looked at Dan Toby, who nodded. 'Last night, sometime last night, Kate, Sir Saul Murdoch died. I found him, in his room, early this morning.'

'What!'

'Yes.' He hesitated.

'You mean someone killed Saul Murdoch? Here? Upstairs?' Kate looked around wildly. 'But no-one knows. I mean, no-one's got any idea downstairs. Why are you telling me? What happened to him?'

'We're trying to find out, Miss Delaney, aren't we?' Dan Toby said calmly. 'It's possible he overdosed on sleeping pills taken with a large quantity of alcohol. A book, one of his own, his last one, I understand—*Vernon Crew*—was found open beside him. A paragraph was underlined. Could you read it out, Milson?'

Detective-constable Milson read from a brown-covered notebook. He read slowly and without expression, as though the well-known lines were written in a foreign language. 'And so I say goodbye to you— midgets, harlots, toytown marionettes. Death is infinitely preferable to lingering in your spoiled city, and the poison cup is nectar.'

'Suicide!' The relief was overwhelming. Kate had thought . . .

'It looked very like it, anyway, Miss Delaney,' said Dan Toby, watching her placidly. 'Would this surprise you at all?'

'Oh, no!' cried Kate without thinking. 'Oh, no, it would be *very* likely. I mean, much more likely than . . . I mean . . . than that someone else had done it, for example, which is what I thought . . .' she trailed off lamely, aware of their watching eyes.

'Yes.' Toby rubbed the corner of his mouth thoughtfully. 'He was known to be suicidal, was he?'

'Well, you know, I wouldn't really know,' said Kate, all too aware of Quentin Hale beside her, and belatedly realising the impact this final disaster was going to have on his planned PR coup for Berry and Michaels. No wonder he looked like death himself. 'I mean,' she went on, as Toby waited, 'he had nervous breakdowns and things, and I'd heard . . . but,' she added eagerly, as a straw to seize upon occurred to her, 'his doctor, his doctor could tell you . . .'

'Oh, yes, we've spoken to his doctor. He wasn't as you might say, knocked sideways to hear about it. He did say, though, that something probably gave Sir Saul a push down the slippery slope.' Toby nodded thoughtfully, his bright blue eyes never leaving Kate's face.

'Mr Hale said earlier that there was a bit of a dust-up at a party last night. You witnessed that, did you?'

Kate nodded vehemently. 'Oh, yes. He was very up-set and went to his room afterwards.' She looked around. She thought they looked vaguely disapproving. 'Everyone tried to persuade him to calm down and not to go,' she said, defensively. 'Quentin did. Every-one did. I mean, we had every reason to, quite apart from . . . Quentin didn't want him saying terrible things to the press this morning, for example. But he wouldn't listen to anyone, and went off as angry and full of threats as if no-one had tried at all.' She glanced at Quentin briefly for approval, but his face was rigid and he didn't respond to her anxious look.

Toby sat, hands on his knees, and appeared to reflect. 'I hadn't actually picked that up, sir, in your statement,' he said to Quentin. 'I mean, that Sir Saul had been making threats. Were the threats directed at any particular person?'

'Oh,' Quentin held up a hand, and a ghost of his confident smile flashed. 'Threat is rather too strong a term, I think, Mr Toby, with due respect to Kate. He was just extremely ruffled and made some general remarks about the company and giving it a bad press, that was all. Nothing violent or really unusual. As I told you, one of our younger authors present unexpectedly at the cocktail party had spoken out of turn, and Sir Saul became rather—rather irrational. He was obviously a deeply troubled man, and the . . . the sad thing that has happened really could have happened at any time, and in any place, in my view.'

'Yes, well, that's one way of looking at it, sir,' said Dan Toby imperturbably. 'Looking on the bright side.' He turned to Kate. 'You know the young man in question, ah . . .'

'Mr Paul Morrisey.' The alert detective-constable supplied the name through a mouth that barely moved.

'Yes, Mr Paul Morrisey,' Toby continued, never moving his eyes from Kate's face. 'You know him pretty well, Miss Delaney?'

'Oh, yes. Professionally, of course, not personally,' said Kate guardedly.

'You sat next to him at dinner last night, I gather. I suppose you heard all about the row—his side of it?'

'Oh, yes, I did. At dinner he was telling the person on his other side, really, Sarah Lightly. But he'd told me before, upstairs. But look, he could . . .'

'At the moment, unfortunately,' Dan Toby rumbled, 'we can't find hide nor hair of Mr Morrisey to be frank about it. According to his housemates, the ones we could get any sense out of, anyway, he never came home at all last night.'

'Oh.' Kate didn't know what to make of all this.

'Yes, so you'd be doing me a favour, put it that way, Miss Delaney,' Toby leaned towards her, smiling, and the leather couch squeaked nervously, 'if you could get me started here by running over what you know. Mr Hale seemed to think you might be able to. You and Evelyn Newell. We've spoken to Miss Newell already. Now, there's no question of blame, in a legal sense,' Toby anticipated her question. 'And as soon as he turns up we'll talk to Mr Morrisey direct, of course.'

'Oh, yes. Sure.'

So Kate began to tell them what Paul had said. They hadn't mentioned the really bad scene, with Tilly and Jack and Barbara. Maybe Quentin hadn't told them. Trying to keep that little pile of dirty linen under wraps, understandably enough. But it was hopeless. Paul wouldn't let himself carry the can for precipitating poor Saul Murdoch's final collapse alone. He'd tell the lot. Quentin was just putting off the evil hour. Anyway, she'd been asked a direct question, and she only had to answer it. She didn't have to volunteer information. God knows, she'd done enough of that already, with the business about Saul's threats. Quentin had obviously glossed over all that. No doubt he thought she'd been incredibly stupid to mention it. She stole a look at him, but he was staring abstractedly, straight ahead, at the closed door.

On the other side of that door the staff of Berry and Michaels carried on their usual daily business, the art department disputed with publicity on the decorations for this evening's party, Sid the odd-jobs man grumbled away his morning, ruminating on his grievances. What a bombshell this affair was going to be. What an occasion for horror, and excited, pleasurable dispute, cups of tea and conjecture.

How would Evie feel? And Malcolm, now presumably escorting Jack, Tilly and Barbara on their round of TV and radio chats, explaining away the non-appearance of the first of the Big Four? Quentin was no doubt thinking of all that, and more. Thinking, maybe, of the green-eyed Amy Phibes, fidgeting at her desk outside. Her reaction was surprising. Strange to see her perfect facade crack over a matter like this. After all, it was nothing to do with her, was it?

10

Toby Takes It Steady

Kate walked down the stairs and back to her office, her mind seething with practicalities, fending off the main issue, the enormity of the death. She'd been sworn to secrecy. Crazily, it seemed to her, Quentin was going to try to hush the whole thing up, till after the party tonight. Only Evie, Amy, Dorothy and Malcolm Pool knew. Sir Saul Murdoch had been 'taken ill' and had left them. That was the story she was to spread and promote around the building. Well, it was sort of true, when you came to think about it, but she didn't feel like being Quentin's propaganda machine, especially as eventually everyone would find out the truth. She turned into the editorial area, thinking. The compromise was obvious. If anyone asked her, she'd give the official line. Otherwise she'd just keep quiet.

One thing she'd have to do, though.

She stopped at her secretary's desk. Mary looked at her, smiling gaily over a pile of manuscripts and mail that reached to her chin. 'Do you want your messages now, Kate, or will I give you ten minutes to get settled?' she said, and laughed. 'Mr Ninish went away, anyway. He wouldn't tell Melissa anything. Said he had to speak to you in person. He left his number.'

'Oh, Mary! Look, Mary, could you help spread the

word there's to be a full staff meeting by the mail desk
at 10.15 sharp? Quentin wants to talk about the party
tonight or something. Absolutely everyone's to be there.
No exceptions, he says. Amy's telling the upstairs people. We're to do this floor, and don't forget the designers are all downstairs in the reception rooms.'

'What about the switch?'

'It's to be left to its own devices.'

Mary raised her eyebrows. 'What a hoo ha. Why do
you suppose he's doing that?'

*Use your imagination, Mary. So a corpse can go down
in the lift and out the back way without anyone seeing,
of course.* Kate shuddered, and pretended she'd
shrugged. 'Oh, well, you know . . .' she said vaguely,
and drifted off towards her office. Mary watched her
go with interest, shrugged herself, and picked up the
phone.

'Look, Mr Hale, don't think I don't understand your
position. I do. No-one likes getting mixed up with dead
people. It isn't good for business, right?' Toby glanced
at Quentin Hale to see how he was taking it. God, the
man was pale as a ghost himself! He lowered his voice
to what he hoped was a reassuring, man of the world
rumble. 'We'll take it as steady as we can. But, sir, we
can't avoid talking to a few people here, including and
especially Mrs Tilly Lightly. If we have to wait till she
gets back from all these interviews, well so be it. As
long as she doesn't do a flit on us in the meantime.
Same applies to young Mr Morrisey. I'd like to know
where he is. If and when he turns up this morning,
we've got to hear what he has to say for himself. We've
seen Kate Delaney, we've seen Evie Newell and at
some stage we'll have to knock off Barbara Bendix and
Jack Sprott.'

He glanced up to meet Milson's disgusted smirk,
and realised that the phrase was unfortunate. He
hitched at his belt impatiently. 'Interview them, that
is,' he said. 'They could have heard something last

night, you know. And the daughter, Sarah Lightly, too. We mustn't forget her, Milson. Write her down.'

'I have everyone's names, sir,' said Milson, exchanging glances with Quentin.

'Of course you have!' muttered Toby sourly. 'Of course you have. Look, Milson, why don't you run along and see if you can find us an empty hole or corner somewhere to set up shop. Maybe Mr Hale's secretary will help you. Make sure it's got a desk and a chair for me, and a pencil sharpener for you. OK?'

Toby watched the door close behind his subordinate with ill-concealed relief. He pulled at his collar, loosening the already crooked tie a little more, and grinned cheerfully at Quentin. 'We'll be as mum as we can about this, Mr Hale. At least until the PM results come in. After that, who knows? But that takes care of the next few days, anyhow. And if you can keep your people's mouths shut, good on you. We've got no objection to that at all. The less publicity the better, as far as we're concerned. You realise, though, we've got to look round. We've got to take the body out, and we've got to seal the room while the PM gets going. There's no getting out of it. It has to happen.'

Quentin nodded. 'I understand,' he said sombrely.

'Good-oh, then.' Toby put his hands on his knees and hoisted himself to his feet with difficulty. He squinted through the window at the bright blue sky. 'Going to be a hottie,' he remarked. 'Good thing you're air-conditioned in here.'

The tall man beside him said nothing. Toby wondered if he'd heard. He left the room, and wandered off in search of Milson, Amy, and a strong cup of tea.

Milson followed Amy appreciatively. Not that he was by any means a womaniser. He never had been particularly keen on women, and that included his wife, who knew it and didn't care. He didn't like men much, either. Or children. Milson had only two passions: his career, and his aviary of lovebirds, on which he lavished all the care and attention he denied the rest of the world. He appreciated Amy because she was neat, clean, cool and efficient. Everything that most people—and his superior was a prime example!—were not. He tried not to let Toby get under his skin, but sometimes the snide remarks and the snubs really pricked him, making him taut with resentment.

It wouldn't be so bad if the old bastard was any good, but he so plainly wasn't a policeman's bootlace that Milson couldn't understand why he'd even got to detective-sergeant. He bumbled through far more by good luck than good management. It was the same story with every case they'd worked on together. Toby had broken just about every rule in the book. He'd forgotten things, and missed things, and then somehow or other he'd tumbled to something no-one else had seen and the case had fallen in his lap. Of course Toby didn't call it luck. He called it instinct. Or sometimes, when he was particularly full of himself, flair. The broken-down old fraud.

'Would this do?' Amy's soft English voice interrupted his angry internal monologue. They had stopped beside an empty office. He glanced around it. Desk, chair, phone, armchair.

'That's fine, Miss.'

'Good.' The girl seemed very tense, now that he looked at her more closely. Even worse than her boss, Hale. Something going on there, Milson thought knowingly. He might not be a participant in the game of life, but he could recognise a player when he saw one. He narrowed his eyes, and was about to speak when a movement further down the corridor attracted his attention. Someone was sauntering towards them. A small person, wearing jeans, looking very out of place. Milson blinked. It couldn't be!

Amy was looking at him curiously. He felt himself flushing, and lifted his chin. He shook his head. 'Who is that?' he asked brusquely, pointing.

Amy glanced, and shrugged. 'Oh, someone who's here from the ABC, doing a programme on the company. It's recently been taken over, you know. She's just the researcher, nobody important. I can't even think of her name . . . oh yes—Verity Birdwood. That's it. She's just getting the facts and figures together, for the real reporters, I suppose.' She turned back to him. 'You know her?' she said, as if this would definitely lower him in her estimation.

'In a way,' said Milson reluctantly. 'We've bumped into one another—professionally.'

Amy Phibes gave him a disbelieving look and left him. As she did so, the small figure in jeans looked up and saw him. Her face broke into a delighted, malicious smile. The thick glasses that shielded her eyes flashed in the light as she drew closer and raised her free arm in an ironic salute. 'Milson the magnificent! What on earth are you doing here? Don't say someone's run off with the Berry and Michaels first editions or something?'

Milson pursed his lips. 'None of your business,' he said hastily.

The woman's face grew intensely interested. She drew closer to him. 'Come on, Milson, what's up? I've got a story on here. I need to know.'

'For God's sake!' Toby's voice boomed along the corridor. 'Verity Birdwood! Where in hell did you spring from? Get out of here!'

'Aha!' The woman grinned gleefully at the sour-faced Milson. She went to meet Toby, squaring her shoulders as if going into battle. Milson groaned to himself. That was all he needed. Verity bloody Birdwood. Miss Nosy herself on the premises. You wouldn't read about it! By God, if Dan Toby let her get round him again . . . ! But surely he wouldn't. Not after last time.

'Now Birdie, it's no use trying to get round me like that,' he heard Toby say. The voice was indulgent. Milson's heart sank.

• • •

Kate had barely sat down behind her desk when Evie appeared at her door. Sober and watchful she came in, shut the door behind her and slumped into a chair.

'So, Kate,' she said, and stared out the window. She looked grey, tired and defeated, as if she'd been up all night. Kate watched her, feeling helpless. This business must have really hit Evie hard. She must feel responsible. She spoke the next thought that came into her mind.

'He probably would have done it eventually, anyway, Evie. He was mad as a meat-axe. He'd tried it before. You know that.'

'I know.' Evie swung round to face her. 'They're taking him out in about twenty minutes, did they tell you? The staff meeting . . .'

'Yes, I know. But Evie, it's looney to try and keep it quiet. How can we pretend he's just sick, when all the time we know he's *dead*.'

'I don't know. I really don't know what Quentin thinks he's doing.' Evie's lips were pale. 'He just won't face reality. I mean, there's this ABC research person, your friend—what's her name?—practically living in our pockets for a start. I told him we should just call the whole thing off. I told him, but he won't listen to me. He's obsessed with this party tonight, and he just won't see reason, and that miserable crawler Pool is going along with it.'

'But Evie, doesn't he see that eventually it'll be announced—where he died and when. And then everyone will know we—'

'Kate, I know!' Evie jumped to her feet. 'It's unbelievable stupidity! I would never in a million years think even Quentin would react like this. But he thinks he can keep everyone quiet, and he won't be told any different.'

'Paul Morrisey won't shut up. They're going to question him, about the fight. And he won't shut up. Why should he? He doesn't owe us any favours.'

Evie snorted. 'Quentin thinks he'll talk him round. He thinks he can talk anyone into anything.' Then she shrugged and half smiled. 'Maybe he can. I don't know any more.'

'Evie, it'll spread. By tonight everyone will know. That sort of thing leaks. It always does.'

Evie shrugged again. She looked exhausted. 'I don't know,' she said. 'He's so determined that it won't leak. Maybe it won't. We are the only ones who know. And I'm not going to say anything. I'm in trouble enough already. I haven't got anything organised yet. I don't want to be out on my ear. If I were you I'd keep my mouth shut!'

'Of course I will,' muttered Kate. 'What do you think I am? I'll be silent as the tomb!'

There was a tap on the door and a small, pale-faced, bespectacled woman with an untidy bush of brown hair stepped into the room. She kicked the door shut negligently with one foot.

'Oh, Birdie! Hi!' said Kate selfconsciously.

'G'day,' said Verity Birdwood, taking a seat and nodding at Evie, who smiled at her professionally. 'How's tricks?' She bent to tie up the lace of a running shoe that had seen better days. 'I'm only in for a couple of hours. Longer, though, if you can get me in with Quentin Hale for an hour sometime, Evie. He did promise, you know, and this is my third day here. It's getting a bit much.'

'Look, I'm sorry, but it's going to be just impossible today, Verity,' said Evie flatly. She exchanged glances with Kate.

'Oh, come on,' mumbled Birdie, wrestling with the lace. Her head popped above desk level again and her amber eyes probed through the thick glasses at their expressionless faces.

'You know!' she said suddenly. 'I knew you would!' She leaned forward, eyes sparkling. 'Kate, tell me! I saw Dan Toby upstairs and that sour-puss Milson. Dan wouldn't tell me a bloody thing with Milson there.

I'll get it out of him eventually but if you know . . .
Come on, what's up?'

'Nothing!' said Evie firmly. 'Absolutely—'

'Oh, Birdie!' cried Kate at the same moment. 'It's
awful! It's Saul Murdoch. He's dead!'

11

Quentin Takes It Hard

'So, that's about all I have to say, people,' said Quentin Hale, glancing at his watch, 'except . . .'

'Oh, come on, come on,' murmured someone to Kate's left, in an undertone. 'Give us a break!'

Kate looked at her own watch. 10.30. No wonder people were starting to get restless. Quentin had filibustered very well, she had to admit that, but after all, how many times and in how many ways can someone actually say, 'Sorry you can't all be with us tonight, folks, but I know you'll be with us in spirit.' He'd managed it a dozen times at least. He showed no sign of the awkwardness he must surely be feeling, though. He stood there addressing his staff from a file-filled corner of the crowded mail room, impeccably dressed as always, with his usual air of rather cold authority, as though everything was going rigidly according to plan; as though no scenes had spoilt the blue and gold atmosphere of his cocktail party last night, no police in crumpled suits had taken notes in his hushed, elegant office, no corpse was being smuggled downstairs at this very moment. It was pretty impressive, really.

She noticed Sarah Lightly hovering on the outskirts of the group. Tall, bewildered and utterly without grace, she looked very vulnerable and out of place. She must have been upstairs in her room ever since breakfast and been hustled down here in case she popped

out at the wrong time and caught them red-handed
putting a body in the lift.

Quentin looked around the assembled troops, smiling slightly, focusing on no-one. ' . . . and, as I said
before, I am very grateful for the cooperation and help
you've all . . .'

The phone at his elbow rang abruptly. His face
didn't change, but to Kate's anxious eyes his hand shot
out to the receiver just a touch too quickly. 'Yes?' he
said, his eyes on the watching crowd. 'Yes.' He paused.
'I'll be right with you, then. Thanks.' He hung up
leaving his hand on the receiver as though the phone
might ring again. 'I'm afraid I'll have to leave it there,
people,' he said. 'Thank you for coming. I'll let you
get back to it, now.'

There was an awkward flutter of claps and a few
murmurs, and people started drifting away. Some of
the more craven hung back, feeling, obviously, that
they should wait for him to go first. But he stood
tightly smiling and nodding at his post, as if seeing
them off, and eventually they too moved on.

Quentin Hale watched them go. He heard again
Amy's tense voice. 'It's done. They're gone,' and the
little sobbing sigh that she gave before she cut the connection, leaving him to answer an empty line for the
benefit of the curious watchers. This business had really shaken her. Well, understandable, considering,
though you could usually depend on Amy's sangfroid.
But you could never tell with women.

Look at how Evie Newell had taken it. Cool as a
cucumber. He hadn't expected that, either. He'd
thought she'd crumble. By God, if she had a shred of
decency she would have. The whole miserable mess
was her fault. But she'd just tightened her mouth and
tucked in her chin and looked out the window.

There she was now, looking grim, with Kate Delaney, Sarah Lightly and some woman he didn't know.
It had been necessary to let the police talk to Kate and
Evie, but it made security more problematical. Security was the great thing now. He hoped to heaven that

they'd keep their mouths shut. Kate would. When he thought about it he was sure of that. She had a priggish streak, and would feel she had no choice. He'd met her type before: they were easy to handle. The Newell woman was another kettle of fish. A mischiefmaker, and resentful of him from the first, to boot. Saw him as an interloper, replacing her precious Brian. Well, they all did, didn't they? All the old hands. Trying to shut him out. Him, and Amy and even Malcolm Pool. He'd known Malcolm would have a rough trot. Ambitious young triers always did. He had himself, in his time.

He'd tried hard enough to be pleasant, but they weren't having any. Cool, and cliquey and polite. They called it dumb insolence in the army. Evie Newell was the worst, though. The others would've come around if she hadn't kept the pot boiling. She wanted him to fail, to scuttle off back home with his tail between his legs. She'd actually said they ought to call the party off, because of Murdoch, cancel the interviews, everything. Well, he'd told her no way. He'd enjoyed that. He'd shown her, he'd show them all, he wasn't going to be made a fool of, by them, by Murdoch, or by anyone. He hadn't come this far, risked everything, for that.

They had all gone now, except for Sid, standing over in one corner watching him with those dead grey eyes, fingering a pile of envelopes. He realised that he was still resting his hand on the telephone receiver, and casually moved it away. He nodded to Sid and walked towards the stairs. The lift would be free again now, but he didn't, somehow, fancy it at present.

As he began the climb he wondered about the woman who'd been standing with Kate and Evie. He couldn't place her. Someone from the computer room, maybe? Oh no, of course. She was the researcher from the ABC. He'd met her the day before yesterday. Not at all the type he'd been expecting. Scruffy little piece. Still, she looked quiet and harmless enough. He'd promised full cooperation. He furrowed his brow.

Imagine taking her for one of the staff! Bad! He should know every member of the staff by name now. He should be getting out of his office more, having more staff meetings and so on. He hadn't done much of a job reconciling them to the Gold Group takeover. They probably thought he was a cold fish. They missed Berry and reminisced about the good old days, he knew that. But he'd been so busy, and they weren't kids, were they? Needing a daddy to smile at them, hold their hands every minute of the day. Silly bunch of twits!

The bitter anger that rose in him made him catch his breath. Unconsciously, his step quickened as he moved closer to the sanctuary of his own domain. They'd talk—he'd talk, she'd listen—and there'd be peace there. Peace, and loyalty and—love. No upset would change that. Nothing he could do, or she could do, would change it now.

It was hard making sensible conversation with Sarah Lightly under the circumstances. Probably, thought Kate uncharitably, it was difficult under any circumstances. The girl gave you no help at all. Why didn't she go back to her room or something? She certainly wasn't enjoying herself here, sitting stolid and mournful in one of Kate's chairs, her heavy hair hanging forward, her hands clasped tight like a schoolgirl's. What a nuisance! Evie needed smoothing down, and Birdie was obviously bursting to talk. But Sarah sat tight, a gooseberry fourth, an immovable impediment to fascinating discussion.

Evie, at the window, glanced at her watch. 'It's nearly eleven. I've got to tape the Miles Harris Show, Kate. Why don't you come and watch? You and Sarah. See how they go.'

'Good idea,' said Kate heartily. 'Come on, Sarah. They might be on first.'

Sarah looked at her blankly.

'Tilly and the others, you know,' Kate urged. 'Your

mum and Barbara and Jack. With Miles Harris. Live. National television.'

'Oh.' Sarah looked down at her hands. 'Oh, yes. I don't think I'll bother, thanks. I . . . um . . . don't really want to.'

Kate looked at Evie who shrugged, and caught the interested flash of Birdie's glasses as she glanced sharply at the girl's dismal profile. 'Well . . .'

'You go,' said Sarah, fumbling for some remnants of social space. 'I'll stay here—if you don't mind, I mean.'

'I'd be interested!' said Birdie brightly. Evie shot her a disgusted look.

The phone rang, and Kate answered. Mary's dry voice spoke. 'Paul Morrisey is here, Kate. He knows you have people with you, but—'

'Paul!' Kate was startled into speech. She saw Evie, Birdie and, strangely, Sarah Lightly, come to full alert. 'Um. I've got to speak to him, Mary. Could you . . . ? No, I'll come out. Just hold him there, OK?'

'OK, Kate, whatever you say.' Mary sounded resigned. This morning's mysteries and shenanigans were not to her liking.

Paul was standing by Mary's desk, hugging a red manuscript folder under his arm. He looked dishevelled, rather manic, and extremely selfconscious. His selfconsciousness increased as Kate walked towards him. He ran his hand through his hair and smiled sheepishly.

'Kate—ah—Hi!'

'Hi, Paul. Look, Quentin's keen to have a word with you. About last night.'

'Oh, yeah?' A flash of concern crossed Paul's face to be replaced instantly by a cynical sneer. 'Going to tell me where to get off, getting up a bigshot like Murdoch, I suppose?'

'No, he just wants your version of things.'

'He could've got that last night, couldn't he? And anyway, I'm just on my way out.' Paul was looking past her, into the office where Evie, Birdie and Sarah stood watching him through the open door. He absently pushed Kate aside and moved forward.

'Hi, Sarah.'

Sarah ducked her head. 'Hi,' she murmured, looking at him through a tangled mass of hair.

'You ready?'

'Oh, sure.' Sarah picked up her shoulder bag and sidled out of the office.

Kate looked from one to the other, puzzled.

Paul stuck his hands into his pockets. 'Last night I said to Sarah I might show her round the city a bit today,' he offered, looking under his eyebrows at Mary, who was ostentatiously tidying her desk.

'Oh. Well, yeah, but look, Paul, what about Quentin?' Kate's mind was working desperately. She must find a way of making him hang around for the police. But how, without spilling the beans all round?

'We'll be back in a couple of hours,' Paul said carelessly, looking everywhere but at her. 'It'll be the first time he's ever deigned to talk to me, after all. He can wait a few hours.' Suddenly he looked her straight in the eye. 'Is Murdoch still here?'

Kate stared at him and he tossed his head like a highly-strung horse. 'Has he talked to the press, like he said he would?'

'No,' said Kate slowly. 'He . . . he's not well. Didn't you hear?'

'I didn't, no.' He laughed suddenly and mirthlessly. 'Hope it's terminal. Arrogant old sod.'

Kate was speechless.

Sarah tugged gently at his arm. 'We'd better go, Paul.'

'Sure.' Paul lifted a finger in farewell, stuck his hands back into his pockets and slouched off, with Sarah trailing submissively behind him. They turned towards the lift, and disappeared from view.

'Something going on there,' said Mary drily. 'That was quick work, I must say. They only met each other yesterday. Still waters run deep.'

'I'll say,' Kate was nonplussed.

'It's two minutes to eleven,' said Birdie. 'Let's go and watch TV.'

The familiar crumpled, friendly face with its famous lopsided grin filled the screen as the Miles Harris theme died away. The face began to talk—easily, intimately, welcoming besotted regular viewers and bored dial-twiddlers alike with the trademark of relaxed warmth that had made this plain man a star. He chatted to the camera for a while, then it pulled back to show that all the time he had had a companion sitting smiling and silent on the couch beside him, a glamorous blonde woman with very long legs and very white teeth. She was the latest in a string of TV hostesses with whom Miles had sat on such couches over the years. Like Fred Astaire, he had had such a long career that his partners kept wearing out and having to be replaced. They got traded in for younger models when the crowsfeet began to show. It didn't matter much as far as Kate could see. Blonde or brunette, they had all been turned out of the same smooth, long-legged mould, and all of them seemed to be called Vicki.

'We have a great line-up, today, Vicki, haven't we?' Miles was saying to his companion now.

'We sure have, Miles,' she replied, smiling fit to bust. 'There's the surrogate IVF mother of twin girls who's going to tell us why she's decided not to give up her babies, a marvellous woman from Perth who's founded a fortune on—would you believe it, Miles?—banana skins . . .'

'Bet she's a slippery customer!' beamed Miles, winking at the camera.

Vicki flapped her hand at him and giggled.

'And,' she managed to continue, her hand on her breast to indicate barely controlled hysteria, 'of course our marvellous home economist Maxine will be here to tempt us all with more goodies from Spain. What a morning, Miles!'

'Too right!' He grinned at her and faced the camera again. 'And of course there's lots more where that came from, folks. Including three very special people I want you to meet. You know their names, you probably know their faces, but it's the books they've written you'll know best. Curious? Good! Three very special people, and I'll be talking to them straight after this break.'

The theme music rose as he settled back and grinned puckishly at Vicki, now apparently overcome afresh by his earlier wit, and remonstrating with him in the gayest and most artificial manner imaginable.

An ad for face cream began. Kate hoped Vicki was paying attention to it. Stave off the crowsfeet a few years longer.

'I would've thought Quentin Hale would be watching this,' said Birdie, looking curiously around the splendid, empty room.

'Oh, he will be,' said Kate. 'He's got a TV in his office, though. He wouldn't come out here.'

'I'm looking forward to talking to him. Now especially.' Birdie's strange, amber eyes were alight with interest.

Evie shifted uneasily in her chair. 'If he found out someone outside this company knew about what'd happened, there'd be hell to pay!' she said querulously. 'I strongly suggest you keep away from him altogether.'

Birdie turned to stare at her, unblinking, through her thick glasses. 'Ssh,' she said reprovingly. 'They're on!'

12

The Miles Harris Show

Make-up had done its best with Jack Sprott. His face was almost normal in colour really, Kate thought, though underneath all the pancake there was a definite greenish tinge. And of course there was nothing to be done about the eyes. But presumably they'd avoid close-ups, and on the whole he didn't look bad—round and cute, just as he was supposed to, and jolly, too, in a dissipated sort of way.

Evie sighed. 'There he is. Hungover, half asleep, but Redcap to the last!'

Birdie ignored her and glanced at Kate with eyebrows raised.

'Garden gnome,' Kate translated dutifully. 'I suppose you've never read *The Adventures of Paddy Kangaroo*, have you?'

'Of course not!' grinned Birdie. 'What do you take me for?'

'Not an ordinary human being, anyway!' retorted Kate. 'Everyone else has read it!'

'I doubt that!' said Birdie coolly, and returned her attention to the screen.

'. . . three best-selling Australian authors,' Miles was saying. 'Thanks for making time to have this chat. I'm sorry to hear that Sir Saul Murdoch, who was to have joined us, isn't well. That's bad luck, isn't it? Still . . .'

'We'll struggle on regardless, Miles,' smiled Tilly

Lightly with her head on one side. She shook back her shining hair.

'Heh, heh, that's right!' said Miles, looking slightly startled.

'Tilly, I have to ask you this. You've been writing about Paddy Kangaroo for how long? Fifteen years or so? Does he ever get on your nerves? Do you ever have the urge to kill him off? Or maybe not kill him off, but send him off into the sunset, as it were?'

'Oh no!' smiled Tilly, putting her little white hand to her chin. 'I love dear old Paddy. What a thing to say, Miles!'

'Liar,' said Evie, grinning maliciously. 'You hate the bucktoothed little bugger. Go on, come clean!'

'Well, you wouldn't be the first writer to want to get on to something new, to get tired of the same set of characters and so on,' said Miles Harris challengingly. He had been advised by his producer to make his interviews more hard hitting.

'Paddy and his friends are my babies,' fluttered Tilly. 'They're part of the family! Part of me!'

'Yuk!' said Birdie, and put her hand over her eyes.

'So we can look forward to more Paddy, and Redcap, and the whole adventurous crew, then!' twinkled Miles Harris. 'More goanna battles, and near misses, and getting home safe and sound. The recipe as before?'

'And getting more feeble and twee every time,' groaned Kate. 'The last one was really—'

''Better than Bindi Mouse, anyway,' said Evie. 'At least the Paddys sell.'

'Ssh!' Birdie waved at them repressively.

'. . . hundreds of letters from children,' Tilly was saying, rather defensively. 'They absolutely love him. But you're typecasting me, Miles, you know. I do write other things. I've actually only done five Paddy stories since the first one. Six in all. But there's the Bindi Mouse books, too, and Kat-Kat the Koala—he's a sweetie, I think—has a wot of twouble pwonouncing his "r"'s.' She giggled, Barbara laughed, and Miles smiled uncertainly.

'You're right,' said Kate. 'She should stick to Paddy. The world does *not* need another Kat-Kat the Koala book.'

Miles turned with every appearance of relief to Barbara Bendix, smiling broadly beside him in Vicki's erstwhile niche.

'We spoke, I think, a couple of years ago, Barbara, when you published your biography of Frederick Manners?'

'That's right, we did,' said Barbara, in her huskiest voice.

'A very controversial book, if I remember rightly,' said Miles, chuckling. 'Is there another one on the boil, Barbara?'

She smiled again, a hungry cat smile. 'Oh yes. I always have several on the boil. It's a matter of which one boils over first, really.'

Miles laughed, and shifted in his seat. Barbara seemed to take up more room than Vicki. 'Someone better watch out, then, Barbara! Can we ask who?'

'Not even my publishers know who I'm working on, Miles. It's better that way. As I said, I've got notes and files on quite a few people. I just work away slowly, you know.'

'You've never worked on a living person, I think, Barbara. Why's that? Surely there are some fascinating living Australians who deserve immortalising?'

'Oh, sure there are, yes. And most of the work I'm doing now is on people who are alive and kicking. But, well, as you know there can be legal problems, Miles, and publishers don't like writs and injunctions. Sometimes, it's better to wait.' Barbara preserved a professional, scholarly tone, but her eyes sparkled with something more like relish.

'Could be a long wait, unless you only look at people you know haven't got long to go.' Miles looked a bit disconcerted. 'Sorry. Makes you sound like a vulture or something.'

Barbara gave him a long appraising stare. 'I suppose you could look at it like that,' she said.

'How do you choose your subjects, then—or should I call them victims?' Miles, recovering, smiled his lop-sided smile, and shared the joke with his audience.

Barbara stirred in her seat. 'Oh, they're just people who interest me,' she said lazily. 'But people who have high profiles too, of course, because then they interest everyone else as well. And because people like that usually have a facade to keep up. I like to try to get behind that facade.'

'The skeletons in the closet, eh?' Miles shook his head, and tutted over human frailty.

'Most people have secrets,' said Barbara, smiling at him. 'Even you, Miles, I imagine. I'll have to look into it.'

Miles chuckled edgily. 'Well!' he cried, and his voice cracked slightly. 'Well, Jack, we haven't had much to say to you, have we? The ladies have kept me too busy here.'

The camera discovered Jack leaning back peacefully in his chair, his short legs barely touching the floor, his eyes closed.

'He's asleep!' whispered Kate watching in horror. 'Evie, he's asleep!'

But at that moment Jack's eyes flickered, and he spoke. 'G'day,' he said gruffly. 'Pleased to be here.'

'Great!' crooned Miles. 'Great to have you, Jack. I have to tell you I swear by your *Gardener's Almanac*. Have you got a new book coming up?'

Jack looked at him vacantly. 'They're doing some-thing or other for Christmas,' he mumbled. 'Something or other. A notebook, or something.'

'*The Gardener's Log Book*, Jack!' Kate prompted im-patiently. 'For heaven's sake!'

'And I'm going to do another one. That'll probably be for Christmas, too. That's about my army days,' Jack continued. 'That'll be a good one.'

'Oh, dear oh dear,' Kate shook her head.

'Ssh,' said Birdie and Evie together, and exchanged unfriendly glances.

'Well, Tilly, Barbara, Jack—it's been great having you. I'll be seeing you tonight at the grand celebration in town, won't I?'

Tilly and Barbara nodded, Jack looked bemused.

'Let's hope Sir Saul Murdoch will be feeling better and can join us. If you're watching, sir, get well soon!' Miles winked sincerely at the camera, and turned to Barbara Bendix. 'Vicki was saying to me earlier that if this was Japan, Sir Saul Murdoch would be a national treasure,' he said.

Jack gave an unmistakable snort of disgust, Tilly a knowing smile.

Barbara raised her eyebrows and laughed. Whether her amusement was caused by the idea of Vicki's having the faintest clue about Saul Murdoch's literary worth or by her quoted sentiment, was not clear.

Miles certainly didn't know, and at this point, didn't wish to find out. With a few more nods, winks and promises of exciting things to come, he bid the camera farewell, until the end of the commercial break.

Three women began to sing about their washing powder to a man in a white coat. Evie looked at her watch, rose and turned off the television set and the video recorder.

'They cut it short. Quentin's a stubborn fool!' she said bitterly. 'He should've cancelled the whole thing. What a disaster.'

'Even without the Saul Murdoch business it was always going to be a disaster,' said Kate. 'I mean, what sort of representatives for us are those three? What sort of impression do you reckon they made on all those people out there? Jack was the worst. He's more or less told the world that we put his books together now. *The Gardener's Log Book*'s going to be a beauty, too. I hope he hasn't wrecked it for us.'

'It was just a throwaway line,' said Birdie. 'Most people wouldn't even have noticed it. I thought the Lightly woman did herself a bit of damage, though.

What a whimsical creep.' She wrinkled her nose in distaste. 'I hate that sort of woman.'

'You're not alone,' said Evie grimly. 'You should have seen Murdoch with her last night. It would've curled your hair.'

Birdie looked at her curiously. 'Tell me,' she said.

Evie shrugged. 'Kate was there,' she said, and got up. 'I've got to get going. I'll see you later, Kate.'

'Bye, Evie.' Kate watched the stocky figure leave the room and turned back to the shiny table top, sighing. She felt tired, heavy and depressed.

'What's up with her?' Birdie leant her head negligently on a freckled hand. Her hair stood out in a wild bush, her pointed face was sharp with interest.

'You know what's wrong, Birdie,' said Kate wearily. 'I've been telling you for a month. You and Jeremy said you were sick to death of hearing about it. Quentin Hale and this little pipsqueak Malcolm Pool—'

'Oh, yes, all that. But surely Evie Newell was expecting a mess. You told me she was. You'd think she'd be crowing "I told you so" from the rooftops. Why isn't she?'

'Well, because . . .' Kate looked at Birdie. How to explain to someone like her? She was Kate's oldest friend, but even at school she'd had little understanding of, and no patience with, ordinary human inconsistency.

'She identifies with the company, Birdie,' she said finally and flatly. 'She's worked here a long time. Despite everything, she doesn't really want to see it hurt. And anyway, she wasn't expecting anything like the real horribleness of the whole thing. I mean, we didn't know poor Sarah Lightly would be involved, for example. And whatever Evie said, I mean, she wasn't expecting anyone to *die*, for heaven's sake! Of course she's upset. I'm upset!'

'Not like her,' Birdie pointed out, unmoved.

'Probably I don't feel so responsible! And anyway, I've got other things. I've got Jeremy, and Zoe, and a life outside. Evie hasn't. Berry and Michaels has been her whole life. It really has. And she's having to watch it fall apart around her. You don't understand, Birdie. She doesn't have lots of friends outside, or a family. She's so alone.'

Birdie shrugged. 'Lots of people are alone,' she said. She spoke casually but there was an edge to her tone.

Kate looked at her quickly, but the light was shining into Birdie's glasses, and she couldn't see the expression in the amber eyes. She wondered for the thousandth time what went on under the mop of bushy brown hair, behind those strange eyes. She took Birdie for granted most of the time. She was just Birdie, as she'd always been. Small, scruffy, irritable and irritating, sardonic, coldly logical, and quite, quite self-sufficient. Birdie was the only person she knew who didn't seem to need anyone. She seemed to Kate, for that reason, invulnerable.

But every now and then Kate had a moment, like this, when she wondered.

'Well, come on!' Birdie's voice cut through her thoughts. 'Give me the low-down before we get company again, will you, Laney? I'm curious. And it'll give me an in with Dan Toby.'

Kate looked at her. No, she'd been wrong. For a moment she'd thought a mask had slipped, but she'd been romancing. The toughness went all the way down with Birdie. It was strange to have such a friend, a friend you never touched, or comforted. A friend who'd seen you cry, and heard your most secret fears and doubts, but who'd never shed tears of her own, or confided. A friend you loved, but who never showed affection to you except, Kate supposed, by staying around.

'I'll tell you all I know quickly, Birdie, but then I've got to get back to work.'

'Well I *am* working. And Quentin Hale told you to give me your *fullest* cooperation, remember? Now, the events leading up to the murder, if you please!'

'Birdie, it wasn't murder. It was suicide. Dan Toby said so.'

Birdie raised her eyebrows. 'I bet he didn't.'

'Well . . .' Kate hesitated. 'He said it almost certainly was, or something. It's the same thing.'

'I wouldn't say that.'

'Birdie, you just want it to be murder!' Kate snapped. 'Someone's dead, you know. A really important man's dead. He was on the edge. He'd had some terrible arguments. He killed himself. OK?'

'Laney, there's no need to get all worked up,' said Birdie reasonably. 'Me knowing about last night isn't going to make anything worse, is it?'

Kate shook her head crossly. Impossible to explain why all this threatened and disturbed her so badly. There were so many reasons . . . Dimly they loomed up at her, inextricably mixed and linked. This was her territory, and Birdie's presence and activity here over the last day or two had been unsettling. Birdie, like Jeremy, and their daughter Zoe, and her other friends, belonged to her world outside Berry and Michaels. Kate played a different role out there. She was in many ways a different person. She liked to keep the two separate.

And Birdie, why was she so interested in all this? This interest in conflict, death—in murder—was starting to seem like an obsession. There was something avid, wasn't there, in her thirst for detail? She wasn't a cop. But how many murder cases had she been involved in now? Three, or four? Was she going to go on and on?

And then what if Birdie's nose, infallible up to now, wasn't leading her astray this time? What if . . . Kate turned her mind resolutely from that thought. She just wouldn't think of that. She sighed.

'Righto. Last night . . .' she began, and Birdie listened, her golden eyes intent, her battered running shoe tap, tapping on the shining table leg.

13

A Little Unpleasantness

'That's it, Birdie. The whole thing. You can see. The poor man had had enough, and he decided to kill himself, and he did. The book, *Vernon Crew*—an awful book, his worst by far—was about a suicide. It's as clear as a bell.'

'Yeah.' Birdie put her hands behind her head and leaned back in her chair. 'Certainly looks like it.' She thought for a minute, and shook her head. 'That's that, then,' she said briskly, and got up to go.

Kate stared at her. 'What?' she said. 'You mean that's it?'

Birdie looked back and shrugged. 'What d'you want?' she said. 'Door locked from the inside, a man previously diagnosed as suicidally depressed dead on the bed with his own sleeping pills and a bottle of plonk beside him, book open with suitable quote marked as a farewell note. Dead several hours when found. Looks like suicide to me.'

'But—'

'Kate, look, I can't stay here talking. I've got to get back to work.'

'You've got to get back . . . Birdie!'

'I'll be in the archives. See you later.' Birdie grinned and strode to the door. She put her hand on the knob. Then they heard the voices.

'Much more comfortable in here,' Malcolm Pool was

saying, over the sound of Tilly's relentless monotone and Barbara's laughter.

'Sprung!' hissed Birdie, and the door swung open to reveal Malcolm, very pink around the ears, shepherding the recent stars of the Miles Harris Morning Show, overexcited, hot, and in one case at least, tired and emotional.

'Oh!' Malcolm's voice squeaked in almost adolescent fashion. He took a step back and trod heavily on Tilly's foot. She huffed indignantly.

'Hello,' said Birdie pleasantly. 'Remember me? Verity Birdwood. From the ABC.'

'Oh, yes.' Malcolm recovered his composure, looked Birdie briefly up and down, and ran his hand over his neat hair. He caught sight of Kate and frowned slightly, then turned and ushered his charges into the room. 'Please find a seat, won't you?' Tilly, Jack and Barbara, staring, spread themselves around the table. Kate noted with amusement that Tilly was still wearing her studio make-up.

Malcolm moved to Kate's side. 'Sorry, but I have to use this room now,' he said in an officious stage whisper, one eye on Birdie.

'We were just going,' said Kate coolly, and walked towards the door.

'Oi, Katie!' bawled Jack Sprott, suddenly coming to life in disconcerting fashion.

She waved at him. 'Hi, Jack.'

Tilly smiled wanly. 'Kate, I'd like a few minutes of your time later, if you could manage it. Sarah has a manuscript she'd like you to look at. Quentin said you were the one to speak to about it.'

Kate's heart sank. 'Sure, Tilly. I'll be in all day. I don't know what your schedule is, but . . .'

'Oh, apparently we're now not needed till this evening,' said Tilly rather stiffly. 'It's a relief to me, of course, because I hate all this sort of thing, and it's already so incredibly hot and steamy outside, it would be *torture* running around. But I really think people are incredibly inconsiderate and high-handed.'

Kate looked quickly at Malcolm. He was rather wild about the eyes, and the tips of his ears burned. She felt a momentary stab of malicious delight.

'Cancellations?' she said.

His lips twisted, and again he looked sideways at Birdie. 'A couple. Nothing that mattered, fortunately,' he said loudly. 'Miles Harris was the big one for to-day.'

Barbara stretched elaborately. 'Could we just see the tape, Malcolm? If we must. We had such an early start, after such a busy, busy night, darling. I'm nearly dead. As far as I'm concerned it's bloody marvellous we haven't got to go trooping off to some dreary radio station. Be a sweetie and let's get on with it! I want a lovely cool shower and a good soft bed.' She held out an appealing white hand, palm up, red-painted nails curved in slightly, like claws. Despite her languid pose she seemed to glitter with energy.

Jack Sprott snorted rudely.

Malcolm seemed to shrink as they watched. He almost scuttled to the TV set.

'Sure, sure,' he gabbled, and began pushing buttons. 'Let's hope Evie Newell has done her job here.'

Disgusted, Kate turned to go.

'Kate, could you or Amy or someone let Sarah know I'm back,' called Tilly faintly, from her chair. 'And ask her to bring the manuscript down?'

'Sarah's out, I think, Tilly,' said Kate, her hand on the doorknob.

'Out?' Tilly looked bewildered. 'Out where?'

'Here we go!' said Malcolm. The Miles Harris theme filled the room.

'Kate, just wait, will you?' cried Tilly excitedly, her eyes on the screen. 'As soon as this is over . . . I need to . . . Kate, don't go, will you?'

Kate sighed. 'I'll wait outside,' she said firmly, and let herself, and Birdie, out of the room. She wouldn't sit through that programme again, not for anyone.

She looked at her watch and sank down in one of the old leather armchairs that flanked the conference room door. 'This day is turning into a nightmare,' she said. 'One of those dreams where you're trying to get ready for something, and the time is going past, and things keep getting lost and broken. I don't seem to be making any progress and it's nearly lunchtime.' She stood up. 'Look, do me a favour, Birdie, and wait here in case they finish, and Tilly panics because I've gone. I'll just slip round and get Amy to ring Mary downstairs for me. OK? Won't take long.'

'Sure.' Birdie sat down in the chair Kate had vacated. It was so large that her feet barely touched the floor. 'You look like Goldilocks in Father Bear's chair,' said Kate, and laughed. Birdie looked at her coldly. 'I thought you were in a hurry,' she said.

Kate left her whistling tunelessly to herself from the depths of the chair and trotted on round the corner to Quentin's office. There was Amy at her post. And with her, drinking coffee, was Sarah Lightly. Kate, surprised, moved closer. The unlikely pair looked up at her approach and both their faces showed relief. Obviously they had had little to say to one another.

'Ah, Sarah. I thought you were out, with Paul,' said Kate. 'Your mum's back. She's in the conference room.'

'We never made it out,' said Sarah flatly. 'No sooner did we get downstairs, than Paul had to come up here. He had to talk to someone, up here. He said to wait.' She took a sip of coffee, expressionless. Kate and Amy exchanged glances.

'You should have come into the conference room with us, Sarah,' said Kate. 'Seen your . . . seen Tilly on TV.'

'No. I didn't feel like it.' Sarah's voice was flat, and she looked down at her hands. Talk about gawky! She was more like fourteen than twenty, thought Kate. She wondered just for a moment whether Sarah Lightly was all there, as they say. Then she marshalled her thoughts. How ridiculous. The girl was just very, very straightforward and simple. It was a shock. And a triumph of heredity over environment, actually, consid-

ering how strongly her mother's example must have
been steering her in quite the opposite direction all her
life.

Kate remembered why she'd come. 'Amy, could you
tell Mary where I am, please? I'll be down in about,
oh, fifteen or twenty minutes.' Amy nodded briskly,
and picked up the phone.

Kate listened to her dealing authoritatively with
Mary. The message sounded much more weighty,
coming from her. Then Kate remembered something
else. She turned to Sarah. 'Sarah, Tilly wanted you to
get your manuscript—the one you brought with you—
to show me, I think,' she said rather diffidently.

Sarah flushed and made a face. 'You don't have to
look at it,' she mumbled ungraciously.

'Well, I'd like to see it. And Tilly's very—'

'Look, you don't have to look at it because of my
mother. I don't want any favours. I've taken it upstairs, and I don't want to go and get it now. I want
to stay here and wait for Paul! He's going to help me
get a dress for tonight. A really nice dress.' The low
voice had risen to a fierce whisper.

Kate held up her hands. 'Look, fine, fine, whatever
you like. There's no rush. I'll explain to Tilly.' She
exchanged glances with Amy again.

'Could I get the manuscript for you, Sarah?' said
Amy smoothly. She may be discomposed today,
thought Kate, almost admiringly, but you'd barely notice it if you didn't know her.

Sarah hesitated. 'I suppose it would save time,' she
said grudgingly at last. 'My mother'll get her way in
the end. May as well get it over now.' She looked
faintly abashed, as if suddenly aware of how inappropriately she was behaving. 'Thanks,' she added belatedly, and began fumbling in her shoulder bag.

But Amy was already slipping past her, slim and
efficient. 'Don't worry, I've got a master key. Just tell
me where the manuscript is, Sarah.'

'In the black case in the wardrobe. A red folder.'

'All taken care of. Don't worry. I'll drop it into the

conference room, Kate.' And in a flicker of gold and cream, Amy was gone.

Sarah stared after her. 'Isn't she pretty?' she remarked without envy or admiration.

Kate hesitated. 'Sarah,' she said lightly, 'would you like me to take you shopping for a dress? I'd be happy . . .'

'Oh, no!' Sarah shook her head. 'Paul knows what would look good. He said he'd take me. And I've got money, if that's what you mean. In the bank. Dad left me some money, you know. I got it when I turned eighteen.' She looked hard at Kate. 'He left me all his stuff. Not that he had much to leave. But he left it to me, not to Mama. I've always thought that was because he really loved me. But now I think it might have been just because he didn't like her.' She stood motionless for a moment, then shook her head roughly.

'You don't have to look after me,' she said. 'I'm good here. Paul will be out in a minute. You'd better go back to the others.'

Thus dismissed, Kate nodded and went. At the end of the corridor she looked back. Sarah was drinking coffee, staring stoically at the wall, waiting.

Back at the conference room, Birdie watched with interest as the door was thrown open, and Barbara emerged.

'Well, I don't know how you can stand it,' she called raucously over her shoulder. 'We all look like death warmed up! I'm going upstairs to have a rest. I'll catch you at lunch.' She flashed Birdie a brilliant, meaningless smile, then winked, turned and leant into the room again. Her voice grew husky. 'Jack, why don't you come up with me? You don't want to see that thing again. Can't I tempt you?' She was in very high spirits, and enjoying herself thoroughly.

Birdie heard Jack growl a reply.

Barbara pouted and shook her shoulders a little. Her breasts jiggled under the thin cloth of her loose black top. 'Oh, go on, Jack. I don't know why you're so sour all of a sudden,' she teased. 'It was a different story last night, you old devil! Isn't that right, Malcolm? Last night I had to have Malcolm to protect me, didn't I?'

'Don't you go on about last night!' roared Jack Sprott, as if tormented beyond endurance. 'I know about you! I heard about you!'

'Better not say any more, Jack,' said Tilly archly. 'She's a dangerous woman. Miles said so. She might write a book about you, mightn't you, Barbara? After you're dead, of course.' She giggled.

Barbara looked at her with slitted eyes, and her top lip curled. 'You'd be a likelier candidate, Tilly,' she said softly. 'I'm sure people would be riveted to hear about your touching relationship with Australia's great man of letters. Baby at home with granny, and all. Another dimension on Tilly Lightly, Queen of the Kids, isn't it?'

'Barbara,' Malcolm interrupted weakly, 'no jokes, now. Let's watch—'

'Who's joking?' retorted Barbara. 'Ah, I can see it now . . .'

'You be quiet, Barbara!' Tilly's voice was shaking. 'You just be quiet. Keep your nose out of my business. If one word of anything Saul said last night gets repeated by you, I'll sue you for every cent you've got! I will, I promise you!'

'Is that right?' drawled Barbara. 'How terrifying!'

'Well, I mean it!' cried Tilly, gratingly shrill. 'Over my dead body you'll ever, ever get your grubby fingers on my life!'

Barbara threw back her head and laughed, but her eyes were angry as she turned on her heel and strode away up the corridor.

Silence reigned in the conference room. Then Malcolm cleared his throat tentatively. 'Ah,' he said, 'ah . . . this is ready to play. So, will we . . . ?' He walked to the door and put his head out. Birdie, swinging her legs in the big upright chair, smiled mildly at him. He shied a little, his blue eyes widening in his flushed and flustered face. Then, forgetting to smile, he pulled the door shut.

Birdie sat on, peacefully. After a moment the Miles Harris theme rose, muffled, from inside the room. She looked up lazily to see Kate approaching. 'You took your time,' she said. 'You missed a scene. They've been at each other's throats here. Barbara Bendix's gone upstairs. The others are watching their performance over again.'

'How could they!' Kate shook her head. 'What were they fighting about? No, don't tell me. I can't stand it. You know, Sarah Lightly was round there. Paul got nabbed after all. He's with your friend Toby now, getting grilled. On this floor somewhere. They must be in the spare office down past Quentin.'

'Stop calling him "my friend Toby", will you?' growled Birdie.

'Well he is, isn't he?'

'Oh, in a way, I suppose. Cranky old bugger. That insect Milson is the one who gives me trouble.'

Kate laughed. 'Don't you like him?'

Birdie grinned. 'What d'you think? And he loves me, too. The jerk!'

'Anyway, Sarah's sitting there at Amy's desk waiting. She's a *very* strange girl. Heaven knows what her book'll be like.'

'It might be good. She might have inherited her mother's talent.'

Kate grimaced. 'That's what I'm afraid of.'

'But I thought this *Paddy Kangaroo* was some great classic!'

'Oh, yes it is. And I suppose I'm being unfair. *Paddy* is terrific, and obviously Tilly's got talent, even if she's got too bored and lazy to show it since the big success. She just irritates me, she sets herself up as such a little-sweetie-pie person, and she isn't at all. She doesn't even like children much.'

'A woman after my own heart! How does she feel about domestic pets? And natural childbirth?'

'How would I know!' snapped Kate. 'And what're you on about, anyway? You said you couldn't stand that sort of woman.'

'Yeah. She's a closet whinger. If she's sick of Paddy, why doesn't she write about something else? No one's stopping her, are they?'

Kate looked uncomfortable. 'Well, no, of course not. But none of her other characters work in the market like Paddy. I mean, the Paddy sequels are much weaker than the original, but they do sell, especially at Christmas. So we . . .'

Birdie leaned back in her chair and shook her head disgustedly. 'So you kind people make it very clear that if she wants her bills paid, Paddy had better prosper and multiply. Oh, I see. The poor woman's trapped! One early success, and she's stuck with it for life! Kate, this book publishing is a depressing business. No wonder she's like she is.'

'Birdie, that's not fair! She could have lived very comfortably just on the original *Adventures of Paddy Kangaroo*. That's where her real income is. She didn't have to write the sequels. She does it as much for the glory as the money. And we do publish her other things—we have. It's not our fault they don't get anywhere, whatever Tilly thinks!'

She jumped as the conference room door clicked open. Tilly Lightly's head popped out. She peered around suspiciously and then smiled graciously as she saw Kate waiting as bidden.

' 'Scuse me,' Jack pushed gingerly past her, and out in the corridor. 'Not a bad show, Kate?' He jerked his thumb back towards the television, where Malcolm was carefully unloading the video tape cassette.

Kate nodded and smiled hypocritically.

Jack wiped his hand across the back of his mouth thoughtfully. 'I think I'll nip on upstairs,' he said to Kate, looking rather devious. 'Have a lie down. Have a bit of a read. See to a few things. Before lunch.' He tottered off.

Tilly looked after him and shook her head gently. 'Poor old Jack. It's so sad, isn't it?' she said, and sighed.

Kate, who had been thinking almost exactly that, immediately felt irritated. 'Oh, Jack's OK,' she said quickly. 'He wouldn't want our sympathy, anyway.'

'No, no, of course not. I didn't mean . . .' Tilly was taken aback and Kate, pulling herself together, hastened to make amends before affront could set in.

'I mean, he's just a natural character. I've known him for years, and he's always been the same. You know, don't you, that everyone calls him Redcap here?' She laughed, willing Tilly to join in. She was disappointed.

'Redcap?' Tilly's brow wrinkled.

'Well, he's so like your Redcap, isn't he? Cute and round and brown. A little gardening gnome who loves flowers and gets stuck into the sap when he shouldn't— you know! It's just a joke,' Kate finished lamely. This was obviously going over like a lead balloon.

Tilly looked at her, and smiled politely. 'I'd never have thought of it myself,' she said stiffly. 'It's amazing what interpretations other people put on your work, isn't it? I'd always seen Redcap as rather a wise little man. Nothing clownish about him. And, I mean, he's not an alcoholic, is he? Nothing like it.'

'No, no, Tilly, of course not. Look, it's nothing,' said Kate, cursing herself for raising the matter. With relief she saw Amy coming towards them with a red folder under her arm. It looked, somehow, rather familiar. 'Here's Amy with Sarah's manuscript,' she said. 'Let's go into the conference room, and we can have a chat about it for five minutes.' She ushered Tilly back into the room, exchanged a few words with the hovering Malcolm, and lifted a hand in farewell to Birdie, slouching by the door with her hands in her pockets.

'See you round,' murmured Birdie, stepping back as Amy reached the doorway.

Kate nodded and saw her turn to go with some relief. It wasn't until Amy had disappeared and Tilly had started her little spiel that she suddenly registered the fact that Birdie had been turning, not towards the lift, but towards Quentin's office. She wasn't going back to work. She was going to look for Dan Toby.

14

Three Authors, Lightly Grilled

In his humble headquarters at the end of the long corridor, Dan Toby put down the telephone.

'He'll be bringing the Bendix woman down in a minute,' he said to Milson, standing stiffly by the wall. 'Keep an eye out, will you? Sprott's next, then Lightly. And you—out! If Hale sees you in here there'll be murder done.'

Birdie drifted to the door. 'Another murder, do you mean?' she enquired. 'Or are you sticking to suicide? Paul Morrisey looked pretty ruffled on his way out, I thought. What did he say? You've hardly told me anything!'

Milson gave her an unfriendly look. 'They'll be here any minute, sir,' he said warningly.

'I'm going, I'm going,' Birdie drawled. She stuck her fingers in her belt. 'It's just I've been round here for a couple of days. Thought I might have picked up something useful to you. Still . . .' She turned to go.

'Give us a ring in an hour,' said Toby, looking fixedly at Milson as if daring him to object. 'I'll see.'

Birdie flashed him a grin and darted out of sight.

Milson shook his head slightly and looked at the ceiling. 'Imagine her turning up,' he said, his tone carefully even.

'Bad pennies tend to,' said Toby, shuffling the papers on his desk.

Milson could stand the suspense no longer. 'You're not really going to talk to her, are you, sir?'

Toby shrugged and smiled, his weathered face creasing into a hundred deep lines. 'Why not?' he said, enjoying the younger man's outrage. 'Any means to an end. Anyone'd be a fool to let prejudice get in the way of information, wouldn't they, Milson?'

Milson shifted his angular frame uneasily.

'She's helped a couple of times, hasn't she?' pursued Toby. 'Stopped us making a big mistake the first time. We bloody ran in the wrong woman, didn't we, in that ABC murder case? She was the one who put us on the right track.'

'She just wanted to get her mate off,' muttered Milson. 'And big-note herself.'

Toby lost patience. 'Milson, you're exhausting, mate!' he barked. 'What do her motives matter, for God's sake! Will you get it into your head? She was right and we were wrong! Hard to take, but there you are. And the only thing that makes me feel good about it is that I did finally have the sense to listen to her before we locked up a completely innocent person and threw away the key. And threw streamers while a killer wandered off to the happy-ever-after, what's more. Pull yourself together!'

Milson thinned his lips. There was no point, none at all, in trying to talk sense to a man who had so little respect for his profession that he could listen seriously to a pushy amateur like Verity Birdwood.

Voices sounded in the corridor. The two men exchanged glances, animosities abruptly shelved.

Toby watched the door keenly. So far he had seen three people's reactions to the news of Murdoch's death. All had reacted differently—Evelyn Newell calm and controlled, Kate Delaney shocked and upset, Paul Morrisey sullen and defensive. Of the three authors he had to see next, Barbara Bendix interested him the least, from a professional point of view. But it would be an experience to meet her anyhow, he reflected. He'd never read one of her books, but he'd seen her on TV, on a couple of panel shows, and being interviewed. She was sharp as a tack, from what he could make out.

In a gale of laughter and a wave of musky perfume, Barbara Bendix swept into the small room, with Quentin Hale close behind. On seeing Dan Toby behind the desk she stopped abruptly, and Quentin almost tripped over his own feet to avoid a collision.

'What's this?' she demanded, her arched black brows drawing together. She pointed accusingly at Toby. 'Cops!'

Toby grinned. 'I never thought I was so obvious,' he said. 'I'm crushed. Aren't you crushed, Milson?'

Milson avoided Barbara's flashing black eyes, and wisely preserved a dignified silence.

Barbara lowered herself warily into the chair Quentin placed for her. She twisted round to look at him. 'What's going on, Quentin? Why didn't you say anything?'

Toby cleared his throat. It was time he attempted to take charge.

'Miss Bendix,' he said soberly. 'I'm Detective-sergeant Toby. I asked Mr Hale to get you because we need some questions answered. We're talking to others, too. The fact is, there's been a problem here this morning.'

'What?' Barbara Bendix put both hostility and boredom into the monosyllable.

'Sir Saul Murdoch was found dead in his room,' Toby said bluntly.

There was a moment's silence. Then a small smile stole over Barbara's face.

'Well, well, well . . .' she mused. 'So he finally pulled it off. What exquisite timing.' She nodded her head slowly. 'Malcolm knew this, didn't he, when he took us out this morning?' she said. The question was obviously directed at Quentin Hale, though she didn't bother to look at him. He cleared his throat.

'Malcolm did know, yes. But I thought it best for him to keep it to himself at that point, Barbara.'

She nodded again. 'He never said a word,' she murmured. 'Sly little devil.' Then the smile crept to her lips again, and she leant across the desk towards Toby. Her perfume rolled over him like a wave. He averted his eyes from the gaping neck of her blouse and concentrated on the long red nails, glistening at the ends of her lightly clasped fingers.

'I heard, saw, tasted and smelt nothing unusual all night,' she purred. 'Anything else you want to know?'

When Quentin had taken Barbara away, Toby found himself breathing out heavily. He wouldn't have been surprised if someone told him he'd been holding his breath throughout the entire interview. What a formidable woman!

'Tough nut, eh, Milson?' he said, to relieve his feelings.

Milson sniffed. 'Thinks she is, anyway,' he answered, and flipped the pages of his notebook over.

Toby felt like making a rude noise at him, but thought better of it. He tapped the desk with his fingertips and whistled softly to himself. Jolly Jack Sprott, the gardener's friend, was next. He'd read all *his* books, anyway. Maybe he could get in a question about that sour little patch by his back fence, where everything he tried turned up its toes. May as well make the most of the opportunity to consult an expert.

But one disappointed look at Jack's red, glistening face and glazed blue eyes banished any fantasy Toby might have had of cosy personal garden consultations. Jack Sprott reeked of whisky, and swayed on his short legs like a man just disembarked after three months at sea in a tub. He was drunk, tired and belligerent.

Toby, abandoning introductions and niceties, told him about Murdoch, and watched for the reaction.

Jack Sprott shrugged. 'Good riddance,' he said defiantly.

'You don't seem surprised, sir?' said Toby quietly.

Jack pursed his lips and narrowed his eyes. 'What

d'you mean?' he said angrily. 'What am I supposed to say? I've seen lots of blokes die in my time. What do I care about that bastard? Heart, was it?'

'Did you see or hear anything at all unusual last night?' Toby doggedly went on.

'No, I didn't!'

'Sure?'

'Course I'm bloody sure. I was in bed. Asleep. Unlike some.'

Toby leaned forward casually. 'Oh, was someone up and around?'

But Jack, blue eyes bleary and cunning, had retreated into tipsy mumblings, and would say no more, and eventually Toby let Quentin take him away.

'He knows something he's not telling,' said Milson, looking after them hungrily. 'You didn't ask about the row last night, sir. Any special reason for that?'

'Well, I didn't just forget about it, Milson, if that's what you mean,' said Toby coldly. 'I decided to wait. He's not making much sense at the moment. Plenty of time.'

'Pathetic to see an old bloke gone to seed like that,' said Milson, looking ostentatiously at his notebook and tapping his teeth with a pencil.

'He's not that old, Milson. Mid-fifties. Not much older than me.'

'Oh yes?' said Milson. He looked up briefly, then dropped his eyes to the notebook again. A faint smile trembled on his thin lips.

Point taken, you worm, fumed Toby. Defiantly he tugged at the strangling knot of his tie. The phone rang and he snatched it up. 'Yes?' he barked.

'Are you ready to see Mrs Lightly now, Mr Toby?' Amy's tense, clipped voice cut through his ill humour. 'Malcolm's taken Mr Sprott upstairs, and Mr Hale said he could bring Mrs Lightly along now, if you like. She's on this floor already, in the conference room.'

'Yes please, love. Wheel her in,' said Toby.

Amy responded politely and cut the connection.

'Lightly's on her way, Milson,' said Toby, and

placed his blunt fingers on the desk before him, vividly aware of the scrawled note, the bitter, angry, threatening note, signed by Tilly Lightly, encased in its plastic bag in the folder under his hands. He watched the door keenly. He was very interested to see how this lady would take the news of Murdoch's death. Very interested indeed.

Two figures appeared at the door. Quentin Hale, tall, powerful, red-faced and stiff, and a tiny, white-faced woman clutching a handbag and a handkerchief.

'Tilly,' said Quentin gently. 'This is Detective-sergeant Toby and, ah . . .'

'Detective-constable Milson,' said Toby automatically, rising to his feet. He smiled in what he hoped was a reassuring manner. 'Please sit down, Mrs Lightly.'

'What's the matter?' Tilly asked faintly. Then a look of real terror crossed her face. 'Sarah?'

'No, no,' Quentin broke in hurriedly, and put his arm around her shoulders, steering her to the chair. 'Tilly, there's nothing wrong. Well, anyway it's nothing to do with Sarah. I would have told you that!'

She sat for a moment, breathing softly, and then shook her hair back selfconsciously. 'Silly,' she said to Toby. 'They told me my daughter was out, and she's not used to the Sydney traffic, and I just thought when he said Detective—you know, police—I suddenly thought . . .'

'I can imagine, Mrs Lightly,' said Toby soothingly, and smiled at her. 'I worry about my son, too. And he's nearly thirty!'

But already the moment of raw feeling had gone, leaving no trace but a slight flush in Tilly's pale cheeks. She tilted her head in a whimsical manner as she smiled in return, and Toby saw, in a flash, the image he had seen in the publicity handout Quentin had shown him a few hours before. Only the flower was wanting.

'I'll leave you, then,' said Quentin formally. 'Tilly,

why don't you come round to my office afterwards, and I'll take you to lunch.'

'As long as I haven't been run in, Quentin! I might have to ask you to get me a takeaway pie with a file in it, mightn't I?' smiled Tilly.

He gave a strangled laugh, and escaped. She turned, daintily composed, back to Toby.

He cleared his throat. Now was the moment. He opened the folder in front of him. 'Mrs Lightly,' he said smoothly, turning the plastic-covered note around to face her, 'did you write this note?'

Her jaw dropped, and she blushed to the roots of her hair. 'Where did you get that?' she almost squeaked, and her hand darted out. He drew the note back to safety, and watched her with interest.

'Did he give it to you? Is he making some sort of complaint, is that it?' she gasped, trembling with anger. 'Well, I can tell you, I'm the one with the complaint. I'm the one. He slandered me in front of a whole crowd of people last night. I've got witnesses! I had a perfect right to ask him to take it back, didn't I?' She was breathing hard, and her small, white fingers clutched desperately at the edge of the desk.

'It's a pretty hard-line sort of a letter, that's all, Mrs Lightly, isn't it?' Toby watched her carefully. 'You say here you could kill him.'

She shook her head angrily. 'Oh, that's ridiculous. It's ridiculous! It's just an angry phrase. He can't possibly claim—'

'Sir Saul isn't claiming anything, Mrs Lightly,' Toby interrupted calmly. 'He's dead.'

Every trace of blood drained from her cheeks. She sat quite still, white as chalk, looking at him with huge, stunned eyes.

'We found the note on the floor of his room,' said Toby. 'How did it get there, do you suppose?'

She licked her lips. 'I put it under his door.'

'When?'

'I don't know. At about 11.30 or so, I suppose. I got up out of bed to do it.'

'Why?'

'I was angry. I wanted to tell him. Make him take back what he'd said. For Sarah. She wouldn't speak to me.'

'You didn't see him? Wouldn't it have been better to ask him face to face?'

'No.' She shook her head slowly, still staring at him as though fascinated. 'I couldn't do that. See him. He . . . hated me. He said terrible things about me. He hadn't changed at all.'

'You're sure you didn't see him, Mrs Lightly?' Toby persisted, watching her closely.

She blinked at him, and frowned slightly. 'No, I said I didn't!'

'I was just making sure. You'll sign a statement saying that?'

'Of course I will!' She was beginning to recover now, and the faint colour was returning to her cheeks.

Toby sat back in his chair. 'Right then, Mrs Lightly. That's fine. Now, if you'll just give Milson your full name and address and so on, he'll type up what you've said and we'll get it over with. Just routine.'

15

Out to Lunch

Toby sat thinking for a moment, after Tilly had gone. She'd wanted the note back, of course, but that was impossible and eventually he'd made her see that.

'Well, she's my pick,' said Milson, jerking his head in the direction of Tilly's retreating back.

Toby stood heavily and lumbered to the door. He looked out. Tilly's small figure was just turning into the corridor leading to Quentin Hale's office. Her back was very straight, and her head high, as though she knew she was being watched. He remembered her face as he'd last seen it, very pale with bright pink patches on the cheeks, the fine lines beginning to disturb the skin around the eyes and mouth at odds with the delicate, flower-like features.

'Maybe,' he said ruminatively. 'We'll see. Could've sworn, though, she got a shock when I told her Murdoch was dead. Were you watching her?'

'Yes,' said Milson in grudging agreement. 'She could have been acting though. She seems pretty good at putting up a front.'

'Oh yes,' said Toby absently. 'I'd say she spends a good part of her life putting up a front. That's what makes it such a shock to her, when the front comes down.'

'Obviously she had a motive,' persisted Milson, refusing to be distracted.

'As did Morrisey, come to that.'

'Yes. Nervy. Belligerent. He'll bear looking into, too.'

Toby stretched. 'They all will. If it's not plain and simple, open and shut suicide, which I'm willing to bet it is.'

'On the evidence, sir?' Milson enquired coolly. 'I wouldn't have thought so.'

Toby winced and hauled at his belt. 'I'm not talking about evidence, Milson, I'm talking about instinct. And let's not get into that discussion again, either. It's tedious.'

And you're tedious, Milson, he thought. *And you make me tedious as well!* He walked back to the desk. The phone shrilled. Birdie had timed it to the minute. He picked up the receiver on the second ring.

Milson looked out into the corridor.

'Why not?' he heard his superior say grumpily. 'Why not? See you at the goods entrance in ten minutes. Fifteen then. OK. Bye.'

Toby replaced the phone gently in its cradle and pulled his tie up not quite enough to disguise the open collar button. 'I'm going out to lunch, Milson,' he said offhandedly. 'You carry on. Do some nosing round upstairs. You can get a sandwich when I come back.'

'Will I get a statement from Sarah Lightly while you're away, sir?' said Milson.

'No thanks. I'd rather do it myself.'

'Excuse me, sir, but wouldn't it be wiser——?'

'Just do what I say, will you, Milson?' growled Toby. 'Hale's probably taken everyone to lunch by now. It's nearly 1.00. They're only going round the corner. Better him than me, I must say. He's a determined bugger. She'll keep, for God's sake.'

'Sir, if this is murder . . .'

Toby fixed him with a steely eye. 'If it's murder, Milson, someone went to a lot of bloody trouble to make it look as though it wasn't and I wouldn't mind their thinking we've taken the bait. If it's murder. And whatever it is, one hour is going to make not a jot of difference to anything. And I'm going out. If that's quite OK with you!'

Milson mumbled, and began flicking through his notes.

Toby brushed past him angrily. As he reached the door, Milson cleared his throat and spoke again.

'Sir?'

'What!' Toby rounded on him, blue eyes almost shooting sparks, but Milson didn't flinch.

'I thought I'd do a check, on the Lightly woman's husband.'

'He's been dead for years, Milson.'

'Yes. But it might be useful to know how he died, don't you think, sir?' Milson blinked, waiting.

'Oh, do what you want,' barked Toby. 'Whatever you want.' He turned on his heel and strode off down the corridor. Milson smiled thinly. That had got under the old bastard's skin all right. He had no feeling for detail whatsoever. And the Lightly woman, he'd felt sorry for her. He was transparent. Silly old fool. He sat down in the chair Toby had just vacated. It was still warm, and his lips twitched with fastidious distaste. He began reading over his notes very, very carefully.

At the other end of the long corridor Quentin and Tilly stood waiting for the lift.

'We'll all feel better with some food inside us, Tilly,' said Quentin heartily. He shot an anxious glance at the wilting figure beside him.

Tilly raised her eyes. 'All this food,' she sighed, 'I'm not used to it. I eat hardly anything, usually. As you can see!' She gestured at her tiny figure, and half smiled. 'I wish I could!' she added, and shook her hair back. 'Sarah would make two of me. And Barbara!'

'Good things come in small parcels, heh, heh!' chuckled Quentin. What a fool he sounded, he thought, but he had learned a thing or two about Tilly, and his instinct hadn't failed him. She smiled at him under her lashes, and tilted her head prettily, watching the golden arrow moving now towards their floor.

'We'll keep the conversation nice and general, now, Tilly,' said Quentin, 'won't we?' He smiled at her and put his hand lightly on her shoulder. 'You'll back me up?'

'Oh yes,' she breathed conspiratorially. 'Don't worry, Quentin.'

With a jerk and a sigh the lift settled before them. The doors were pulled back. Barbara Bendix, broadly smiling, and Jack Sprott, swaying and definitely the worse for wear, stood behind the hulking figure of Sid. Malcolm Pool, very pink and scrubbed, stood beside him. The smell of whisky hung like a cloud around them.

'Hello,' said Tilly brightly, stepping in. 'You're all here!' She wrinkled her nose slightly and half-turned to look at Jack.

'Malcolm gathered us up, didn't you, darling?' said Barbara Bendix, twinkling.

Malcolm twitched and grinned. Jack looked sourly at them both, and at Tilly. Perhaps whisky didn't agree with him as well as champagne did. He was obviously fed up with this whole enterprise.

Sid growled and everyone looked at him, disconcerted. But it seemed that he was just clearing his throat. He shut the doors with a clatter, and the lift began its descent.

Despite the little fan that whirred busily above Sid's head, the air was oppressive. Hot, stuffy and heavy with the mingled smells of Jack's whisky breath and Barbara's musky perfume. They stood in silence, shoulder to shoulder, watching the gold arrow.

It crawled down to one, jerking and clatting. Sid opened the doors.

To Quentin's chagrin Birdie stood waiting there, hands in her pockets. Beside her, but rather definitely not with her, was Evie, freshly combed and lipsticked, and Sarah Lightly.

Sid shook his head heavily. 'Can't do it,' he said to no-one in particular. 'Too many for one trip.'

'Oh! Oh look, we'll walk down,' said Evie, blinking at the crowd. 'We'll meet you down there.' She turned to Birdie. 'You don't mind walking down, do you, Verity?' she added firmly.

'Sarah! Where have you been?' cried Tilly. 'I've been worried about you.'

Sarah shrugged. 'I've just been here,' she said vaguely. 'I meant to go out, but I couldn't, in the end.'

'I gave you-know-what to Kate Delaney,' coaxed Tilly. 'I'll tell you all about it at lunch.'

'Come on!' growled Jack, from the back.

Sarah shifted from foot to foot. 'Actually, I don't really want any lunch,' she mumbled. 'I wasn't going to stay, and now I've seen you up here I don't need to come to the place at all, do I? You don't mind, do you?' she added, addressing Quentin directly.

He smiled and mouthed non-committally.

'Quentin's booked!' said Tilly sharply. 'Don't be silly!'

Sarah shuffled her feet, and shook her head again. Her big hands were tightly clasped.

'Oh, let the poor girl skip lunch if she wants to, Tilly!' shouted Barbara from the back of the lift. 'It doesn't matter.'

'It doesn't matter, Tilly,' said Quentin, smiling tightly, and glancing at Birdie, still standing beside Evie, and studying, apparently, a poster on the wall.

Tilly shrugged and turned her heart-shaped little face away. 'She can do what she likes,' she said bitterly. 'Different things matter to different people, and obviously you don't agree with me, Barbara, but to me it's always been very important to stick by your promises and not let yourself or other people down.'

There was a shocked silence. Barbara just grinned

wolfishly, but Jack stood on his toes to peer at Tilly with furious, red-rimmed eyes.

'You're a fine one to talk, aren't you?' he bawled. 'It's all right to sneak round with fancy men behind your husband's back, though, isn't it? That's OK, is it?' His eyes began to water and his voice to tremble. 'Do the best mate that ever drew breath down, that's all right, is it? But stand up some stuck-up big-wig for lunch, and that's some bloody disaster, is it? You bloody women!'

Tilly went white.

'Jack!' Barbara laid her hand on his arm. 'Shut up. You don't know what you're talking about.'

He shook her hand off and glared at her. 'Shut up, yerself!' he shouted. 'Know what I'm talking about? I know what I'm talking about. You'd be bloody surprised what I know. Bloody women. You're all the bloody same, when it comes down to it. Like a lot of she-cats when a tom comes round. Screaming for it, the lot of you. And the bloody smooth bastards who hang round for the pickings. They're just as bad. They're not real men. Real men like Rabbit Lightly, and Wombat O'Neil and . . . and . . . they were real men. And where are they? Dead and buried.' He gave a huge sob, and his eyes welled over. 'And bloody forgotten,' he whispered, and turned his face to the wall.

There was a horrible silence.

Evie glanced at Malcolm, who seemed frozen to the spot, and moistened her lips. 'Jack, why don't you and I have a sandwich quietly together up here,' she said calmly. 'You probably don't feel like a big lunch. Then you can get upstairs and have a little sleep. How about that?' She held out her hand to him.

'I'm not going upstairs,' fumed Jack, refusing to look at her. 'I want to have my say about the bloody goings-on in this place. D'you hear that? I'm not going to be shut up like—'

'Sid!' barked Quentin, his eyes on Birdie.

Birdie looked quickly, had time for a split second glimpse of the people in the lift, clustered, huge-eyed faces, goggling at Jack's shaking shoulders, and Sarah's wild eyes. And then Sid, scarlet-faced, had crashed the doors shut, and the lift had disappeared.

The cafe was crowded and hot, despite the air-conditioner roaring in the corner. Birdie and Dan Toby lunched together at the back, in extreme physical discomfort, trying to keep their knees from touching under the tiny table.

'Well,' said Birdie impatiently. 'What's happening, Dan?'

Dan Toby rolled his eyes and stirred his tea. 'You could ask me how I am, or if I had a good Christmas, or something, Birdwood,' he complained, 'before you get going on the rough stuff. No finesse, that's your trouble. You'll never get a good man to love you if you don't learn to be a lady.'

Birdie snorted. 'What would you know about good men! Come on, we haven't got all day. What's the story? Murder, or suicide?'

'The PM wouldn't even have started yet. Fingerprints and so on still being checked. No evidence it's anything but suicide so far.'

'What do you think?'

'It looked like suicide.'

'But?'

'Keep your voice down.' Toby glanced around the crowded cafe, eased his bulk in the flimsy chair and took a sip of tea. He looked at Birdie, fascinated and intent, facing him over the cramped table top. Her chestnut hair stood up in a bush at the back of her head, her thin freckled hands clasped her cup tightly, and her thick glasses flashed as they caught the light. The first time he met her, a few years ago, he'd thought she was the plainest little piece he'd seen since high school. All she lacked was braces on her teeth. Funny. She didn't look nearly so plain to him now. Now he knew what went on under that tangled curly hair, knew how sharp were those amber eyes behind the glasses. Little witch. He found himself smiling, and quickly frowned, to disguise it.

But Birdie had sensed his mood, and played her best card. 'Look, I know Milson doesn't think you should talk to me, Dan,' she said innocently, 'so if you'd rather . . .'

'Bugger Milson!' growled Toby. He gulped at his tea, burning his tongue. 'Milson's a pain and a bore.'

'Well, why don't you just fill me in, Dan,' said Birdie persuasively. 'And then I'll tell you what I've picked up. Might help.'

'Might,' he said grudgingly.

Their waitress brought their lunch. 'Smoked turkey salad on rye,' she said, sliding a plate in front of Birdie, 'and steak sandwich and chips,' she added less approvingly, and clattered down Toby's choice. 'Mind-the-plate-it's-hot!' she ordered, a second too late, and withdrew.

Toby sucked his fingers ruefully. 'I hate these places,' he mumbled. He looked again at Birdie and reached a decision. 'OK,' he said. 'You're on. Again. Why not? But this time don't rile Milson. It makes my life a misery. And when and if I say it's time for you to butt out, you butt out! Agreed?'

'Of course, Dan!' exclaimed Birdie sweetly. 'Anything you say.'

He looked at her bland expression and had severe misgivings. He pushed his plate towards her. 'Go on, then, have a chip. And let's get on with it. Now, basically, we've got the two options. Suicide, and murder. Accident's not on. Suicide was my pick, when I saw the bloke. But then . . .'

'You met the other inmates, right?' Birdie grinned at him, and took another chip.

'An excellent choice of word. Yes. I met the other inmates, and started to wonder. Of course,' he looked at her cunningly, 'even before that, there was the note.'

'What note?' Birdie sat up eagerly.

'The note in Murdoch's room.'

'Tell me! Tell me!'

Dan Toby pulled happily at his tie, leaned forward and began to talk.

16

A Bird's-Eye View

A seagull fixed Dorothy Hale with a cold yellow eye.
She shrugged her shoulders and showed it her empty
hands, and it stalked off on spindly red legs to join its
more successful friends clustered round a late-lunching
pair of office workers. She looked around the park, almost deserted now, settling into the long stillness of a
weekday afternoon. She wondered in a detached way
why there weren't more people here, to take advantage
of the cool breeze that frisked off the harbour waves.
The breeze petered out by the time it reached the hot,
crowded streets, the sweating, jostling shoppers and
tourists, all so busy and determined on their various
errands.

She had no errands. She had bought the few things
she needed before coming here. Neither, apparently,
did the student reading under a tree near her have anything urgent to attend to, or the man lying staring at
the seagulls, white shirt and dark trousers formal
against the green. They shared the public grass, the
public breeze, carefully private in their idleness.

She glanced at the building opposite, and at her
watch. 2.25. Too early to go back to the apartment.
Quentin might find her there and quiz her about not
going to lunch. She'd claimed she had things to do,
but really it was just that she couldn't face the thought

of sitting with those people again. Not after last night. Not after this morning.

A boy and a girl, pacing by the stone sea wall that held back the harbour, moved into her line of vision. The boy carried a battered briefcase. His other arm was round the girl's shoulder, and their heads were together. They were talking, very seriously—or at least, she now saw, he was talking and she was listening intently, nodding as he gestured with a bony hand, his eyes crinkled against the harsh sunlight. She almost smiled. She remembered that. Some things didn't change.

The couple stopped, and glanced up, across the trees, towards the city. She followed their eyes, and realised with a start that they were looking, as she had done, at the Berry and Michaels building. You could see straight into the windows from the park. She looked back at the couple and realised who they were. Tilly Lightly's daughter, Sarah, and the boy who had had the drink thrown over him last night. Paul Morrisey. She shrank back against the hard bench, her heart fluttering, her hand feeling for the plastic shopping bag at her feet. But they were too absorbed in each other to notice a dumpy little woman on a park bench. Matching their strides, heads together, they began walking again, around the duck pond, over the little bridge that spanned a narrow stream, and out of sight.

Dorothy Hale sighed. A seagull fixed her with a cold yellow eye. She shrugged and showed it her empty hands. She looked at her watch. It was 2.30.

In the magnificent reception rooms on the ground floor of 'Carlisle', Kate listened to a tale of woe.

'We've got other things to do, you know, Kate. The whole art department's been down here the whole bloody day. It's bloody ridiculous! We're book designers, not interior decorators!' Kate looked at the art director and wondered whether to try to placate him, or to agree heartily. Her conscience got the better of her.

'Never mind, it'll all be over after tonight, Dave. And you wouldn't have wanted anyone else in charge of it, would you? It's looking really good, anyway. The big pictures look good, don't they? Especially the old ones.'

He nodded grudgingly. 'Not bad.'

'Where's Malcolm's banner?'

'Unfortunately it had an accident,' said David blandly.

'What do you *mean*? You're not serious, Dave? It cost hundreds of dollars! Malcolm will have a fit!'

'It fell in the sink, and ran,' said David turning away. 'Shame. Still, these things happen.'

Kate snorted with horrified laughter. 'David, how could you *do* such a thing?'

David shrugged. 'It was orange and purple,' he said, and wandered off.

'Kate! Could you give me a hand a minute?' Lulu teetered on a ladder by the door to the big kitchens at the back of the building. Kate ran to steady her, and support from below the huge mounted print she was holding.

'Thanks.' Lulu turned back to her task.

'Nearly finished, aren't you?' said Kate hopefully, looking around.

'Nope,' said Lulu cheerfully. 'Hours yet, I reckon. Is that straight?'

'It'll do. Yes. It seems OK.'

Lulu carefully released the print and backed down the ladder. She brushed her hands on her jeans and stood back. Saul Murdoch's huge, haunted image stared out at the elegant room. Kate exclaimed, and Lulu looked at her curiously.

'Oh, I was just wondering . . . why you've put that there, Lulu?' Kate said quickly. 'Why not in the front room?'

'Dave wanted it out of the way a bit,' said Lulu tolerantly. 'See, it's not that good quality? It's a sub-stitute print. We had to get it done again in a rush this morning. The first one was really nice, too. It's a real shame. That Sid shouldn't be let near our stuff, Dave says.'

'Sid says he didn't damage anything. He told me,' said Kate slowly. She was grappling with the rather creepy coincidence. Saul's picture, and Saul himself, gone in one night.

'He would,' said Lulu scornfully. 'You just have a look, Kate. Put his big boot right into it. It was all right before he carried it down yesterday. You look. It's out the back. Next to the bin.'

Kate walked slowly through the old-fashioned kitchens, to the back door.

She stood thoughtfully by the big silver garbage bin and inspected Saul Murdoch's damaged image. The photograph, a blow-up of the studio portrait that Malcolm had displayed to them in the conference room six weeks before, was disfigured by a huge crease that ran right across the nose and mouth. How could Sid have done such damage, and not noticed? Yet he didn't usually lie about things like that.

She jumped as a hand touched her shoulder.

'Take it easy,' grinned Birdie, and then the grin faded. 'Hold on, what's this?' She peered at the damaged print.

'It got wrecked,' said Kate, grimacing. 'Isn't it a ghastly coincidence?'

'How? What happened to it? Looks as if it's been kicked in, or something.'

'Does a bit, but I don't see how Sid could have done that without knowing it, do you?'

'Sid's hardly Mr Sharp, but no, I don't.'

Kate shrugged. 'Well,' she said, 'it happened.'

Birdie frowned and turned to survey the gleaming kitchen, freshly scrubbed in honour of the evening's festivities. Boxes of food stood beside the preparation benches, crates and cartons of drink were stacked close to the bar on the other side.

Lulu stuck her head in at the door. 'See?' she bawled. 'Told ya!'

Birdie turned to look at her. 'Where was this print, before?' she asked.

Lulu stared at her. 'Leaning up against the grog there, out of the way of the cleaners,' she said. 'They were all there . . . well, there were only four of five down by then, you know? The rest came down this morning. We didn't let Sid bring them. Dave says—'

'Was this one at the front?' Birdie asked and her glasses flashed.

'Yeah.' Lulu looked disgusted. 'He never even tried to hide it. Thick as a brick.'

Birdie sauntered over to the mountain of cartons and regarded it, hands behind her back. Kate followed her, raising her eyes and shrugging at the curious Lulu. 'What's up?' she demanded, but Birdie ignored her, and began pushing at the boxes with her foot. There was a double row of cartons at the front, then a triple row, with a double layer at the back against the wall.

Birdie bent over the middle tier, trying to reach something at the back. She lost her balance and tripped, nearly dropping forward on her knees.

'Birdie, you'll break the grog, look out!' cried Kate. But Birdie stood up looking pleased with herself.

'Voilà!' she said, and walked round to the edge of the wall of cartons. She squatted down, stood up with a bottle of whisky and grinned. 'Thought so,' she went on. 'The Scotch is at the back.' She moved out of the way and Kate took her place by the wall. A carton towards the middle of the back row had been torn open. She peered inside. It was half empty. She looked up at Birdie, wordless.

Birdie nodded. 'At least three gone, wouldn't you say? Plus the one I've got. Someone's been having a go at this lot. Three guesses who.'

Kate shook her head. 'You're saying that the big pictures were leaning against the pile of cartons, and someone fell forward on them trying to get to the back and nick some grog without anyone noticing. You're saying it was Jack, I presume. But that's impossible,

Birdie. He was paralytic last night. He would've gone straight to sleep.'

'Not necessarily,' said Birdie reasonably. 'He said he did, but Toby seems to think he's keeping something back. And these old boozers can recover surprisingly fast, you know. Especially when they've got a raging thirst and know where there's some grog to be had. *Did* he know?'

'He probably did. Malcolm gave them all the grand tour when they arrived, and the stuff was delivered before that.' Kate sighed. 'You must be right. I've been wondering how he's managed to stay so drunk. I thought he must have brought a huge supply with him. The old devil. He's so little and tubby, too. He would've fallen just like you did, and probably kicked Saul's picture then as well, just to add insult to injury.'

She looked at Birdie suspiciously. 'You haven't changed your mind, have you? About . . .' She glanced behind her, but Lulu had got bored with their detecting and returned to work. 'About Saul. That it was suicide, because it would be crazy to think—'

'I'm saying nothing about Murdoch's death at all, Laney,' said Birdie briskly. 'I'm saying something about bent portraits and missing whisky. OK?'

They walked out of the kitchen together, dodged Lulu and Dave, several hundred metres of streamers and a swarm of incoming caterers, and began to climb the stairs.

'Where have you been, anyway?' asked Kate curiously.

'With Dan Toby,' said Birdie, watching her feet. 'We had lunch together up the road. They did talk to Paul Morrisey, like you said. Apparently he was quite calm about the whole thing. Said everyone knew that Murdoch was a case and could have done himself in at any time. But he got a bit snakey when he worked out that Quentin had kept quiet about Murdoch's little fracas with Jack and Tilly. And when Quentin came in and tried to make him promise he wouldn't say anything he laughed in his face. Dan said Hale was so red he thought he'd explode, by the end of it. Said he was looking at Paul as though he was a creature from another planet. Couldn't understand his attitude at all.'

'I'm sure the feeling wasn't mutual,' said Kate drily. They reached the top of the stairs and walked past the deserted mail desk. Sid was nowhere to be seen. Off somewhere nursing his grievances, presumably.

'Anyway,' Birdie went on, 'Dan reckons Paul eventually calmed down and sort of said he'd keep quiet. As did Barbara, Tilly and Jack.'

'I wouldn't bet on that, myself,' said Kate. 'With Jack especially.'

'You'd be right,' said Birdie, and told her about the scene in the lift. Kate sniggered, and then looked rather ashamed of herself.

'I shouldn't laugh,' she said. 'It's all so terrible. And I never thought I'd say this, but I'm starting to feel really sorry for Quentin.'

'Are you joking, Kate? After everything you've said?'

'Oh well, I know. But poor Quentin, he had this whole thing worked out, and he was getting so excited about it all, and now absolutely everything that could possibly go wrong, has. Even his little floozie seems to have got cross with him over something or other. His whole, cosy little world's breaking up. And he's dealing with it in this very brave way, keeping a stiff upper lip, and chin up and all that, and—'

'Kate, sometimes you're extremely irritating, d'you know that?' snapped Birdie. 'You're talking about the man as if he's a little boy. It's patronising and stupid. The man's your enemy, isn't he? Don't get sucked into sympathising with him or he'll have you on toast. He hasn't got where he is by being a fool. He's probably got there by being extremely manipulative and ruthless. I'm warning you.'

'Oh, thank you,' said Kate as coolly as she could while she felt her cheeks burn. 'I haven't got where I am by being a fool, either, Birdie. People have different ways of coping, you know.'

Birdie regarded her tolerantly. 'Did I tell you how Paul Morrisey spent last night?'

'No,' Kate said, still cross.

'Apparently he fell asleep waiting for a bus, and then woke up and spent the rest of the night just wandering around the city. That's what he says, anyway.'

'Why would he lie?' shrugged Kate.

'Why indeed?' Birdie walked over to the window. She stared out for a few minutes in silence.

Kate picked at her loaded in-tray disconsolately. Sarah Lightly's manuscript had joined the growing pile on her shelf. She supposed she had better deal with it first.

'Oi.' Birdie leaned forward and pressed her nose against the glass. 'Hey, Kate, come and look.'

'What at, for goodness' sake!' snapped Kate.

'Out there. Over in the park. They're all over there. Promenading in unlikely groups! Oh, come and look, Kate. I wish I had some binoculars!'

'I wish you had some work to do!' grumbled Kate. But she did get up to look. Somehow it was horribly fascinating to see the gradual unfolding of this appalling exercise in folly. She supposed Malcolm and Quentin had decided a walk in the park would cool and soothe—and presumably keep old Jack off the bottle.

She leant on the deep window sill and looked out. Yes, there they were, like characters in a french farce seen through the wrong end of a telescope.

Across the road, behind black iron railings, the park slipped down to the Harbour and spread in green bands to the left and right of 'Carlisle'. Great groves of palms and shrubbery provided secret places, paths curved through banks of flowers, over the twisting stream, and out of sight. But clearly visible on the broad swathe of grass directly opposite, shielded only by some low bushes and the rose garden, Tilly Lightly, Barbara Bendix, Jack Sprott and Malcolm Pool walked gravely and in full view.

Behind them, the solid figure of Evie trudged,

shoulder bag swinging, deep in conversation with Amy. Presumably Quentin had decided to give each of his problem authors a personal watchdog. Perhaps he hoped that this would stop them talking too much about Saul's death, and the police. What could the conversation at lunch have been like? It was almost impossible to imagine how Quentin had carried it off.

You couldn't see the expressions on their faces from here, of course, but at least they were still on the premises. Or in its environs, at any rate, Kate thought. As she and Birdie watched, the group drew together, hesitated, and then split up, into pairs. From where Kate stood it looked as though they'd decided on some bizarre game of hide and seek.

Birdie spoke: 'Evie and the others are keeping them separated,' she said gleefully. 'That must've been Quentin's idea.'

She was right, Kate thought. Evie was leading Jack off in one direction, Barbara and Malcolm were sauntering in another. Amy and Tilly, strangely enough the most unlikely pair of all, stood awkwardly hesitating for a moment, before strolling towards the sea wall. No doubt Tilly had said she wanted to feel the clean wind in her hair, thought Kate maliciously.

'I wish I could hear what they're saying,' fretted Birdie.

'I'm glad I can't,' said Kate crossly. 'It's a horrible situation, and they're horrible people. Well, except for Evie, of course. Oh, and poor old Jack, I suppose, though he's being pretty awful at the moment.'

'I think they're fascinating,' said Birdie. 'And the situation's fascinating. And besides,' she turned to Kate with a challenging look in her eye, 'didn't Quentin say I was to have the run of the place, so I could get a really good programme going? Why else am I here?'

'Birdie! Don't be ridiculous! You couldn't use any of this!' Kate looked at the shabby, untidy figure beside her. Birdie shrugged. 'We'll see,' she said airily. 'After all, I do have a duty to my employers, Kate.'

'Since when!' jeered Kate. 'You just thrive on mess and scenes and tension, that's all. It's revolting. You're like one of those extra-terrestrial vampires who live on human beings' life forces, instead of blood.'

'What on earth are you talking about, Kate?'

'You know, the ones who just stare at people and they collapse from within and go all wrinkled like prunes. Haven't you ever seen one of those movies?'

'No I have not,' said Birdie, grimacing. 'Your taste in films is incomprehensible to me, and I can do without the lurid description, too. And the actions, if you don't mind.'

'If you saw more of life, Birdie, you'd know more about human nature than you do,' Kate responded. She stood on her toes to catch a last glimpse of Jack and Evie before they disappeared behind some bushes.

Birdie stared at her coldly. 'That's a ludicrous remark, Kate. I've seen more of real life than you'll—'

'Oh, yeah, I know you've seen things. The sort of things that get in the news, and money and big business, I suppose, because of your father and everything.'

'Well! What d'you want!' Birdie was too miffed even to object to the reference to her high-profile father, who was usually out of bounds as far as conversation was concerned, even in private.

Kate shook her head. 'But I don't mean that sort of thing. I mean the things that most people just know because they've lived ordinary lives.'

'Oh, I see.' Birdie was scathing. 'Like pop songs and horror movies and soap opera stars and—'

'Yes, if you like,' snapped Kate. 'And cooking and gardening and . . . and the latest kids' slang, and how to clean tortoiseshell . . .'

'Kate, have you flipped your wig?' Birdie stared at her friend in frank amazement.

'No, I'm simply saying that most people know those things, and you don't. And I'm sure it puts you at a disadvantage.'

Birdie snorted. 'Oh, yes, I've found it an enormous

disadvantage, in my calling, not to know how to clean tortoiseshell.' She turned back to the window and peered out at the park again.

'You haven't even read one book by those people you're so keen to spy on, have you?' Kate persisted, the bit between her teeth.

'I've read several of Saul Murdoch's books,' said Birdie loftily. 'Look at that. Tilly and the Phibes woman are having a real old natter, there. Hard to imagine what they'd have to say to one another, isn't it?'

'You read those books at school!' pursued Kate. 'And that was only because you had to, or you'd have failed. I remember!'

'Novels are a waste of time,' muttered Birdie, eyes narrowing as she watched the park. Then she appeared to lose interest. 'The Murdochs were boring, anyway. You thought so too, I remember *that*.' She looked at Kate for a moment, and the strange amber eyes behind their thick spectacles were thoughtful. 'But you're right, of course, Kate, I should keep in touch more. Give me some books now.'

'What for?' exclaimed Kate, looking at her askance.

'To read!' said Birdie patiently. 'Give me a Bendix scandal, and Tilly Lightly's masterpiece—Jumpy, or whatever it's called. And one of old Jack's things, too.'

'You're going to read them now?'

'Why not? It's a lovely day—a touch on the hot side, maybe, but it looks nice over there. I'll find myself a shady spot, and really get into some popular culture. Come on! Don't waste time!'

Shaking her head, Kate went to the shelf and picked out a dog-eared paperback copy of the *Gardener's Almanac*, with Jack Sprott leering from its cover in front of a blazing display of spring annuals, a large format *Paddy Kangaroo*, its hero sitting up, grinning toothily on a bright yellow background, and a thick black and silver tome that was Barbara's demolition of the late, great, Frederick Manners. She tipped them into Birdie's arms.

'Birdie, you're impossible!' she sighed wearily.

Birdie grinned. 'You're very unreasonable, Kate,' she said. 'I'm only following your advice.' She walked to the door, the books tucked under her arm. At the door she paused. 'How *do* you clean tortoiseshell, by the way?'

'Sesame oil works quite well,' said Kate primly.

Birdie nodded thoughtfully. 'Oh, right!' she said. 'Well, that is a good thing to know. Now I'm prepared should any emergency arise.' She gave a royal wave, and disappeared.

Kate looked after her sourly and returned to her desk. She did not look out of the window again.

17

Hide and Seek

Amy walked beside Tilly, smiling automatically, controlling efficiently as usual, the mixture of impatience and boredom that her job so often entailed. The efficient Amy Phibes. She almost smiled. Efficient in everything, except the things that mattered most. And for how long, she wondered, would her control hold? She saw it these days as almost a thing outside herself, operating without her direction. And if she didn't consciously exert the control, then she had no way of knowing how reliable it was, or when it might simply crack, as it nearly had this morning.

'Naturally,' said Tilly, for the third and fourth time, 'this isn't anything to do with you personally, Amy. I'm not blaming you.' She hesitated and went on, probing for a reaction. 'And, I mean, I can see you have a special loyalty to Quentin Hale . . .'

Amy felt with relief her eyebrows lift in cool enquiry, her mouth stay steady.

Tilly gave up and, sighing, looked around, at the blue of the Harbour, the green of the park. 'It's such a beautiful day. It seems so sad . . .' her mouth wobbled suddenly. 'It was a shock, that's all, hearing about it like that. And really so awful to think none of us was told.'

'It was done with the best of intentions, Mrs Lightly, that's all I can say,' soothed Amy. She wondered how many times she would have to say those words before the flow of complaints would cease.

Tilly looked over the water and sighed. 'Really, I think I almost knew last night that Saul had reached the end of the road,' she said softly. 'I lay awake, thinking about him and the old days, for hours last night. I just lay there, and I lay there, more or less till dawn, I think.' She smiled wanly.

'Oh, look, isn't that your daughter over there?' exclaimed Amy, delighted to sense a diversion. 'Over there with . . .'

Tilly squinted shortsightedly at the group under a tree to the left of the path ahead. She wrinkled her nose in annoyance, nostalgia and mournful musing forgotten. She quickened her steps. 'She's with that boy from last night!' she whispered to Amy. 'She takes up with the weirdest people sometimes. And the woman, who's that?'

'The researcher from the ABC,' said Amy. 'Verity Birdwood.'

'Oh yes, I met her earlier,' said Tilly, still in that conspiratorial undertone.

They joined the group under the tree. Birdie seemed pleased to see them, and if the same couldn't be said for Sarah and Paul, Tilly appeared not to notice. Amy was amused to note that despite her references to weird people and the suggestion of undesirable influence, Tilly responded even to Paul's rather understated maleness with a redoubling of the fey, frail manner she had perfected. Her voice softened, she looked up into his face with that characteristic tilted chin, and huge, limpid eyes. Beside her Sarah seemed even larger and clumsier than usual. The long, dark hair hung coarse and dull beside Tilly's shining mouse, her tall, robust figure looked masculine and gawky, straining at the seams of her frilled print blouse and skirt. As if she sensed this she began to hunch her shoulders, and almost to glower.

'I was telling Amy,' Tilly was saying, 'how upset I

was we weren't told earlier about Saul . . . not, of course, that I blame her personally.'

Paul shrugged. 'I don't care much either way, really,' he said coolly.

'Oh,' Tilly recovered quickly. 'Well, you didn't really *know* him, I suppose. Poor Saul. He was so—I don't know, so full of life when I first knew him. All he wanted was to write. I understood that so well. And he left a book as his farewell. Oh, poor Saul.' Her voice trailed off wistfully and she cast her eyes down.

Birdie saw Paul and Sarah's eyes meet over the bowed head and knew that for once Tilly was wasting her time, playing to the wrong audience.

After a moment or two Tilly raised her head. No-one had responded to her cue. She looked at Sarah reproachfully, but the girl met her gaze with no trace of guilt or concern. Tilly's brow puckered slightly. Then she tried again.

'You know, I was telling Amy that I think, somewhere in my unconscious mind, I must have known what was happening to Saul. I didn't close my eyes last night. Not until almost dawn. I just lay there, and lay there—you know how I can be, Sarah. I just lay there, and I've been thinking—I suppose it'll always haunt me—that if only I'd just got up and gone over and talked to him, maybe he wouldn't have felt so alone, and maybe . . .' Her voice trailed off again, and she turned to look unseeingly at the Harbour.

Again Paul and Sarah's eyes met, and this time Paul's lips twisted wryly and his eyebrows rose. Sarah's cheeks flushed and she moved uneasily. She looked . . . embarrassed. That was the only word to describe it. Birdie regarded them curiously. Tilly was turning it on, all right, but still their reactions were rather extreme.

Amy Phibes made a sudden movement. She had been so still that for a moment Birdie had forgotten she existed. She looked white and strained, and had clearly had enough of Tilly. 'Mrs Lightly, Tilly, I think, since we've found Sarah I might leave you for the moment. Take the opportunity to pop back to the office and see if I can help at all. There's so much . . .'

'Oh, yes, of course, Amy. You don't need to look after me, though it's been so nice of you. I'm really fine.' Now Tilly was being gallant.

Amy looked at her watch. 'You'll still meet the others for tea at the kiosk, won't you? At 4.00? I'll be back by then, to, ah, to see to everything.'

Tilly smiled graciously. 'Oh, we'll be there,' she said.

Amy nodded to the others and turned away with obvious relief. They watched her cut across the grass, hurrying unsteadily up the slope in her elegant high-heeled shoes.

Paul tossed back his lank hair. 'Hurrying back to Quentin baby,' he sneered.

Sarah laughed loyally and rather loudly. Tilly looked at her, and again her smooth forehead puckered, as though she had lost something, but didn't quite know what it was.

'Are all the others here too?' asked Birdie, looking guilessly at Tilly.

Tilly shrugged her thin shoulders. 'Oh, yes,' she said carelessly. 'They're all off somewhere. Evie's being so nice to that Jack Sprott, you've got no idea, and he's so drunk! It's awful. He should be sleeping it off in his room, not walking round in public.'

Birdie tutted. Tilly ignored her and turned to Paul and Sarah, standing shoulder to shoulder now, towering over both her and Birdie and apparently perfectly at ease with one another.

'Let's run back to the water!' she urged girlishly. 'Come on! I'll race you!' She slipped off her shoes and picked them up, slinging them over her shoulder and smiling roguishly up at Paul. Her little bare toes wriggled in the grass.

He cleared his throat uncomfortably. 'Ah, look, no, I've got to be going, really,' he said. 'Got to get back home, and get changed for tonight. Coming, Sarah?' He began to drift away.

Sarah picked up her bag, ducked her head at Birdie and her mother and began to follow.

Tilly took two steps after them, grimaced, hesitated. 'Oh, Paul!' she called.

He stopped and turned around.

'Your new book—Evie was telling me about it. I've just forgotten what it's called now.'

'*Unexpected People,*' said Sarah possessively, chin up.

'Oh, yes . . . ah,' Tilly moved forward another step, 'I'd really love you to sign me a copy. Would you mind?'

He flushed and looked awkward. 'No, no. Yeah, of course, anytime,' he mumbled. 'I've got a few copies at home. I'll bring you one.'

'I'll pay for it, of course,' persisted Tilly, standing on her toes.

He blushed even more deeply. 'Oh no, no. I've got plenty. I'll bring you one.'

'Oh, thanks, Paul. I'm dying to read it. I'll tell you what, fair exchange. I'll give *you* a signed copy of *Paddy Kangaroo!*'

'*Mama,*' exclaimed Sarah, 'he wouldn't want that!'

Paul mumbled.

'Oh, why not?' trilled Tilly. 'Why not? Well, I suppose it's not great art, Sarah, but Paul knows it's an art in itself, writing good children's books, don't you, Paul?'

'Sure,' said Paul offhandedly.

'Good,' smiled Tilly. 'Tonight we'll make an exchange. I'll ask Kate or Evie for a copy. They've always got *Paddy* in stock. Which is more than you can say for my other books.' She sighed and addressed him solemnly, writer to writer. 'It's just laziness. Easier, you see, to sell the household name. You'll have to watch that, Paul. You've got to keep on at them all the time. Publishers! Just because everyone's read *Paddy*, and knows its name, that doesn't mean it's the best thing I've done, does it?'

'Everyone hasn't read *Paddy*, actually, Mama,' Sarah broke in, childishly scoring points. 'Verity hadn't read it, had you?' She appealed to Birdie. 'She was reading it when we met her down here. And Quentin Hale hasn't. And Jack Sprott hadn't. Malcolm gave him a copy this morning, so he could. And I'll bet Amy Phibes hasn't. I'll bet half of Berry and Michaels hasn't!' She stopped, breathless and aware she was sounding spiteful and immature.

Tilly looked stunned and almost frightened, but Paul tossed his hair from his forehead impatiently and pulled at Sarah's arm.

'Come on, Sarah,' he said. 'What does it matter? We've got to get going.' He nodded abruptly at Tilly and Birdie and moved quickly away. Sarah trailed after him rather forlornly.

Birdie came up beside Tilly and cleared her throat tentatively. Tilly jumped and turned to look at her. She frowned slightly. Why was this boring little person still here? She was being quite irritating. Tilly was always irritated by people who were the same height and build as she was. They spoilt the effect of her petite fragility, making it seem more commonplace. And anyway, she would rather no-one had heard that particular conversation.

But Birdie looked at her calmly through her thick spectacles, her pointed, freckled face quite devoid of criticism or curiosity. 'I've been reading *Paddy the Kangaroo*,' she said. 'I'm enjoying it. Very amusing.'

'Oh, good,' said Tilly flatly. She limped to a nearby seat, threw her shoes on the ground, and sat down. She began picking unhappily at the soles of her feet, pulling out the round, brown prickles that stuck there.

Birdie watched her, amber eyes twinkling. 'Bindi-eyes?' she asked sympathetically.

'Yes,' snapped Tilly.

Birdie nodded. 'Better to keep your shoes on, really,' she said.

Tilly didn't answer, and after a minute, Birdie wandered away.

●　　●　　●

Deep in a grove of palms nearby, Jack Sprott, with the help of the illustrated *Gardener's Almanac*, was lecturing Evie on growing palms in containers. 'See, if they'd just hold off with the water, Evie, they wouldn't get into trouble. It's all in here, in black and white. But oh no, they're always fussing around with their 'nice drinks', like the plant's a cat or something and before they know, it's turned up its toes and they're complaining!' He tapped the book and shook his head heavily. A lock of grey hair fell over his forehead, clinging to the beads of sweat there.

Evie nodded. It was hot and still in the palm grove. Her mind wandered, and for a momen⁺ she almost forgot where she was, and why.

Jack sniffed, shut the book, and reached for a crumpled, checked handkerchief. He wiped his nose, and his forehead, and stuffed the handkerchief back into his pocket, his watery blue eyes staring vacantly ahead.

'Hot work out here, isn't it?' he complained. 'Look, Evie, I think I'll get back to the flat now, if you don't mind. I feel like a bit of a lie down.' He licked his lips with a sticky tongue.

Evie looked at him sharply, marshalling her thoughts in an instant. 'We're meeting the others at 4.00, Jack, for tea.'

'I don't want tea, and I don't want to meet them,' grumbled Jack. 'Those women get on my goat, 'specially Rabbit Lightly's missus. If I never saw her again it'd be too soon. Had enough of her at lunch, flapping her mouth. Had enough of her last night, if it comes to that.' He lowered his voice. 'I read some of her so-called famous book, the kangaroo one, before lunch. By God, I never saw anyone give themselves airs they didn't deserve like that one! Stuck-up, dishonest little tart she is. You heard me tell her off, Evie. Women like her don't know they're alive. They should be more than told off!' His small, stubby hands closed into white-knuckled fists.

'Well, it takes all sorts, Jack,' said Evie soothingly. She looked at him curiously. She had known Jack

Sprott for years, and wouldn't have said there was a vindictive bone in his body. But there was real dislike in his face now. Real resentment, as though Tilly's affair with Saul, all those years ago, was a blow to him personally.

'You ever been married, Jack?' she asked on impulse.

His face darkened. 'Not so's you'd notice,' he said, and the corners of his mouth turned down. He turned his head away from her.

There's a story there, she thought briefly, but couldn't stop to ponder it. There was too much else to think about.

'I haven't either,' she said lightly. She tried again to distract him, as they walked further into the palm grove. 'You seemed to get on OK with Barbara Bendix last night, though, Jack. She's quite a character, isn't she?'

He blinked at her sullenly. 'I suppose you could call her that,' he said. 'We'd have had another name for her in the army.' His eyes narrowed, and he shot a meaningful glance in her direction.

Evie looked blank. Jack sniffed and walked on in silence. Suddenly he seemed to make up his mind about something. He stopped dead and clutched at Evie's arm. She could smell the alcohol on his breath. Whisky from this morning, wine from lunch. Just the fumes made her head reel. How on earth could he still walk and talk with that much alcohol in him? And she was sure he had a flask in his jacket pocket. He was probably dying to get into it. He leaned closer, and she had to force herself not to pull away.

'Women like her make me sick to my stomach!' he breathed. Again his mouth thinned, tightened and turned down at the corners, so that his red, gleaming cheeks knotted into hard lumps.

Evie moved her hands helplessly. She felt quite sick herself. She cleared her throat.

'I don't quite understand, Jack,' she said, as casually as she could.

He hunched his shoulders impatiently. 'Ah, what does it matter?' he said, and wiped his mouth with his hand. 'I need to get back to the flat. I don't want to hang round here.' He looked at her, inspired. 'And I need a gents,' he said firmly.

'We're due to meet the others soon, Jack,' said Evie slowly. 'Come down this way. I'm sure there's a loo along here.'

She led him, complaining, down the palm-lined path. They turned a bend, and there, tucked away out of sight, was a little public lavatory, its doorways modestly facing away from the path. Dark shrubs half obscured it from view, and the stream running nearby gurgled and rippled just enough to remind people what had made them come this way.

Jack fidgeted, and looked vaguely embarrassed.

'I'll wait for you here, Jack,' said Evie briskly.

He grumbled something under his breath and began to trot towards the demure brick building, his feet kicking up the leaves and mulch that obscured its narrow pathway.

She turned her back, put down her heavy shoulder bag, and stood in the shaded silence. Dimly she heard the sound of the traffic from the city, the cry of a seabird from the Harbour. She glanced at her watch. It was 3.30.

Amy Phibes and Tilly Lightly sat drinking tea on the verandah of the park's refreshment kiosk. Yet again, Tilly asked the time. It was, thought Amy, one of her more annoying affectations never to wear a watch. She glanced at her own and stifled a sigh.

'It's 4.15,' she said. 'I don't know where the others have got to. Would you like another pot of tea, or—are you sure you don't want anything to eat?'

'Oh, no, thank you, Amy. I couldn't manage it.' Tilly shook back her hair. 'I had some water while I was waiting for you.'

'I'm sorry I was late,' said Amy, paying her dues.

Tilly half smiled. 'Only five minutes,' she said. 'You shouldn't have rushed and got all hot and bothered. No-one else did.' She looked at the table top and scratched at it with a fingernail. Her hands were very small and thin and white, and very clean, the nails clipped short, pink and unvarnished, like a child's hands.

Amy felt huge beside her. She curled her own long fingers around her teacup. She felt Tilly was looking at her hands, comparing them unfavourably with her own, noting that the bright red nail polish was chipped, and one nail broken. She hadn't had time to see to that before rushing to keep the 4 o'clock date. And now the others hadn't even bothered to turn up on time. Not even Malcolm. Tilly put her chin on her hand and stared moodily out at the shimmering afternoon. It was still very hot, though shadows were beginning to steal over the paths and grassy places. The little breeze from the water had dropped, and the humid air hung still and sticky around them.

There was an unrestful silence. At last Tilly sighed, stirred and spoke.

'I may as well pop into the ladies while we're waiting. I didn't stop on the way in, not wanting to be late. I needn't have bothered, obviously.' She stood up and looked around restlessly. 'Do you know where it is?'

Amy pointed. 'Over there, behind that screen.' She watched as Tilly picked her way through the tables, keeping clear of the people sitting around them.

A few minutes' peace. She needed it. She would be so glad when all this was over. So glad. She dropped her eyes to her clenched white hands, and willed them to loosen and relax. She thought of her fragrant, uncluttered corner on the second floor of 'Carlisle'. She'd felt safe and secure there, as well as efficient and organised. Now, she wondered whether she would ever be able to recapture that calm. She looked at her watch. 4.20. Where on earth was everyone?

'Oh, well, finally!' said Tilly in a low voice, sliding back into her chair, and indicating with her eyes a very hot and bothered-looking Evie, threading her way through the tables towards them.

'Where is everyone?' she demanded, reaching them. 'My God, it's so *hot*! I'm melting!'

'Well, *we* don't know,' snapped Tilly, showing a flare of bad temper. 'No-one's turned up, except us.' She craned her neck to look behind Evie. 'Where's Jack Sprott?' she asked.

'I wouldn't have the faintest idea where he is,' growled Evie, flinging herself into a chair. 'The old devil's given me the slip. I've been looking for him for three quarters of an hour. He went into the public loo out there,' she gestured vaguely out into the park, 'and I waited, and he never came back. I went in and looked for him in the end. I thought he might have collapsed or something. But he wasn't in there at all. He must've come out and nicked off, or never gone in at all, which wouldn't surprise me. I've been all round the park in the blazing heat, back to work, everywhere. He's hiding out in some pub, I'll bet you, drinking himself silly.'

Amy looked shocked. 'But tonight . . .'

'I know, I know,' Evie said, through gritted teeth.

'Have a cup of tea,' suggested Tilly with annoying solicitude. 'Don't look so worried, Evie. Malcolm won't bite you.'

Evie lifted her chin, blushing angrily. 'Malcolm! I don't give a continental what Malcolm thinks, I can tell you!' she sneered, and then realised where she was, and with whom. 'Oh, sorry, I didn't mean to bark at you, Tilly.'

Tilly lowered her eyelids and said nothing.

Evie looked round desperately for a waitress, and caught sight of Malcolm, edging sheepishly towards them. He looked rumpled and somewhat disconcerted, but he put his shoulders back as he approached, and essayed a cheery smile.

'Sorry I'm late. Where's Jack?' he enquired, eyes darting round selfconsciously.

'Where's Barbara?' countered Evie.

They looked at one another for a moment.

Tilly gave a low laugh. 'Has Barbara caught you napping too, Malcolm?'

His face flamed, and for a moment he was speechless. Then he cleared his throat. 'Barbara must have gone . . . gone back to her room, I think. We, ah, got separated.' He pounced at Evie. 'But look, you're not saying Jack's not here?'

'He gave me the slip, yes,' said Evie steadily. 'I've looked, but I can't find him anywhere. We'll have to go back to the office and hope he turns up there.'

Malcolm lowered his head till his forehead rested on the table top. 'What have I done to deserve this?' he wailed. It was a strangely theatrical gesture for the controlled, sharply groomed Malcolm Pool to make, and the three women regarded him curiously.

'It's par for the course,' said Evie gruffly. 'He'll turn up, and so will Barbara. They wouldn't miss the party.'

Malcolm raised a pink-stained face and ran grubby fingers over his close-clipped hair.

'The party,' he said, almost to himself. 'I'd almost forgotten about that.' He shook his head, and, to their surprise, laughed boyishly.

Evie fidgeted, and looked under her eyelids at his skewed tie and flushed, vulnerable face. People cracking under pressure always embarrassed her. She hadn't thought, she really hadn't, that Malcolm would lose his nerve quite as quickly as this.

18

Party Time

Dan Toby hoisted his feet onto his familiar, battered desk and unwrapped his first hamburger. It had been a long, hot day, what with one thing and another. He could have gone home, and the thought of the wilting plants and dry grass, yearning for the sprinkler, made him feel guilty, but still somehow he preferred a hamburger and chips in the brightly-lit clutter of the cop-shop on night shift to the sweet stillness of the suburbs tonight.

He chewed thoughtfully. There'd been nothing in the evening paper about Saul Murdoch, so presumably Quentin Hale had been successful in keeping the lid on the thing. Extraordinary, really. The man had nerve all right. You had to admire him for that. Even when his staff let him down as badly as they had this afternoon, letting Jack Sprott slip through their fingers, for God's sake, he hadn't faltered. Just went colder and quieter, and calmly asked if the police would help track Jack down. Which of course they were only too happy to do, under the circumstances.

The chips weren't salty enough, so he began eating them in bunches, to maximise the taste. Strange co-incidence, meeting up with Verity Birdwood like that. She had the knack of turning up in unexpected places, and oh dear, how she got up Milson's nose! Chuckling to himself he crumpled the empty chip bag and looked

up, straight into the dark, narrow face of Milson himself. He jumped violently, nearly upsetting the chair.

'God, Milson, don't sneak up on me like that!' he
complained to cover his confusion. 'I thought you'd
gone home.'

'I'm sorry,' said Milson patiently. 'I didn't want to
interrupt your dinner.' He looked pointedly at the
shameful remains of Toby's high calorie, salt-filled,
cholesterol-ridden binge. Milson was proud of his
straight, spare figure. He lived principally on raw veg-
etables, wholegrains and water. 'Like one of his bloody
parrots,' Toby was wont to say scornfully, at the same
time making occasional shamefaced but mighty efforts
to emulate his example.

'I've been catching up on some paperwork,' Milson
remarked. 'And I called Berry and Michaels, by the
way, sir. Jack Sprott still hasn't arrived, and the party
starts in . . .' he consulted his watch, '. . . seven minutes. I was wondering if it was a good idea to go over
there. Mingle with the crowd. Unobtrusively, of
course.' He waited.

'You'd be about as unobtrusive as a giraffe in that
lot, Milson,' said Toby rudely. 'And frankly I don't
see how we could justify it. Birdie's there. She'll keep
an eye out for us.'

Milson's lip curled in disdain. 'She wouldn't know
what to look for. I'd like to keep close to Morrisey,
Bendix and Lightly. And Sprott, of course, if he turns
up. One of them might slip up.'

Toby shook his head. 'Milson, what do you think
you're playing at? You're making a mountain out of a
molehill, mate. I admit when I met those weirdos this
morning even I started thinking murder was on the
cards. But I've calmed down since then, and thought
about it. Look, they found no evidence that anyone'd
been in Murdoch's room, did they? I've seen the reports. And being mad as snakes doesn't necessarily
qualify people for being murderers, does it?'

'What about the note?' said Milson stubbornly. 'The
Lightly woman . . .'

'Did you find out about her husband, by the way?'

'What? . . . oh yes,' Milson said with studied indifference. 'His car was wiped out by a truck in the bush somewhere. Truck driver got five years. Still, it was worth checking. She did write that note.'

'Milson, if you were going to murder someone, would you leave a threatening note on the floor of the bloke's bedroom for the cops to find?'

'She could have forgotten it. Or she could have been trying a double bluff.' Even Milson knew this was a bit thin.

Toby sighed. 'And Morrisey didn't look like a murderer to me. He looked like all-talk-no-do. The simmer in silence sort. And the building was locked up tighter than a drum when the others went home. He couldn't have got in to do it, even if he'd wanted to.'

Milson tried another tack. 'Bendix could've . . .'

'Bendix hasn't got the shadow of a motive.' Toby was enjoying himself. 'And Sprott? Well, he's a possibility, if he hadn't been so drunk he could hardly stand up. I can just imagine Sir Saul Murdoch entertaining him at midnight, can't you? They had so much in common.'

'Sir . . .'

'You forgot Sarah Lightly, Milson. The best pick of all, in many ways. But her mum was sharing a room with her, and she says she was awake most of the night, and that Sarah didn't stir.'

'Well, she would, wouldn't she, sir? Say that?'

Toby paused, and thoughtfully rubbed his salty lips with the back of his hand. 'Maybe she would. Maybe she would. We'll see. We'll have a word with her in the morning, Milson.' He heaved his feet from the desk, stuffed the evidence of his dinner into the overflowing waste-paper basket, and ostentatiously picked up a pen.

'I have some paperwork to catch up on now, Milson,' he said loftily. 'If you don't mind. And I wouldn't ring Berry and Michaels again if I were you. The party's probably starting round about now.'

•   •   •

'What a fiasco, Evie.' Kate, painted, perfumed and in her best dress, put her arm round her friend's shoulder.

Evie looked steadily ahead, without acknowledging the gesture. 'I told Quentin it wouldn't work. I tried to tell him. Now he knows I was right, doesn't he? He'll listen another time.'

'There mightn't be another time. If he's made a laughing stock over this, people will start talking about the takeover all over again. He was supposed to calm things down. He might get into real trouble. Even get the chop!'

'We can hope. And help. Tonight I'll give the press the word—oh, not about Saul. Just about things being badly managed and so on. As if tonight isn't a prime example! You do the authors, the agents and Birdie. That ought to help get the snowball rolling.'

'Evie, we can't do that!' exclaimed Kate. 'Evie, what's got into you?'

'This is war, you gutless wonder!' whispered Evie furiously. 'You can stand by and be a lady if you like, but don't expect me to!'

Kate looked around the elegant reception rooms. Cedar furniture glowed softly in the lamplight, summer flowers filled the fireplaces, the huge photographs of great Berry and Michaels authors, past and present, hung from the picture rails, trailing red and white ribbons. In the kitchen beyond the reception rooms the caterers chatted quietly and did fastidious things with slivers of lemon rind. The waiters put out glasses in readiness. It didn't look like a fiasco, but in a few minutes people would start arriving. The great party would begin. Without Jolly Jack Sprott. Without Sir Saul Murdoch. Only a disgruntled Tilly Lightly and a malicious Barbara Bendix would be present to hold up the banner of the Big Four.

'The Big Two—doesn't sound too good does it?' she murmured. But Evie didn't smile.

'Jack might still turn up,' Kate went on hopefully. But an inner voice answered her. Better he doesn't, now. Much better. He's drunk as a skunk for sure, and if he was peeved before, he'll have worked himself into a frenzy by now. Better for Quentin if he stays away, however embarrassing it all is. She put the thought into words.

'Better, really, when you think about it, that Jack stays away now, Evie, wouldn't you say? Given what he's been like. And better, really, I mean from that point of view, that Saul isn't here either. Given he was so angry and was going to tip the bucket on everything.'

Evie shrugged. 'In one way, I suppose. But in another . . . I don't know. Quentin'll have to work overtime to explain two non-appearances. It makes a nonsense of the whole Big Four thing. Malcolm, of course, has completely dropped his bundle. I knew he would.'

'Where is he now?'

'Who knows? Who cares?' Evie shrugged.

They watched as a film crew wandered into the room, carrying camera equipment and lengths of cable. The crew looked around vaguely, wiped their foreheads and muttered to one another disapprovingly. Kate and Evie walked over to them.

'Can we help you?' asked Evie.

'ABC,' said a tall boy with curling orange hair and a gold earring. 'Verity Birdwood anywhere round?'

'I don't think she's here yet,' said Kate, feeling vaguely guilty on Birdie's behalf. She glanced at her watch. 'Shouldn't be long.'

He said nothing, but drifted back to the group waiting by the door and shook his head. They all put their equipment down and relapsed into waiting positions, leaning and squatting where they stood.

Evie and Kate looked at one another. They had attended many such parties together before—launching parties, mainly. Launching parties pretending to be nothing else, launching parties disguised as press con-

ferences, literary lunches, gourmet breakfasts, tours of
the building, club meetings, concerts, wine tastings,
poetry readings—anything that Brian Berry and Evie
thought might drag the surfeited, maddening, unreli-
able press in and earn the book in question a few lines
in a paper, a few words on the radio, a minute or two's
TV time. The first appearance of one untidy journalist
with a notebook, let alone a TV crew, was the signal
for a certain sense of relief, a relaxed feeling, as though
everything was now going to be all right.

There had been one or two occasions, etched forever
in their memories and laughed over only when very
safely passed, when no journalist with a notebook had
come, and no TV crew. When, indeed, no-one had
come at all except the poor author, the celebrity who
had been invited to launch the book, and such mem-
bers of the staff who could be contacted from the
nearest phone.

But tonight, Kate would not have minded being ignored by the media. Tonight, when they had so much
to hide, it seemed that they were going to be inundated
with those who would delight in uncovering the anom-
alies, the rivalries, the mismanagement endemic to this
whole affair. For here came Tilly, laughing low and
meaningfully, her white Chinese shawl trailing behind
her, a flower (from the vase by the lift, Kate was sure)
held loosely in her little white hand. And by her side
was Malcolm and a girl with an intense expression and
a cassette recorder, and Barbara in a scarlet dress so
revealing, and jewellery so extraordinary, and perfume
so overpowering, that she looked like the personifica-
tion of Lust in The Seven Deadly Sins as devised by
Cecil B. de Mille.

The ABC camera crew shuffled backwards to let the
procession pass, and Kate saw them exchanging glances
and raising eyebrows ever so slightly, and looking
around for further stimulation. Looking for Jack
Sprott, presumably, for they would know by now that
Saul Murdoch had unfortunately been taken ill, and
could not join the party after all.

But no squat, gnome-like figure advanced through the doorway. Only Quentin, resplendent in dinner jacket, imposing and cold. He displayed not a quiver of nerves or indeed humanity, which nevertheless both accompanied him in the person of Dorothy, walking tentatively inside a stiff, dark green dress and looking pale and scared to death.

A waiter came around with drinks, music rose in the background, Quentin expressed casual approval of the decorations. Malcolm nodded vehemently and began to explain about the perfidy of the design department, and the fate of the banner. More people arrived: staff, authors, agents; Miles Harris, crumpled face flashing the well-known smile, looking so much smaller than he seemed on TV, and escorting a wife, or girlfriend, who looked exactly like all the Vickis, though her name was Fleur. And there was plenty of press. The flash cameras were at the ready, the best profiles were being assessed. There was already one TV camera trained on Quentin who was examining with exaggerated interest the giant photograph of Tip O'Flannagan, in pride of place above the fireplace, while Tilly Lightly and Barbara Bendix stood on either side of him like two grotesquely mismatched fire dogs.

'Who's that?' someone said. Kate turned to look, and stared.

At the door, startling and splendid, stood a tall, dark figure. Sarah Lightly was transformed, in a long black dress, her mass of hair bound in a plait round her head and a single plain gold bracelet pushed high on a strong white arm. Beside her was Paul Morrisey, his hand under her elbow, possessive and almost smug, as though he had been the only one sensitive enough to see this girl's potential, and was therefore her mentor and guide by right until he said otherwise.

'Sarah!' called Barbara Bendix irrepressibly from across the room. 'You look fabulous!' Sarah smiled at her. But her eyes swept over her mother glassily, and she followed where Paul led, keeping close beside him as he pressed into the crowd.

Evie had slipped away, and was chatting calmly to an old friend from one of the radio stations. Kate saw to her relief that Birdie had arrived and had presumably briefed the people from the ABC, because they had disappeared from their places by the door and were setting up shop down by the kitchen. The big room was filling fast. People were happy, excited and dressed up. The champagne was flowing, the noise was rising, and the air growing thick. Maybe, after all, it wasn't going to be a fiasco. Maybe Jack and Saul's non-appearances were just going to be taken in that easy-going Australian way as 'one of those things', a bit embarrassing for the incoming pom, Quentin Hale, but not the more disturbing for that. Well, it might happen that way.

And Quentin would come out of the show un-scathed, against all odds. He was certainly looking strong, confident and in perfect control. Tilly and Barbara were handfuls, in one way, but nothing like as bad as they were likely to have been with Saul and Jack around. Quentin must have a guardian angel, who turned disaster into strength for him.

'Kate, hello!' Priscilla Penn, the illustrator, beamed at her over a glass of champagne. 'What a lovely party!'

Kate turned to her with pleasure and rising spirits. Well, it *was* a party, and there were all these people to see and talk to. So many of them had become friends over the years. So many of them she hadn't seen for ages. Why not relax and enjoy, as she would have done had this been one of their old style get-togethers, with no Big Four (or Big Three, or Two) and no Malcolm Pool to loathe, Quentin Hale to fear, or Amy Phibes to resent. She began to chat to Priscilla, and the circle of familiar faces who soon joined them. She had an-other glass of champagne, and another, and soon she had entirely forgotten to look with a shiver at Saul Murdoch's brooding portrait by the kitchen door, or worry about Barbara or Tilly, or to shoot quick glances at the doorway, fearing to see the squat, swaying figure of Jack Sprott with his new bitter face, looming out of the shadows.

After an hour she found herself standing beside Dorothy Hale, who was kindly, if rather absently, listening to Sylvia de Groot's reminiscence of her skiing holiday in Switzerland. It was rather difficult to imagine Sylvia skiing. She was very small and dogged, and the antithesis of those snow bunnies who cavorted in TV commercials for shampoo and peppermint products—all legs, hair and teeth. But skiing it was, for Sylvia, and everyone, from Sid to Lulu, had seen the holiday snaps: fuzzy, white photographs of lots of people they didn't know, and a few of Sylvia herself, posed in goggles and beanie and shiny, padded jumpsuit, and looking strangely foreshortened, as though she was standing in a hole.

Fortunately, Sylvia didn't have the photographs on her at this moment. She was making do, though, in her inimitable way, by describing them in quite minute detail. Emboldened by champagne, Kate broke in on her monologue to greet Dorothy and express relief at the apparent success of the evening. But Dorothy, though she smiled obediently, not wanting to disappoint, or to appear to be rude, did not respond to this well-meant overture. She looked, if anything, frightened by it, and began looking around in an uncomfortable, hesitating way, as though checking the exits in a strange place that had a reputation as a firetrap. Kate heard her own voice flatten and hesitate, and Dorothy, turning, caught her eye and put her hand to her forehead. 'I'm afraid I have a bit of a headache,' she said apologetically, in her soft English voice. She wasn't good at lying, Kate thought.

19

Long Shadows

A hand on Kate's arm made her start slightly. Tilly Lightly stood beside her, head on one side, smiling enigmatically. 'Think how many parties this room has seen in its time,' she said. 'You can feel the spirits! I was just saying to Verity,' she drew an expressionless Birdie into the circle, 'that I often feel the other dimension now. It's not frightening—it's rather nice! Oh, hello!' she beamed at Sylvia de Groot, who beamed delightedly back. Tilly's social manner, never very restful, was definitely tuned tonight at too high a pitch. Kate hastily made introductions.

'So you're Sylvia!' Tilly exclaimed. 'We've been corresponding for such a long time, haven't we? And we've never met,' she explained to Dorothy Hale. 'Sylvia's always so kind, explaining the little worries I have about my royalty statements. I'm such a fool about things like that. I'll never be a businesswoman, I'm afraid.' She smiled and shook her head ruefully. 'That's why writers will never be rich, I suppose. The business details are just the last things on our minds, so the publishers can run rings around us.'

Sylvia woke from her happy, flattered social dream to make a startled protest.

Tilly laughed, and shook her hair back. 'Oh, Sylvia, not *you*. You just carry out your orders and do your job, I know that. It's my own silly fault for being so impractical, and thinking so little about the money side of things.' She wound her shawl, waif-like, around her shoulders and shrugged ruefully. Even Kate, who knew how ruthlessly Tilly negotiated her contracts, and how piercingly and perseveringly she pursued every possible anomaly in her royalty statement, to poor Sylvia's frequent chagrin and despair, was almost taken in.

Dorothy Hale looked at her doubtfully with faded blue eyes, but said nothing.

'You look tired, Dorothy,' cooed Tilly. 'This must have been a strain for you. And the heat must be worrying you, too.'

'Oh,' said Dorothy, rousing herself sufficiently to display a little spirit in the face of this attack, 'oh no, I've hardly done anything to help, I'm afraid. Quentin and Malcolm—oh, and Amy Phibes, of course . . . they've really borne the brunt.'

Tilly nodded sympathetically and put her hand on Dorothy's. She leaned forward.

'That can be a strain in itself, though, can't it?' she breathed. 'Having just to stand, and watch, and to be able to do nothing.'

Dorothy stared at her, and slowly withdrew her hand. Absently, she wiped it on her dress.

Tilly tried again. 'Quentin was telling me that you have a roof garden, Dorothy. That must be wonderful.'

Dorothy nodded.

'It is lovely,' Sylvia de Groot broke in eagerly. 'Sometimes we have office lunches up there, don't we, Kate? Or . . . at least, we used to, before . . . I mean, when Brian Berry was living there.' She flushed. 'It was different then, of course,' she bumbled on, one eye on Dorothy, 'because . . .' She plainly couldn't think of a 'because', and her voice trailed off miserably.

Dorothy rose to the occasion. 'We must start doing that again, then, mustn't we?' she said. 'Quentin and I only ever go up there on weekends. Otherwise, it's just empty, except for Sid, who does the watering. I think you should feel free to go up there, all of you, for lunch, if you want to. We don't lock the stairwell door, or anything.'

Kate looked at her gratefully. What a truly kind woman she was. But what would Quentin say about her offering his garden to the staff for sandwiches al fresco? She had a feeling he wouldn't be too impressed.

Tilly Lightly clasped her hands, 'Oh I'd *love* to go up now,' she said eagerly. 'It's so hot and stuffy in here. I tried to persuade Quentin to take me before, but he said he had to stay down here. Evie was *just* as boring. And Verity wouldn't come with me either, even though I gave her people a lovely interview,' she tossed her head archly at Birdie, 'and she really owed me a favour.'

Birdie looked uncomfortable. 'Oh, well, I . . .' she muttered. Kate looked at her in amazement. What had happened to Birdie the amused, the confident?

Tilly threw up her chin, and shook back her hair. 'You're all stick-in-the-muds,' she proclaimed, 'aren't they, Sylvia?' Sylvia de Groot tittered uncertainly.

Sometimes, thought Kate, Tilly was so irritating that she actually set your teeth on edge. She noticed with a relief she never would have believed possible that Malcolm, Barbara and Amy were edging towards them. Malcolm, flushed and purposeful, was in the lead and on reaching them he ducked his head perfunctorily at Dorothy Hale and then spoke directly to Tilly, ignoring everyone else.

'Tilly, could you come over here for a minute? The speeches are going to start soon, and Quentin thought we should all be together, just over by the door, there.'

'Oh, heavens!' Tilly cast her eyes to the ceiling. 'All this fuss! I'll be so embarrassed! And it's not as if I'm very important in all this. Barbara, you go.'

'Well, of course I'm going, Tilly,' said Barbara impatiently, 'we all are. It won't take long. Quentin wants us. Come on.'

Tilly looked at her tremulously, bit her lip, and pressed her handkerchief to the side of her mouth. 'Barbara, you're used to all this hullabaloo and you're good at it. And you love it, you've got to admit. It doesn't offend you, or worry you, all the flattery and so on. But I just feel myself shrinking inside.'

Sylvia de Groot made a comforting noise, and Tilly smiled at her gratefully, and laid a little hand on her arm. 'See? Sylvia understands.'

Barbara laughed unpleasantly, and Tilly's brow furrowed. 'No, honestly, Barbara,' she said. 'I hate all this sort of thing. Sarah and I both do.'

Barbara laughed again, and glanced at Sarah, standing very tall and upright in her black dress, talking to Paul and another intense-looking man on the other side of the room.

'Could have fooled me,' she drawled.

Amy bent forward, her fair hair swinging. 'Whoever is coming, we'd better get back, Malcolm. Quentin wants—'

He gestured impatiently.

Tilly watched, head on one side, and then bowed her head. 'Oh, all right,' she said resignedly. 'I don't want to let anyone down. As long as you promise I can be excused as soon as the speeches are over. I'm absolutely determined to see Quentin's roof garden in the moonlight, and no-one's going to talk me out of it!' She looked around and tossed her head waywardly.

'Why in God's name should anyone try to stop you?' Barbara hissed. 'You can drop dead as far as I'm concerned.' She turned on her heel and pushed her way through the crowd to where Quentin stood, adjusting his tie and looking expectant. Malcolm, after a nervous glance at the watching group, followed her. Amy stood waiting by Tilly's side. Tilly shivered, wrapped her shawl more tightly round her shoulders, and then impulsively leant towards Sylvia de Groot. 'Come with me, Sylvia,' she pleaded. 'Oh, go on. I really need moral support. I can't face that crowd alone.'

'Oh, heavens, I don't think I . . .' stammered Sylvia, immensely flattered but dreading Quentin's reaction should she intrude upon his circle of honour.

'Don't worry about it!' cried Tilly, suddenly gay and careless. 'Who has a better right than you anyway? You pay us all, don't you?' She laughed at her little joke and took Sylvia's arm, leading her in triumph to Quentin's side. Amy set her perfectly shaped lips. She looked not so much at Kate as through her.

'I find it difficult to like that woman,' said Dorothy slowly.

Kate looked at her in surprise. She had never before heard Dorothy say an even vaguely negative thing about anyone. Dorothy saw the look and grew slightly pink.

'Not that I know her, of course, so I shouldn't really say anything,' she said hastily. 'Obviously she's very clever and everything. Barbara Bendix, too. But, with all that's happened . . .' Her blue eyes still rested on Tilly, now chatting vivaciously to Quentin, while an awkward Sylvia hovered in the background. 'I mean, you'd think,' she said with more energy, 'that they'd be thinking less about themselves, not pushing themselves forward, and quarrelling and so on, as if nothing's wrong at all.'

'Yes,' said Kate thoughtfully. She became aware of a certain tension in the air, and looking up caught Dorothy and Amy eyeing one another. She realised that this was another first. Usually Amy and Dorothy kept well away from one another, and when they were in the same group, never looked at one another, or exchanged more than the briefest social pleasantries.

'I must go,' said Amy quickly. 'See you later.' She slipped away into the crowd.

Dorothy moistened her lips. 'I think I'll go upstairs and fix my hair,' she said to Kate and Birdie with careful nonchalance. She, too, moved away and they saw her edging towards the door.

Birdie surveyed the room curiously, and remained silent.

'You know,' said Kate at last, 'I really thought to-night was going to be a disaster. But it isn't, is it? No one seems to have even noticed that Jack isn't here, after all that.'

'Oh, of course they have!' said Birdie. 'Everyone's talking about it. What else would you expect? They're all killing themselves laughing!'

'No, they're not!' said Kate. 'No-one's said a word to me about it. Not a thing!'

'Of course they wouldn't talk to you about it, dopey. They're not talking to anyone from the company about it, except for your mate Evie who's actually raising the subject all over the room.'

'Evie is? She isn't really, is she?'

Birdie raised her eyebrows. 'Why on earth not? She's obviously got an axe to grind. Anyway, she's only stirring a pot that was already bubbling nicely all by itself. Everyone can hardly wait for Quentin's speech.'

'Well, I don't know,' said Kate glumly, 'I really don't!'

'Don't know what?' trilled Priscilla Penn, waltzing by. Kate grabbed her arm and she wheeled in a very small circle to face them, triumphantly holding aloft an intact glass of champagne.

'Priscilla, you've met Birdie,—Verity Birdwood—haven't you? Old friend of mine. Well, she's been saying that everyone's talking about Jack Sprott's not being here, and I was just wondering what you . . . because you didn't say anything to me about it, so I didn't think . . .'

Priscilla, her kind, middle-aged face dewy with champagne and flushed with the heat of the room, put a hand on Kate's arm without a trace of embarrassment. 'Oh, well, Katie,' she said, 'we couldn't really gossip about it to you, could we? I mean, it's your party. But of course everyone's terribly curious about where he is. Especially after all the publicity and fuss about them being your four best authors, or whatever it was, and now they aren't here, are they? Well, half of them are, but it's not the same, is it? And I must say that some people I've talked to are being a bit sarcastic about it all, because they didn't much like, you know, not being one of the chosen, I suppose. This stuff about all your authors being represented by the Big Four hasn't gone down very well. Paul Morrisey, who's getting around with Tilly Lightly's daughter— what a stunner *she* is, isn't she?—anyway, he seems very bitter.' She pondered, and drank a little champagne. 'Of course, he's very young,' she finally pronounced.

Kate could see Malcolm fussing around with a microphone, and Quentin looking grimly expectant. The long-awaited speech was obviously about to occur. She had opened her mouth to suggest they move to a good vantage point, which, from her point of view, meant one where she could hear but not be seen, when Priscilla went on.

'And I must say, without mentioning Sir Saul Murdoch, of course, who everyone knows is a genius and everything, that the other three aren't exactly the sorts of people most of us would want to represent them. I mean, would you, Katie?'

'Priscilla, I agree with you!' whispered Kate, throwing discretion to the winds. 'Evie and I thought it was a terrible idea! But Quentin's new, you see and he didn't know . . .'

'Why didn't you tell him then?' enquired Priscilla reasonably.

'You may well ask,' said Birdie drily. They both looked at Kate who, blushing miserably, could think of nothing to say.

Kind-hearted Priscilla finally smiled and shook her head. 'Never mind,' she said. 'Ours is not to reason why. And it's lovely to see everyone. I was even quite pleased to see Tilly although I must say, a little of her goes a long way!'

Her voice took on a new edge. 'She's always *terribly* sweet to me. So sweet it really sets my teeth on edge! It's worse every time I see her. She was *so* patronising about my alphabet book. Told me very seriously that the cover 'let it down', as she put it. She honestly thinks she's got this marvellous design sense. She's had one good idea in twenty years and that qualifies her to criticise me. And have you *seen* those ghastly wall plaques she's let them do—you know, 'Melissa Sleeps Here' and so on. They're all over town, with the madly grinning Paddy Kangaroo, looking even more like a giant fat-tailed rabbit than usual, with a nightcap and candle? Oh, they're so vile! And she has the cheek—' She broke off, looking flustered. 'Oh, dear,' she said, holding a hand up to her flushed cheek, 'I've done it again. I don't know why I let her get under my skin! I always swear I won't.'

'She gets under everyone's skin,' said Kate despairingly. 'Saul Murdoch's, Barbara Bendix's, Jack's . . .'

'I wonder whether Jack'll turn up at all tonight,' said Priscilla, glad to get on to less personal ground. 'I suppose most of us oldies know exactly what he's doing now. I thought at the time it was a bit funny, you deciding to put him in the limelight again, with his problem, poor old boy. Of course you probably don't know this, Kate, but I used to illustrate his first gardening columns! In the *Sydney Morning Star*, forever ago.'

'Priscilla, you never told me that!'

'Oh, well, it wasn't exactly a career highlight, Katie,' Priscilla laughed. 'But I've known Jack since those old days. He'd only been doing the gardening bit full time for a couple of years then. He took the nursery over from his old dad, you know. And the columns, well, they'd only been going a week or two!'

'Gosh, it's a small world,' said Kate wonderingly. Birdie rolled her eyes. She leaned towards Priscilla.

'Do you know how he came to suddenly write the book? The original one, that made his name, before the gardening columns?'

'He took over the book when he took over the nursery. His dad died with the book just started, so Jack with on with it and it was published in both their names.'

'Yeah, that's right!' said Kate. 'I remember now. I've seen that book. It's out of print now, very old fashioned, of course, but I remember the sad little story in the foreword. Yes, I'd forgotten all about that.'

'It's amazing to think,' said Priscilla, 'that he was in the army, and wasn't going to go into the nursery at all. I mean, it's been such a success, hasn't it? Although, poor old Jack, they say he's been getting worse, with the drinking and everything, lately, and even his garden's going to rack and ruin.' She paused to draw breath.

Someone tinkled a spoon against a glass to attract attention.

Quentin cleared his throat.

Birdie leaned close to Priscilla's ear. 'Why did he leave the army?' she whispered.

Priscilla, a deep silence falling all around her, mouthed and pointed to Quentin, who was looking around waiting for every single person's attention. But Birdie frowned, beckoned, and leant towards her, so that Priscilla felt herself impelled to bend her head again, and answer. She looked straight ahead and merely breathed it, so Birdie had to strain to hear.

'His wife. Left him. While he was in Vietnam. Took baby, little boy. Some man. Didn't even tell him. Letters just stopped coming, Jack said. When he got back they'd gone into smoke. He was drunk when he told me. He never saw his son again. There was an accident. His son died in it.' Priscilla's kind eyes were brimming over. She wiped them with the back of her hand. 'He told me that was when he left the army, and went to work for his dad. But he only talked about it to me the once, you know. And I'll tell you what, I'm glad. He was still so angry, filled with rage, even after a couple of years. Quite unlike himself. Bitter. Murderous, really.'

'Ssh!' said someone behind them, and Priscilla flushed and put her hand over her mouth. Kate glanced at Birdie, but she was staring attentively at Quentin, as he began to speak. Kate looked around the room. It was warm and well-lit as ever, but the shadows in the hall crept forward and back as the antique lights began to swing from their expensive brass chains. Outside, a southerly wind was rising.

20

The Short Way Down

Quentin's speech was polished, professional, and very, very long. Perhaps, Kate thought, his strategy was to bore his audience so thoroughly that it would go into a trance and fail to notice how the Big Four theme, so integral to the celebration as planned, had subtly been transformed into The Great Berry and Michaels Authors of Past and Present.

Some present authors, anyway, seemed gratified by the change, and willing to overlook past slights. Others just wanted the speech to end, so drinking and chat could recommence. Still others laughed up their sleeves with malicious glee and composed witty articles, essays, descriptions and letters in their heads, and were delighted with the bon mots thus conjured up. So all in all there was quite a little thunderclap of applause when Quentin had finished, and he stepped back, gratified and sleek, showing nothing of the relief he surely must have felt.

'He's the world's most boring man!' Birdie said in an undertone. Kate shrugged wearily. She felt flat. The speech and its aftermath had been an anticlimax. She told herself that she should be relieved that her fears of scenes and ridicule had been unfounded, and that she should be feeling celebratory. But somehow the evening had a stale, sour taste now. For if there had been some sort of demonstration against the tone of this affair by those present, some acknowledgement that it was unacceptable to large numbers of them, it would have been at least a fitting climax to the months of frustration, resentment and doubt. And, in a way, it would have been a vindication, and celebration, of a time, not long gone, when Berry and Michaels was an Australian company, proudly independent, sturdily eccentric, profitable against the odds, and run by book people, not accountants or marketing men. As it was, it seemed, no-one really cared.

'Some of them seem to like it better!' she said aloud, watching Tilly turning her face up to Quentin's, and twisting the now rather raggedy flower against her lips.

'What?' Birdie was also watching Tilly, with a curious look on her face.

'Doesn't matter.'

Priscilla, suddenly back in a party mood, went off in search of a waiter. People were milling and talking all around them, heady with freedom after their period of enforced, respectful silence and inactivity. The caterers were laying out supper now, on the long tables at the end of the room, and already small knots of the more alert, and hungry, guests were drifting in their direction.

Kate, light-headed with overtiredness and champagne, blinked at the eddying crowd. Familiar faces greeted her, laughed, talked, moved on. Familiar faces moved in the crowd. She saw Sarah, tall and sullen, glaring at her mother across the room. She saw Tilly herself, talking earnestly to Sylvia de Groot, who was smiling and nodding like a puppet. She saw Quentin, cold and impeccable, lay his hand once, lightly, on Amy's bare white shoulder, and then reflexively look around to see if anyone was watching. She saw Dorothy, in her stiff, dark green, lift her chin and stare determinedly at Barbara Bendix, who was laughing out loud while Malcolm hovered anxiously at her side. She saw Evie, watching them, her face a mask. And then it was as if she was seeing them all at once, frozen in time, a collage of faces that would stay in her memory for years after, rising up when she least expected it, to chill and terrify, and make her remember.

Supper satisfactorily over, the crowd began to thin. Most of the real celebrities had departed even earlier, laughingly pleading ruinously early engagements the following day, very aware of the need to conserve their energy and to ration the reflected light of their glamour in the comfortable knowledge that the gathering was the poorer for their departure. With them went the camera crews, the social columnists, the photographers. Now the very old, the very far from home and the responsible with babysitters to think of, were drifting away.

Kate was saying goodbye to Priscilla Penn at the front door when Paul appeared from nowhere and grabbed her arm.

'Kate, sorry, can you come?' He began to pull her away without further ceremony. She glanced at him in surprise. He was white and sweating.

'Paul, what's wrong?'

'Kate, just come!'

She held up an apologetic arm to Priscilla, still hesitating in the doorway, and went with him.

'Paul! What *is* it?'

'The roof. Sarah. Come.'

They ran up the stairs. Paul wouldn't wait for the lift. Kate became breathless quickly and tried to slow down, but he grabbed her elbow with a bony hand, and propelled her forward, till the entrance to the roof garden was ahead of them. Then he stopped, and put her in front of him, hanging back white and gasping, while she pushed open the door, and stepped out into the sweet-smelling darkness.

Sarah Lightly huddled against the parapet at the far end of the building. They ran towards her. Her black hair hung in wisps around her ears and she clutched a book against her breast with desperate hands. She was sobbing quietly but as soon as she saw them coming she started to laugh, in the hysteria that had driven Paul for help. She laughed and laughed, her mouth horribly stretched over her teeth, tears streaming down her face so that it shone in the pale moonlight.

'Sarah! Stop!' Paul was on his knees beside her. 'You'll hurt yourself. Stop it!'

She doubled over, the laughter coming in painful, silent shudders, her head flapping helplessly, her nose running, her black dress gaping.

'What's happened to her? Paul, what have you done?' cried Kate, terrified and repelled. 'Sarah, be quiet! Sarah!'

'I haven't touched her!' yelled Paul. 'God, you don't know what's happened! You've got to help me, Kate. Get her out, downstairs. Come on, come on!' And he began tugging and pulling the girl's heavy body, trying to make her move.

'Paul!' Kate shouted, his panic shocking her almost as much as Sarah's hysteria did. 'Leave her alone! I'll get Tilly. I'll get—'

Sarah jerked her head violently. 'Get Tilly!' she shrieked. 'Get her? Oh, God! Look!' Her face was distorted with fear and horror, her finger stabbed the air. 'Look over . . . down. Down. Look!'

Kate looked over the parapet, into the narrow laneway that ran beside the building and her stomach lurched. Around a garbage bin, far below, something white and shapeless was crawling. She almost cried out, and then she saw it for what it was—Tilly's Chinese shawl, ripping and flapping in the wind. She almost laughed in relief, and then her eyes moved on and the laugh choked in her throat. There was something else in the alley, directly below where she stood. Something small, twisted and broken, pale limbs sprawling, and still as death.

She turned back to Paul speechless with horror. He nodded wildly, and pulled the book from Sarah's clutching hands.

'This,' he whispered, 'this was on the wall.'

It was a copy of *The Adventures of Paddy Kangaroo*, open at pages 64 and 65. A paragraph had been marked in the margin with thick black pen. It was only a short paragraph. Kate read it, and fear clutched at her heart.

'Oho,' laughed Paddy, launching himself into the air. 'You just watch me, all you blokes. You see? I can fly . . . I can . . . oooer-er . . . he-l-p!' There was a sickening thud as he hit the ground.

They stood in paralysed silence, staring at one another. The cool southerly wind blew around them, the thick shrubs and low trees that crouched together in the centre of the roof garden tossed and cracked in shadow.

With a sharp click the stairwell door opened. Light streamed from inside the building like a beacon, picking them out as they clutched one another by the parapet. Still they stood breathless and unmoving. Sid's hulking figure loomed in the doorway. His voice hailed them, roughly.

'What's going on up here, eh?' He was breathing heavily. 'Who's that out there? That you, Mrs Lightly?'

Sarah gasped. Paul's arm closed on her wrist and pulled her upright.

Kate licked her dry lips and called out. 'Sid! It's Kate Delaney. Wait there a second, will you?'

She took Sarah's other arm. 'We'll have to go down and tell Quentin. Get the police. Come on, quickly. Before someone on the street . . . sees.'

They stumbled along with her, towards the light. Behind them the bushes rustled. Kate kept wanting to look behind her, but forced herself to move forward, quickly, not showing a second's hesitation, in case Sarah again lost her head. Her heart was beating fast and hard, but at least she knew what they had to do. Downstairs. Quentin. Police. Ambulance.

They reached Sid, standing lowering and resentful. He looked at the dishevelled Sarah with disapproval, but moved aside to let her and Paul pass. Kate paused beside him. 'Sid,' she said, as calmly as she could, 'could you please shut the door behind us and then stay here, and stop anyone else going onto the roof?'

'I can't do that,' said Sid sullenly. 'Mr Hale's told me to make sure Mrs Lightly's all right, and tell her he can't come up. Isn't she out there? What was all the yelling about? That bloody beatnik try something on the girl, did he?'

'Ssh. No . . .' Kate was whispering urgently. 'Sid, could you just wait?'

He shook his head slowly. 'Can't be done,' he said stubbornly. 'I can't stop Mrs Lightly going up there. Mr Hale said—'

'Sid, Tilly Lightly's been up here already. Please.' This was like a bad dream, thought Kate. She couldn't think straight. Somehow she felt she couldn't tell Sid what had happened. The proprieties seemed to demand that Quentin was told first. But no-one must go onto the roof. Tilly had been murdered. She couldn't have just fallen. And the book . . . The police would want to seal off the roof, to try to find some clue, up there, as to who might have . . .

'She's been?' Sid looked at her narrowly. 'That was a bit quick, for all the damn carry-on, wasn't it?'

Kate shrugged, and turned to join Paul and Sarah sagging, exhausted, against the stair-rail.

And then they heard the footsteps. Someone else was coming to the roof garden. Kate straightened her shoulders and put her arm around Sarah. They would have to carry this off somehow. Get downstairs, get Quentin, get . . .

The footsteps reached the landing below them. A figure began toiling up the last flight of stairs, looked up and saw them.

'Oh, hello there,' smiled Tilly Lightly. 'You

shouldn't have waited!' She hesitated and looked at them whimsically, head on one side. 'What's the matter? You all look as though you've seen a ghost!'

Sarah Lightly began to scream. And this time, she wouldn't stop.

21

The Gilded Cage

They sat in Quentin's elegant living room, numbly drinking coffee. They waited, for an explanation, or a development, or for the next blow to fall.

Dorothy Hale had served them herself, rejecting all offers of help. She was frankly pleased to have something to do, and moved around quietly offering cream and sugar, and a plate of chocolate biscuits, suddenly mistress of her own home, and a steady, warm and comforting presence in the midst of chaos and calamity. Her husband, standing alone by the window, obviously felt it too, for he took the cup she tentatively offered gratefully, and patted her hand as it withdrew. She returned to the group sitting around the coffee table with a slight pinkness in her cheeks. She still looked plump and middle-aged, but the sweet-faced girl she must once have been peeped out for a moment from her glowing eyes. Well, what do you know? thought Kate. She wondered if Evie and Birdie had noticed the little exchange. She stole a look at Amy, sitting motionless on the couch opposite. She was pale as chalk, and sipped automatically at her coffee, taking no notice of Malcolm, blinking feverishly on one side and Paul Morrisey, glowering on the other. No joy there.

Tilly and Sarah Lightly had long since been bundled off to talk to Dan Toby alone. Kate doubted they

would reappear now. They would be in their room, or
at the police station, maybe. Anyway, they wouldn't
be coming up for coffee and biscuits with the others at
this late stage.

It was midnight. Half an hour ago the last guest had
been ushered out, name and address taken, promise
not to travel in the immediate future extracted. Quentin and his troop had moved upstairs to get away from
the streamers and the posters and the flowers, and to
get away from the small, shrouded body outside: the
flash cameras, the spotlights, the ambulance.

Quentin had been asked to identify the body. But,
shaking his big head in stunned bewilderment, he'd
had to call for help. She'd fallen on her face, and he
wasn't familiar enough, he couldn't be sure. Only a
couple of months he'd been here, and he couldn't . . .
So it was Evie in the end, who confirmed what Kate
had already guessed, and at last Sylvia de Groot, royalties manager, devoted employee of Berry and Michaels for seven years, was driven away from 'Carlisle'
for the last time.

They didn't speak. There was a policeman standing
by the lift. He was staring into space, as though engaged in private cogitation, but none of them really
believed that. Why else had he been posted there, but
to listen to whatever they might say?

And anyway, what was there to say? As individuals
they had little enough in common, and under circumstances like these, the social niceties that provided a
meeting point at more ordinary times were wildly in-
appropriate. Kate wondered whether the others had
realised why they had been selected out of the crowd,
and asked to remain for further conversation with
Detective-sergeant Dan Toby. Surely they did. And
yet, she herself had wondered earlier, and had asked
Birdie. Birdie had looked at her quizzically, her glasses
flashing as they caught the light. 'I'm here, I imagine,
on a whim of Dan's. But all of you—oh, Kate, why do
you think? Because you were at the party last night.
When Saul Murdoch . . .'

Oh, yes. When Saul Murdoch snarled at Tilly, out-raged Jack, fascinated Barbara, threatened Quentin and attacked Paul. When Saul Murdoch stormed off, vow-ing to pillory them all, and then went back to his room and took an overdose. Took an overdose, in a glass of wine, and left a marked page of one of his books as a farewell note.

The police had taken charge of the copy of *Paddy the Kangaroo*, found by Sarah and Paul on the parapet. They'd put it in a plastic bag. Presumably they'd test it for fingerprints. But they knew where it had come from. It was stamped 'Publicity' on the title page, and Malcolm thought, was almost sure, it was the copy he'd given to Jack Sprott, only this morning.

Kate considered this fact without surprise. Nothing now had the capacity to surprise her, it seemed.

Birdie sat beside her looking pale, unobtrusive and very slightly bored. In Kate's experience, this was an infallible sign that she was thinking hard, and paying close attention to everything going on around her. She had made some slight concession to the formality of the evening by wearing a loose embroidered black coat over black trousers, and a pair of odd little black shoes with straps. Tap shoes, thought Kate suddenly. That's what they looked like. Beginner's tap shoes. Somehow they gave the whole outfit an air of being a dress-up, and the black drained all colour from the freckled, clever face.

Kate saw that Quentin was also watching Birdie. Uncomfortably. He must be remembering how he had promised full cooperation, asked Kate to give her all the information she needed to prepare for the docu-mentary. It was too late to back out now, but surely, he must be reasoning, this little librarian type wouldn't want to cause the company trouble. This bizarre affair would be off-limits in the projected programme. He'd see to it, fix it, later.

Quentin's heavy pink face was sober, but his shirt still glimmered impeccably white, and his silk tie re-mained competently knotted around his strong neck.

He stood with his back to the window, facing his blue and gold room, and the people in it, apparently quite at ease. But a muscle in his cheek twitched as the lift doors clattered and opened.

Eight faces turned to watch Dan Toby and Detective-constable Milson move from the lift to Quentin's side. They spoke to him for a moment, then faced the others.

'Sorry to have kept you waiting, folks,' said Toby serenely. 'I know it's late.' He cleared his throat. 'As you're all aware, there was a fatality earlier tonight. As a matter of routine, I have to ask each of you a few questions. Nothing to get het up about,' he added, his calm gaze sweeping the room.

Beside him Milson straightened slightly, and peered down his beaky nose at them with eyes like cold little river pebbles. Nothing reassuring about Milson, thought Kate. The two men were very unalike. She wondered if they played 'good policeman/bad police-man' when they were grilling suspects. Well, she'd soon know.

'We're to assume, are we,' drawled Barbara from her armchair, 'that you believe one of us to be responsible for this death?'

Toby stroked his chin and returned her challenging stare with a quiet smile. 'Not necessarily, Miss Bendix, no,' he said slowly.

'Then why have you chosen to ask us to stay be-hind?' persisted Barbara, impervious to the combined efforts of everyone else in the room to will her to si-lence. 'It's obvious what you think—and it's obviously ridiculous!'

'We won't be jumping to any conclusions, Miss Bendix,' rumbled Toby firmly, 'and I suggest no-one else does, either.'

Barbara subsided with a shrug. 'It seems odd to me,' she said, looking at the ceiling, 'that Tilly Lightly has apparently been allowed to go to bed, and her daughter too, and yet they were the people most concerned in the whole thing. Frankly I don't see why you have to look any further than those two for your explanation, though plainly you intend to.'

'Barbara!' Evie began an exhausted protest, but Dan Toby remained silent, and Barbara, waving red-tipped white fingers at Evie, went on.

'It's only what we're all thinking, Evie. It's logical. It's clear as a bell.' She looked around with knitted brows, and leant forward. 'Tilly's white shawl was found near Sylvia's body. This could mean one of two things. Either Tilly was up on the roof with Sylvia and Sylvia fell, or was pushed over, pulling Tilly's shawl down with her, or, Sylvia was up there by herself, wearing Tilly's shawl, as I understand Tilly says was the case, and someone pushed her over by mistake, thinking she was Tilly. That could happen. It was dark, and the shawl is distinctive, and they were about the same height, weren't they? And the only person with any kind of reason to kill Tilly Lightly was Sarah Lightly. The rest of us might have felt like killing her. I know I did. But extreme irritation isn't really a good enough motive for murder, is it?' She reached out and took the last chocolate biscuit.

'You'd better be quiet, Barbara,' snapped Evie. 'That's libel.'

'Slander, actually,' smiled Barbara. 'Don't try and teach your grandmother to suck eggs, Evie darling. The libel laws are very familiar to me. I spend my life trying to avoid spiking myself on them.'

'Then perhaps, Miss Bendix, it'd be better to keep the rest of your theories to yourself,' said Toby severely. 'Mr Hale has kindly offered his study for our use. You could make your statement now. Milson?'

He strode to the study and held out his arm invitingly. Barbara sighed, shrugged, and hauled herself up from her chair. She winked broadly at Paul Morrisey, who pointedly averted his eyes, and undulated to Toby's side. Milson, looking disapproving, brought up the rear.

The strange trio disappeared into the study, and the door closed.

'Barbara Bendix,' said Kate, 'is really . . .'

'Well, she's handling it better than the rest of us, anyway,' said Evie. She lowered her voice. 'She looks to me as though she's got something cooking, actually. I wonder if she knows more than she's telling.'

Kate glanced uneasily at the policeman by the lift. Evie saw her looking and grimaced.

'I'm not saying anything special, Kate. I'm just saying she looks a bit too elated, under the circumstances. Let's face it, she'd have no reason to, you know, do anything to Tilly, or Sylvia de Groot—or to Saul, if it comes to that. She knows she's not in the running as suspect number one. She's in the clear. So why shouldn't she tell whatever she's got up her sleeve?'

'She's a stupid woman,' said Paul Morrisey loudly. 'Stupid, and a troublemaker. It's ludicrous to say Sarah could have pushed someone over a building. The whole idea's absurd. Anyway, I was with Sarah the whole time. She couldn't have done it.'

'Well, who did?' Evie put the question into words. 'They seem to think it was one of us.'

'They can't,' whispered Dorothy Hale.

'Obviously they do,' said Birdie pleasantly. 'And what's more they think whoever it was killed Saul Murdoch too. Or, as Barbara says, why are we all here?'

Amy stared at her as if noticing her for the first time. 'I can't imagine why we're here,' she said coldly. 'I don't think they know what they're doing. In England the police don't throw their weight around like this.'

'How would you know?' retorted Evie rudely.

It would have been impossible for Amy's face to grow any paler, but her lips tightened and her eyes darkened, and she stared at Evie as if she hated her.

Quentin turned from the window and seemed about to speak, but his wife forestalled him. She was very pale and her earlier composure had deserted her.

'Don't, please, Evie,' she begged and put her hand to her forehead. 'We're all upset. Let's try to keep calm, shall we?'

'Sorry, Dorothy,' Evie said in a low voice. But she didn't look at Amy, who sat very upright and frozen-faced while Malcolm and Paul fidgeted uncomfortably on either side of her.

The study door opened and Barbara wandered out into the room, yawning ostentatiously. 'I can go now, I gather?' she said to Milson, who had accompanied her. He nodded shortly and she smiled. 'I'm for bed, then.' She lifted a hand. 'Thank you, Dorothy, Quentin. A fascinating evening. See you all in the morning—I hope!' With a wicked smile she made for the lift.

Malcolm stood up, as if to follow her, but Milson blocked his path. 'Carruthers there will escort the lady down, sir. If you could come this way?'

Malcolm shied like a skittish horse. He ran his hand over his short-cropped hair and blushed. 'Oh, sure,' he said, and walked towards the study door looking rather lonely and young, the tips of his ears burning.

'Not so cocky now, are we?' Evie breathed vindictively. But Kate was by now feeling sorry for Malcolm Pool and couldn't join in the celebration of his chagrin, so she didn't answer. She suddenly felt stifled in this air-conditioned, airtight apartment high above the rowdy, humid streets.

'Dorothy, would you mind if I made more coffee?' she said, standing up abruptly. She waited for Dorothy's nod and then turned to Birdie.

'Could you give me a hand, Birdie?' Birdie raised her eyebrows, but obligingly heaved herself up and followed her to the tiny kitchen off the living room. Kate pushed the door behind them.

'I just wanted to know,' she said, fiddling with the coffee maker, 'what you think.' She looked at Birdie expectantly. Birdie prowled around, peering at the gadgets that lined the kitchen benches.

'This is all very lavish, isn't it?' she said. 'I didn't know book publishers lived like this.'

'Most don't!' said Kate waspishly. 'Not here, anyway. But listen, we haven't got long. What do you reckon? And don't get smart. About poor Sylvia, I mean. It was meant to be Tilly, wasn't it? Everyone knew she was going up to the roof. They thought she was going alone. She'd asked Quentin and Sarah and everyone to go up with her, and they wouldn't, but at the last minute she asked Sylvia, and Sylvia went. She would. She adored Tilly. And when they got up there it was cold, because the southerly had come up, and Tilly gave Sylvia her shawl to put on and she went down to her room to get another one. So Sylvia was standing there, in the white shawl, and someone . . . someone came, and just pushed her. Thought it was Tilly and pushed her. And left the book, with that bit marked, about flying . . . and falling.' Kate's stomach lurched. She shivered and pressed her hands against the heating jug of water.

'Well?' said Birdie, waiting.

'Well . . . well, Birdie, if you agree with that you must have stopped thinking that Saul Murdoch killed himself.'

'Oh,' Birdie recommenced her prowling. She went over the sink top to examine the garbage disposal unit. 'I don't know, Kate,' she said calmly. 'It looked like suicide. Everything points to suicide.'

'But Sylvia, that wasn't . . .'

'No. That wasn't. That wouldn't make sense.'

'And the wall's too high for it to have been an accident, isn't it?'

'Yes.'

'So now,' Kate swallowed, 'now there are two people dead. And if all had gone as it was meant to, it'd be two of Malcolm's Big Four. Someone . . .'

'Laney!' Birdie looked at Kate seriously and held up a cautious hand. Suddenly she began to speak, rapidly and forcefully. 'If I were you—I don't want to put you off, or make you angry, or anything, Kate, but if I were you, I'd keep out of this. Leave it to Dan Toby. You might think he's slow, but he's an expert, and he's the best person to handle it. We're dealing with something here that's dangerous. You should keep a low profile, and not say or do anything that'll attract attention. Right?'

Kate stared at her. 'You're saying . . .'

'I'm saying to be still, be careful, keep your head down. I'm not sure what's happening, but it's all very odd, and very dangerous. That's what I'm saying.'

'You think whoever it is might . . . go after someone else? It's not finished?'

'I'm sure it's not finished. Laney, they'll be waiting for that coffee. Aren't you going to . . . ?"

'Oh, yes,' Kate poured boiling water into the coffee maker and turned to set out fresh cups and saucers. Her hands trembled slightly and the cups rattled. Suddenly she thought of Sylvia, and her eyes filled with tears. She felt the tears well over, and run down her cheeks. She could feel Birdie watching her back, and concentrated on not letting her shoulders shake. She swallowed, and breathed evenly. When she was sure her voice would be steady she spoke, without turning around.

'Do you think Dan Toby knows . . . who?'

'Not yet. But he's got a few ideas. And I have too. He'll tell me, when it's my turn to go in. He'll tell me what he thinks, and I'll tell him.'

'Tell me. Now!'

Birdie shook her head. 'Kate, I can't. You've got to keep out of this. You've really got to. There's nothing you can do.'

Kate grabbed the tray and made for the door. 'I don't know what you think you're playing at!' she whispered angrily. 'Don't treat me like a half-wit, if you don't mind.'

'Well don't act like one! Leave it to Toby and me!' ordered Birdie.

They looked warily at one another.

'Toby'll talk to all of us, right?' Kate spoke reasonably. 'He'll take notes, he'll think about them. He'll look at the roof, and the pavement, and Sylvia, and Saul again, I suppose. And he'll look at Saul's book, and the copy of *Paddy Kangaroo*, and all that. But I don't see how he's going to get any further. What more can he do?'

Birdie looked at her in surprise. 'Well, Laney, he can do the most important thing, for a start, can't he? He can find Jack Sprott.'

22

Conspiracy

An hour later Birdie sat with Dan Toby in Quentin's study. They sat facing one another over the glassy-clean antique desk, and leaned forward like conspirators. The dark-browed Milson sat slightly to one side, staring into space.

'We'd better make this quick,' said Toby, pulling at his tie to loosen it. 'They're wanting to get to bed in there, Hale and his wife. Any thoughts?'

'A few,' said Birdie carefully. 'But you're the one who's heard all the statements. Where did they get you?'

'Not far. They all admit to knowing Tilly Lightly was going up to the roof. She'd actually tried to get Hale, her daughter, Evie Newell and Barbara Bendix in turn to go with her. They all say they refused for one reason or another. The others heard her say she was going to skip supper and go up for some air.'

'They all admit that?' Birdie's glasses flashed in the lamplight.

'Yeah,' rumbled Toby. He stroked his chin thoughtfully. 'No choice, really. She apparently more or less told everyone, making a big thing, Barbara Bendix said, of the fact that she wasn't hungry, and couldn't face the plate of food some flunky had given her. Bendix said something bitchy about it. What was it, Milson?'

Milson riffled the pages of his notebook, put a long

finger on the page, and bent the book back. 'Tilly thinks having an appetite like a bird, as she puts it, makes her seem more interesting, I suspect. I bet she gutses sweet biscuits on the quiet,' he read. 'Her loss, anyway. I ate hers as well as mine, and it was delicious!' He flipped the book shut again.

Toby looked quizzically at Birdie. 'No love lost there,' he said.

'No,' agreed Birdie. 'But it must be said, Dan, that Tilly got up everyone's nose. If anyone said differently, they're lying.'

He looked at her calmly. 'No, no-one claims to love Tilly Lightly,' he said. 'Well, Quentin Hale was pretty non-committal. So was Malcolm Pool. You can understand that, I suppose. And Hale's secretary, what's the name again?'

'Amy Phibes.'

'Oh, yes. Well, she wouldn't admit to having any feeling about her one way or another. Implied it wasn't her place to have feelings. She, by the way, was like a cat on hot bricks, wasn't she, Milson? Bundle of nerves.'

'Hiding something,' Milson offered briefly, his eyes on his notebook.

Toby nodded. 'Maybe. Anything to say on that, Birdie?'

'Office gossip is she's on with Quentin Hale,' Birdie said shortly. 'She's only been with the company a couple of months—he hired her after he'd been here a week or so. Brian Berry's secretary left when he did. Phibes is not much liked.'

'No, I can see other women wouldn't be very taken with her,' murmured Toby slyly.

Birdie gave him a sharp look. 'It's her personality, not her looks, that's the problem, I think you'll find,' she said tartly.

He grinned, pleased to have got a rise out of her. 'Anyhow,' he went on, 'just to fill you in, all of them say they thought Tilly Lightly was going up to the roof alone. No-one noticed Sylvia de Groot was missing from the party. And no-one noticed that anyone else was missing, either. I'll have to go into it all more thoroughly, Birdie. Milson'll do one of his famous time and motion charts for us, won't you, Milson?' He grinned teasingly at his subordinate who remained expressionless.

Toby suppressed a sigh and continued: 'But it seems to me, mate, that everyone was busy gasbagging and getting into the eats, and it's going to be bloody hard to prove definitely that any one of them was out of the reception rooms for ten minutes or so. That's all it would have taken, I reckon, to get up the stairs, push the lady over, and get down again. As I say, no-one even noticed Sylvia de Groot was gone. There were hundreds of people present, Hale said, at the time.'

'And the time was?'

'The doc said she probably went over round 10.45. Body discovered about half an hour after death, which was instantaneous, of course.'

'You should be able to pinpoint where people were just by checking all the other people tomorrow, Dan. The people they were talking to can vouch for them.'

He shrugged comfortably. 'To a certain extent, yes,' he said. 'But everyone's as vague as hell about the time. A good proportion of them would've been half blotto by then anyway. We'll do our best.'

Milson gave a barely audible sniff.

Toby looked at him sharply and straightened his shoulders. His fingers reached for his tie, and he tightened it peevishly.

Birdie sat forward. 'Did you get into the Saul Murdoch business again with any of them?'

'With a few of them, I did. Bendix, Tilly Lightly, Sarah Lightly, Hale and his wife. The people who were actually staying in the place. All of them say just what they did before. They heard nothing.'

'The girl, Sarah, said she heard a board creak outside her room half an hour after she went to bed,' Detective-constable Milson intoned, tapping his book.

'For what it's worth,' grumbled Toby. 'And that,

my little friend—not you, Milson, you needn't be insulted—brings us round to the disappearing gardener, Jack Sprott. You reckon he went downstairs in the night to nick some whisky from the kitchen?'

'I'm sure he did. And damaged Saul Murdoch's picture in the process, as I said.' Birdie paused. 'No word about him yet, presumably?'

'Nothing. The bars are being checked, the usual hangouts. His house is being watched. But we're on it, Birdie. I agree with you, we've got to get hold of him fast. He could be playing a bloody dangerous game, if he's as tanked up and unbalanced as you and your mate, Kate Delaney, say. For a start, we have to check his story through again, about last night—well, the night before last, as I guess it is by now. Last we heard he was written off and out of commission the whole night. Heard nothing, saw nothing, said nothing to no-one. Now it seems he's been wandering around the building in the dark. Probably nothing in it, but why didn't he admit to it?'

Birdie put her hand on her chin. 'Embarrassed?' she tried.

'Possibly.' He hesitated, and looked at her shrewdly. 'Your friend Kate Delaney seems a bit spooked, Birdie. She doesn't know more than she's telling, does she? D'you know her well?'

'Since school,' said Birdie briefly. 'I'm sure she's not hiding anything.'

'She seems concerned about Jack Sprott.'

'I told her I thought he had to be found. Also, she's worked with him for years. She's quite fond of him, I think. I think she'd get fond of Attilla the Hun if she spent enough time with him. Jack Sprott isn't particularly likeable, as far as I'm concerned. She says he used to be different. Meeting up with Tilly and Sarah and the others seems to have affected him badly. I told you about his wife and son?'

Toby nodded, his face grave. 'After a bit of beating round the bush Kate Delaney told me too. She was upset. She said she'd been worried about him, and had wished he'd turn up for the party but now she was glad he hadn't, because if he'd been there we might have suspected him of pushing Sylvia de Groot over the parapet, thinking she was Tilly. Now, she said, whatever we might have suspected about Saul, and she wouldn't blame us for thinking Jack was a reasonable suspect if we'd dropped the suicide idea, we at least couldn't blame him for the second death because he wasn't there.'

He sat calmly watching Birdie's reaction. She sighed. 'I told Kate to keep out of it,' she said, almost to herself. 'She'll get herself into trouble.'

'Oh, not quite that, I don't think,' said Toby thoughtfully. 'But she might be in for a nasty shock, whether she stays in or out, Birdie.'

Birdie raised her eyebrows. Her glasses caught the light. 'It's like that, is it?' she said.

'You know it is,' rumbled Toby. He began shuffling the papers in front of him, and then pushed his chair back and abruptly stood. 'Let's get out of here,' he said. 'Big day tomorrow.' He waited until Milson was safely turned away, collecting his jacket and documents, and jerked his head towards the street, miming raising a glass to his lips. Birdie grinned and nodded.

At the lift the uniformed policeman was still at his post. He looked unperturbed by the fact that Quentin and Dorothy were watching him from the living room couch, and Sid from just inside the lift. He preserved a disciplined silence until they reached the ground floor and proceeded to the front door. Then he allowed a sigh to escape him. Milson looked at him sharply, but Toby smiled.

'Had enough of that, had you, Carruthers?' he said.

The man nodded, a bit abashed. 'I think that big guy, Sid, is a bit, you know, short on screws in his think saucepan, sir. Could feel his eyes boring into the back of my neck the whole time I was standing there. Odd bloke.'

Toby turned to Milson. 'The others have packed up and gone, I gather? Find anything?'

Milson shook his head. 'No-one hiding anywhere in the building, sir.'

'The guest rooms were checked?'

'Yes. And their bathrooms.'

'One thing, sir,' said Carruthers, eager to join in. 'You know that Jack Sprott's room and Saul Murdoch's room were connected by the shared bathroom? Well, one of the doors was missing a part. When I tried it, it pushed open quite easily from the inside, although it looked locked.'

Milson leaned forward, eyes snapping. 'Why wasn't I told about this?' he demanded crossly.

'Why didn't we notice it before? That's the important question, Milson,' said Toby quietly, and Birdie felt his tension as he asked the next question. 'Whose side was the faulty door on, Carruthers?'

'Saul Murdoch's, sir,' said Carruthers, surprised.

'So you mean,' broke in Birdie, quite unable to keep out of it any longer, 'that you can get into Saul Murdoch's room just by pushing on the bathroom door from the inside?'

Carruthers nodded, after shooting an enquiring glance at Toby to see if he was free to answer her.

'This is incredible!' muttered Milson furiously. 'Who was responsible for checking that room last time?'

Toby held up a hand. 'We'll find out in due course, Milson. Don't let's waste time looking for scapegoats now.'

'Apparently the lock seems fine from Murdoch's bedroom itself, sir,' said Carruthers anxiously, making it clear that he at least knew who was going to be held guilty of the oversight. 'It was only when you went into the bathroom and tried it from the inside that you realised it was broken.'

'And of course,' said Toby slowly, 'everything pointed to suicide, so there was no real need to look for other ways into the room, was there?'

'What about now, sir?' Carruthers asked.

'Well . . .' Toby opened the front door and looked

thoughtfully out to the almost deserted street. The wind had dropped now, and it was still a little too warm for comfort as the old brick buildings released the heat baked into their walls during the long, hot day. 'In one way, nothing's changed,' he said. 'But in another—'

'Everything has,' Milson cut in with satisfaction. 'And we've got another body on our hands as well. If you don't mind me saying, sir, I did suggest we go full on, on this, at the time. But you—'

'Milson, you make me tired,' said Toby abruptly. 'You're always so right!'

He walked grumpily out into the street. Birdie slipped out after him.

'I presume,' Toby turned back to the unfortunate Carruthers. 'I presume you had the wit to fingerprint the door?'

The man nodded vehemently.

'Find anything?'

'Ah, no, sir. After we gave Hale the go-ahead this afternoon the bathroom was cleaned, by the regular cleaners, top to bottom,' croaked Carruthers, looking wild about the eyes.

Toby nodded resignedly, turned away, and then turned back again. 'Carruthers, did you search the roof garden?'

Milson lifted his chin and looked scornful. 'I saw to that myself, sir, of course.'

'Of course,' breathed Toby. He slung his jacket over his shoulder and trudged off down the street. Birdie put her hands in her pockets and followed at a safe distance, whistling tunelessly to herself.

Milson watched them go, shaking his head. Then he turned to confront the hapless Carruthers.

23

Talking It Through

'Where do we find a bloody drink around here at this time of night?' demanded Toby as Birdie caught up with him.

She shrugged. 'We could go to the Cross,' she said, matching her stride to his.

'Give us a break, Birdie!'

They marched on, going nowhere. Birdie hated walking. She considered her options, and made a decision.

'Come back to my place,' she said, carefully casual.

He stopped dead and stared at her. 'Darling, this is so sudden,' he said.

She ignored him, and hailed a cab cruising along the opposite side of the road. The driver made a lazy U-turn in the deserted street and pulled up beside them. They got in.

'Fourth Street, Annandale,' Birdie said briefly. She didn't look at Toby. 'It'll only take ten minutes at this time of night,' she observed.

'Fine. Fine.' Toby settled back, grinning to himself.

Birdie caught the driver glancing at them in his rear-vision mirror. The expression in the dark eyes was incurious and world-weary. Ill-assorted couples were this man's bread and butter, on the night shift.

•   •   •

'Wine, whisky, gin or coffee?' asked Birdie, flicking on the light and slamming the front door behind them, shutting out the night.

'Whisky.' Toby blinked. It was very odd, to be in Birdie's house. He couldn't remember ever thinking about her having a private life, away from the city offices, the cafes, bars and streets that were her usual day-time haunts. But here was the place she spent her time when she wasn't harassing bureaucrats and businessmen, or shuffling papers or briefing reporters or arguing with the latest person who wanted her to drop a story she'd got her teeth into.

The house was tiny, must be only one bedroom. A single-story terrace crowded up to its neighbours, hidden from the narrow street by a mass of overhanging shrubs and small trees that clustered behind its miniature front fence. Funny. You'd think with her father's money she'd do herself better for than this.

They walked down the short hallway. Bedroom, thought Toby, looking in at the door on his left. But the light from the passage streamed in on a desk heaped with papers and books, a computer, and a row of filing cabinets.

Birdie turned on another light. 'Sit down,' she said brusquely. 'I'll get the drinks.'

Toby sat. And stared. 'How long have you had this?' he said at last.

'I don't know. Seven or eight years, I suppose,' Birdie answered. She poured a couple of drinks, and came back to him.

'Must've cost a packet.' Toby took the glass from her, and drank.

She said nothing, but looked unemotionally around her. The whole of the back part of the tiny house had been knocked into one big L-shaped room, partitioned only by glass doors from a paved courtyard where green leaves nodded in the moonlight.

The floors were polished boards, the walls were lined with books. A tiny kitchen area nestled cleverly in one corner, conspicuously clean and tidy. Probably never used, thought Toby. Table for eating, chairs, one big rug, paintings, the big, soft couch on which he sat, two other armchairs, coffee table. A million dollars' worth of stereo equipment. And in one corner, a baby grand piano.

'D'you play that?' he said.

She looked away and nodded. 'Sometimes.' She was already regretting her impulse to bring him here.

'Where do you sleep?' he asked curiously.

She raised her eyes to the open loft above the kitchen, saw him take in the plain red-covered mattress, the reading light, and the huge skylight that opened the roof to the stars.

He crinkled his eyes at her. 'You're full of surprises, kid,' he said softly. Then he grinned. 'You're safe from old blokes like me up there, anyhow. I'd never make it up that ladder.'

'Give it a rest, Dan,' she muttered.

He looked at her, bemused. 'Sorry,' he said, not having the faintest idea why he should be.

She shifted uncomfortably in her chair and then suddenly shrugged and grinned. 'Look, come on, let's get on with it,' she said in her normal voice. 'Talk it out and we'll see what happens.'

Toby rubbed a tired hand over his forehead. 'The fact is,' he said, 'I got the thing arse-about, didn't I? Murdoch's medical history, the locked room, the pills—his own pills—the marked book, all of it . . . well, I went through the motions, you know I did, but the fact is in my gut I bloody felt it was suicide. I gave them all a bloody easy run. Even Lightly, and I had her letter threatening him under my bloody hand. Even Morrisey, who'd practically had a fist fight with him, and Sprott, who was best mates with the man whose wife he seduced. And Sarah Lightly! My God! You'd think I'd have learned not to assume anything by now. After all these years. Milson did say—'

'Oh, forget about Milson for five minutes, Dan,' Birdie interrupted, frowning over her glass. She tucked her legs under her in the armchair. 'You can talk to them all again, can't you? They're all still around.'

'And another person's dead.'

'So? Look, if the thing tonight had any meaning at all, it's that we're not just dealing with a loon who kills anyone he or she comes across, or with a particular motive that relates to just one person. If we're talking about two murders, we're talking about two linked murders.'

'Yeah. I'd got that for myself,' said Toby gloomily.

'Well, that means that as far as motive's concerned, whatever you might have thought about motives for Saul Murdoch's death by itself, they wouldn't apply to this death, would they? Whether the victim was supposed to be Tilly, or Sylvia?'

'Sarah Lightly?'

'Well, possibly. She might have wanted to make it a double for daddy, I suppose.'

'She was in a hell of a state tonight,' said Toby thoughtfully. 'She thought it was Tilly who'd gone over all right. They had to get a doctor to calm her down.' He gulped at his drink. 'Still . . .'

'Morrisey says he was with her all evening.'

'She only needed an excuse for ten minutes, to go to the ladies, powder her nose, anything.'

'Maybe.' Birdie stirred. 'Why don't we forget motive, then, and talk about opportunity? That might take us further. Murdoch first.'

'The point is,' Toby fingered his glass, 'we now know Saul Murdoch didn't die in a locked room. He died in a room you could get into from a bathroom connecting with Jack Sprott's room on the other side. Puts a different complexion on things, doesn't it?'

'Go on, Dan,' said Birdie calmly. 'You knew before that that locked room stuff wasn't really solid. There are master keys in the building, that open all the doors. Quentin Hale has one for a start, and there must be others.'

He nodded. 'There are five altogether,' he said, 'and six people with access to them. Hale, and therefore Dorothy Hale, Amy Phibes, Evie Newell, Malcolm Pool—he doesn't usually have one, but he's got it just for this affair, on loan from the chief accountant. There's one other they keep locked away, and it's still there, safe and sound, Hale says. So those people'd be the first ones I'd have been looking at, as far as opportunity was concerned. And that would have been ludicrous,' he hesitated, '. . . well, with one exception. But now . . .'

'Now it's anyone with access to Jack Sprott's room. Anyone could've slipped in there while he was downstairs, for example,' said Birdie, thinking it out rapidly. 'It's ten to one he didn't lock the door after him.'

'That's right. But the trouble is—'

'How would they know the door was faulty in the bathroom?'

'I wish you'd stop finishing my sentences, Birdie,' exclaimed Toby. 'I'm quite capable of doing it myself, you know. You remind me of blasted Milson.'

'Sorry. Bad habit.' Birdie grinned.

Toby tapped the coffee table thoughtfully. 'Well, leaving that problem aside, all the people who slept in the building overnight could be regarded as having access to that room, couldn't they? We'd better go from there. Limits the field a bit, anyway.'

Birdie opened her mouth to speak, but thought better of it. Toby seemed a bit touchy. Better, perhaps, to wait a while before pointing out to him that there were a few complications he hadn't thought of.

He gazed thoughtfully out into the courtyard. 'Leaving aside the problem of the bathroom door, and looking at it cold, you'd have to say that Sarah Lightly was a pretty hot contender, Birdie.'

'She's got Tilly, lying awake till dawn, to vouch for her the first night, and Paul Morrisey clinging close beside her for the second. And surely there's an even hotter contender. Other than the one we both know about but are not mentioning, for some reason.'

He looked at her sharply. 'We'll see,' he said.

'It's still the simplest solution of all,' said Birdie,

watching him. 'You don't need any fancy theories. That front door was wide open, and unattended a lot of the time.'

'Well,' Toby hesitated, 'yeah, well . . . you're right. He's got to be questioned. I said that.'

'You've got to find him, first,' said Birdie.

'Don't worry.' Toby drained his glass and lumbered to his feet. 'He'll turn up.'

And Jolly Jack Sprott did, in fact, turn up, quite early the following day. Two boys, preparing to take an unauthorised holiday from school, crossed the little stream in the park in the sparkling morning and penetrated the shrubbery that lined the water upstream. Seeing a comfortable-looking pile of leaves under a rhododendron, they exclaimed at their cleverness in finding such an excellent, sheltered spot to enjoy the iced doughnuts with which they'd provided themselves, and wait out the hour until school had safely begun. The doughnuts never got eaten, though. The police found them later, icing melted, stuck to the white paper bag that the younger boy dropped when he screamed and ran.

And they found Jack Sprott, too. His head was in the creek. His body was roughly covered with leaves and grass clippings. He had been dead for some considerable time. Beside him, face down, lay *The Gardener's Almanac*. Dan Toby lifted it carefully and read the marked paragraph.

General planting instructions:
Place in the prepared hole, fill and press down firmly. Water well, and cover with mulch.

'Cripes,' said Toby. He felt a shiver run down his spine.

24

Method in the Madness

Kate heard the news in the car radio, when she was still ten minutes from the office.

'Concealed in shrubbery . . . drowned . . . a police spokesman said . . .' Kate put her foot on the accelerator.

Sid was at the front door, wearing sunglasses, ushering in staff, repelling the press and other interested parties. Kate couldn't remember ever before being grateful for his hulking, uncommunicative presence. He almost smiled at her as she slipped past him. 'In you go, Kate,' he said, in an avuncular way. 'Go straight upstairs.' He was, she realised, taut with excitement and very much rising to the occasion.

She met Lulu on the stairs.

'Kate, have you heard?' Lulu's eyes were popping.

'Yes, I heard it on the radio,' Kate panted. It was the first time she had spoken to anyone since hearing the news, and she caught, with a little shock, the quaver in her own voice.

'But you didn't—' Lulu pursued her, all agog, the errand that had started her down the stairs forgotten, '—you haven't heard what else they're saying. Everyone's saying that he wasn't just mugged or anything. Everyone says he was knocked off by the same person who pushed Sylvia off the building last night. And you know what else?'

'Lulu . . .' Kate knew what was coming, and couldn't bear to hear it. Lulu, however, was not going to be put off, not for anything. She followed Kate down the corridor, whispering piercingly.

'They say Saul Murdoch isn't in hospital at all!' She paused triumphantly for effect, and looked behind her before delivering her final shot. 'They say *he's* dead too. The three of them, dead. And we never knew a thing about it. Quentin kept it quiet. Can you believe that? We're partying on and Quentin just stands there, knowing there's some loony on the loose. Great, eh?'

'Lulu, it . . . I'm sure it wasn't like that,' Kate protested weakly.

'It was! It was!' Lulu grabbed her by the arm. 'Everyone's running round like chooks with their heads cut off. You wait. There's cops everywhere. Quentin's going round looking like he's dying himself. Looking round for Evie to handle the press for him. He's woken up to that turd Malcolm Pool in a big way. All he wants is Evie now. But she can't get him out of it, can she? No-one can. Dave reckons Quentin's cooked his own goose. Dave reckons he's had it.'

'Lulu,' Kate pulled away, 'I've got to go. I've got to see . . .'

'Well, you watch out!' hissed Lulu. 'Dave reckons we should all go home. I reckon they'll send us home when the cops are finished, don't you? They should. My mum's already rung up. She wants me to go home now, but Dave reckons—'

'You'd better stay till you're told you can go, Lulu. I'm sure there's no . . .' Kate paused. She had been going to say she was sure there was no danger. But why not? Why, when as Lulu said, three people already lay dead.

'Well,' Lulu turned to make her way back to the stairs. 'If I was Tilly Lightly or Barbara Bendix, I wouldn't be hanging around here, I can tell you that. I'd be out of here so fast.'

Kate bit her lip and walked on to her office. Mary was not at her usual post. The phone rang forlornly, as though it had been ringing for some time and had given up hope of ever being answered. Kate walked straight past it. She looked up and down the narrow passageway that led to the other editorial offices. There was no-one to be seen. Everyone was presumably lying low, or talking in the kitchen. She didn't want to talk to anyone, except, maybe, Evie.

She sat down at her desk and rang Evie's extension, without much hope. But the phone was answered straight away.

'Evie Newell,' said the voice, crisply, as if this was just another day.

'Evie, it's me.'

'Kate! Where are you?'

'In my office. I've just come in. I heard . . . about Jack on the radio. Isn't it . . . ?'

'Yes.'

'Do you know what happened?'

'He drowned. In the creek in the park.'

'Was he drunk? Oh, poor Jack!' Kate felt the hot tears in her eyes and shook her head angrily. No point in crying now, you fool, she told herself savagely. A bit of sympathy yesterday, or the day before, yes. A bit of attention then might have helped. But now . . .

'He was drunk,' said Evie's voice brusquely. 'But he'd also hit his head. And the police say it looks as though someone pushed his head into the water. He was unconscious, or as near to as didn't matter, and his head was pushed into the creek. There were the marks of it, on the ground they said.'

'Oh, God!'

'Then, whoever it was covered him up with leaves and stuff.'

'Oh, Evie. Evie, was there a book, like the others?'

'Yes.' Evie sounded weary. 'Some . . . instructions . . . were marked. For planting bulbs, or something.'

Kate felt her heart leap. She swallowed. 'Evie, where're Barbara and Tilly?'

Evie sighed. 'They're upstairs. And they're not

happy.' She gave a snort of mirthless laughter. 'To put it mildly,' she added.

Kate started a little as her door began to open. Then Birdie's tousled head appeared in the crack and she relaxed.

'Kate,' Evie spoke again, rather impatiently, 'Kate, I've got to go now. Quentin's asked me to handle the press, and I have to . . .'

'Oh, yes,' Kate watched Birdie sidle in and take a seat, looking at her inquisitively. She felt as though she must be reacting inappropriately. Evie was managing to be quite businesslike about all this. 'Where's Malcolm?' she asked, stupidly.

'Malcolm's off with the fairies,' said Evie flatly. 'As you'd expect. And when he's finished doing all that, he'll be distancing himself from Quentin so fast it'll make your head spin to watch him. You wait.'

'Oh, Evie, he won't. Even Malcolm wouldn't . . .'

'Well, Quentin obviously agrees with me, Kate.' Evie's voice was curt. 'It was me he rang at home this morning, not Malcolm. He's asked me to handle everything.'

'Oh . . . well, about time,' said Kate lamely. 'Well, I'll see you later.'

'Right. Bye.' Evie hung up without further ado.

Kate slowly replaced the receiver, and turned to meet Birdie's watchful eyes.

'You've heard?' she said helplessly.

Birdie shrugged and nodded.

'It's mad!' sighed Kate. 'Saul Murdoch, Tilly Lightly—or her stand-in, anyway—and now poor old Jack. It's unbelievable! Who could be doing this? Why?'

'You've got the order wrong, actually,' said Birdie mildly. 'Toby reckons Jack has been dead since yesterday afternoon. He was the second victim, not the third.'

'Oh, and I kept waiting for him to turn up at that stupid party, and hoping he wouldn't. I was scared he'd be an embarrassment. And now . . . he was dead all the time.' Kate covered her face with her hands.

'Yes, well, we were all taken by surprise, if it comes to that. Jack was pretty high up in the running as the killer, actually,' said Birdie, half-smiling. 'Toby's very put out. His only consolation is that Milson was caught out as well.'

'Birdie, it's no joke, this!' exclaimed Kate. 'Poor Jack!'

'Will you still publish the calendar thing, and the war diary?' asked Birdie inquisitively. 'I mean, will they be less or more valuable now?' She pulled Jack's battered green book from the manuscript pile, and flicked through it.

'Less, I suppose. I don't know, really. We'll go ahead with the log book for sure, but we were never going to do the memoir, Birdie—unless, I suppose, Jack really put the pressure on.'

'Why not? It looks quite interesting to me,' said Birdie argumentatively, waving the green book back at her. 'You should read it!'

'Look, what's up with you, Birdie? Stop picking at me! I feel bad enough. I don't expect Jack and the others to mean anything to you, but you could at least not be so cold about it!'

Birdie raised her eyebrows above her glasses, marked her place with her finger, and adopted her most supercilious tone. 'There's no point in getting emotional about it, Kate. That won't solve anything. And they do mean something to me now, in a way. I've read their books . . . well, some of them. I'm sorry about old Jack. He obviously wasn't a bad bloke, at least in his prime. That book of his you gave me is a really nice thing, and even this isn't bad. I can see why people trusted him, and I can see he was a real expert in his field, in his day. And I've read *Paddy the Kangaroo*, and I agree it's good, and funny and all that— nowhere near as wet as most of the things I remember reading as a kid. So Tilly can't be all bad. And Saul Murdoch—well, I've never liked his stuff much, and that latest one, *Vernon Crew*, is a shocker, but still . . .' She went back to her reading.

'Yeah, still! None of them were hotshots any more, but none of them deserved to die!'

'No-one deserves to die, Kate, do they?' said Birdie sententiously, without raising her eyes from the page. 'And three people have. The question is—'

'Who did it? Who's out there?'

Birdie looked up again. 'I don't think anyone's "out there", Laney,' she said slowly. 'I'm sure it's very much someone "in here".'

'But . . . it's mad!'

Birdie leaned forward. 'Look, it may very well be mad. But there's method in the madness. It was cleverly done. Whoever killed Jack did it at a time when almost anyone could have done it. Just about every possible suspect was in the park when he was, in the same general area, and alone for some part of the time. Same sort of thing for Sylvia de Groot.'

'And Saul?'

Birdie wrinkled her forehead. 'Saul's more problematic. I don't see . . .'

'Then we have to look at motive, don't we?' exclaimed Kate impatiently.

Birdie shrugged. 'Well, Sarah Lightly has the most obvious motive. As Toby pointed out.'

'Only for her mother, maybe Saul. Not for killing Jack,' Kate protested. 'She seemed to like Jack.'

'He might have seen something, mightn't he?' said Birdie slowly, as if trying to convince herself. 'The night Murdoch died. While he was wandering around. He might have seen someone coming out of Saul's room, or out of his own room, for that matter. Someone sneaking back, or out, after using Jack's room and the bathroom to get to Saul.' Her voice trailed off, and she shook her head impatiently. 'No, that can't be right!'

'I don't see why not!' Kate leaned forward. 'That's what could have happened. And Sarah could have got upstairs and pushed Sylvia off the roof, without anyone noticing. She could . . .' Then her face fell. 'Oh, but wait a minute, that's no good. She's the one person

who had someone with her all the time, at the park.
Paul said he was with her all the time, didn't he? And
he took her off shopping, and to his place, after that.'

Birdie nodded. 'Yeah, that's right. I saw them go.
And at the party, Kate. She wasn't alone then either.
She was sticking to Morrisey like glue. And of course
the night before . . .'

'She was sharing a room with her mother, and Tilly
said she hardly slept all night, so she would have heard
if Sarah went out. So . . . that's that.'

Birdie nodded thoughtfully. 'Pretty airtight, all
right,' she said.

There was a knock on the door. Tilly, serious-faced,
came into the room, with Sarah trailing after her. Kate
felt a stab of panic. Had they heard anything? Surely
not. Both of them were pale and very nervy-looking,
as you would expect, but they didn't seem to be angry
or upset in any but a general way.

'I'm sorry to interrupt, Kate, Verity,' said Tilly
fretfully, 'but I thought you might be able to help us.
Quentin's locked away upstairs, with the police, I
think. And Malcolm's with Barbara Bendix in her
room, and won't even speak to me. And Evie's just on
the phone all the time, and really . . .' She seemed on
the point of tears. Kate stood up and smiled as reassuringly as she could.

'Oh, dear, you poor things, I'm sorry. Sit down.'

Tilly leaned back in her chair. She looked exhausted. 'I want to see if Sarah and I can get a plane
back home today,' she said. 'Could you organise that,
Kate? Please? I've had all I can stand. I can't bear any
more of this.'

Sarah shifted in her seat and looked out the window.

'I'll do what I can, Tilly,' said Kate gently, 'but it's
possible, I suppose, that the police won't let anyone
go home yet. You know, they might want everyone to
be . . . on hand, for the moment. Mightn't they,
Birdie?'

Birdie, ostentatiously deep in Jack's manuscript, grimaced as though she was the last person to know the answer to such a question.

'But that can't happen!' insisted Tilly. 'Kate, I'm in danger of my life! They've got to let me get away!'

'She should go,' volunteered Sarah, looking at Kate. 'She's a nervous wreck. Oh!' She stood up abruptly. 'Paul!' she called, waving through the doorway. 'In here!'

'Oh, Sarah, honestly. Give it a rest,' murmured Tilly. 'Can't we just . . . ?' She glanced sharply at Birdie, still apparently paying no attention to anything but the book in her hand.

But Paul was in the room. He stood awkwardly in the doorway, shaking back his lank hair. 'I nearly didn't get in,' he complained to Kate. 'Your lift driver, or whatever he is, seemed to think I was from a newspaper or something. What's this about the old bloke? Jack? Someone said he was dead. That isn't right, is it?'

'Yes, it is,' said Tilly, her voice trembling with painful energy and aggravation.

Paul looked unnerved. 'Who did it?' he asked simply.

'We don't know,' said Kate, trying to look at no-one in particular. 'It could be anyone. Any one of us, I mean.'

'Of us!' Paul looked indignant.

Birdie cleared her throat and smiled lazily at Tilly. 'You look very tired, Tilly,' she said, with an air of changing the subject. 'You look as though you've hardly slept.'

'I haven't,' said Tilly, lifting her huge eyes to the ceiling and casting them down again. She shivered, and clutched her jacket more closely around her chest. 'I sleep so lightly anyway, and after what happened to Sylvia . . . I can't get over it.' She bent forward a little and shivered again.

'Mama!' Sarah patted her shoulder awkwardly, and Kate saw her worried eyes meet Paul's. For a moment their look held, and when she looked away, doubt and fear had gone.

'We'll go home, Sarah, as soon as we can. Kate'll fix it for us, won't you, Kate?' Tilly dabbed her mouth with the handkerchief clutched in her hand.

'I . . . I think I'll stay here for a while, mama,' said Sarah, holding herself very still.

Tilly twisted around to look at her. 'You're not serious?'

Sarah nodded. 'I know you want to go. But I want to stay for a while. I can stay at Paul's, can't I, Paul?' She appealed to him, and he nodded, unsmiling, watching Tilly.

'Well . . .' Tilly seemed nonplussed. She shook her head slowly. 'We'll talk about this later, sweetie, OK?''

''Yes. But I'm staying,' said Sarah childishly.

Tilly's lips tightened. 'Paul could be busy, you know, over the next couple of days.'

'Oh?' Paul drew himself up a little, and raised an insolent eyebrow. 'Why's that, Tilly?'

'Well, because, frankly, I'd say you're the perfect suspect for them, Paul. You had the terrible argument with Saul. You obviously don't like me. And since you seemed to have such a chip on your shoulder about Malcolm's Big Four idea, for all they know you could have taken your spleen out on Jack Sprott, too. You were in the park at the right time, as I understand it.'

'I was with your daughter. In the park, and at the party last night,' said Paul. 'And, if you want to know, most of the night before, as well.'

Sarah caught her lip between her teeth. Her pale cheeks flushed crimson. 'Just talking!' she blurted out, and covered her mouth with her hand.

'That's impossible!' cried Tilly. 'Sarah was asleep, in with me. I saw her there. I got up, I may as well tell you, to write Saul a note. I wanted him to . . . to tell everyone how they'd misunderstood what he said. About me, and him. I put it under his door and then I got back into bed and I just lay there, tossing and turning—'

'You didn't at all, mama. You didn't!' Sarah's voice was almost wondering. 'You're playacting, just like Saul Murdoch said you did. You weren't lying there awake! You got up and wrote that note and put it under his door. You came back and took your pills. And you went to sleep. You were fast asleep by midnight.'

'And snoring!' said Paul cruelly.

'Yes.' Even Sarah was a bit ashamed by this betrayal.

Tilly's cheeks were crimson. She stood up, pushing her chair back. 'How could you know that! Even if it were true!' she said.

'Because I told him,' cried Sarah, burning her boats. 'Because I checked, and you were sound asleep and snoring too, though not very loudly,' she added, biting her lips at the look on her mother's face. 'I went out and met Paul, you see, downstairs, like we'd arranged at dinner. I locked the door after me . . . I was away for hours, and you never knew!'

'You . . .' Tilly struggled to find words.

'Not that we were doing anything,' Sarah said loudly. 'I mean, anything wrong. We were talking. About my book, and his book, and other things. I gave him my manuscript. He said he wanted to read it. And he did read it, mama. He read it, and he liked it. He doesn't think it's a good try. He thinks it's *good*.' Again the dark blush stained her cheeks, and she ducked her head, and blundered out of the room.

'Paul, you didn't tell the police you were here on Monday night. You told them you were wandering around the streets,' said Kate, staring at him.

His face twitched, but he forced a smile. 'There seemed no need to confess, given that Sarah was involved. She was jittery, thinking, understandably,' he shot a look at Tilly who preserved a furious silence, '. . . that people might misunderstand. She wanted someone to talk to. So did I. There was nothing in it. She just slipped down and opened the door for me, and we sat in that front room, where the party was last

night, and spent a couple of hours, together, by ourselves, that's all.' He shrugged. 'It was no big deal.'

'It seems incredibly underhand to me,' said Tilly
icily. 'Sarah's a young, inexperienced girl, and you took
advantage of it. I think that's vile.'

Paul looked at her with dislike. 'I did not take advantage of Sarah in any way. And if it had been a
matter of taking advantage, I can only say that she was
so used to being pushed around, and people taking advantage of her, that you of all people shouldn't be surprised. And as for being young, she's no younger than
you were when you took up with that swine Murdoch,
as I recall.'

Tilly stood up. 'That was completely different,' she
hissed.

'Yes,' jeered Paul. 'Sarah isn't married.'

Tilly pushed her chair back and left the room, without another word.

Kate and Paul looked at one another. Birdie closed
the green book with a snap, and tossed it back on the
shelf.

'Well!' she exclaimed with relish. 'How about *that*!'

25

Truth Will Out

'Paul, you'll have to tell Toby about this,' said Kate at last. 'You should've done it before.'

'I will tell him. I told Sarah I would.' He looked strained and young now that Tilly had gone, and his anger had left him. His hands trembled and his sensitive mouth twitched. 'It wasn't important before, see, because everyone said Murdoch had suicided. And then when that woman went over the roof, I didn't really know whether I should say something or not. But now that Jack Sprott's been killed, I've got to . . .' His voice trailed off, and he looked at them helplessly.

'Did you see or hear anything while you were sitting downstairs?' asked Birdie calmly. She didn't seem too surprised by the revelations of the past few minutes.

He seized on the straight question with relief. 'That's just it,' he said. 'We thought we heard—well, we *did* hear—someone walk down the hall, and the front door open and close. We didn't see who it was. We were sitting in the front room, in the dark, with the door shut. We just sat very quietly. We were more concerned about being found ourselves, by whoever it was, than satisfying our curiosity.

Kate sat forward. 'Paul, that's terribly important! Birdie, we've got to tell Toby straight away!'

'What time would that have been, Paul?' Birdie was looking intent.

He wrinkled his forehead. 'It was dark, and I couldn't have seen my watch, even if I'd thought to look. But I guess we'd been there about forty minutes or so by then, and Sarah let me in about 12.30. We'd decided on twelve, but she'd heard someone, she thought, walking outside her room earlier, and she'd hung on a bit because of that, and to make sure her mother was really asleep.'

'So, going by that, it would have been about 1.15 or so, that you heard the person going out the front door,' said Birdie slowly. Her eyes were calculating behind her spectacles.

'I suppose so.'

'You didn't hear the lift, Paul?' asked Kate.

'No, no we didn't. We just heard the footsteps. Would we have heard the lift from there?'

'Oh, yes,' said Kate. 'It's terribly noisy. You'd easily have heard it, even with the door shut.'

'So whoever it was came down the stairs, presumably,' said Birdie, 'not wanting to advertise themselves by using the lift. Well, well. This is interesting.' But she looked rather grave.

'And you didn't see Jack, at all, did you, Paul?' asked Kate. 'They think he came downstairs sometime, and went into the kitchen.'

He shook his head, and then looked alert. 'While I was waiting for Sarah to let me in, I did see a light go on, somewhere at the back of the building, on the ground floor. I saw a glow through the curtains. I thought it was her, at first, come down early, but the light went off after about five minutes.'

'That must have been Jack. That fits.' Birdie half smiled. 'Lucky they missed each other, wasn't it? The two guilty consciences sneaking around in the dark.' She noticed his stony expression and controlled her own. 'What time did you leave, do you think?'

'About 2.30. I looked at my watch under the street-light outside, because I wanted to get some coffee, and I was wondering where I'd find a place open.'

'When do they think Saul Murdoch . . . ?' Kate bit her lip.

'Obviously, they can't pin it down exactly, and the post mortem isn't finished,' said Birdie. 'But they think it was between midnight and 2 a.m. when he took the stuff that killed him. He took it with wine from the fridge in his room. There were a few traces of the drug in the glass, but not in the bottle. It makes it difficult. Mind you, someone could have organised a drugged glass of wine earlier, for him to pick up and drink in the night, but that seems very unlikely to me. So chancy. And I don't see how anyone could have made him take all those pills. He would have had to be tricked into it.'

'They could have held a gun at his head,' suggested Kate.

Birdie shook her head. 'I can't see that happening. Not with the crew of people we're dealing with here.'

'Then it must have been someone he trusted, surely,' said Kate. 'Or someone he would talk to or wouldn't be scared of, anyway.'

'The same applies to Jack Sprott,' said Birdie slowly. 'Again, it must have been someone he was actually sitting with, or talking to, who could take advantage of him being drunk to push him over so he hit his head, and then roll him half into the creek.'

Kate shuddered. 'Maybe it was an accident,' she said desperately.

To her surprise, Birdie nodded. 'Could have been,' she said. 'Could have started out that way, anyway. But there's no doubt at all that he was deliberately shoved into the water, however he was put out to it originally. You can see the marks. It wouldn't have been hard to do. He was on a slope, very close to the water. Anyone could have done it. No special strength needed or anything.' She tightened her lips, and fell silent.

Paul stood up. 'I'm going to find the cops,' he said. 'They're with Quentin, apparently.' He flicked his hair back and gave Kate an anxious smile. 'I'll let you know how I get on—if they don't haul me off in a paddy wagon on the spot!'

'Oh, you've decided to give yourself up, have you, Paul?' Barbara Bendix grinned mischievously in the doorway. 'Sorry, couldn't help overhearing. What on earth's wrong with Tilly? I just saw her upstairs. She's cross as two sticks, muttering about being deceived and made a fool of to that poor daughter of hers. More worried about the fool part, of course. I had to know more, good little journo that I am. What *has* poor Sarah done?'

'Barbara, this isn't the time—' urged Kate.

'Oh, stop it,' cried Barbara. 'What's the point in being so priggish and discreet now, Kate? Absolutely everything's going to come out. You may as well let me in on it. It'll be handy for me, later.'

'You're a ghoul!' said Paul Morrisey, flushing to the roots of his hair.

Barbara looked at him coolly. 'That's a typical, elitist response,' she said. 'The fact is, however much you people want to deny it, more people read my books in one month than will read your sensitive little scribblings in a lifetime! And that's because people want to know the truth about public figures. They want to know what's behind all the PR flim flam and the servile interviews. They've got a right to know, whatever you and your kind think!'

Paul stared at her, his mouth twitching. 'I'll see you later, Kate,' he said, and pushing past Barbara he left the room. Barbara came in and sat down in the chair Tilly had vacated. She was heavily made up, and shimmering with energy.

'If it wasn't for books like mine, no-one would ever know how pathetic and false some of these absurd public figures are!' she said vehemently, fixing Kate with angry eyes. 'And why should they be allowed to get away with it? The Saul Murdochs, the Tilly Lightlys, the Jack Sprotts of this world, why shouldn't they be held to account?'

'It's their books that matter,' said Kate bravely.

Barbara leaned forward and her black eyes flashed. 'Jack Sprott didn't even write his own books any more,' she said with venom. 'You just kept turning them out for him, didn't you? He was a drunken old fraud.'

'He wasn't!' Kate's eyes began to fill with tears. 'He knew everything there was to know about plants and growing things. So we put a few calendars and things together for him—so what! There was no need for him to do much on those anyway, and all the information was from his books. So he didn't write any more—so what! Saul Murdoch hadn't written anything for years, either.'

'I know,' sneered Barbara. 'He was another has-been.'

'They'd both written what they had to write,' said Kate, suddenly calming down as the truth of what she was saying gave her confidence. 'They didn't have to prove a thing. They need not have written another word.'

'You're very gallant in the old boys' defence, Kate,' said Barbara lightly. 'Why is that, I wonder?' She looked at Kate with devastating inquisitiveness, then pounced. 'You're guilty!' she crowed.

Kate jumped. 'What do you . . . ?'

'You're guilty, because you knew, you must have known, what would happen when this Big Four thing came off. You must have known it would be a disaster. You and Evie were setting poor little Malcolm up. You sat back and let it all happen—bugger what it did to Saul, and old Jack. I saw you that first night, trying to get away from Jack as hard as you could wriggle. You could see what a pathetic old case he was then, without any trouble. Why pretend now? And now you're feeling guilty, because you let him be invited, because you exposed him to ridicule, because you didn't comfort him when he was miserable, or even read his bloody memoir and have the politeness and gumption to just reject it and put him out of his misery. Now he's drunk himself to a standstill and drowned himself in the creek! Well, feel guilty if you like, but don't take it out on me!'

Kate sat and looked at her in silence. There was nothing to say. She looked over to the pile of manuscripts lying waiting for her recommendation or rejection. Jack's battered, green book lay shabby and slim where Birdie had dropped it, topping the pile of plump, shiny folders, manila envelopes and bundles of quarto paper banded together with string. It would never be published now. That would have disappointed him.

Barbara's sharp gaze followed hers. She raised her eyebrows. 'I'd better let you get back to work,' she purred. 'You seemed rather behind with your reading.'

The phone rang. Kate picked it up wearily. It was Amy Phibes. 'Could you come up and see Quentin, please, Kate? Now, if possible, he said.' Her voice was very controlled.

'Sure. I'll be right there,' said Kate. She stood up gratefully. 'I have to go upstairs.'

Birdie slipped from her chair. 'I'm going that way,' she said brightly. 'I'll come with you.'

Barbara smiled sweetly at her. 'Still sniffing out a story, Verity? Surely you've got more than enough on Berry and Michaels by now.'

'Oh, every little bit helps,' said Birdie, in her most diffident voice. Barbara's eyes flickered over the shabby little figure, took in the jeans, the shirt, the pale, pointed face and the mass of brown hair tucked carelessly back behind her ears. She almost shook her head, but instead turned her smile to Kate.

'Would you mind if I used your phone while you're away, Kate? I have to make a few calls.' She opened her eyes wide. 'If you aren't too furious with me, darling,' she added challengingly.

'Go ahead, Barbara,' said Kate flatly. 'Whatever you like.' She got up and left her office, seething. Birdie followed.

'I could kill that woman, honestly!' Kate strode along the corridor towards the lift.

'Someone might save you the trouble, if the present pattern continues,' murmured Birdie at her shoulder. 'Here, slow down, will you?'

Kate stopped abruptly. 'Birdie, what do you think you're doing? Why are you shadowing me like this? Do you know something I don't?'

Birdie looked away. 'I'm not sure,' she said evasively. 'I think so. I've got to talk to Toby. If he's spoken to Morrisey . . .'

'Which he should have done by now,' said Kate. 'Well, if he has . . . what?'

'Well, he might feel ready to do something, that's all.'

'But Birdie, Paul couldn't have done it, nor could Sarah, because they were together at all the right times. They weren't lying. You could see that. And you aren't going to say they did it together, because that would be just ridiculous.'

'Stop putting words into my mouth. Of course that would be ridiculous.'

'Then—oh, you mean about someone coming down the stairs, the night Saul died? But that could have been anyone, really.'

'Well, not really anyone, if you think about it.'

Kate started walking again. 'Stop talking in riddles,' she said angrily. 'I've got to get upstairs.'

'I'm coming with you.'

'Birdie!'

But when Kate reached Amy's uncluttered corner, the pale green eyes registered no surprise at seeing she had a companion.

'You're both to go in,' she said indifferently.

For the second time in two days, Kate entered Quentin Hale's immaculate office. Again Dan Toby and Detective-constable Milson sat cushioned in pale grey leather at the end of the room.

Quentin was standing, looking out the window, across the park. He turned to face them as they came in. He looked very tall and strong, but his face wore the bewildered look of a hurt child.

'It seems, Kate, that we're nearly at the end of this,' he said. He crossed over to her, and put his hand on her shoulder. 'Sit down,' he said. 'And don't worry, or be concerned about anything else except the truth. Will you do that?'

Kate nodded and gripped her hands together to stop them shaking. What was happening here? She sat down in the armchair Quentin indicated. It was very deep and soft. She had to perch on the edge to keep her feet on the ground. Quentin and Birdie remained standing, Birdie leaning against the wall by the door, Quentin behind her chair. She felt his presence there, heavy and watchful. Dan Toby shifted in his seat, and nodded at her comfortably.

'Now, Miss Delaney, we've got a few questions for you. We think you can help us.'

'Me? But how? I don't . . .'

He smiled and raised his eyebrows, and Kate fell silent.

'You've worked for Berry and Michaels for ten years, I think, haven't you?' he began.

She nodded, watching him.

'It would have been a shock to you, and to the staff in general, when the company was taken over so suddenly and when Mr Hale, here, became the managing director, in place of Mr Brian Berry?'

Kate felt herself blushing. She was glad she couldn't see Quentin's face. 'Well, yes it was,' she admitted awkwardly.

He nodded, still smiling reassuringly. 'It'd be very natural for some of the longest-serving people to be upset, even angry, under the circumstances.' He waited.

'Yes, that's right,' said Kate. Honesty was the only way to go at this point, she thought.

'Now, Miss Delaney, Mr Hale says that the decision to bring Sir Saul Murdoch, Tilly Lightly, Jack Sprott and Barbara Bendix together this week was his, and that the idea was young Malcolm Pool's. He says he has a feeling you didn't approve. Is that so?'

Kate's heart thudded. 'Yes.'

'Why?'

Kate took a deep breath. 'It was because I didn't think those particular authors should be brought together, and into the limelight. Malcolm and Quentin didn't know what they were like.'

'And you did?'

'Well, more or less. I'd never actually met Saul Murdoch, but . . .'

'You knew him by reputation?'

'Yes.'

'And you knew that he and Tilly Lightly had had a relationship at one time, and weren't, shall we say, the best of friends?'

'I had heard that,' said Kate carefully.

'It wasn't generally known?' Toby was looking down, smoothing the blunt creases in his baggy grey trousers.

Kate shook her head. 'Only a few people here knew. Well, only Evie Newell and me, actually, by that time. It was just old gossip, you know.'

'And Saul Murdoch's rather rocky mental state—that wasn't generally known either?'

'Well, I assume some people outside knew about it,' said Kate defensively.

'But Mr Hale and Malcolm Pool wouldn't have known, necessarily,' prompted Toby.

Kate lifted her head. If she was going to get the sack she may as well say her piece properly. 'No,' she said. 'They wouldn't have known. Or about Jack Sprott having an alcohol problem, if that's going to be your next question. They wouldn't have known, as most people wouldn't have known, because Evie Newell, who is a superb publicist, though she mightn't look slick and vibey and all that, protected them and found ways of promoting their books without exposing them.'

Toby nodded calmly. 'So you and Miss Newell knew the situation, and you were to all intents and purposes the only ones who did. I gather from Mr Hale that Miss Newell also spoke up against Malcolm Pool's idea, when it was discussed at a meeting. But he says that after that one time she didn't mention the matter again.'

'No,' said Kate stoutly. 'Quentin had put Malcolm in full charge of the celebration, and asked Evie to assist him. Evie decided that under the circumstances she'd just . . . let things take their course.'

'And she persuaded you not to try to put a stop to it either.'

'I tried to warn Quentin, in the first place,' said Kate. She could feel her face burning, and looked out the window to avoid Toby's eyes, and the impassive face of Birdie, who was still standing by the door. 'But he wouldn't listen. To me or to Evie. And I was angry, I suppose, because of that. I've regretted it very much, since.' She heard Quentin give a sigh that was almost a groan, but couldn't bring herself to turn and look at him. She braced herself for the next question.

'Evie Newell has been with the company fifteen years, I think?'

'Yes. That's why she knew all this background. She was very close to Brian Berry.'

'She knew the four authors involved very well, and their books?'

'Well, of course.'

'When Sir Saul Murdoch died and Mr Hale decided to try to keep the matter quiet and go on with the celebration, did Miss Newell speak to you at all, about her reaction?'

Kate looked at him in confusion. She couldn't work out where this was all leading. 'She . . . she didn't approve,' she began slowly. 'She thought it should all be called off. She was surprised that he'd even consider going on with it.'

'She hadn't thought he would?'

'Well, no. I mean, no-one would, would they? I mean . . .' Kate bit her lip. This was getting worse and worse. 'Why are you asking me all this?' she exclaimed. 'You should ask Evie. She'd be much better able to tell you . . .'

'Oh, we'll get round to that, Miss Delaney,' said Toby calmly.

The phone rang. Kate still couldn't make herself turn around, but she heard the click as Quentin answered it.

'Thanks, Amy,' he said. 'Ask her to wait, will you?'

Toby looked at him over Kate's head and nodded with satisfaction.

'Well, I think we can let you get back to work now, Miss Delaney. I'd appreciate it if you wouldn't mention our conversation to anyone, for the moment.'

Kate stood up. 'Have . . . has Paul Morrisey spoken to you yet?' she asked hesitantly.

He smiled at her. 'Oh, yes,' he said. 'We had a few words with Mr Morrisey just before we called you up.'

'Oh.' Kate, still confused, turned to go, and found herself face to face with Quentin Hale. They stared at one another.

'I'm sorry,' she said. It was all she could think of to say. He returned her look gravely. 'I'm sorry, too,' he said. 'It was my fault. None of this need have happened. As it is . . .'

Toby cleared his throat warningly and after a quick glance in his direction Quentin guided Kate to the door. 'I'm coming with you,' he said. 'I . . . have some things to do upstairs.'

He opened the door and ushered Kate and Birdie through ahead of him. Evie was standing by Amy's desk. Her eyes were bright and she held a sheaf of papers in one hand. Kate hadn't seen her look so alive and intent since Brian Berry left. She looked mildly surprised to see Kate, and simply smiled at her briefly before moving to Quentin's side.

'Quentin, I have the statement here, if you'd like to . . .'

Quentin bent forward a little. 'Evie, I have to go upstairs for a minute,' he said gently. 'Could you just go in? I'll be down shortly.'

Silently she looked at him, and at Kate, and a slight frown crossed her face. Dan Toby appeared at the office door. 'Could you spare me a few minutes, Miss Newell? While you're waiting?' he said politely.

Evie looked once more at Kate, squared her shoulders, and followed him into the room. The door closed.

Quentin gave a sigh. 'So,' he said, 'that's that. What a bloody waste.'

Kate looked at him wildly. 'What do you mean?'

He put a hand on her arm. 'Come upstairs, Kate,' he said.

'We'll ask Dot to make us a cup of coffee. Verity will come too, won't you, Verity?'

Birdie nodded, and moved to Kate's other side. 'Come on, Laney,' she said gruffly. 'Let's get out of here.'

26

Revelations

'It all fitted, Kate.' Quentin looked morosely into his coffee cup. 'You just have to turn the thing around, and look at it from another angle, like Dan Toby did. From the end result, backwards.' He smiled briefly at her confusion. 'End result? I'm in a Godawful pickle. I can't believe that head office won't recall me. And who wanted that more than Evie.'

'But that . . . that's not proof.'

'No, of course it isn't, Kate,' said Birdie quietly. 'But there were other things. Evie had a key to the building, so she could have let herself in after all the others were upstairs after dinner on that first night. She knew Saul well enough for him to just let her into his room, and to sit talking to her quite calmly. She was the only one who did. Plenty of opportunity to doctor his drink. Then she could have simply gone down the stairs and let herself out, unheard by anyone. Except that Paul and Sarah were sitting in the dark in the front room, but she wouldn't know that. Then, she was with Jack Sprott in the park, wasn't she? Again, he would have been quite happy to sit and talk to her. She says he gave her the slip, but we only have her word for that, when you come to think about it. She was late back to the rendezvous point, half an hour late, according to Tilly and Amy. And . . . well, she could have easily slipped upstairs on the night of the party to dispatch someone she took to be Tilly Lightly.'

'Birdie, this is . . . I can't believe it. It can't be true!' Kate was shaking. The coffee cup rattled in its saucer, and she tried to steady it without success.

'I don't think it can be true, either,' said Dorothy Hale surprisingly. 'And what's more, I don't believe the police will ever prove it is. Not unless and until Evie actually confesses. Which I'm sure she won't do.'

'Dot!'

'Well, Quentin, it's the truth,' cried Dorothy, her voice trembling. 'Australian courts can't be all that different to English courts, can they? I know what I'm talking about. When the evidence is circumstantial like this, they need a confession to prove guilt beyond reasonable doubt. A jury wouldn't convict.'

'They've been known to,' observed Birdie.

'Yes,' Kate agreed, thinking of some celebrated cases of recent memory. But she eyed Dorothy uneasily. Why was she so certain of her ground? And then she remembered. Of course, Quentin, and presumably Dorothy, had been somehow connected with a scandal involving a violent crime, in England. She still remembered the spiteful glee with which Evie had told her about it. It was one of the reasons Quentin wasn't 'quite quite', as far as the old school ties who ran the Gold Group were concerned.

'Well, I don't see how any jury could convict, in this case, without a confession,' cried Dorothy hastily. 'You know yourself, Quentin, that if Daphne hadn't said she'd done it they'd never have . . .'

'Dot!' Quentin's warning cry penetrated her self-absorption. Her hand flew to her mouth.

Quentin shook his head hopelessly. 'I'd rather this went no further, Kate—and Verity,' he said heavily. 'But just to put the record straight, Dorothy's sister, Daphne, was involved in a tragic accident, a few years ago. She—'

'She killed her husband.' Dorothy's blue eyes were fixed on his. 'He was a brutal man. He deserved ev-

erything he got. He was a violent, drunken beast, who
terrorised Daphne for years. It wasn't an accident,
Quentin, what's the point of lying about it? It was all
over the papers at home. They could look it up and
find out. It's amazing they don't already know. And
why be ashamed of it? Any woman would have done
the same.' She looked directly at Kate. 'He'd started
on their daughter,' she said flatly. 'He came home
drunk and started ordering her around, and when she
stood up to him he knocked her down. She was just
eighteen. He'd always left her alone before but I suppose poor Daphne wasn't much sport for him any
more. She was so cowed and terrified. Well, the worm
turned at last. He went to sleep that night and he never
woke up. He never woke up. In the morning Daphne
rang the police, and then she rang me. She said, "He's
dead, Dot," just like that. And by the time I got there
the police were there too, and he was dead in bed with
the kitchen knife through his chest. He'd been dead
for hours. And Daphne was saying over and over, "I
did it. I did it. I killed him." Like a gramophone record.' Her shoulders slumped, and the faded blue eyes
stared unseeingly at the floor.

'What happened to her?' whispered Kate.

'She was found not guilty of murder,' said Quentin
heavily. 'They said she'd killed him while of unsound
mind.'

'They sent her to an asylum,' whispered Dorothy.
'They said she was getting better. Then she killed herself. Killed herself. Poor, beautiful Daphne.'

Quentin put his hand on her shoulder. 'That's
enough, Dot,' he said gently. He looked at Kate and
Birdie almost pleadingly.

Kate nodded and stood up. 'We'd better go, Dorothy,' she murmured. 'I'm . . . I'm sorry about all this.
That you've been reminded. Sorry you had to go
through it. It must have been . . .'

Dorothy looked up at her with swimming eyes. 'No,'
she said in such a low voice that Kate had to bend
down to catch her words. 'It's good to talk about it

sometimes. It's harder, really, being out here, away from the family, and people who know. It's a terrible strain. I thought it would be better for us to be away, but I don't think so, now. When they send us home it'll be easier. Better. When we're home again.' She took a deep breath and tried to smile.

'I should be the one apologising, Kate,' she said. 'Carrying on like this. But listen,' she leaned forward, 'don't worry about your friend. She'll be all right. There are lots of other people who could have done it.'

'Well, we'll see,' boomed Quentin, with a terrible, assumed heartiness. 'Maybe next they'll be saying I've done it, Kate, or you!' He clapped his hand on Kate's shoulder, and began guiding her to the lift. Dorothy followed with Birdie.

'At least we'll be spared that,' she said, trying hard. 'You two were both sitting working like beavers in your little boxes, all afternoon while the others were in the park, weren't you? I can be witness to that!'

Quentin laughed stiffly, and glanced at the others. He stabbed impatiently at the lift button. The gold arrow began to move.

Dorothy put her hand to her forehead. 'Yes, well, I'll go and have a little rest, I think. Goodbye, Kate. Goodbye . . . ah . . .' She smiled at Birdie hesitantly and wandered off towards the bedroom.

The lift doors opened. Dan Toby and Detective-constable Milson stepped out, almost colliding with Birdie and Kate, preparing to step in. They untangled themselves with mutual apologies and stood eyeing one another. Finally, pulling himself together, Toby nodded formally at Quentin standing frowning in the background.

'Sorry for coming unannounced, but we've finished downstairs for the moment, sir,' he said.

'Is Evie arrested?' Kate asked the question with lips that seemed stiff. It was hard to articulate.

'No, no, nothing like that yet. She's been helping

us, certainly, but we've laid no charges.' Toby smiled imperturbably. Milson's lip curled.

'Oh, I'd thought . . .' Quentin hesitated. 'I mean, I'm glad, for Evie, but . . . I was totally convinced. It seemed to me she was the only one who—well—hated me enough to want to drive me away, back to England.'

'Are you sure?' Birdie spoke to Quentin, but her amber eyes behind the thick spectacles were fixed on Toby, as though she was trying to convince him of something. 'Are you sure it's a matter of someone hating you, Quentin?'

They all looked at her. Quentin puzzled, Toby impatient, Milson positively sneering. 'Well,' said Milson coldly, 'it would hardly be a matter of someone *loving* Mr Hale, would it?'

Birdie ignored him and again spoke to Quentin and Toby. 'I was just thinking logically about the question,' she said loftily, 'and it seemed to me that if someone wanted Quentin out of the way, and wasn't averse to a spot of murder, the simplest thing for them to do would be to kill him, and have done with it. Why kill three people, when one would have done?'

A baffled look crossed Quentin's face. He blinked, and brushed the back of his hand over his eyes and forehead. Slowly he turned to Toby. 'I hadn't thought of that,' he said slowly.

Toby was impassive, but Kate suspected the thoughts that were racing behind his placid brow. 'That's one way of looking at it, of course,' he rumbled.

Milson frowned and poked his head at Birdie in that rather offensive way he had. 'When it comes to murder, Miss Birdwood, you'll find people aren't as conveniently logical as you seem to think. Impulse and opportunity play an important part, especially linked with strong motive. It may simply have been easier to get to the people who were killed, than to Mr Hale. Mr Hale, after all, has rarely been alone over the past few days. His wife has been with him at night, his secretary right outside his door during the day. He has been well guarded.'

'He was alone yesterday, during the afternoon,' Kate pointed out, irritated. 'Amy was in the park, and so was Dorothy. Anyone could have got to him then.'

Quentin made a convulsive movement, instantly controlled.

Toby ignored him, and looked at Kate with interest. 'Was Mrs Hale in the park?' he asked lazily. 'Dear, oh dear, I'm getting confused. I don't remember that from the notes, do you, Milson?'

'No,' said Milson sharply. 'Mr Hale stated that Mrs Hale did not go to lunch, or to the park, because she had some errands to do in the city. She confirmed this.'

'That's quite right,' barked Quentin. He didn't look at Kate, who felt her cheeks begin to burn.

Toby crinkled his eyes at her. 'Why did you think Mrs Hale was in the park, Kate?' he enquired.

She squirmed, not even noticing that he was using her first name. She opened her mouth to speak, but couldn't.

Birdie spoke crisply. 'I think Kate assumed it because Mrs Hale said a few minutes ago that she could be a witness to the fact that her husband and Kate were both working in their offices yesterday afternoon. Kate knows Mrs Hale often goes to the park in the afternoon, and usually sits where she can see into the Berry and Michaels windows. She assumed that's what happened yesterday. A fair assumption.'

'Rubbish!' Quentin Hale was obviously furious, angrier than Kate had ever seen him. Involuntarily she took a step back.

'I think I should speak to your wife now, to clear the matter up, don't you agree, sir?' Toby was very courteous but firm.

'No I bloody don't!' snapped Quentin. 'Dorothy is resting, and I won't disturb her. What possible relevance can it have?'

'Everything has relevance, sir,' said Milson coldly.

'Thanks, Milson. Just leave this to me, will you?'

Toby didn't take his eyes off Quentin's face. 'Please call Mrs Hale, sir. I'd appreciate it.'

'I'm here!' They turned, and saw Dorothy walking slowly towards them from the bedroom. She had changed into a pink-flowered dressing gown and pink slippers and looked small, faded and vulnerable. 'What's the matter?' she asked.

'Dot, go back to bed, love,' urged Quentin, but she stayed where she was, staring at the group by the lift, blinking anxiously.

'Mrs Hale, you were in the park yesterday afternoon, weren't you?' Toby spoke gently.

'I . . .' Dorothy's blue eyes were wide and frightened. She was like a rabbit caught in a shooter's spotlight, thought Kate, feeling disturbed and almost revolted by Toby's slow persistence, Milson's cold attention and Birdie's avid interest, all focused on this defenceless creature.

Not quite defenceless, though. Quentin stepped between his wife and the enemy, and took her arm. 'Back to bed, Dot,' he said casually, as if they were alone.

'Mrs Hale!' Toby raised his voice just enough to penetrate the barrier Quentin had set around her by his nearness. She jerked her head and looked at him.

'You were there, Mrs Hale, weren't you,' he repeated. A statement, not a question.

'Yes,' she whispered, and her eyes welled over with easy tears. 'Quentin, I'm sorry. I'm so sorry.'

'Dot, for God's sake!' Quentin glanced horrified at Milson, writing busily in his brown-covered notebook.

'I . . . I haven't been all that well, Quentin.' The blue eyes were pleading. 'You know, I told you—I hate it here. I told you, but you wouldn't listen, Quentin. It would be better, so much better, at home.' The tears trickled down Dorothy's soft cheeks, and she tried to rub them away with her fingers. 'I couldn't stand those—people—anymore. I couldn't stand the strain. Oh, I've let you down, Quentin. I've brought you such trouble, and you've stood by us and now . . .'

Kate gripped Birdie's arm. She remembered her

quiet question, *Are you sure it's a matter of someone hating you, Quentin?* and Milson's sneering reply, *It would hardly be a matter of someone loving Mr Hale, would it?* She looked at Dorothy's soft, faded face, and Quentin's flushed, stern one, and saw between them the smooth white and gold image of Amy Phibes, pale green eyes cold and blank. She saw Dorothy, dumpy in powder blue, on that first night, staring across the room—at Amy, and talking to Jack Sprott, about women fighting for what they loved, as desperately as men fought in war.

Birdie gently disengaged her arm and stepped forward. She looked insignificant enough beside the towering, be-suited men, and her thick glasses gave her an owlish look. But the strange amber eyes were clear and intent, and she gave no sign of being anything other than completely self-possessed.

'If you don't mind my interrupting,' she said clearly, 'could I just say that I think we could be taking what Dorothy is saying a little too seriously. She—'

'Birdie, be quiet, please.' Toby was very cold. He turned to Dorothy Hale, trembling like a fluffed-up sparrow in her flowered dressing gown, and spoke gently.

'You wanted to return to England, Mrs Hale. Very much.'

She nodded.

He hesitated. 'Would I be right in thinking,' he said, choosing his words, 'that some of the strain you have been under over the past months has been because of Miss Amy Phibes.'

Quentin Hale literally jumped. His wife gasped, and colour suffused her face. She licked her dry lips.

'I . . . I don't know what you mean,' she said.

'Well, I think you might, Mrs Hale.' Toby looked at her almost pityingly. 'I was thinking that part of your reason for wanting to remove your husband from Australia might have been to bring to an end a relationship you felt was, perhaps, closer than it should be, with Miss Phibes.'

'What!' Quentin Hale rounded on Toby, incredulous rage vivid on his face. 'What in God's name do you think . . . ? The girl's my—'

'Quentin!' Dorothy clutched anxiously at his arm.

'No, Dorothy! This has gone far enough! Love, don't you realise what's happening? What he's saying? He's hinting you might have killed people! To get me sacked and sent back home. He's saying,' fiercely he spoke directly to Kate, 'he's saying this, about Amy, because . . . that's what people are saying round the bloody office. That's it, isn't it?'

Kate looked at him steadily. She couldn't look at Dorothy. 'Yes,' she said awkwardly. 'People think you are close.'

'Close!' he laughed wildly. 'Close! We're close all right. And do you know why?'

Dorothy held up her hands to stop him, but he ignored her. 'For your information, Kate, and for the information of all your grubby-minded little colleagues, Amy is Dorothy's niece—her sister's daughter. You've heard about her. Her father was a violent bully, her mother stuck him with a kitchen knife and died in a bloody madhouse, and Amy was left to us, to try to give her some sort of life. We thought—a new country, a new chance. *Her* picture had never been published. She'd been kept right out of it. She followed us out here and she came to work for me. Why?' He glared defiantly at Toby. 'Because she couldn't get a bloody work permit, couldn't get residency, in this God-forsaken place. So we had to have her here, and keep it quiet so buggers like you wouldn't turn up and bloody deport her. And Dorothy,' he put his arm around his wife, and drew her against him, 'Dorothy, who apologises, who says she failed me because she couldn't bring herself to sit down to lunch with a mob of squabbling egomaniacs, Dorothy, who you seem now, like lunatics, to be suspecting of murder, has been going through hell, like Amy, *with* Amy, whenever a copper puts his nose near the girl who she loves like her own daughter, and who she's supported and propped up on the quiet all this time, like she's supported and propped me up—always!'

He looked at them all, breathing heavily. 'Please go away, now,' he said. 'Just go away.'

27

Paperwork

In the lift, Birdie looked at her toes and whistled tunelessly to herself. 'If that's your way of saying "I told
you so", Birdwood,' said Toby, 'I'll thank you to put
a sock in it. I wouldn't forget I'm twice your size, if I
were you!'

Birdie looked at him thoughtfully. Milson straightened his tie. 'We may still be on the right track, in my
view,' he said. 'Hale put on a good show, and presumably we were on the wrong track as regards the girl.
But nevertheless . . .'

'There's no nevertheless about it, Milson,' said Toby
heavily. 'We got—I got, I admit it—carried away by
the fact that the lady told a little white lie. Look, I
know the truth when I hear it, and so do you, surely,
after all this time. All that woman was worried about
was her husband knowing she'd skived off lunch, and
then that we'd find out about the girl and tell Immigration. She's a bundle of nerves all right, but she
never killed anyone.' He ran his hand over tired eyes
as the lift stopped at the second floor. 'I'm buggered!'
he said, to no-one in particular. 'Milson, we'll see a
few more people and then move out for a while, back
to the station. We'll go through the notes and reports
a-bloody-gain. I'll find a rhyme or reason for this business if it's the last thing I do.' He paused, then stepped

out of the lift. 'If there *is* a bloody rhyme or reason,' he growled.

'Oh, there is,' chirped Birdie brightly. 'There is, and I'm starting to see it. In fact, I think I've got it!'

'You do, do you?' said Toby slowly.

'Yeah,' she grinned challengingly. 'Wanna hear it?'

'No!' he bellowed.

The lift doors shut on his indignant face. Birdie stuck her hands in her pockets, leaned against the wall and smirked at Kate.

Kate sighed. 'I suppose it's useless asking what you meant by that.'

'Useless. I mean, look, I could still be wrong!'

'Nice of you to admit it. And sensible, since you've been wrong twice today already!'

The lift doors opened on the editorial floor. Birdie stepped out looking injured. 'I wasn't wrong, if you don't mind! It was Toby. I admit I'd wondered about Evie, very reasonably. But by the time Toby was all geared up about her I'd started to have my doubts. She knew Tilly and Sylvia de Groot really well, for example. I couldn't imagine her mixing them up for long enough to manhandle Sylvia over the ledge.'

'And . . .' Kate hesitated. She didn't want to say anything that might bring Evie under suspicion again, but she had to know. 'You don't think that Sylvia was killed *as* Sylvia, as the royalties manager, for example, or a witness, maybe, to what happened to Saul, or Jack?'

Birdie shook her head. 'No,' she said. 'I can tell you that much. Sylvia died because she was unlucky, because she was Tilly Lightly's build, because she was wearing Tilly's shawl, because she went up to the roof, in the dark. She didn't die because she knew something. She didn't know anything.' She clenched her fists slightly. 'It's Sylvia de Groot I'm angry about,' she muttered.

Kate looked at her in surprise. Birdie, faced with murder, could be worried, tense, curious, absorbed, enthusiastic—a whole range of things. But anger? That was something new. She wondered.

They walked in silence past the bank of editorial files. In the locked archive beyond, every book Berry and Michaels had published sat in its original jacket, and the oldest, most precious files lay in rows of fire-proof cabinets, waiting their turn for a dogged re-searcher's eye, a solicitor's copyright investigation.

Birdie paused. 'I think I'll stop here and do some work,' she said unexpectedly.

Kate stopped with her. 'You never thought it was Dorothy?'

'No!' Birdie was contemptuous. 'I don't know what Toby was thinking about! Well, he wasn't thinking, that's the point!'

'But you said yourself it wasn't necessarily a ques-tion of someone hating Quentin, didn't you?'

'Well, it's not! Look, where's the file queen—Betty, or whatever her name is? Could you find her for me? I have to get to work. I might need the archive as well as the more recent files.'

'OK, OK!' Kate walked back to her office rather crossly. Sometimes Birdie could be pretty hard to take.

Betty was nowhere to be seen. Not in the kitchen, or the ladies, or in any of the rooms Kate passed on her abbreviated circuit. Still feeling put out, she walked back to her own office with the cup of tea she'd made herself.

Mary was at her post, looking harassed. 'Oh, you're back!' she observed rather shortly. 'Where've you been?'

Kate stared at her. 'Where've you been?' she re-torted. 'You could've shot a gun through here when I came in!'

'That'll be next, I suppose,' retorted Mary, grimly shuffling papers. 'First the authors, then the staff. Sounds logical!' She looked up, and their frightened eyes met. 'Sorry,' they both said together. Mary cleared her throat.

'Tilly Lightly's rung from her room a couple of

times, Kate. She wants to know what arrangements you've made to fly her home. She says you promised.'

'I didn't. I'll ask Evie about it, if she's there. Oh, and could you try to find Betty? There's someone who wants to use the archive.'

Kate went into her office and shut the door. She needed to think. Or think rationally, more to the point. She should ring Evie first. Tell her the heat was off. Or did she know that already? Tell her about Tilly, wanting to get home, panicking up there in the guest apartment with only Sarah for company, and Barbara Bendix in the next room, working, with Malcolm as bodyguard. Working! How anyone could! She was superb, Barbara, like that. Kate sat at her desk. The papers had been slightly disturbed. She frowned, and then remembered that Barbara had made some calls from her phone earlier this morning. She'd straightened papers as she'd talked. She was an organised person, for all her vivacious carry-on. Must be, to produce the books she did, because for all their sensationalism, and racy style, and Barbara's glamorous public persona, they were based on very solid research.

Kate lifted the phone and dialled Evie's number. 'It's me,' she said quietly, as Evie answered. 'You OK?'

'Oh, yes.' Evie sounded exhausted, but her voice was quite steady. 'I've got the heebies, though. Where've you been? I've been trying to ring you. I think that policeman, Toby, thinks I killed Saul and the others. He kept asking—'

'Evie, he doesn't think so,' interrupted Kate. 'At least, he might've but I think he's gone off the idea now. I've just seen him.'

Evie's sigh hissed through the phone. 'God, I don't know,' she said. 'I feel . . . I don't know . . . this is frightful, Kate! When Saul was found I sort of just assumed he'd done it himself. It seemed so likely. But the others, Jack! And I feel . . . I seem to have only just realised, Kate, that someone's *killing* people. Someone here. Who?'

'I don't know, Evie!' exclaimed Kate.

'Toby says it's someone who hates Quentin.' The voice was flat and tired. 'That means . . .'

'Birdie says he's wrong,' Kate said quickly.

Evie snorted. 'How would she know? My God, it seems years since Hale started here, years, and it's only been a couple of months. I really wonder . . .'

Kate's attention wandered as Evie's voice fell into a familiar drone of complaint. She didn't feel like hearing criticism of Quentin Hale right now. Everything was in turmoil. There was so much work to be done. So much time had been wasted over the last few days. She had to pull herself together. Her eyes wandered despairingly over the piles of letters to be answered, reports to be read, manuscripts to be accepted or rejected. Again she heard Barbara's jibe, *a bit behind in your reading, eh?* Her brow wrinkled. She had a feeling there was something she'd forgotten. Or something not quite right in the familiar scene.

'Are you there?' Evie's voice had risen impatiently.

'Oh, yes—'

'Well, answer me. Will you tell Tilly, or will I?'

'What?'

'Oh, Kate, you *weren't* listening! That she can't go home yet. But she can go to a hotel if she wants to.'

'She will.'

'Of course she will. If she's got any sense! More money spent! Hale'll send this place broke before he's finished.'

'Hmm. We'll have to pay for Sarah too, of course. And Barbara.'

Evie laughed nastily. 'Barbara's not yelping, not yet, anyway. She's got other things on her mind. I rang her. She says she's working happily up there. Well, we all know what that means!'

'What?' Kate was puzzled, and for a moment gave the phone her full attention.

'For goodness' sake, you're an innocent! Look, I've got to go. I'll catch up with you later. Take care.'

'You too.' Kate put the phone down and put her head in her hands. This was all too hard. She remembered her tea and began to drink it, looking out the window.

Out in the park, the morning shadows had disappeared. Again the sky was relentlessly clear and blue. The trees and shrubs clustering thickly around the path of the stream hid the place where Jack Sprott had been found. Hid, too, the cordon the police had thrown up to protect the area and the clues to the murderer's identity that might yet be lying hidden in the earth and the undergrowth.

Jolly Jack Sprott. Kate remembered his high spirits on that first night. How he'd scandalised everyone. She almost smiled at the recollection of Malcolm Pool's face, frozen with a mixture of embarrassment, horror, panic and baffled rage as he saw all his finely-woven plans for triumph unravelling and collapsing before his eyes. Poor Malcolm, you could almost feel sorry for him if he hadn't been so ruthless and underhand in his dealings with Evie. But that night she'd had her revenge. Jack drunk, Tilly and Barbara sparring, Saul raving about exposing them to the press. How Malcolm must have panicked and dreaded the coming of the morning and that particular humiliation.

People were walking in the park, now. Kate watched them idly, as she'd done the day before. Then she'd seen the authors and their minders wandering on the green. Now—she leaned forward and squinted against the sunlight—yes, Sarah Lightly and Paul Morrisey walked close together down one of the paths, deep in conversation. So Sarah had abandoned Tilly yet again. Kate frowned. That, actually, wasn't such a good idea, just at the moment. After all, there was a killer at large.

Still, Kate thought, Malcolm's up there with Barbara so . . . Strangely, the thought stuck in her mind. And the longer it stayed there, the less reassuring it became. She put her cup of tea down carefully, and tried to push the thought away but it wouldn't go. She hesitated, then quickly picked up the phone and rang a number.

The ring sounded hollowly on the empty line. She

found she was gripping the receiver with a damp hand, and looked at it almost in surprise, jumping as the phone clicked and Barbara's voice barked a greeting.

'Hello? Who is this? Hello?'

'Oh,' Kate found her voice at last, 'Barbara, it's Kate Delaney here. I—um—I was just checking that you were OK.'

'Oh yes?' Barbara sounded amused. 'Checking I was still alive and kicking, were you? How thoughtful.'

'Barbara, is Malcolm there?'

'No, he's not, Kate. He was here, but he had to go off and do something or other for Evie.'

'Oh, right. You're OK, anyway?' Kate felt a fool. Now all she wanted was to end this conversation.

'So far, yes. Only getting peckish. When's lunch?'

'I don't know. Evie will. She'll give you a ring.'

'Right ho!'

'Well, OK, I'll go then, Barbara.'

'Wait on, would you like to speak to Tilly? Check she's still casting a shadow, as they say? You can kill two birds with one stone that way. Oh, sorry, unfortunate phrase.'

'Tilly's with you?'

Barbara gurgled with laughter. 'Fear of death makes strange bedfellows, Kate. Speaking metaphorically, of course. Sarah abandoned Tilly, Malcolm abandoned me, so we joined forces. Despite the copper in the corridor, we're feeling a bit edgy. Hold on.'

'Kate?' Tilly's voice shook slightly. Kate's lip curled. After Barbara's breezy exuberance Tilly's melodramatics were even more repellent than usual. She could make a bit of an effort!

'Hello, Tilly, just rang to see all was well,' she said heartily.

'Oh yes.'

'They'll be organising lunch soon.'

'Right. Right. That'll be nice.'

Kate relented. The woman was a pain all right, but after all, the experience she'd had over the past few days would shake anyone's nerve. Barbara was the odd one, really. 'Tilly, would you like me to send someone to get Sarah for you? She's in the park. It wouldn't take—'

'No!' The word cracked in Kate's ear, making her jerk away from the receiver. Then, hastily, Tilly spoke again, more quietly. 'No, thanks, Kate. I'm fine. Really. Let Sarah have her walk.'

Kate shrugged. Well, at least she'd offered. 'All right. Well, I'll go, Tilly. I may see you at lunch, OK?'

'Yes, OK.'

The phone went dead. Kate clicked her tongue. She hated people who hung up in your ear like that. She realised that she'd forgotten to tell Tilly she could move to a hotel. Still, she'd find out at lunch. Strange she hadn't asked again about going home. It wasn't like her to miss an opportunity to nag.

Kate looked at her watch and sighed. She had an hour, maybe, till she was called for lunch. She seized a bundle of papers from her in-tray, and plunged, with relief, into the oblivion of paperwork.

28

Birdie Pulls Strings

'Sandwiches and coffee upstairs, Quentin's flat, fifteen minutes!' Birdie's dry voice penetrated Kate's pleasurable, if guilty, immersion in a charming, unpublishable manuscript about an old farmer and his accident-prone duckling and other assorted animals.

Kate looked up. Birdie's eyes were sparkling gold behind the thick spectacles, and her face wore the sharpened, alert look of anticipation that meant things were moving, and moving her way.

'I wouldn't have thought Quentin would feel like entertaining,' she said carefully.

She wrote 'No' on *Quacking Up in Mossy Ridge* and slid it on the reject pile. She saw the author's name, Ninish, on the outside of the folder. Mr Ninish had called to see her yesterday. How long, long ago that seemed now.

'Toby persuaded him,' said Birdie cheerfully, and looked around the cluttered office with a superior smile.

'Oh, you two have made up, have you? What have you got up your sleeve? Who's going to lunch?'

'You, me, Quentin and Dorothy, of course, Amy, Malcolm, Evie, Tilly, Sarah and Paul, Barbara, Dan and the unpleasant Milson. It should be . . .' Birdie's voice trailed off. She bounded into the room, her pose of casual omniscience abandoned.

'Kate, has anyone been in here this morning? Alone? Except you?'

Kate looked at her blankly. 'Mary, I suppose. And Barbara Bendix used my phone for a while, when I went upstairs. I don't know of anyone else, but anyone could. Why?'

'Doesn't matter.' Birdie was at the door again, her face anxious. 'I've got to go.' She disappeared, and Kate heard her feet thudding on the carpet as she rushed away.

Fifteen minutes later Kate presented herself as bidden at Quentin's unlikely luncheon party. Only Tilly, Dorothy, Amy and Malcolm Pool were there.

'Hello, all!' Kate's attempted social cheer was speedily punctured by Tilly's wan nod, Malcolm's abstraction and Dorothy's tremulous manner. Amy, standing by the window, hadn't even turned her head.

Kate looked at her watch selfconsciously.

'You're right on time, Kate,' said Tilly. 'No-one else is here yet. Malcolm brought me up far too early it seems. Dorothy wasn't even ready.' She looked at Malcolm accusingly.

Dorothy mumbled a half-hearted disclaimer. Malcolm shifted uncomfortably in his deep chair. He still had that slightly hunted, dishevelled look Kate had noticed over the last few days. It was an extraordinary transformation, really, Kate thought. Brash, bumptious, self-confident Malcolm Pool. Recent events had shaken him, it seemed, to his core, made him vulnerable. Made him far more likeable, too. Even his eyes had lost that over-alert predatory look.

'Where's Barbara?' she said to Tilly. 'I thought you two were sticking together.'

Tilly shrugged. 'I had to go down to the art department to talk to David. I had to talk to him before I left. The policeman in our corridor kindly escorted me. Malcolm came and picked me up from there, and we came straight up. I don't know where Barbara is.' She paused for a moment, and hunched her thin shoulders. 'I hope all's well,' she said at last. 'I mean . . .' she fell silent.

Kate felt a flutter in her stomach, and saw Malcolm's eyes widen.

'Here comes the lift now,' said Dorothy hopefully. 'That'll be her, surely. She'll be with the others.'

They watched the arrow move and come to a stop. The doors opened, and a crowd of people stepped out into the room—Evie, Quentin, Birdie, Sarah and Paul, Milson and Toby. No Barbara.

There was silence in the room.

'Where's Barbara?' said Kate. Her voice sounded odd, as though someone else was speaking. She swallowed and tried again. 'Barbara isn't here.'

Toby looked around, a slight furrow in his brow. He looked at his watch and his frown deepened.

There was a breathless silence, broken by a thunderous knock and a muffled shout from the firestair door.

Quentin reached it in two strides, and opened it. Barbara, resplendent in black and white stripes, and striped hoop earrings, with a huge red handbag over one shoulder, almost fell into the room, followed by Sid, who was resentfully balancing a large platter of sandwiches on his heaving chest.

'I met the food on the way up the stairs,' she hooted. 'Poor Sid is nearly expiring. Quentin, you've got these people scared to death of you, darling. He came all the way up on foot because he was scared of being late, and the lift was tied up!'

Sid shot her an unfriendly glance but said nothing. He set his tray down in the kitchen and removed himself from the flat as rapidly as was humanly possible.

Barbara plumped herself down on the couch opposite Tilly, who ignored her. She grinned mischievously around the silent group.

'This is all a bit funereal, isn't it? What's up? Lunch, I hope! Sarah, I *love* that T-shirt!'

Dan Toby cleared his throat and stepped forward.

'Now we're all here,' he said, rather ponderously, 'I'd like to say a few words. Our investigation has moved along somewhat, and—'

'Look, I'm terribly sorry to interrupt,' said Barbara, without a trace of sorrow on her face, 'but would it be possible to have a drink? I'm absolutely dying for one . . . dying for one!' she laughed.

'Barbara!' said Evie automatically.

'Of course, Barbara.' Quentin moved towards the kitchen, glad, perhaps, of something to do.

'Whisky and soda, please.'

'Right. Tilly? Drink?'

'Oh!' Tilly shrugged and shivered, hunching her shoulders inside her thin jacket. 'Oh, nothing, anything—whatever everyone else is having,' she babbled. Then she bit her lip and visibly pulled herself together. 'Whisky and soda will be fine, thanks,' she said.

Toby stood, almost tapping his foot while orders were taken and delivered. Barbara ignored him completely, jumping up, insisting on helping, spilling drinks, mixing up orders and generally playing the fool. She was in high spirits for some reason, thought Kate, and her good humour was strangely infectious, subtly lightening the atmosphere. Finally she took her place again, clattering Tilly's drink and her own on to the coffee table with a flourish, and leaning back to grin at Toby's sour expression.

Kate found herself smiling too. Thanks to Barbara's antics a lot of people were looking more relaxed now, despite the situation. But Toby was remorselessly sober, and his eyes were watchful. And true to form Tilly's little pinched mouth was turned down at the corners and she gazed at Barbara from her corner of the couch, clutching her drink and the inevitable balled-up handkerchief to her narrow chest, as though Barbara was some sort of monster of insensitivity who might attack her personally at any moment.

Again Toby cleared his throat. He had refused a drink, and a chair, and now stood rocking, heels to toes, toes to heels, his hands clasped before him. Kate

felt a stab of fearful excitement in her chest. She looked
round for Birdie. There she was, slouched on a chair
by the wall. Almost certainly she knew what Toby was
going to say. Almost certainly it had something to do
with her mysterious comings and goings of this morning. But she was giving nothing away, and if Toby was
her puppet, operated by remote control, he gave no
sign of it. He looked very solid, very official, and very
serious.

'I have asked you to be here, all of you,' he began,
'to tell you that I believe I now know the person responsible for the tragedies that have occurred. I know
who was responsible, and I know the reason behind
the killings.' Someone in the room sighed. Kate
thought it was Dorothy Hale. Barbara, with a toss of
her head, finished her whisky in a gulp, belched and
raised an eyebrow at Tilly.

'Drink up, Tilly,' she whispered. Tilly lifted her
chin and deliberately placed her brimming glass on the
table, pushing it away from her with a fastidious finger. A strange mixture of expressions chased each other
across Barbara's face—confusion, anger and, bizarrely,
grudging respect, all gone in an instant to be replaced
by the familiar insolent confidence.

'If I can have your full attention, please.' Toby
raised his voice. 'We began this investigation with certain information gleaned from various sources, and I
have to admit that we, or rather I, began to look at the
scenario in one particular way, which turned out to be
a one-way, dead-end street.' He looked at them soberly. 'I believed,' he said, 'that the deaths of Saul
Murdoch, Sylvia de Groot and Jack Sprott came about
because of someone's desire to ruin Mr Quentin Hale,
or in any case to have him removed from this company
and recalled to England.'

Kate saw Barbara look with interest at Evie, who
had her own eyes firmly fixed on her hands clasped in
her lap. Dorothy and Amy, standing together, exchanged glances and felt for each other's hands.

'I had to consider the pattern, you understand,'

Toby went on. 'It was a perfectly clear pattern. Two of the four authors brought here to participate in a big public relations exercise, very important, as I understand, to the new management of this company, have died, one in very suspicious circumstances. And a third person is dead too. A person who bore a superficial physical resemblance to Mrs Tilly Lightly, another of the Big Four, and was wearing a distinctive article of Mrs Lightly's clothing at the time of her death in the darkness on the roof above our heads.' He glanced up to the ceiling as he spoke, and Kate found herself involuntarily looking up too. She remembered Birdie so uncharacteristically fierce, saying, *It's Sylvia de Groot I'm angry about!* and felt Tilly shiver beside her.

'In each case, in each death,' Toby went on, 'a book by the writer who was the object of the attack was left near the body, with an unpleasantly appropriate passage marked. In the case of Saul Murdoch, the words were carefully underlined. In the two other cases they were bracketed off more hastily, in the margin. This recurring motif has added a bizarre aspect to the case. I admit I have only within the last few hours understood it as something other than simply the expression of an insane obsession.'

The room was very still. People stood or sat with glasses in their hands in a parody of social well-being. Light streamed in through the windows and the vibrant blue sky outside was savage with heat. But in the air-conditioned, sealed box that was Quentin's apartment, it was cool and civilised. The elements were safely excluded.

But that meant that they were shut in, too. With each other, and the monster of fear and suspicion that had sat down with them, and made itself at home.

Toby hitched at his belt and glanced at Detective-constable Milson, upright and expressionless on the other side of the room.

'There hasn't been the opportunity for a steady-as-she-goes approach in this case,' he continued, 'because frankly it's likely that the killer will strike again at any

moment. The killings have been of a particularly callous type—a preying on the weak and defenceless—
and the vanity of a killer of this sort is generally fuelled
by success, so that further deaths seem easy and inevitable.' He looked around sharply, focusing on each
individual, as if looking for reaction, but no-one
stirred.

'These murders,' he rumbled, deliberately looking
down at some notes in his hand, 'are a direct result of
one person's strong emotion. But the emotion was not
hatred for Quentin Hale, or Berry and Michaels. It
was fear. The fear of losing something of enormous
importance to the person concerned: livelihood, and,
more importantly, a place in the sun, as one of my
colleagues put it. The person concerned is in this room
now, and must know that we—I—know their identity.'

A shuddering sigh, like a breath of wind, passed
around the room. Kate found that her hands were
clasped so tightly that they'd begun to ache. Dorothy
was gazing at Toby with frightened eyes, her arm
around Amy's slender waist. Amy herself was utterly
still. Her corn-coloured hair swung over her cheek like
a bird's wing, hiding her face. Malcolm had his eyes
on Quentin. His mouth hung open slightly. Barbara
fingered her empty glass, raised her eyebrows at Tilly
and looked at the full glass standing untouched between them on the coffee table.

'Have it!' muttered Tilly exhaustedly, turning her
head into the corner of the couch. Barbara grinned and
grabbed the glass. She stood and wandered to the windows, stopping by one of Quentin's absurdly glossy
pot plants and turning to scan the room.

Toby refused to be diverted. He looked around
sombrely and suddenly dropped his formal manner. 'I
won't allow another killing,' he said loudly and
abruptly. 'I will, for preference, make a charge with
the little evidence I now have, and work night and day
to make it stick. I will do that, make no mistake. So
what I'm saying is, the game's over. It's over. A con-

fession now will save a lot of drawn-out misery for everyone, and could help when you come to trial.'

Suddenly Birdie started forward. 'Dan!' she cried sharply.

There was a paralysed silence.

Then Sarah screamed, and pointed, and Malcolm, eyes starting from his head, stumbled forward. But they were too late. With glazed eyes, and a terrible smile still fixed on her face, Barbara Bendix, half-full glass still clutched in her hand, had crashed in a writhing heap on the softness of Quentin's gold carpet.

'Get back!' barked Toby. He rushed to the terribly contorted body and bent over it, shielding it from the horrified onlookers. 'Birdie, here! Milson, ambulance!'

'Poison!' Malcolm was screaming now. He rounded on Quentin. 'You gave her a poisoned drink. You bastard. You . . .'

Quentin was white as chalk. He gripped the back of a chair, as though he might fall. He shook his head slowly as if to clear it, and moistened dry lips.

'No, no! She poured it herself. The whisky . . . both the whiskies . . . she poured . . .'

Toby stood up and faced them. The body on the floor was quite still now. 'She poured both the whiskies,' he said grimly. 'She drank one, and gave the other one to Mrs Lightly.'

'But Tilly wouldn't drink it,' Kate said slowly.

'She . . .' Tilly pointed a trembling finger at Birdie, still crouched by Barbara's body, 'she told me not to. She said we were going to be told who . . . She told me not to take anything to eat or drink from . . . from Barbara. She told me.' She put her face in her hands and for once, Kate thought, the shaking sobs that racked her body were genuine. Sarah moved swiftly to her side and bent over her, clumsily patting her arm.

'If you don't mind, Mr Hale, we'll clear the room,' Toby said. They saw that he was holding a glass in a handkerchief.

'Some sort of cyanide, I'd say,' he said briefly.

The phone rang and he strode towards it, lifting the

receiver under Quentin's nose without apology. 'OK. Good. Send them up,' he said curtly, and hung up.

Kate shuddered. She looked over to the huddled figure on the floor. Birdie still knelt beside it, as though on guard, but there was no movement in the hand that clutched at the carpet as strongly as Barbara Bendix had clutched at life. There was no sound, no movement, nothing.

29

CRYING FOR A KILLER

'But why? Why?' Tilly asked Toby fretfully, as they tramped down the firestairs, with Kate and Birdie trailing behind and Milson bringing up the rear. 'Why would Barbara want to kill me, and Saul, and Jack Sprott? It doesn't make sense! She had everything. She was the only one of us who . . . who still seemed to be writing things she liked and that really sold.' She checked herself. 'I mean, not that mine don't *sell*,' she added, glancing hastily behind her at Kate. And then she smiled faintly, as though for once she'd caught a glimpse of herself as others saw her.

'It'll all come out in the inquest, Mrs Lightly,' said Toby gently, as they reached the landing on the third floor. 'Look, why don't you let Kate and Birdie take you down to the coffee shop now, to join the others?'

'You're going into Barbara's room now, aren't you?' Birdie cut in.

He nodded formally, but said nothing. His hand was steady on the doorhandle. Milson waited impassively beside him, ignoring them.

'I want to see,' said Birdie directly. 'You owe me that, Dan, you know you do. You can't refuse.'

'I certainly can,' he said grimly. Then he looked at their expectant faces, glanced at Milson's rigid profile, raised his eyes to heaven, and suddenly capitulated. 'All right!' he said. 'All right. But you know what we'll find.' He straightened his shoulders, and opened the door.

The curtains were drawn across the windows in Barbara's room, and Toby had to switch on the light so that they could see. Brightly-coloured clothes littered the chairs, coffee cups and papers and files were scattered on the desk around a portable typewriter. A suitcase in one corner of the room yawned open and shoes and underwear spilled out from it onto the floor. The room was so redolent of Barbara's personality it seemed alive. Toby stood aside, holding the door open for them.

Kate shivered, and Tilly was very white, but Birdie stepped forward eagerly.

'Stand back and don't touch anything,' Toby said in a low voice. He moved quickly to the bathroom door, opened it and looked searchingly inside. Then he turned abruptly and made for the desk. He flicked through some papers, opened a file, and gave a grunt of satisfaction. He beckoned.

'Here,' he said quietly.

Kate and Tilly crept together to his side, and looked where Toby's blunt finger was pointing.

They saw a grubby file, thick, and filled with handwritten and typed notes. Hours, days, months of work. Toby turned the pages. Meticulously recorded interviews, reviews, newspaper clippings, photographs, comments. All featuring one name. Saul Murdoch. Thousands of words, hundreds of pages, a case history building up. And on the paper by the typewriter, hastily typed notes. Saul Murdoch again, but this time with another name leaping out at them as well. Matilda Lightly—Tilly Lightly—the bare bones of the pathetic little twenty-year-old affair sketched out. And in the typewriter a nearly completed page headed 'In at the death' and beginning 'The night Saul Murdoch died, I met him for the first time . . .'

Tilly drew back. 'She was writing a book about Saul,' she breathed. 'Her new book.'

Birdie nodded. 'Once he was dead, she could go for it, you see. Rush to finish it. And she could say what she liked.'

Tilly shook her head vehemently. 'Not about me she couldn't,' she cried angrily, her voice ringing in the hushed room. 'I told her I'd sue her for everything she had! You heard me. I told her, over my dead body she'd . . .' She broke off, and her hand crept to her mouth.

Toby nodded slightly. 'Quite,' he said. 'An unusual motive for murder, but all quite logical, in a mad sort of way. If you and Murdoch were dead, no-one could stop this book being written and published. Jack Sprott must have seen something that first night. We'll never know now.'

'And she needed the book,' said Kate sadly. 'Everyone knew that. She'd already spent the advance. Oh, God!'

'And there's something else,' said Birdie. She pointed, and Toby drew from under a scarf a copy of *The Adventures of Paddy Kangaroo*. Tilly gasped. She looked very near breaking point.

Holding the book by its edges, Toby began to flick through it. Here and there passages were underlined fastidiously in black ink, and numbers were scribbled in the margins.

Kate felt sick. The book was the second copy from her office. It had been in her office this morning. She looked at Birdie.

'Picking out passages that might prove useful, it seems,' Birdie said. 'But as it happened events moved faster than expected.'

'Barbara was with Tilly here this morning!' Kate burst out. 'She could have killed her then, easily.' She turned on Toby. 'It was what you said upstairs! It drove her to it. You threatened her!' She felt her eyes prickle with tears. Crying for a killer. She knew she was being absurd.

'Kate, the poison was in the glass before any threats were made. It wasn't a matter of being driven to it. It was simply a matter of taking the first available chance to kill without being the obvious suspect! My God, Kate, innocent people have died, you know. And today another innocent nearly got a stomach full of cyanide!' snapped Birdie brutally. 'All because of one woman's giant ego.'

'I know. I know. It's just . . . sad. A waste.' Kate looked at the litter of papers, the vivid clothes, through a haze of tears. She thought of Barbara's wicked smile, her irrepressible tongue, her famous appetites—for food, drink and young men. All gone. 'She was so strong, and funny. And she was so full of . . . life,' she finished lamely.

Birdie looked at her seriously. 'So was Jack. So was Sylvia, in their own ways,' she said. 'Who said only the strong and funny and beautiful have a right to life?'

Toby reached forward and pulled back the curtains. The afternoon light streamed in, and caught Tilly, small, bony, faded, overacting even now, in a golden pool. Kate almost smiled through her tears. Nothing very strong or beautiful or funny about Tilly Lightly. But she had survived.

'OK,' said Toby. 'That's enough. Carruthers'll give the whole place a good going over later.'

He ushered them out of the room. Milson, standing outside, looked down the hallway away from them, with the air of one turning a blind eye to unbelievable folly.

'I'll get Sarah for you, Tilly,' Kate offered, but Tilly shook her head.

'No,' she said very quietly. 'She won't come home with me. She won't forgive me.' She lifted her chin. 'But I'll be fine,' she said. 'Paddy and I will be fine. And Sarah will come around. When she's ready.' She smiled and bit her lip, in the old way, and made a graceful exit into her own room, closing the door bravely behind her. Kate felt like laughing, and crying, but of course did neither. A third alternative had occurred to her.

'How about a cup of tea?' she said to Birdie and Toby.

Birdie grinned. 'The universal panacea, eh?' she said. They looked at one another in silence for a moment.

And then they heard a scream, and a bang and a shout, and Toby had wrenched open the door to Barbara's room and hurtled inside.

Against the light streaming through the window two figures struggled. Detective-constable Carruthers, red-faced and streaming with sweat, and Tilly Lightly.

'What are you doing here, Mrs Lightly?' barked Toby.

'I forgot something!' screamed Tilly. 'This man attacked me. Let me go!' She jabbed Carruthers viciously in the chest with her elbow.

He flinched, but held on gamely. 'She came through the bathroom, like you said, sir. She pulled that out from under the mattress,' he gasped, ducking his head at a battered green book on the floor at his feet.

'Ah,' said Toby. He bent down and picked up the book. 'Is this what you forgot, Mrs Lightly?'

She stared at him, her mouth working. There was an exclamation from the room next door.

'Milson!' called Toby. 'Have you got it?'

Milson pushed past Kate and Birdie to join him. He held out Tilly's handbag, open. Tilly gave a startled yelp, and backed away. Toby followed her, smiling benignly. 'The things women keep in their handbags!' he said. He tipped the bag slightly, to show her the white plastic bottle rolling around inside it.

Kate gripped Birdie's arm and craned her neck to see. Tilly was backed up against the window, eyes dilated, staring at the objects in Toby's hands.

'You recognise it, don't you? The bottle of fericyanide crystals?' Toby continued, still in that pleasant, reasonable voice.

'It was in the art department's photography section this morning, before your visit, the art director tells us, but now it's in your handbag. Funny place to put a deadly poison, Mrs Lightly. Dangerous. And this!' He tapped the book. 'It's someone else's property, you know, Mrs Lightly. What were you going to do with it?'

Tilly swallowed, and licked her lips. Her huge eyes darted right and left. 'Barbara . . .' she swallowed again. 'Barbara must have . . .'

Kate heard a rustle behind her. Felt a hand on her shoulder. She spun around.

'Oh yes?' drawled a familiar, husky voice. 'What must Barbara have done?' And Barbara Bendix, fiercely smiling, pushed into the room.

Tilly whimpered and strained backwards against the wall. 'You're dead! You . . . so much of it, you drank. You must be . . . !'

'I would be, if I'd drunk it, Tilly. But there's a sick pot plant upstairs now, instead.' Barbara took another step forward. 'I might be a greedy old trollop, but I'm not so stupid as to take a bait from you! I'm not as easy a mark as Sylvia, or old Jack. Besides, I was warned. Someone's been on to you for quite a while, sweetie-pie!' She jerked her head at Birdie, hovering in the shadows.

Tilly's teeth began to chatter. She hugged her arms to her narrow chest. 'It's not true! I didn't do anything! He was drunk! He fell over and bumped his head. The creek was right there. What did you expect me to do? He was going to tell. I had to do it!'

Birdie moved forward. 'And what about Sylvia? That was an accident too, I suppose, Tilly, was it?' she said coldly. 'You chose her because she was little, like you. You dressed her up in your shawl. You flattered her, and pretended you liked her, and you tossed her over the bloody roof, didn't you? And she'd done nothing. Nothing!'

Face distorted with rage, Tilly lunged at her. 'It was going to be you!' she spat, hurling herself forward, beating against Toby's restraining arms to get at

Birdie, hands reaching to claw at her eyes. 'You! You should be dead now! I'll kill you now!'

'That's enough!' thundered Toby.

Then the room was full of police, and Tilly was dragged, screaming, away.

30

Grateful Ghosts

'Well, Barbara, you've missed your calling, that's all I can say.' Dorothy Hale shook her head. 'I can't imagine how you did it all so convincingly.'

Barbara preened herself delightedly. 'Ah, well,' she said, casting her eyes down modestly.

'What a ham!' scoffed Evie. 'Writhing and gasping like a baddie in a B-grade movie!'

'Evie, you cried buckets!' retorted Barbara complacently. 'I saw you. Ah, it's nice to know you're beloved!' She leaned back on the couch, and stretched languorously.

Evie snorted. 'Don't let it go to your head.'

'Listen, Birdie, you've got to explain some things!' Kate cut in.

They were sitting again in Quentin's living room. Quentin and Dorothy, Amy, Malcolm, Evie, Barbara, Kate and Birdie. Dan Toby and the disapproving Detective-constable Milson had gone, Sarah Lightly had been ushered away by a selfconsciously supportive Paul, and Quentin had sent the staff home too, so that the building below them was empty, and a Sunday afternoon peace had settled on the deserted corridors.

Birdie took off her glasses and polished them on her T-shirt. Her beautiful amber eyes, unshielded for once, stared short-sightedly out at the fading blue of the sky.

'I was stupid, really,' she began, and shook her head.

'For quite a while I let myself be taken in by the idea that the murders were a series. All that business with the marked books. So much so that I didn't argue with Dan nearly enough when he fixed on Evie. I think I was thrown off balance. I'd been convinced Saul Murdoch suicided, you see, so the night of the party, when Sylvia, a Tilly look-alike, died, and the *Paddy Kangaroo* book was found, I got rattled, and I forgot to think.'

'But Birdie, Birdie,' Kate broke in impatiently. 'Tilly *couldn't* have killed Saul. That's what I've been thinking. She *couldn't* have. She wouldn't have left a note she wrote to him there for the police to find. And she was locked in her room at the time he was supposed to have drunk the stuff. Sarah said she was definitely asleep, and snoring. She *couldn't* have killed him.'

Birdie looked at her pityingly. 'Haven't you woken up yet, dopey?' she said. 'She didn't kill him. No-one did. He killed himself, just like I always said he did. I must have told you a dozen times.'

'But, I thought . . .'

Birdie sighed deeply. 'You didn't think,' she said flatly. 'If you had you'd have seen that it was far more likely that Saul Murdoch had done himself in, than that someone killed him. He was teetering on the brink of a nervous collapse. He'd had a lot to drink, and a harrowing argument. He'd attempted suicide several times before. And there was no evidence that anyone else had entered his room. Also, there were people wandering around those corridors at the vital time. There would have been enormous risk involved in walking to his room. And he was demented with fury. He'd hardly be likely to sit down peacefully and drink with someone, except maybe for Evie, and I'd decided it was illogical to suspect her. She was sensible enough simply to bump off Quentin and be done with it, to get rid of him!'

'Oh, thanks very much!' said Evie and Quentin together.

'The point is,' Birdie went on, ignoring them, 'that

once I cleared my mind, and refused to be bamboozled by the series idea, I could look at the whole thing rationally. If Saul had in fact committed suicide, and the other deaths were murders, that meant that someone was trying to conceal a motive that had nothing to do with a mad vendetta against the Big Four. The killing of Sylvia de Groot puzzled me very much. There were some funny things about it. Sylvia was small, but she was dark and fairly chunky. Even at night, and wrapped in Tilly's shawl, no-one who knew Tilly at all well could have mixed them up at close quarters. That let out the obvious suspects—Sarah and Evie—as far as I was concerned.'

'I thought it might be Jack,' Evie said sadly.

'Yes!' Birdie turned to look at her. 'I thought about Jack too. But then this morning it became all too clear that he couldn't be the one. In fact, Jack was the first murder. Jack was the one whose death was made to seem in series with Saul's. After realising that, things started to move into place, for me at least. Toby was falling for the idea of Evie like a ton of bricks at the time.' She smiled reminiscently, and a trifle maliciously, and looked at the toes of her battered shoes.

'I thought again about last night, the party, Tilly. Tilly asked quite a few people to go up with her to the roof. But she only asked people who were busy and in the thick of things—Quentin, Evie, people like that. She didn't, for instance, directly ask Kate, who might have gone to be obliging. And she didn't persist with those people. Just asked, and breezed on. But then she made a bee-line for me. And she went on and on about the bloody roof. That afternoon, in the park, she'd acted like I was beneath her notice entirely. Now, suddenly, we were best friends. She was so determined I started to think she was loopy!

'Anyway, finally she gave up on me and battened on to Sylvia. I didn't think much more about it, then. But this morning, when Dan Toby made some offensive remark about me being small—thank you, Dan!—I suddenly realised that I'd have been an even better substitute Tilly than Sylvia. And then I became convinced that Tilly had set up the murder of "Tilly Lightly" because for some reason she had killed Jack. She'd met him in the park as he was ducking off to hide from Evie and have a quick snort, and she'd sat with him, till he drank himself silly, then pushed him into the creek. He had his book with him. She saw the possibility of linking his death with Saul's, and took it. This would both conceal her motive, and put her out of the running as a suspect, because she thought Sarah would vouch for her not having left her room the night Saul was killed, and she'd realised that the note she'd left in Saul's room had in fact made her seem innocent, rather than guilty, of his death. What would put the lid on it would be another "Big Four" murder—and the easiest murder to arrange was her own.'

There was a shocked silence. Birdie looked around. 'Yes,' she said bitterly. 'That's how I felt. She just took another human being and used her as a stage prop. Utterly callous, utterly self-regarding. With no sense of other people's rights and feelings at all. Which fitted in completely with everything else I'd observed and heard about her—her marriage, her relationship with her daughter, her general social behaviour, everything. Which brings me to—'

'Her motive!' exploded Kate. 'For goodness' sake, why? Why kill Jack Sprott?'

Birdie smiled. 'If you'd been a good *hardworking* publisher, Kate, you'd know,' she purred, enjoying the moment. 'Barbara knows, don't you, Barbara?'

Barbara grinned, and bounced out of her chair. 'I do,' she said briskly. 'But I'm not going to tell, or hang around while you tell it. It would be so embarrassing! I loathe being shown up in front of people. Malcolm, sweet boy, let's away, shall we? I'm awfully tired! Being poisoned really takes it out of a woman.'

She stretched out a careless hand and Malcolm Pool, to Kate's enormous surprise, shuffled to his feet and took it.

'You're all pink, darling, like a little cherub,' she cooed, leaning over and ruffling his hair. He stood and blushed even more deeply, gazing at her helplessly.

'Goodbye, Quentin, darling. Catch up with you soon. When I've finished the Saul opus,' cried Barbara, spinning round to Quentin and offering her other hand to him.

Quentin Hale, absolutely lost for words, gulped and nodded. He eyed Malcolm in a disconcerted fashion. Barbara looked around happily.

'We'll be at the Hilton for a few days. Then—don't say you haven't told Quentin yet, Malcolm? No? You naughty boy! Well, Quentin, I'm afraid I'm stealing your boy wonder from you. I so need him, darling. He said he'd come home with me and be my personal publicist and secretary for a little while. Take the pressure off, you know? You'll be glad, darling, in the end. My book will be finished so much more quickly if I have Malcolm to organise things for me!'

She smiled sweetly and Quentin, eyes wide, smiled and nodded mechanically.

'Oh, good!' cried Barbara. 'All's forgiven! 'Bye, Evie, 'bye all!' She swept to the open lift, and Malcolm trotted after her, carrying her bag. She put her arms around him as the lift doors closed and they were lost to view.

'My God, what a terrifying woman!' exclaimed Quentin Hale.

'She'll eat him alive,' said Evie with grim satisfaction. 'Couldn't happen to a nicer bloke!'

Kate sat open-mouthed. 'I had no idea!' she breathed at last.

Evie laughed wickedly. 'You know Barbara! And he is quite good-looking, I suppose. In a spivvy sort of way.'

Dorothy Hale was looking shocked, Amy fastidiously repelled, Quentin bemused. But Birdie grinned. 'I was sure from very early on that something was going on between those two. Barbara was in very high spirits and Malcolm seemed to have lost his bearings completely. And of course I knew Barbara liked her men young. They're more bossable that way.' She considered the question seriously. 'And prettier,' she added composedly.

'Birdie!' exclaimed Kate.

Birdie turned to look at her, glasses glittering dangerously, and Kate fell silent.

'Barbara never thought, you see, that there was any doubt about the murders. She thought Saul had suicided, Jack had just fallen in the creek dead drunk and Sylvia had been taken for Tilly by Sarah Lightly. She had it all worked out. She said it to all of us. She never for a moment thought she could be a suspect, though Saul's death was so very convenient for her, because she knew in her own mind that she had an alibi for both Saul's time of death, and for Jack's. When I finally tackled her this morning she was very surprised and amused to think a case could be made out with her as number one suspect A. Because the night of Saul's death, and in the park when Jack died, she was with Malcolm Pool. Very much with Malcolm Pool, actually.'

'You mean it was *Malcolm* that Sarah and Paul heard creeping out of the building that first night?' exclaimed Evie. 'The police thought it was me!'

Birdie nodded. 'That's right. I think Jack heard them in Barbara's room, too. He was very cross with Barbara the next day. Dear little Malcolm must be exhausted. Behind bushes in the park, up in her room, anywhere and everywhere, anytime. Barbara has considerable energy. No wonder he was looking frayed around the edges.'

'Poor bugger!' said Quentin with feeling. Dorothy laughed explosively, then guiltily covered her mouth with her hand.

'Anyway,' said Birdie, 'by the time I spoke to Barbara I was sure that Tilly was the murderer, and that Barbara herself was in real danger. The fact that Barbara had a cast-iron alibi in the case of Jack Sprott meant that I could ask her to do the bit of play-acting up here quite safely, even if I was wrong about Tilly. Good old Dan didn't like it much, but he agreed it was the best way to get the thing cleared up quickly. He agreed that Tilly seemed the likely villain, but we really had no hard evidence against her. We had to get her to break down and confess.'

'Tilly said you'd told her there was going to be a showdown, and warned her not to take anything to eat or drink from Barbara,' said Kate slowly. 'You did that to—'

'To give her the idea, of course,' Birdie broke in, 'that she'd be safe if she could poison something she was supposed to drink, and then get Barbara to take it, as if by accident. Then I gave her the perfect opportunity, with Barbara's help. Drinks, with Barbara serving, and a crowd of witnesses. She couldn't resist it! Here was the chance to kill Barbara, and make it look as if Barbara had been actually trying to kill her, had failed, and had suicided to avoid being brought to justice. She knew I'd be there to back her up. She had the bottle of fericyanide crystals she'd nicked from the photographic studio in her handbag. She tipped some into her handkerchief. Then she just held the hand-kerchief in her hand like she always does, all balled up, and dropped the crystals into her whisky and soda. They're orangey-brown and wouldn't show. Then she put the glass down, brimming over nearly by now, though no-one but Barbara and me noticed that, and pushed it towards Barbara, tempting her to take and drink it. Barbara would've, too, if I hadn't warned her.'

'Birdie,' Kate put out her hands in appeal, '*why* did Tilly kill Jack Sprott? And why did she try to kill Barbara?'

'Dan Toby told you earlier. To protect her liveli-hood, and her place in the sun. First Jack, then Barbara, threatened the thing she cared about most in the world.' Birdie looked at Kate ruefully. 'You, Kate, and you, Evie, should have picked it. You had every opportunity. But I guess you just accepted things as they were, and didn't question, simply because you've been in this business so long.

'To me as an outsider, though, there was something very odd about Tilly Lightly, queen of the kids, creator of that funny kangaroo and his troop of assorted animals plus one piss-pot of a garden gnome. Once I'd read *The Adventures of Paddy Kangaroo* for myself it was very clear to me—there was absolutely no way that Tilly could *ever* have written a book like that. Or even come near to it.'

'What!' Kate, Evie and Quentin shouted out in one voice.

She smiled pityingly at them. 'Don't you see? It's so obvious. You all knew she didn't have a genuinely funny bone in her body. Whimsy, yes. Humour, no. No way. You all know she supposedly produced this outstanding manuscript after two very ordinary little stories and one complete flop. You know she hasn't written anything worth a crumpet since. You know Paddy's the story of a group of mates who get into all sorts of scrapes adventuring in the bush far from home. You heard Sarah and Jack talk about Alistair Lightly's funny stories, wacky humour—'

'Birdie! Are you saying Tilly's *husband* wrote *Paddy Kangaroo*? That she sent it to Berry and Michaels as her own work, after he was dead?' exclaimed Kate.

'Of course,' said Birdie calmly. 'Only his book was called, I'll bet, "The Adventures of Big Rabbit", or some such thing. He wrote it about his wartime mates, with himself, "Rabbit", as the main character.

'Tilly's letters of the time, in the archive, lay the story out quite clearly. Her third "Bindi Mouse" book was rejected by Brian Berry, who hadn't, I'd say, thought much of the two that his father Gerald had published earlier. Tilly wrote back very bitterly, appealing to old Gerald, and saying she was now a widow with a child to support. Gerald wrote to her and said, try something new, dear little girl, I have faith in you, and so on. No help from that quarter.

'So there she was. She totally lacked the talent to

produce anything more original than Bindi Mouse look-alikes. She was a fair illustrator, but incapable of an original thought, as far as writing went. And in her heart she knew it.

'And under her hand she had Alistair Lightly's book. The book she'd kept to herself because she knew it was good, and she was jealous, just as later she was jealous of Sarah, her daughter, for producing what Paul Morrisey at least seems to find a very interesting and highly original novel.

'So, she just typed out Alistair's manuscript, substituting "Paddy Kangaroo" for "Rabbit" all the way through, and changing all the other names. "Jack" the garden gnome became "Redcap", for example. Then she redrew his amateurish, funny little sketches in her own style, though the influence is there for all to see—I don't know how many times I've heard people say Paddy looks like a big rabbit, with his long front teeth. He does, too.'

'He does . . .' Kate shook her head in wonder. 'Jack, the old joke about Jack looking like Redcap! He *was* Redcap! No wonder Tilly wasn't happy when I told her the joke.'

'No wonder,' Birdie grinned. 'She must have been appalled to find out Jack had been in Vietnam with Alistair.'

'But Jack hadn't ever read Paddy. Until,' Kate broke off.

'Until he looked at the copy Malcolm had given him, before lunch on the day of his death,' Birdie nodded. 'His wits might have been a bit blurred with whisky by then, but when he started to read Tilly's masterpiece, he started to smell a rat. Or a rabbit. The rabbit gang was a joke of Alistair's, in Vietnam. He recognised the characters, the drawings. He attacked Tilly in the lift, remember? And in the park he met up with her while he was giving Evie the slip and decided to tackle her about it properly. That's why they were talking. And he was drunk, and fell over, just as she said, and she saw her chance, and . . . finished him off in the water.'

'And came to meet me at the kiosk, with hands as clean as if she'd just washed,' said Amy, pale in the fading light. 'But she said she hadn't been to the bath-room . . .'

'She didn't know, you see, that Jack was going on more than memories,' said Birdie, leaning forward. 'Because no-one, in her presence, had said that Jack had kept a diary.'

Kate's heart leapt. Jack's memoir! That was what had been missing from her office this morning, after Barbara's visit. The battered green book had been missing from the pile. She opened her mouth to speak, but Birdie was too fast for her.

'Jack's diary was more than a diary, as I saw when I read it this morning. It was a journal for the whole unit. Lots of his mates had added bits and pieces to it. "Rabbit" Lightly had. He'd done pictures of Jack, and himself, and the gang—"Lizard", "Boney", "Wom-bat" and the rest. And he'd spun some little yarns about the gang, too, some true, some clearly made up. And when you look at those, you know where *Paddy* came from. Its authorship is as clear as a bell.

'Barbara took the diary from Kate's office, this morning, hoping to get some dirt on Tilly's husband for her book about Saul Murdoch. And she worked out about *Paddy*. She compared *Paddy* with the diary, and marked the similar passages. As soon as I saw the diary gone from Kate's office, I knew what she'd done.

'And, she told Tilly. See, she didn't think for a mo-ment Tilly was a murderer—only a fraud. She told Tilly she'd suppress the diary if Tilly would hold back from suing her over the Saul Murdoch book.'

'That's all very well,' exclaimed Evie, 'but Barbara would never have kept such a juicy bit of dirt to herself forever. No matter what she said.'

'Of course not. And Tilly knew that! That's why Barbara was in real danger. I told her after Tilly was safely away downstairs, and she finally believed me.

She'd put the diary under her mattress. She'd told Tilly she was going to keep it there, and not to bother trying to steal it. Tilly had to get the diary, even with Barbara dead, before the room was thoroughly searched. So, when she thought we'd gone, she crept back to get it, through the bathroom door Dan had thoughtfully unlocked for her while we all watched. She didn't know we were onto her, and that Carruthers was crunched up in the wardrobe the whole time, waiting for her. The rest you know.' She leaned back in her chair and tipped her head back. She looked tired.

'This is incredible!' Quentin Hale got up restlessly and paced to the window. Then he turned around. 'Even if the book was Alistair Lightly's, she would have inherited the copyright, wouldn't she? So . . .'

'No!' cried Kate, suddenly enlightened, 'because Alistair left everything to Sarah, in trust till she was eighteen. She told me. She got a few hundred dollars. But the *Paddy* royalties are worth a fortune!'

'In a nutshell,' said Birdie, closing her eyes. 'That's the whole story.'

'Mind you,' said Kate to Birdie, as they walked down the stairs later, 'it wouldn't have been nearly as successful, you know, if it had been "Paddy Rabbit". *Paddy Kangaroo* is much stronger, for this market.'

'Spare me the publishing wisdom, Laney, I beg of you,' pleaded Birdie. 'I've had enough over the last week to last me all my life. I don't know how you stand this business. A more clumsy, chancy, inefficient racket I never did see. You take on these manuscripts you just think will sell, you make them into books at enormous cost, then you pay a fortune to have them transported to bookshops, who seem to sort of rent them because they can send them back whenever they like. You pay the authors a pittance, the company makes a pittance, on investment. It's very odd. A very inexact science. I don't know how you stand it.'

'Oh, you know,' murmured Kate vaguely, as they reached the editorial floor. 'I just like it . . . Birdie?'

'Yes.'

'Why do you think Dorothy's so protective of Amy? I mean, it was a terrible thing, her mother killing her father like that, but . . .'

'But what?' said Birdie, looking at her watch.

'It seems excessive—bringing her out here, and everything. And she—Amy—she's so strange—cut off.'

'Kate, how would I know?' demanded Birdie. 'People take things in different ways.' She looked down at her shoes. Whatever she thought, she wasn't going to tell Kate. She watched Kate shrug and walk on, leading the way to her office through the silent corridors. She thought about Dorothy's compassionate, troubled face and Amy's closed one. Thought about the psychology. Thought about Dorothy's sister—a weak, pretty, cowed woman finding the bully she had married stabbed to the heart and her daughter holding a knife standing above him. Thought about that woman cleaning the girl up, putting her to bed, taking the knife in her own hand, calling the police, saying 'I did it, I did it,' over and over again, so no one could suspect, having found at last a way of protecting the daughter she had failed for years, and of forgiving herself for her cowardice.

Dorothy would have guessed. She knew her sister. She knew Amy. She would have guessed at once. But she would have gone along with her sister's wishes. She'd have understood what she wanted. She'd love and protect Amy till the day she died, shielding her from the curious, trying to help her to fight the terrors that must menace her peace. And Quentin? Without understanding, he'd support his wife, because mutual support was the lynchpin of their lives together—here, or back home, whatever their differences. She thought about that, for a moment.

Kate turned to look at her friend. Birdie seemed tired—and strangely forlorn. 'I'll just get my things,' she said brightly, 'and we'll go for a coffee, eh? Or come home to dinner.' She picked up her handbag and began to flip through the day's letters still lying at the top of her in-tray. She was pleased to see that Mary had already typed up the morning's letters, and sent away the rejected manuscripts with the usual depressingly brief preprinted message.

'I don't know,' Birdie kicked the edge of the desk. She looked around. 'Anyway, let's get out of here. All these books get me down. As I said, I don't know why you stick at this business. It's all guesswork and gambling. None of you seems to have any real, concrete idea what makes one book sell and one not.'

'Of course we do!' said Kate breezily. 'We have instincts. They come from experience. You wouldn't understand.'

She got to the last letter in the pile. Oh, dear. It was from Mr Ninish, the author of *Quacking Up at Mossy Ridge.*

'Dear Miss Delaney, I did call to see you yesterday morning but you were unable to see me. Of course, I should have rung first, but I live locally and I tried my luck in person! Anyway, having also failed to contact you by phone yesterday afternoon and this morning, I thought I'd drop you a line.'

She shook her head.

'See, Birdie, look at this. This poor man Ninish has no idea. His manuscript—it's a dear little story, but we couldn't possibly do it. No commercial potential at all.' She scanned the letter to its close. Poor Mr Ninish would get his rejection note on Monday. He would be so . . . her eyes stopped, ran back a line. *I thought you might like to know . . . just signed . . . ABC TV series . . . quite excited . . . I have had approaches from other publishers . . . so would appreciate your phoning . . .* Kate's fingers tightened on the letter, Birdie was looking out the window . . . 'That name's familiar some-

how,' she was saying idly. 'Ninish, Ninish, oh yes—
some TV series about an old farmer and a duck they'd
just signed up at work. Couldn't be the same bloke of
course. They say this guy's the new James Herriot.
The BBC's co-producing with them. They say it'll be
huge. I wonder who's got the book for that?'

Kate could find no words to answer her.

They walked down the stairs. *Oh hello, Mr Ninish,*
rehearsed Kate in her head . . . *so glad I caught you . . .
terribly busy week . . . clerical error . . . ha, ha, . . . yes
. . . love it . . . come in and discuss?*

As they left the building, the traffic snarled on the
hot, black street, the birds argued in the tops of the
palm trees in the park, and the first lights went on.
Birdie shut the door behind them. And in the conference room, up on the second floor, the Berry and Michaels ghosts whispered gratefully in the gloom.
Tonight, they had lots to talk about.

GRIM PICKINGS

BY JENNIFER ROWE

Kate and her husband, Jeremy, usually enjoyed the Tenders' annual harvest. But this season something was gnawing away under the rosy surface like bitter rot.

Aunt Alice was really getting on—so forgetful. Had she really sprayed the trees with pesticides just before picking? And Betsy, her niece, was more desperately manipulative than ever. Odd, too, were Betsy's strangely detached husband, their mousy daughter-in-law, and their beautiful daughter Anna, home since the scandalous breakup of her marriage.

This year you couldn't even eat the apples off the trees—with the spray and all. But Anna's estranged husband obviously missed the warning. He was found sprawled in the orchard with four discarded apple cores next to his lifeless body.

Any way you slice it, there's a rotten apple in Aunt Alice's orchard. And suddenly the pick of the harvest could be a very clever killer.

Experience Murder Most British with Marian Babson

Murder at the Cat Show

A glorified cat show is about to become an exhibition of grand larceny, catnapping, and murder.

❑ 28590-4 $3.95

Murder Sails at Midnight

Four wealthy women sail from New York to Genoa aboard an Italian luxury liner. As the passengers frolic in the sumptuous elegance of her staterooms and cabarets, a killer stalks the decks under a full moon.

❑ 28096-1 $3.50

Tourists are for Trapping

A luxury tour with a premium price tag. Now conspiracy, perjury, and murder have just been added to the itinerary.

❑ 29031-2 $3.99

Available at your local bookstore or use this page to order.